Chloe James is a pseudonym for Fiona Woodifield, who is the author of *The Jane Austen Dating Agency*.

LOVE IN LOCKDOWN

CHLOE JAMES

avon.

Published by AVON
A division of HarperCollins*Publishers* Ltd
1 London Bridge Street
London SE1 9GF

www.harpercollins.co.uk

HarperCollins*Publishers*
1st Floor, Watermarque Building, Ringsend Road
Dublin 4, Ireland

A Paperback Original 2021

First published in Great Britain by HarperCollins*Publishers* 2020

Copyright © HarperCollins*Publishers* 2020

Chloe James asserts the moral right to be identified as the author of this work.

A catalogue copy of this book is available from the British Library.

ISBN: 978-0-00-843057-3

Typeset in Sabon by Palimpsest Book Production Limited, Falkirk, Stirlingshire
Printed and bound in UK by CPI Group (UK) Ltd, Croydon CR0 4YY

This book is produced from independently certified FSC™ paper to ensure

For more information visit: www.harpercollins.co.uk/green

In writing *Love in Lockdown* I hope I have done justice to what has been a really tough time. I'm aware that reading about lockdown will bring up a lot of difficult emotions for many. *Love in Lockdown* is at its heart a love story, and a love letter to community – not a story about the virus itself, and it does not go into specifics around the medical or political side of the story. This is not to diminish these aspects of lockdown, but because I wanted to tell a story that reflected the courage, hope and love that can come out of darkness. So many of us have pulled together during lockdown, and this is the experience I hope you'll find reflected in this book.

To Marianne, Grace, Madeleine and Francesca with love

'I like being alone, but I want someone to be alone with, if that makes sense . . .'

PROLOGUE

It's funny how in this world we all rush about like hordes of teeming worker ants, focused on our individual errands, together but not together, our paths coming close. They may sometimes cross, yet so often we aren't even aware of it.

Jack is intent on his own troubles, his dark head bent low into the torrential wind and rain driving relentlessly into his face. The fateful papers are clutched to his chest in a simple plastic wallet. Not very classy, but he can't afford leather after all the solicitor's fees.

Besides, 'there's nothing more we can do at this point,' the incredibly serious, smartly suited man had said with a sigh. Honestly, did he really have to be so dismal?

'You'll soon bounce back, mate – you're like a rubber band,' he could hear his brother Sam saying. Sam is four years older than him and therefore supposedly more mature, but can usually be relied upon to create comedy

1

even in the most hideous of situations. 'When life gives you lemons, just make a darn good gin and tonic,' is one of his favourite sayings.

Everything is a bit of a mess now, though, just when Jack thought he'd got his life all worked out. It had all been going so well. Finally he had been having some fun, being normal, right up until he blew it. Maybe he should have stayed in Greece; he'd been happy there – not settled with a family like Sam of course, but at least he'd had a good time. He remembers his first day in Agios Nikolaos, learning how to make Ouzotini. The Greek people treated him like family. The endless blue skies, the brilliant white of the ancient buildings glistening in the sun, the banter in the taverna had all been exhilarating. He wished it could have gone on forever.

Especially on days like this, though to be fair the weather seems to match his mood. He pulls his hood further over his head and huddles deeper inside his coat against the onslaught of rain, as a car races past and splashes water up his leg.

Greece had been wonderful, but he'd missed Sam. And now Sam is going to be a dad, and 'Uncle Jack' has a certain ring to it. He wouldn't want to miss out on that. Not that it had been an easy decision. After years of medical tests, sheets of rules, special diets and regulations, Greece had been the sanctuary he needed. But it was an escape, running away from reality. Sam knew that and unlike their parents, he had vaguely understood. 'Main

2

thing is you got it out of your system, mate,' he had said. But on the upside, Jack loves his job at Soho. It's a laugh and there's a terrific crowd of regulars, especially on a Saturday night. His daiquiri is legendary, so deceptively simple to make but incredibly difficult to get the balance right. He'd learned that on his course and it was well worth all the practising.

Jack hurries across the street. It's not long until his hospital appointment – nothing serious, just his regular blood test. He hopes they are more accurate than usual when they jab the needle in. His veins are all too prone to playing hard to get and afterwards he often looks as though they have been using him for target practice.

His phone blasts out.

'Where are you, mate?' Sam asks. 'I'm driving into the car park.'

'I'll meet you inside,' says Jack. 'The solicitor took longer than I thought, boring old sod.'

'You're always bloody late. Any news?'

'No of course not.'

'What a surprise! See you in ten.'

Jack is half-running towards the multi-storey – he's going to be far longer than ten minutes. No one minds lateness if you've achieved what you needed to, but it had been such a waste of time. He cuts through the street and round the corner, slap bang into two women who are hurrying the other way.

One is carrying a pile of magazines and papers, most of which spill onto the rain-soaked pavement.

'Oh, for goodness' sake!' she shouts.

'I'm so sorry,' Jack says, attempting to scrape sodden pages off the unforgiving cobbles.

'It's fine,' the woman, who has a choppy blonde bob, says tightly. *It obviously is not at all fine*, thinks Jack. The wet magazines in his hand are covered with images of brides resplendent in various white frothy dresses, now looking splodgy, the colour of the print running into the white.

Next to her is another young woman – although it's difficult to tell really, as she is dressed in a navy mac, hiding most of her features – but she bends instantly to help pick them up.

'This would never have happened if we had left on time,' the blonde complains.

Her companion sends an apologetic grin in Jack's direction. All he can see is her eyes, but he can tell by the way they crinkle at the corners that they're full of amusement – she is obviously used to this complaint.

'My brother is always saying the same to me.' He smiles at her over *Brides and Setting Up Home*, but she is too busy picking up papers to notice.

'I can't apologise enough,' he continues to the angry woman who by now has managed to retrieve most of her pile of magazines. 'I feel really bad. Can I help you to get somewhere?'

'No thanks,' she comments abruptly, but then appears to reconsider. 'Thanks anyway. We're here now.' She indicates the bridal boutique to the side of them and pulls open the door.

'Good luck with that!' Jack mutters under his breath, but oblivious she dashes into the shop.

He is sure he hears the friend respond, 'You said it,' as she follows behind, but her words are drowned by the tinkling of the shop bell and the passing traffic. He's left looking at her retreating back, wondering if he imagined it. He watches them in the shop for a split second, laughing at something, both the picture of excitement in spite of their wet gear. He is struck by their hopeful happiness. He looks at his watch and braces himself for Sam's usual rant about how he's always late.

Inside the shop, Jess gingerly deposits her magazines on the ornate desk.

'What a terrible afternoon.' Valerie, the assistant, bustles towards them.

'Awful. I hope we don't have weather like this on my wedding day,' says Jess, indicating the sodden and crumpled magazines.

'They look a bit worse for wear,' Val remarks, 'but don't panic, I've plenty more where those came from.' She goes to the back of the boutique and returns with a veritable mountain of shiny new glossies.

'Thanks so much.' Sophia throws her wet mac on a nearby stand.

'Now make yourselves comfortable, my dears. Would you like a lovely glass of bubbly or a hot cup of tea and we'll get started on some more designs you like the look of?'

Within minutes they are happily ensconced on the chaise longue, sipping from long elegant flutes of champagne whilst checking out gowns in the magazines.

'Now I know you had a couple of favourites last time you were here, but I do have a few that are new in only this week,' Val says, appearing from the back room under a mound of frothy fabric and lace.

'Ooh I like the look of the one on top there,' says Jess.

'You have great taste – that's a Bella Morilee. Very simple, with a gorgeous circular train.'

'I love the simple styles,' states Sophia, 'rather than too much decoration. Makes a bit of a statement, don't you think?'

'Maybe,' Jess muses, contemplating the satin dress on its fabric-covered hanger. 'I'll try it on.'

Soon there's a lot of muffled grumbling and expostulating coming from the changing room. 'I've got the strap stuck round my arm and I can't move,' calls Jess. Val deftly rearranges the thin strips of fabric so Jess can actually move, then she wafts out of the fitting area, the simple dress curving effortlessly out from her waist. 'What do you think?'

'I don't know,' says Sophia, her head on one side. 'What do *you* think?'

They both look at each other for a second; words aren't really necessary. 'I'm not sure,' they both say at the same time.

'Maybe it's a bit too plain,' Sophia says. 'Even though I like the diamante belt.'

'I agree.' Jess swoops off to try another new style, kindly handed to her by the ever-patient Val.

'Your wedding dress has to be absolutely right,' she tells Jess. 'You'll know when it's the one.'

Jess returns in a sheathed robe with a plunging neckline. 'Wow,' Sophia says. 'That's pretty spectacular.'

'I don't know,' says Jess, turning this way and that and peering at her reflection in the mirror. 'It feels a bit too, well . . . revealing. Don't you think it is?'

'Maybe. But you look incredible in it.'

'I just think I'll be worrying everything is going to fall out in the middle of the service.'

They both giggle. 'Maybe not then,' Sophia admits. 'We don't want to upset the older guests.'

Three dresses later and still nothing is quite right. 'It's no good, I'm going to have to try on the Madi Lane dress again,' Jess says disconsolately.

'Which, the rose or the drape?' asks Sophia.

'Both,' they say at the same time, then laugh.

Of course Jess looks gorgeous in each of the gowns, apart from a puffy dress with far too much ruching. They discard the meringue but they're left with a huge pile of possible winners. 'Which one feels like *the one*?' asks Sophia.

'I don't know,' ponders Jess. 'This is such a big decision.' To many it's just a dress, but for Jess it means everything. She wants to be the centre of attention, just for once, to look and feel amazing. This is her wedding day and it's got to be perfect.

'Why don't you try each of them again, this time with the shoes and the veil?' suggests Val, hovering eagerly, refilling their champagne glasses with a generous hand, no doubt with the hope that a little inebriation might soften the sting of the high price tag for this particular collection. Having done so, however, she speedily trots off to replace the bottle in the back room; she doesn't want them so tipsy they spill sparkling wine on the dresses.

Jess goes back into the changing room before reappearing in the rose dress. She looks beautiful but Sophia can sense she's not in love with it. 'Now the next,' she says, idly flicking through a magazine. Something about one of the brides attracts her notice. She's laughing, her long brown hair cascading down her back, and her cute husband is holding her hands and smiling into her eyes. The backdrop is of a stunning beach in the Maldives, or somewhere like it. Sophia swallows and quickly turns the page. She can't get upset here, this is Jess's time – but she can't help thinking that this could have been her, if only . . .

'Well, what do you think?' Jess returns in the draped Madi Lane dress, the first one she ever tried on, funnily enough. It is breathtaking; layers of lace cascading down from the bodice showing off Jess's figure to perfection. The finespun trim on her delicate veil is hovering gently on her shoulders, tiny gems sparkling in the shop lights like dewdrops. She looks stunning and this time she knows it.

'So, do you have your answer?' asks Val anxiously, sensing an imminent, highly lucrative sale is finally within tantalising reach.

'I think we do.' Jess smiles across at Sophia. 'This is the one, I can just feel it.'

'It's perfect. I love it,' agrees Sophia. 'You look amazing and Zach is one incredibly lucky guy.'

'I'll make sure he knows it,' Jess says with a laugh, swishing back into the changing room in a flurry of cream fabric.

Sophia goes back to her magazine, but the print blurs and swirls in front of her eyes.

'Are you all right there, love?' asks Val, taking the discarded dresses in her arms.

'Yes, I'm fine,' says Sophia with an attempt at a smile. She doesn't feel fine; she feels a bit weird, a little out of it, even. Just like on that fateful day that changed everything. She had worked so hard; everything was all mapped out perfectly: her successful high-powered job, her future marriage to Ryan. And then in one brief episode, the course of her whole life had changed. Four minutes, that's all it had taken – well, four minutes and thirty seconds to be precise. Because on that day, Sophia had suffered her first epileptic seizure.

It's okay not to be okay – that's what they say. And of course it's true, but it's a weird fact that in this world, sometimes you can feel alone even when you're together.

CHAPTER 1

Sophia

'This is totally ridiculous,' I say, staring disconsolately at the row upon row of empty shelves, where the loo rolls should have been.

This is actually a crisis of epic proportions; shortage of toilet roll is a problem for the two of us in our flat at the best of times. We use it for pretty much everything: clearing up spillages, wiping the door handles with disinfectant (a regular occurrence these days) and for make-up emergencies, so we get through a fair bit.

'We're on our last roll,' Erica says at the other end of the phone, confirming my worries.

'I knew I should have stocked up, but I thought the reports were exaggerated.'

'Obviously not – it just takes one national crisis and everyone is reaching for the loo roll,' comments Erica.

'Anyone would think it's a stomach bug.' I poke about desperately to see if by some miracle a small pack of toilet rolls has hidden itself behind the tins. 'We'll have to improvise. What did they use in wartime?'

'Newspaper I think, but I don't fancy that much – it would be flipping uncomfortable.' Erica laughs. 'And we could hardly flush it down the loo after.'

'Doesn't bear thinking about,' I say with a chuckle.

'I've got to be on shift in a few hours. Have you seen my tunic?' asks Erica. I can hear her rummaging about for her midwife's uniform; she'll be trashing the place.

'It's hanging up ready in the wardrobe,' I say.

'You're a star, Soph. Just grab something and get yourself back. I need to be early tonight as we're short-staffed and last time we ate dinner together, I was late.'

'No surprise there then,' I remark but get off the phone hurriedly in any case.

Three-quarters of an hour later, I arrive in the scrubby little car park at the flats. Thank goodness the parking has got a little easier since the lockdown – fewer people coming in and out and at least the idiots who sometimes park in our lot so they can walk to the shop are stuck in their homes. I guess we have to be grateful for any positives we can find in this situation. I unpack the car and trudge past the bin bags, piled against the rusty garage fronts. One of the bags has spilled open and half the rubbish is scattered all over the ground, including some condom wrappers and an empty box of Viagra. How embarrassing, everyone seeing the contents of your bin. I'm relieved it's not mine – there would be far too much alcohol for one thing.

I carefully balance a beautiful picture of a rainbow one of the children insisted on my bringing home, on top of my shopping, delicately so as not to damage it, and trudge on up to the second floor. I am not risking the lift, which has broken more times than I can remember. I figure they won't have any repair men free to come and fix it in the current crisis.

I thump on our door and, after a pause, Erica opens it with her elbow, tying her hair high on her head in a neat ponytail.

'Couldn't give us a hand could you?' I pant as I blunder in, spilling packets of salad, veg, crisps and sweets in that order. I always figure a balanced diet means a treat every time you have something healthy.

'Just let me finish my hair, so I don't have to wash my hands again. The skin's beginning to peel off,' Erica tells me, disappearing back into her room.

I begin the usual procedure of hand scrubbing. I already used the obligatory antibac on leaving the shop, but you can't be too careful. Then begins the rigmarole of unpacking the shopping on a certain area of the table, which will be carefully wiped once it's all put away.

Erica reappears, looking smart in her blue uniform, make-up and hair immaculate. 'Have you got enough tissues here?' She laughs, unpacking five boxes. 'Are you getting a cold?'

'No, they're to deal with the current loo roll crisis,' I explain, 'at least until I get online to order some.'

'That's brilliant,' says Erica. 'I might take some to work; we're running short of supplies.'

'As well as midwives?' I ask ironically.

'It is a problem . . . Jenny has underlying health issues so she's having to self-isolate and I think there are a couple of others in the team who aren't going to be able to work at all.' She pulls open a packet of crisps and starts munching.

'Hang on a minute, they've got to last all week.' I laugh.

'Onto wartime rations now, are we?' asks Erica with a grimace.

'At the rate we get through snacks, yes.'

'Okay, well I won't eat my usual two packets at once then. What's this rainbow?' She indicates the painting I've carefully propped on the sideboard.

'This?' I lift it gently and hold it up against the wall. 'Isn't it wonderful? I need to put it up on the balcony.'

'Excellent idea,' replies Erica, finishing the crisps in one last enormous mouthful. 'Did one of your pupils create that or did you do it?'

'No it's better than I could do. We've been hard at work all day – the kids did an amazing job. This was Freya's. It's sweet isn't it?'

'Yes I love the bright colours, although I'm not sure about the orange, red and neon green right next to each other. It's cheery though. How old is she?'

'Eight,' I say, carrying the artwork onto the balcony. 'Have we got any string?'

'You've got to be joking . . .' She pauses. 'Might have some wool or something, in your old sewing basket? Not that you'd know, because you've never used it!'

'I did, years ago. Anyway Mum probably hoped I'd maybe use it for teaching the kids.'

I rummage about and manage to find some wool that isn't too scrappy and tie the resplendent rainbow on the railings, facing out towards the courtyard below.

'Don't you think it might get wet if it rains?' asks Erica.

'It hasn't rained for weeks,' I say indignantly – and it hasn't. The sun has shone for days now in some cruel irony of nature, given the hideous situation we all now find ourselves in. The birds have been singing, gathering bits of fluff from the courtyard below ready to make their nests. Spring has well and truly sprung and yet the whole of mankind is battling against a pandemic. I can't help but think this scenario would give Alanis Morissette inspiration for an entirely new song; the situation is so ironic.

'Will you do the clap at work?' I ask Erica, standing back to admire my handiwork, albeit from up above and therefore the wrong way up.

'You mean clap for ourselves? Bit bizarre.'

'That's a bit sad,' I say. 'No, I mean for everyone. You're clapping the NHS workers but also people in the shops and all the key workers.'

'Of course I will, unless I'm in the middle of delivering a baby – I don't think the mum would be too chuffed trying to push and yelling for more gas and air if I just stand there clapping.'

'Yeah, maybe that wouldn't go down too well.' I smile. 'It must be so tough for these mums. I wouldn't want to be expecting a baby right now.'

'Me neither,' says Erica. 'In fact, after what I've seen in the maternity unit, I'm completely rethinking the whole having kids thing. Are we having tuna pasta? I haven't got long.'

'It'll only take ten minutes.' I pop the kettle on and grab a pan. 'Can you chop some cucumber for the salad?'

'I guess . . .'

Erica is terrific, but she doesn't really do cooking or washing. In fact, she doesn't do a lot round the house at all, but she's lovely to live with all the same. I bet she makes an amazing midwife. She's totally unflappable and to be fair she also makes a mean cup of tea.

'Are you still kicking the dads out?' I ask, opening a tin of tuna.

'Yep.'

'Seems a bit 1960s. Mum told me they did that all the time – that and shoving babies on the bottle at the slightest inclination.'

'No choice; can't risk infection. It's for the babies' sakes as well. I try to make them feel as though they've got a friend in the room, though.'

'I can imagine, and to be fair I'd rather have you there than any man.'

'Thanks.' Erica pops a piece of cucumber in her mouth.

'But I'm not sure that's much of a compliment considering you hate all men at the moment.'

'Not all men,' I protest indignantly, 'just most of them!'

We down our food as we often do, in front of the TV. We've got quite into that drama *Quiz* about the guy who cheated on *Who Wants to Be A Millionaire?* by getting someone to cough when the right answers were read out.

'That wife is a bit scary,' Erica remarks.

'Yes, to be honest I think she put him up to it,' I comment.

'Must have driven them mad; people coughing wherever they went for the next ten years.'

'Yes, it's a good job there wasn't a virus outbreak then – the studio would have been empty.'

The dulcet tones of Dua Lipa blast out. 'Can't you change your ring tone? I've heard that so many times,' Erica complains.

'I love it,' I say, grabbing my phone. 'Besides, it gets me moving better than Joe Wicks. Oh, hi, Jess. How's it going?'

'Good thanks. Well, as good as it can be considering,' Jess replies.

'Yeah I know what you mean. It is a bit weird isn't it? I can't believe it's been a month since we went shopping at Greenham.'

'I know. It all felt so normal. Little did we know what was coming. I've had the most frustrating day too. The server keeps going down and we've had so many calls.'

'How annoying. I guess it's because everyone's on the system. I s'pose at least business is going on?' Jess works for a marketing company and used to have regular battles with her boss about working from home (it was apparently against company policy) – until the actual lockdown that is, which of course enforced it.

'I don't want to talk about work – it's totally boring. I've had an idea.'

This sounds ominous.

'Mmm,' I say noncommittally. Jess is fab and I adore her, but I can tell this is her *I'm-about-to-start-trying-to-manage-your-life* tone.

'I happened to come across this app the other day that could have been designed for you.'

I know exactly what kind of app she means and it will certainly not have been designed for me. 'Jess, we've been all through this. It's kind of you but . . .' Erica has her jacket on and gives a little wave from across the room. 'Just a mo, Jess – bye, Erica, take care won't you?' She gives me a sympathetic smirk as she vanishes out the door.

'Erica's just off for her shift. She's amazing – I would hate to go and deal with birthing women, especially in the middle of a pandemic,' I gabble to Jess, hoping it might distract her from the conversation.

'Yes, but we're all different aren't we, Soph? Anyway, Hinge is a dating app that helps you meet someone *nice* and *normal*. Even you can't go wrong. How about it?'

'Hinge? Sounds like something to do with a door.' I'm

trying my best, but there's no distracting Jess when she gets like this.

'Ha-ha, come on, Soph.' She hears my silence, which is hopefully deafening. 'Okay so maybe you haven't heard of it; you are getting on a bit now.'

'Thanks a lot.' I roll my eyes. 'It's nearly time for the NHS clap. Don't you think you'd better go and get ready?'

'It's only seven-thirty and we only have to go to the window. It's really not that far.'

'Yes, but I need to make sure my hands are warmed up ready for my best clapping,' I say.

'It's too late anyway,' says Jess.

'What do you mean? It's not 'til 8 p.m.'

'No, the dating thing. I've done it, I've signed you up to Hinge. You're welcome.' As always with Jess, it's a fait accompli. I remember the time we vaguely discussed getting Mum and our stepdad a holiday weekend away as a surprise and before I had confirmed I could pay my share, she had booked it and paid the deposit. Jess has a heart of gold but goes at everything at a hundred miles an hour.

It's a fact that she doesn't ever give up. I hate dating apps. I have managed to avoid Tinder so far, having heard too many horror stories. It's so not my thing. These people could be anyone; how do you know the photo is even them? I'm a bit old-fashioned. For me there's something so impersonal about meeting online.

'Jess, it's very thoughtful, but you know how I feel about apps. I was going to get back into dating slowly;

19

I have this idea of actually meeting someone in person, getting to know them properly. I had it all planned.'

'Yes, but now we're in the middle of a lockdown you're kind of limited for options, hon.' My sister is ever practical.

'It's so frustrating,' I admit. 'I was all geared up for a fresh start. Joining some fitness groups, book clubs – you know the sort of thing.'

'Not going to happen now for ages, so you're going to have to get creative and Hinge is quite good actually. Danni at work used it. She's been going out with this guy for six months now and he is really nice and normal.'

'Well that's a start,' I say with a laugh, 'except you know I am far from normal – it's way too boring. And I would rather meet someone first. God knows who you find on these apps. They could be a stalker.'

'You're going to have a hard job finding a stalker in the current situation. Most people aren't able to go out,' Jess tells me. 'And in any case, Hinge is really cool. It's not like other apps – it's not random and you can only contact a certain number of people. Also, you have to have things in common or it won't let you contact each other.'

'Why is it called Hinge anyway? If you're unhinged you're not allowed to join?'

'Yeah right. I don't know but I've just pinged across your account details.' My phone bings at the arrival of a message.

'Thanks, it's good of you,' I say patiently, wanting to throttle her, but I know she'll never change. 'Is Mum okay?'

Miraculously, for once my tactics work and Jess is momentarily distracted. 'Yes, I spoke to her yesterday. She's been having trouble with Uncle Jim though.'

'Oh no, is he poorly again?'

'Well, you know how his stomach is?' I think the whole world is au fait with my Uncle Jim's stomach. It seems to have a life all of its own. I'm surprised he doesn't send out a Christmas letter dedicated solely to the ins and outs of his digestive system. He is about ninety-three and one of the most dapper old gentlemen you have ever met, always in a smartly pressed shirt and tie, whatever time of day you might find him, yet he is also one of the most difficult. He usually has something wrong with him, but as soon as my mum tries to help, he won't take the medicine. He really needs to go into a nursing home, but staunchly refuses and instead lives in a block of flats for older people, where they seem to have a competition going for who can be the most awkward and cantankerous.

'I thought Mum sent him some medicine that would build him up a bit?' I say.

'Yes she did, but it was rather awkward because I took the stuff round, to save Mum, and left it outside Uncle Jim's flat, as of course I couldn't go in. Apparently after I'd gone, one of his neighbours, Geoff – you know, the one who lives in the flat next door and is ninety-eight, the one Uncle Jim looks out for?'

'I remember.' How could I forget? He's always getting

21

into some trouble or other despite my ill, elderly uncle's expert care.

'He got hold of the box of sachets prescribed to build up stamina after being ill, and he ate three of them.'

'Oh no.' I stifle a laugh. 'I mean that's terrible. Was he all right?'

'He was fine, probably better than he had been in years, but Uncle Jim was furious with him, said he'd stolen his medicine and there was a right old ruckus. Without intervention it would have truly been a case of Zimmer frames at dawn. Mum had to calm him down – apparently she was on the phone for ages!'

'Poor Mum, as if she hasn't already got enough to do at work.'

'She said it's really busy at the surgery although they're trying to do most of the appointments online to minimise contact.'

'It's a worry isn't it? I wish now that she had a job where she worked from home. It would be a lot safer,' I say, 'and just imagine if she'd had her way – you'd have been working on the front line too.'

'Someone's got to do it, although I was never cut out to be a doctor. I hated science anyway. You should have stepped up to the plate as the prodigal daughter,' Jess replies staunchly.

'That was never going to happen. Science was the only GCSE I had to retake and in any case she was perfectly happy with my career in law. It's the whole teaching thing she has issues with.'

'I guess, but you can understand it was a bit of a shock to her after putting you through years of law school. I'd have loved to have an opportunity like that.'

I sigh inwardly. This is an age-old argument. Neither Mum nor Jess get the whole career change thing. For ages they just thought I was having a momentary crisis, which they expected to resolve along with the cessation of my seizures with the epilepsy meds, with the happy result of me going back to my legal career and everything returning to normal.

As always Jess is oblivious. 'I've got to go now, but before I speak to you next I want you to try the app.'

I get the sense the world could be ending and she'd still remember to check.

'I'll speak to you tomorrow,' I say.

'I'll be asking questions,' Jess replies and with that she's gone.

Half-heartedly, I click on the link she's sent, but quickly exit it again. I can't face it – it's simply not the right time to meet someone now. It's typical, just when I'm finally considering making some sort of effort to at least try to regain my trust in guys. They can't all be unreliable and shallow, influenced totally by success and looks. There must be some genuinely nice blokes out there somewhere; it's only a matter of finding them.

I glance at the clock: 7.50. There's just enough time to clear up the remains of dinner and get ready for the clap for the NHS.

At 7.55 I am ready. The door to the balcony is open

and I potter about just inside, not wanting to look as though I don't know what I'm doing. I'm not sure why. It's not like anyone will see me. I fiddle with a couple of bits, picking them up and putting them down again.

I go back out again at 7.59. Should I start? Is it like a thing when everyone automatically knows when to begin? Will I be able to hear anyone else? I peer down into the courtyard but it's empty as usual. Perhaps I'll just start clapping on my own. I check my phone and as I am looking, it changes to 8 p.m.

As if by magic the clapping starts – first quietly, from one side of the courtyard, then the next, and from above, until all around me the air is full of clapping. It's a rousing chorus of applause ringing out round the court-yard and beyond from the streets of the city, echoing far and wide. It's simply beautiful.

Before I realise what is happening, the tears start streaming down my face. So many people everywhere, kept apart, yet we are all responding in the same way. We are clapping together in one united group for our incredible fellow human beings out there right now on the front line, risking their lives for us all, battling to save people from this hideous virus. Erica, Mum, and so many others – people we care about and are terrified of losing. I hate this isolation from friends, family, even strangers, from normal human contact. I am sobbing now; a raucous, noisy broken sound and I can't stop.

'Hello? Are you okay?'

24

Now I've completely lost it – I'm beginning to hear things.

'Hello?'

I stop crying for a second and glance over my shoulder. No, there's no one there. Thank goodness no one has broken into the flat, though the door's locked and who would try burgling someone in the middle of the clap for the NHS, when everyone's in? I really am losing it.

'I just wondered if you were all right?' The voice comes again, definitely from outside. I look down into the courtyard. It's deserted.

'Hello?' I say tentatively, my voice husky after the crying.

'I'm up here,' says the voice.

'You're the voice from above?' I say. I mean, it could be comic if it weren't for the fact I'm so stressed about everything.

'Yes, I live in the flat above.'

'Oh.' That's a relief; there's a perfectly normal explanation. 'I thought I was hearing things,' I admit. Good grief, now he's going to think I'm really weird, whoever he is.

'You probably thought I was the voice of doom?' He laughs; it's a nice sound actually.

'Maybe. I'm sorry, did I disturb you? That's really embarrassing.' How awful, my blubbing must have been super loud for some random person to feel they had to ask if I'm all right.

'Not at all, the clapping was really moving – made me want to cry too,' he says.

'Well you were a lot quieter than me,' I say wryly.

'Not difficult,' he jests. 'Was it just all too emotional or is there something wrong?'

It's strange talking to someone I've never met, outside on a balcony when I can't even see him.

'It was emotional, but I guess I'm also scared,' I confess, sniffing and trying not to. In a way it's easier to be honest when you can't see the person you're talking to.

'We all are I suppose. I mean, it is sort of scary being told to stay in and that people are getting really sick,' the voice says matter-of-factly.

'I know, but I'm so frightened something's going to happen to my mum – she's a doctor – and my flatmate's a midwife. I guess the whole emotion of clapping for them brought home to me how much danger they're in. I can't bear the thought of losing them.' I wipe my nose with one of the new tissues; good job I bought so many as I have a feeling we're going to need them.

'I'm sure they'll be okay; they're doing their best to keep things safe as they can in hospitals and surgeries. Surely your mum's doing most of her appointments online?'

'Yes,' I call back up into space, 'she is, and Erica is pretty sensible. They give them masks and stuff.'

'Then you need to try to stop worrying about them as much as you can. Sometimes it's worse for the people at home, as they have more time to fret than if they were actually doing the job.'

'Thanks, I guess you're right. I never thought of it like that.' I sniff.

26

'What do you do anyway?' he asks.

'I'm a teacher – I'm looking after some of the key workers' kids who still have to come into school,' I say.

'Bet that keeps you busy then?' he asks.

'Very, though I've only got six from the whole school. I love it, but I'm sorry for them. They worry about their parents too. You'd think they wouldn't as they're little, but sometimes children surprise you – they understand more than you would think. Freya asked me today if her mum was going to come home and what would happen if she got sick. She's a single parent, all Freya's got.'

'That's tough, but all you can do is stay strong for these kids, I guess. But you have to let it out sometime, so I'll let you off having a noisy blub on your balcony and disturbing my quiet beer and packet of crisps.'

'Rude!' I chuckle.

'That's better,' he says. 'At least you can still laugh, which is a good sign. I bet the kids are entertaining too.'

'Yes they're so funny,' I reply. 'Milo, who is five by the way, asked me today why we can't just call up Spider-Man to come and entangle the Cornyvirus in his web and tow it into space!'

'Interesting idea.' He laughs.

'We should recommend renaming it to the government for the next update meeting. Talking about the Cornyvirus would seem much less sinister.'

'I'll tell Boris next time he calls.'

'Yeah right,' I reply with a smile. 'I could do with

27

setting you on my sister Jess too; she's also a complete stress-head at the moment.'

'About the virus?' he asks.

'No, about her wedding. She's talked of nothing else for the last year and although I love her dearly, she's making me wish that the government would ban all weddings until at least 2025!'

'Not a Bridezilla?' he asks.

'Maybe a bit,' I admit.

'But when's the wedding? Surely it can't go ahead at the minute?'

'No, she's had to cancel the physical wedding reception. As you can imagine, she was totally devastated, and I was gutted for her. Although she can be really annoying, she put an incredible amount of work in. So the service will be on Zoom.'

The guy above really laughs now – I like it, a deep chuckle. 'My God, I've never heard of such a thing. There really is no stopping her then!'

'Absolutely not.' The whole Hinge conversation reverberates disturbingly in my mind. 'She is a real human dynamo, Jess.'

'Well, good for her – although it sounds as though she might leave everyone steamrollered in her wake.'

I'm silent for a moment, as I've tried talking to Mum and Erica about Jess but it's difficult. In spite of her pushiness, she does really care and I adore her. When the chips have been down, Jess has always been there for me yet she doesn't always get where I'm coming from, especially not since my illness. It's odd because no one really understands the love-hate relationship you can have with your own family – yet this random man, who is just a voice (for all I know he doesn't even have a body) has hit the nail on the head.

'I haven't offended you have I?' comes the voice.

'No of course not, it's just that right now a little of Jess seems to go a long way!'

'Always does where weddings are concerned, but I'm intrigued anyway . . . How is she going to manage the service?'

'Good question, but she's got it all sorted.'

'Naturally. Is there a huge wall planner and a bumper executive Filofax?'

'No, but she has three huge lever arch files, two apps and a *Countdown to your Wedding Plan* she has distributed to all of us.'

'Oh wow, this woman means business. What does the groom say about it all?'

'He just said he's going to turn up.'

'That's a good start.'

'It seems pretty unavoidable, considering he already lives with her and they're in lockdown.'

We both laugh.

'To be fair though, he would need to hire security, if he let Jess down – we're really close,' I say, feeling disloyal.

'I get it,' he replies. 'I have an older brother who is great, but he thinks it gives him a free ticket to tell me what to do all the time.'

'Siblings, huh?'

'Yep . . . I'm guessing Jess and her fiancé don't live with you then. That might be a bit crowded?'

'No, you're right, it would be a nightmare!' I reply.

'At least you get a break from it then,' he says and I can hear the amusement in his voice.

'True, but then I miss her too.'

There's a silence and after a while I wonder if he's still there. 'There's only one thing for it,' he says eventually. He's obviously been thinking.

'What?'

'You're going to have to exercise your human rights.'

'Human rights?' I reply, puzzled.

'Yeah, your basic human right to not answer your phone or respond to texts.'

'But what reason can I give? I can't exactly say I'm out, when I'm always either at school or at home.'

'Hmmm good point. The lockdown has taken away the excuse of being unavailable when you are generally pretty available,' he says contemplatively. 'You'll have to say you were in the loo or cooking dinner or something.'

'That's only going to work for half an hour at the most.'

'Fair comment. You could just not get back to her and pretend you've left the country.'

I laugh. 'During a lockdown? You have not met Jess; she'd get a SWAT team scouring the entire planet, social distancing or not.'

He chuckles. 'You've got me there. I'm going to have

to give it some thought. I too have several large files and a planner, so I'll get back to you.'

'Okay sounds good,' I reply. Although the sun has been staying out a little longer now the clocks have gone forward, it has finally vanished for the night. 'It was nice to meet you and thanks for putting up with my emotional outburst. I'm going to go in now as it's getting cold and dark.'

'Yeah and these flats aren't posh enough for outside lighting.'

'Or for anything else,' I say. 'Bye then and thanks for the chat.'

'That's okay, I enjoyed it.'

There's silence and I wait momentarily to see if he's going to say anything else, but he doesn't. I shiver again as it really is cold and I get quickly back in the warm.

I hear the balcony door above shut a split second before mine and wonder if he hesitated too; maybe he too was waiting to see if I said anything else. Strange I never knew he lived there. I suddenly realise I don't know anything about him. I was so busy talking about my own troubles I didn't ask him about himself. I don't even know his name!

Perhaps Jess is right: Hinge is the only answer. This lockdown and social distancing malarkey is making me incapable of having even the simplest conversation with a guy.

CHAPTER 2

Jack

I wake with a start, my heart pounding, with an unaccountable feeling of impending doom, as though I should be somewhere or doing something. Groggily I peer round the pillow at my silent alarm clock and the slow realisation dawns on me that I haven't got to be anywhere and in fact I can't go anywhere even if I wanted to. Just like yesterday and the day before and the day before that. I lie there gazing disinterestedly at the ceiling. I don't feel like doing anything at all.

Perhaps this is what happens to people when they get old and retire, unless they are one of those active individuals who take up golf or petanque or something, they just end up staying in bed longer and longer until one day they simply can't get up. Like the four old grandmas and grandads in *Charlie and the Chocolate Factory*. That's it – it's all over. I think I've been on my own too long. In rebellion against my thumping head and in active

33

defiance of the hideous future I have predicted for myself, I leap out of bed and wish I hadn't. How many Old-Fashioneds did I drink last night? Too many, judging by the fact my feet no longer feel as though they belong to the rest of my body. Yet it can only have been a couple; it's not as though I can get away with much these days.

For the next ten minutes I blunder about randomly, trying to find a shirt and manage to slip up on my iPad, which I'd left on the floor by my bed. Not a bright idea in view of the fact I've only narrowly managed to avoid smashing it to smithereens. I should really take more care of it. There's no way I could get another if I break this one. I pick it up gingerly and place it on charge, upended and propped against a table leg. For some unaccountable reason, this is the only way it will charge now. The wire seems to have broken and it will bing incessantly otherwise. The first time it did it, the other day, I spent at least ten minutes wandering round the flat, trying to work out what was making the noise. Well at least it gives me something to do today; I'll get online and order a new charger.

I wander into the kitchen, flick on the kettle and rummage about for some coffee. Great, there's only decaf left; this is getting desperate. I add a double quantity hoping it will somehow help the situation and stare dispiritedly at the now-stale loaf I have available for breakfast. It's not very appealing to be honest. Maybe I'll make eggy dip to moisten it, unless . . . I search hopefully about in the fridge . . . nope, I'm out of eggs.

34

It reminds me of that stupid advert where the woman gets in late from work, looks casually in the fridge and conveniently finds a courgette, a couple of eggs and some old cheese and whips up a meal out of almost nothing. It's all very well unless you don't have any eggs. In fact, I think it was an advert for eggs.

Okay, this is really sad. A couple of weeks ago I was living my best, well *nearly* my best life, laughing with customers, whipping up cocktails in one of the coolest bars in the district and now here I am obsessing about whether or not I have an egg in the fridge, with just a scrap of bread and a scraping of Marmite all that stands between me and starvation. I put the bread in the toaster and examine the couple of bags of crisps I have left. I could eat one now, but then there won't be any for the long evening ahead and what about tomorrow?

I haven't been able to get a food delivery from the supermarket until two weeks' time. Until then I've got a problem. I'm just going to have to keep getting online and trying for slots. Perhaps if I try first thing in the morning? If I wanted to take this really seriously, I could set my alarm. But that's a bit too keen, and the day will stretch even longer ahead of me. At this rate, I'll be forced to turn my entire sock drawer into a puppet show cast of *Hamilton* and perform a one-man version of the hit musical on YouTube.

I wander back to the bedroom to grab my iPad so I can at least try to check for delivery slots again, but it's still on one per cent. I plug it back in and attempt to prop the lead up with a book. It bings several times defiantly at me and then seems to be charging.

Back in the kitchen smoke is coming out of the toaster. I sprint towards it and desperately press the emergency eject button – this is the last slice; I can't waste it even if it has completely turned to charcoal. It pops up and looks vaguely edible. I'll scrape some of the burnt bits off with a knife. Whilst I am trying to do this, the bread, which in any kind of normal life would have been relegated firmly to the bin several days ago, gives up and collapses into several pieces.

I stand and munch at the Marmite-coated remnants, which are okay actually, when swigged down with large gulps of coffee, whilst peering out onto the courtyard. There's no one out there; it's unnaturally quiet. It's been like this for the last couple of weeks: weirdly silent, no sirens even, as though people have stopped calling ambulances, the world has ceased to turn, waiting for some invisible storm to hit, but we are none of us sure what.

I wonder what the girl downstairs is up to. I haven't heard a sound, so I assume she's probably gone to work. I glance at the clock: 8.59 – ten minutes after the last time I looked. It's as though time is going in slow motion since I've been stuck in this flat. I guess she would have to be in school now. I picture her standing in front of a small group of children, all sitting obediently two metres apart in different parts of the classroom. I wonder what she looks like. I picture her as fairly tall, with dark hair and maybe a smattering of freckles, to match her smiley voice. What am I thinking? I have no reason to have any idea what she looks like. Maybe I drank too much and imagined all of it; perhaps she doesn't even exist. Somehow the thought upsets me and I feel bereft.

My phone rings out and I hurry to pick it up, excited at the thought of speaking to someone, then hastily put it back down again. It's Laura, and she phoned last night too. It's no good, I can't face speaking to her. It's only going to be more of the same harassment and somehow I feel even more trapped locked down here in this flat, unable to go out or get away from her constant haranguing.

As a distraction, I start to tidy the kitchen, not that there's much to clear: a pan from last night's stir-fry and the chargrilled corners of toast. There's a sound from outside and excited by the prospect of something interesting actually happening for once, I hurry to the balcony. It's a woman pushing a bike across the courtyard and heading back out towards the main road. She's middle-aged with vibrant red hair. I don't think that could be her – she sounded young. I finally understand what makes dogs sit with their paws up on the sofa, staring out the window of their houses – it really is the most social interaction you get when you're stuck in. I often wave to a dog in one of the ground-floor flats, or rather I did when I was allowed out. Back in the day. I laugh at myself, at the thought of telling potential future grandchildren what it was like to have to stay inside like a prisoner for months on end.

'Keep busy,' Sam said when I spoke to him the other

day, so I'm going to clean up the flat. Since there's nothing else to do. It's pretty disgusting. I don't think I've cleaned it for weeks, but then I hate cleaning at the best of times. I get out the hoover, rummage about in the cupboard for polish. There isn't any, just some pink rubber gloves. What are they doing there? Then I remember, my mum insisted on giving them to me when I moved in. Probably a joke. I unpack them from the wrapper and put them on. They feel really bizarre.

I take hold of the hoover and start to move it round the floor. It's quite fun actually, but I need something to make it more interesting. I flick on Freddie Mercury. The iPad is cooperating even though it's only just made it to ten per cent.

I shout 'I Want to Break Free' while whizzing the hoover under the sofa. I make myself a wig out of a tea towel, catching sight of myself in the mirror – I look brilliant. And if I don't, no one is here to tell me otherwise. Whoever knew housework could be such a laugh.

I hear something strange interfering with the music – my phone is buzzing and vibrating round the table. I check it isn't Laura again. Thank goodness it isn't. It's Sam on FaceTime.

'How's tricks?' I say cheerfully, answering it.

'What the heck have you got on your head?' Sam asks.

Oh no – he can see me. 'Nothing mate, just doing some clearing up.'

'With a pair of pants on your head?' he asks.

'Yeah, erm well my hair's getting in my eyes so I

popped it back with whatever's nearest. It's actually a tea towel,' I say, as if that makes anything better.

'And the pink gloves?'

'What? Oh,' I snatch off the rubber glove. 'Well, you can't be too careful with germs.'

'We'd seriously better hope this lockdown doesn't last long – you're totally losing it. I mean, for a start, since when did you care if the flat is tidy?'

I throw myself down in the chair, exhausted after my short burst of activity – it's seriously true that the less you do, the less you are able to do. 'I'm pretty bored.'

Sam laughs. 'You must be.'

'How's Tina?'

'Clearing up also. There must be something in the air; she's been scrubbing the bath since first thing this morning. It's not like anyone's used it recently.'

'I guess she's getting ready for the baby,' I suggest.

'Yeah it's called nesting or something. Apparently it means it's not far off.'

'Exciting times. You still going to risk the hospital?'

'No choice with a first baby. Means I won't even be allowed in the room with her though.'

'That's tough. I guess you'll be cheering on from the sidelines then. Can you use Zoom or something?'

'Hardly, it's probably against health and safety or something. To be honest with you I don't really mind; I just wanted to be there for Tina. I was going to stay up the top end anyway.'

'Coward!'

'Says you. You'd run a mile.'

'To be fair, it's scary stuff. But life-changing.' I'm silent for a moment. 'I envy you though. You've already got Tina and now you're going to have a little one to keep you company.'

'I bet you're finding things quiet there still. No calls from the solicitor?'

'No, and yeah it is a bit. For me to have to tidy up – it's pretty desperate. I feel like I'm copping out somehow. Useless. I watch the news and people are all out there helping and I'm stuck in here hiding away.'

'For good reason.'

'I know, but it doesn't help. It's so boring. Dan's got himself a job as a delivery driver as he was made redundant and Matt is still working to get stuff packaged. It feels like everyone's busy except me.'

'Why don't you get out your guitar again? You must have it there with you.'

'Haven't played for ages.'

'All the more reason to get it out now.'

'I guess. Still me, myself and I though.'

'It's the way it's gonna be for a while. But you've got us and we can Zoom when the little one's born.'

'Yeah that'll be nice.' There's a silence. 'I did speak to someone downstairs last night.'

'I hope you didn't get near. You've got to keep yourself safe – you know what the specialist said.'

'I know.' I love Sam, but he gets overstressed. 'I didn't even see her.'

'Her?' he asks.

'I heard someone crying when I was out on the balcony last night, after the NHS clap, which was really cool by the way.'

'I know, I thought hardly anyone would be doing it, but you could hear it all round our street. It was great.'

'Afterwards there was this sobbing, so I called to the person down below and we got talking.'

'Trust you, Jack.' Sam raises his eyebrows and gives me one of his big-brotherly looks. Bizarrely I've missed them. 'There's no keeping you away from the chicks, is there?'

'No, it wasn't like that; it was simply nice to hear someone's voice. To actually have a conversation, other than on the phone, with another human being.'

That was the point; it had somehow made me feel less alone, talking to someone here in the building, so nearby, even if we couldn't see each other. I find myself wondering if she'll be out there again later. Perhaps I'll have my last packet of crisps on the balcony at the same time tonight, just in case.

CHAPTER 3

Sophia

'I'm sorry about the change of plan, but chocolate crispy cakes are really yummy too,' I say apologetically to the six pairs of hopeful eyes staring at me and my bag of goodies.

'Chocolate crispy cakes yessss!!!' shouts Milo. I smile affectionately at his cheeky face under the mop of fair hair; I can always rely on him to be enthusiastic.

'What about the fairy cakes?' Freya asks.

'The thing is, I can't get flour anywhere because the shops have run out,' I explain. 'So fairy cakes will have to wait for another day.'

'But then we can't put sprinkles on them.' Freya looks miserable. 'I wanted to surprise Mum with something pretty.'

'Well,' I say thinking on my feet, 'I think you'll find that, first of all, chocolate is full of magnesium and other good things that will help your mum be an even better nurse than she is already, and secondly, we have some other little goodies in here we can use to decorate them.' I tip the bag up and out fall some decorative paste butterflies, silver balls and pink edible flowers.

Freya and her friend Lola shriek. 'Please can I use the butterflies?' asks Freya.

'I like the flowers,' calls Lola.

'I'm just going to do mine plain with lots and lots of chocolate,' says Milo decisively. 'My mum needs extra chocolate 'cause she was really grumpy this morning.'

'You can all do them as you like,' I say with a smile. 'What about you, Alfie?' It's always hard to get eleven-year-old Alfie to say much.

'Am I allowed to do cakes?' he asks. 'I thought they'd just be for the younger kids.'

'Of course not,' I say. 'They're for everyone. In any case, I expect your parents are in just as much need of chocolate cakes as anyone else?' My current class is made up of all ages as they are the children of key workers.

Alfie nods shyly.

'What about you, Pritti?'

'My mum loves cakes. She makes them all the time.'

No pressure then. 'It will be nice for you to make her some in that case.' I have a hideous flashback to the time I volunteered to make cakes with the reception class during teaching practice. The look of horror on the headteacher's face when she happened to come into the room, which was mostly decorated with icing sugar and

44

flour, as well as the children who were pretty much covered, will probably stay with me forever.

Pritti smiles. 'I don't think she's made crispy cakes before.'

I notice Zane peeking at the bowls and ingredients with a worried look on his face. Zane is only four and a cute little lad, but always painfully shy. I hoped he would come out of his shell more with fewer students in the class, but if anything he's become even more timid. Hopefully he'll enjoy it more once we get the chocolate out. You can't really go far wrong with these. Or at least I hope not, as I think of Pritti's mother, who is a professional pastry chef. I start to put out the ingredients, making sure Zane has some pictures to follow to make it easier for him. It's been a real struggle to get all the utensils because of course we have to have six bowls, six spoons – six of everything, basically, or we'll never keep up social distancing.

'So I've placed a bowl on each table and next to it all the things you will need to make your mixture. When I call your name each of you will come up and I'll use the plug-in hob to melt your chocolate. Of course we will have to make sure we keep two metres apart – the length of a broom.' I point at the chart on the wall.

It works more smoothly than I'd hoped and after an hour, each child miraculously has a plate of chocolate crispy cakes next to them.

'Can we eat them now?' asks Milo, a crispy cake poised halfway into his open mouth.

'You can have one, once you've each gone and washed your hands again, but take the rest home for your parents. They've been working hard and deserve them.'

'But, Miss Trent, Zane has eaten nearly all of his.'

Oh, good grief. While I've had my back turned, Zane has eaten four of his cakes. They say it's always the quiet ones you have to watch. I really hope he isn't going to be sick.

'Did he really eat all of them?' Jess asks with a laugh, on FaceTime that evening. I am exhaustedly slumped on my sofa eating my own batch of chocolate crispy cakes.

'Most of them.' I chuckle. 'I just hope he isn't sick when he gets home or his mum will be after me. I gave him a load of spares I made so at least he got to take some for his family – if he didn't eat them on the way home.'

'I don't know how you do it,' says Jess, 'spending all day surrounded by kids.'

'I'm not exactly surrounded,' I say amused. 'There are only six of them in at the moment. Anyway, they're brilliant; they say what they think, unlike most adults. And it's a good excuse to do fun stuff.'

'Wish you could send one of those cakes down the phone,' Jess groans. 'They look delicious.'

'They are.' I finish popping another cake in my mouth and put the others to one side. I feel mean eating them in front of Jess. It seems rude somehow. This lockdown has taken away any pleasure in eating with people, other than those you are with. It's all very well saying we can

FaceTime or Zoom, but there is something so basic about our need to be together, to eat and celebrate special events with each other, not in our own separate little universes. 'How are the plans going?'

'Good. I've finished paying for the dress, the suits are sorted and the hotel has kindly agreed to refund the reception.'

'Decent of them.'

'I guess they haven't any choice.'

'No, but I kind of feel sorry for hotels, restaurants and bars; how are they supposed to make a living?' I wonder.

'You feel sorry for everyone. That's your trouble; you're too soft.'

'Not really, but I do imagine how other people might feel about things.'

'Good job you didn't keep working as a lawyer then.'

I stay silent for a moment. That was a little near the bone. I enjoyed working in law. I had worked so hard for my legal career. I earned my way with relentless graft and hours of burning the midnight oil. I can still visualise all the pages of legal clauses, the Latin names and ream upon ream of legal jargon and provisos. At times my room-mate would struggle to find me behind the mountainous piles of books I would be lost behind. But I guess Jess is right: in the end, I wasn't ever really suited to it. Much as I blame the epilepsy.

'Sorry, I didn't mean to offend you,' she says as an afterthought.

'It's okay.' Although it's not really, but there's no point in trying to explain it to Jess. I attempted it a couple of times, soon after my diagnosis, thinking she would understand, as she so often had with other things in the past, but she really didn't get it. So I have learned to smooth it over. Make it all appear to go away. It's so much easier for everyone else that way, especially since the meds have been keeping the seizures under control. 'I love what I do,' I continue, 'and there's no going back now. Kids are far less demanding than divorcing couples anyway.'

'True.' Jess giggles. 'And at least you can put them on the sun on the reward chart, if they're good, or on the naughty step if they're bad.'

'There is no naughty step any more,' I retort, stifling a yawn.

'How're the new meds?' she asks.

'Better.' Thank goodness they are, as well. 'That hideous feeling of exhaustion has diminished a little. The last ones were awful. I felt drugged all day. As long as I take these the same time every evening I'm a tiny bit better. The mornings are still hard as I feel most tired then, but the exhaustion sometimes wears off during the day. Other times it doesn't. It kind of feels as though you've been out on the razzle every night and you have to work through it all morning until by about lunchtime, things feel a little better. Other times I stumble or lean on the wall because I feel sort of off balance, but it only happens occasionally.'

'It's a hard price to pay to avoid having a seizure,' Jess says.

'It is, but there isn't any choice is there? The thought of collapsing in front of the entire class is not a good one. They'd be terrified.'

'Not a pretty sight, but the staff would manage. I mean it must happen.'

'It just can't happen. I'd have to leave my job. I'd feel as though I had traumatised the kids; they would be afraid for me to teach them.'

'It really can't be that bad. I know it's a bit embarrassing but . . .'

'One of my colleagues at Price Maberton told me I looked like I was doing the running man, the last time I had a seizure, let alone the fact he was totally freaked out because I had been eating a biscuit at the time and he was worried I would choke. It made me almost feel ashamed of even having to talk about it – as though I was an annoyance to everyone else. Also, I don't want to be "Sophia with the epilepsy". I want people to see beyond that.'

'Fair enough. I think you're best on the meds then.'

'Yes and at least they work at the moment. Viv's niece at school still has them occasionally in spite of the meds.'

'What a nightmare that must be. I suppose you have to be grateful for small mercies.' Jess sighs. Then she brightens a little. 'Anyway, it's all the more reason why you need someone nice to take care of you. How did you get on with Hinge?'

How annoying. I thought she'd forgotten about it. 'I've been really busy,' I mutter.

'Not that busy,' she says in a stern tone. 'You just don't want to do it.' I'm silent for a moment, hoping she's got the hint. 'Okay, I'll have to think of something else,' she declares breezily.

We chat for a few more minutes before I get off the phone. I need to make sure everything's washed ready for tomorrow, as my best shirt has a stain on it. I'm pondering the idea of cooking up some mince and making a cottage pie, which would at least do for two nights, then I could have a night off tomorrow.

As I pootle about, clearing things off counter tops and sorting clothes, I wonder about the guy from last night. I haven't heard anything since I got in, but I guess that's not surprising, given Erica was here earlier, crashing about with her stuff before rushing off to her shift, and then I've been on the phone. I open the door, wander out onto the balcony and stand there looking down into the courtyard. It's all quiet. I consider going back inside and watching something on TV but it's a warm evening and it seems a shame to spend it indoors. Then I hear a noise. Up above.

It sounds as though his balcony door is opening. 'Hello?' I call quietly.

Nothing.

'Hello?' I call a little louder this time.

'Hello?' comes the voice from above.

'Oh, hi.' I smile, ridiculously pleased that he's there. 'You're back.'

'I haven't really gone anywhere,' replies the voice.

50

'No . . . I guess it's quite difficult at the moment,' I say.

'How were the kids today?' he asks.

'Great, thanks.' I feel inordinately pleased he remembers our previous conversation. 'We all made chocolate crispy cakes.'

'Sounds delicious.'

He sounds wistful, hungry even. 'I wish I could send one up to you, but I'm not sure how.'

'Don't worry, I'm okay – I have my emergency packet of crisps left.'

'Is that all?'

'I do have an Old-Fashioned as well.'

'I've never tried one of those,' I admit.

'Well it's not a proper one – I haven't all the ingredients – but it's refreshing.'

'Ooh I'm jealous,' I say.

'I've had an idea. Give me ten minutes and I'll be back.'

I smile to myself, wondering what his idea could be; there aren't really a lot of options currently. As I stand on the balcony an older guy, still fairly upright, with a silver moustache and wearing an old green jacket combined with smartish trousers, walks across the courtyard and through the archway across the other side. I've seen him walk through here before but I don't know where he lives. I know pretty much all the residents in this block so I don't think he lives in the flats. He must come from one of the nearby houses. He seems to go out about the same time every night. It makes me feel sad for him somehow; he cuts a lonely figure, in spite

51

of the purposeful nature of his walk. I wonder if he has a wife or if he lives by himself. It must be so hard for anyone coping with this lockdown living in total isolation. I would hate it.

The man upstairs has only been gone a minute or so – I have time to pop on the veg for the cottage pie while I wait. I go in and peel, rinse and chop the carrots, then soften them with the onion and a clove of garlic. The mince is just browning nicely and I'm about to add the tomatoes when I hear a noise from outside. I go back out onto the balcony.

To my amazement, a box has appeared, just below the parapet of the upstairs balcony. It looks like the end of a cardboard Budweiser box, hanging from what appears to be a bright yellow skipping rope.

'Have you got it?' calls the voice.

'Just a mo, keep it steady,' I say, trying not to laugh. I rush forward to grab the box, which is dangling precariously and at high risk of tipping out its contents, which on closer inspection turn out to be a glass of something with a slightly old-looking piece of lemon and a cherry on a cocktail stick. Miraculously it hasn't spilt.

'Oh wow!' I exclaim and carefully remove the glass, placing it on the little table on the balcony. 'This looks amazing.'

'Hope you like it!' There's a warmth to his voice and I wonder if he's smiling.

'I'm sure I shall.' The box starts to rise up again towards the balcony above. 'Hold on a minute!' I call.

'Don't pull it up yet, incoming!' I rush into the lounge and grab a handful of chocolate crispy cakes and place them carefully in the box. 'Okay,' I say standing back, 'pull away.' The box disappears, wibbling up in the air. At one point it tips at a precarious angle and I'm worried the cakes will scatter over the courtyard below. He manages to balance it again, though, and the trusty Budweiser box disappears from view.

'Chocolate crispy cakes!' he shouts. 'What a result – I love these.'

'Cheers!' I say taking a sip of the cocktail. 'Mmm, that is so good. What is it?'

'Well, it's my own invention at the moment as I haven't got half the usual ingredients.'

'Tastes pretty darn good to me. I'm not sure it will go with the cakes.'

'I can tell you it does,' he replies. I have to strain to make out his words; I reckon he's got a mouthful.

'They are pretty moreish,' I agree, tucking into another one myself. I can always make another batch tomorrow. 'Good grief.' I suddenly remember the mince and as I run inside the flat, I am almost knocked backwards by an acrid smell of burning. 'For goodness' sake!' The contents of the pan have stuck fast to the bottom in a blackened mess. 'So much for being organised,' I lament to no one in particular, scraping the burnt meat into a bowl just in case any of it's salvageable. This is all going horribly wrong. I was only trying to be organised so things would feel a little more under control, a couple of dinners prepared in advance so I don't have to worry about cooking when I get in from work, and I can't even manage that.

'Everything all right?' calls the voice.

I walk back outside. 'Yes – no, not really, I've just burnt tea for the next two days and I might have ruined my favourite pan.' I take a comforting sip of my cocktail.

'That's a bit of a crisis. Is it totally trashed or can you save some of it?'

'It's pretty blackened.'

'Looks like you're going to have to live off cocktails and cakes.' We both laugh.

'Could be worse I guess. Where did you learn to make such amazing cocktails?'

'In Greece. I lived in Crete for a couple of years and did a bartending course.'

'Oh wow, that sounds amazing. I've not been to Crete but I've visited Santorini and it was just beautiful.' I refrain from adding that the memory is tinged with sadness, as it was my last holiday with Ryan. We had stayed in a gorgeous apartment with a shared pool. Our days had been spent exploring the cobbled streets, swimming in the glass-smooth water and making love in the cool white cotton sheets within the sanctuary of the air-conditioned stone-clad apartment. It's been many months since we broke up, yet I still miss him, the feel of him, what we had together. Now I feel so bereft. Five years is a long time to be together for it to end so abruptly, just like that.

'Santorini is stunning.' His voice breaks in on my

thoughts. 'I went on a day trip from Crete once. I didn't like the cable car ride much though – it felt really dodgy.'

'I avoided that.' I smile at the recollection, trying not to think of Ryan. 'The donkeys looked safer to me.'

'You're braver than me; they looked every bit as lethal as the cable car.'

'Yes, they were a bit twitchy and fidgety,' I acknowledge. 'And it seemed to take forever to get up the cliff path. At one point I was worried I was going to have to dismount and carry the poor donkey.'

He laughs. 'It was awfully hot there, even for carrying just a scrawny donkey.'

'Baking. I needed one of your cocktails. When I got to the top I drank three jugs full of iced water.' Ryan had laughed at me, as I had sprawled against a cooling wall in a shady spot to recover. I had laughed too. Everything seemed so much simpler then. We had been two young people having fun. With difficulty, I drag my thoughts back to the present.

'Did you always want to be a barman?' I ask.

'No, funnily enough I wanted to be a sports therapist. I was all set to go to college. I was looking forward to the course but . . .' He breaks off suddenly.

'But?'

'Things changed. Greece sounded fun, less responsible. It was easier to run away instead I guess.'

'You could always go back to it, if it's really what you want to do. It's never too late. Our local college has an excellent reputation for Sports Science.'

'I guess.' He goes quiet and I worry I've touched a nerve.

'What made you come back from Greece anyway?' I ask, to change the subject a little.

'My brother Sam,' he says simply. 'And a few other things.'

'Does he live nearby?'

'Sort of – he's about an hour away.'

'That's nice. It's good not to be too far away from family, but maybe not too near either? If my sister Jess lived any closer, it would be a complete nightmare.'

'I know what you mean.' He laughs. 'I'm glad Sam's around though. He's about to become a dad.'

'Exciting – when's the baby due?'

'In the next couple of weeks.'

'Not long then. How's Sam's wife doing? It must be stressful in the middle of this whole business?' I know I would be terrified giving birth in the middle of a lockdown, although I guess it would be exciting as well. This birth would be a small moment in history, a snapshot from a major human drama. Ryan and I had discussed having kids several times. He wanted to have children and so did I, until I was ill that is; it made everything so much more complicated. Now our dreams feel as flimsy and transient as a gossamer-thin spider's web flickering in a thunderstorm.

'Tina? Yeah, she's doing okay, though Sam says she's driving him mad with frenetic scrubbing of everything in the house. Even the cat's running scared in case he ends up with a good bathing.'

I laugh. 'That's quite normal, as I understand it. My flatmate Erica's a midwife and she says all sorts of strange behaviour is completely run of the mill when dealing with pregnant women.'

'From what Sam says, I think she's right. Tina has insisted on reading Shakespeare to the bump at least once a day as well as the Quantum Theory of Physics – apparently she figures he or she needs to be fully rounded – at the same time as eating mustard and gherkin sandwiches. Most bizarre.' He pauses a second. 'Nice for you to have company – when your flatmate's not at work.' He sounds envious.

'Are you on your own up there, then?' I wonder if he has a girlfriend living with him.

'Yep, at the moment. I used to have a flatmate but he moved out. I was about to advertise for a new inmate and this all happened.'

'What a pain – you must be fed up then. How are you coping on your own? I guess at least it's peaceful?'

'Yeah maybe a bit too quiet for me,' he admits.

'Are you still working?'

'Nope, the bar's shut.'

'Oh, of course.' I feel really stupid now. 'Which bar is that?'

'Soho.'

'Oh, I know it.' I've been several times with Erica. I wonder whether I might have seen this guy there, amongst the admittedly fit and smartly uniformed barmen. 'It's great in there, nice atmosphere.'

'Yeah it is good, and our cocktails are second to none.' I can feel the pride in his voice.

'I can tell.' I take another sip. 'I haven't been in there for ages.'

'You'll have to pop in when we've reopened.'

'That would be lovely. I can't wait to have a night out again with the girls.'

'It all seems a long time ago now, doesn't it?'

'Going on a night out?'

'Going out at all.' The raw tone of despair paired with utter resignation in his voice is painful to hear.

'Are you stuck in then?'

'Yeah, pretty much.'

'Oh that sucks.' I wonder why he's having to stay in. He must be shielding for some reason, but I don't like to ask why.

'Yeah it does. I've got kidney disease, so I'm in the high-risk category. Not that I've got a letter to prove it or anything. But doctor's advice. You know how it is.'

'I do, actually.' I know all too well. It was with mixed emotions I had read the letter from the hospital.

We would like to inform you that there are no known additional risks associated with catching Covid-19 if you have epilepsy. If, however, you have any concerns, please call the Epilepsy Team.

In spite of this supposedly reassuring letter, I had been in a quandary about work. After all, no one really knows how this virus affects anyone. It's an unknown quantity, especially for anyone with any kind of underlying condition.

58

For anyone told to shield, it must be terrifying. 'How are you coping? How are you getting food and stuff?'

'I'm okay. I managed to get a delivery booked for a couple of weeks' time.'

'But what are you going to do until then?' I'm horrified now.

'I do have nice chocolate cakes that a kind person sent me.'

I laugh. 'No, seriously, do you have enough? If you ever need anything . . .'

'No, I'm fine.' I don't believe him at all. I'm getting the sense that he's the type of independent guy who doesn't like to ask for help. It would be admitting weakness. He's been through a lot by the sound of it; it's hardly surprising he feels this way.

'I'm going to Tesco tomorrow. Why don't you drop me down a list? I bet there must be some things you need.'

'I did eat my last crust of toast this morning,' he admits after a pause.

'Right: bread, what else?'

'I have a terrible craving for crisps, beef-flavoured ones, and Super Noodles; I love them. But I can't possibly ask you to get all those things.'

'Look, it's nothing. Write me a proper list with everything on it and send it down.'

'It's really kind of you – that would be brilliant! But I feel terrible. You've already got a lot on your plate.'

'Honestly, it's no trouble. I insist.'

'Okay then. I'm really grateful, thanks. But there's one thing, other than the fact you must let me give you the money.'

'That's fine – what's the other thing?'

'If you're kindly doing some shopping for me, I'd like to at least know your name?'

'Sophia.'

'Jack.'

'Nice to almost meet you, Jack,' I say – and it is. It really is.

CHAPTER 4

Jack

I go back inside as Sophia says she needs to go and try to salvage her dinner, but I leave the door to the balcony open, just in case. I like her name; it suits her.

I flick on my iPad and check all the major supermarkets' delivery slots, but they've got nothing sooner than my trusty slot on April 1st. I hope Sophia really is happy to shop for me. I feel bad asking her, but she didn't seem to mind. I peer in the cupboards and make a list, crisps and peanuts at the top – not that they're the most important, but at the moment they feel as though they are. Perhaps I should put staples at the top of the list, like bread and noodles and the other stuff at the bottom with a disclaimer: *only get if you don't mind.*

I tear off another bit of paper and rewrite the list with little notes next to what's urgent and what is just an extra luxury. I even add a few illustrations. I survey my handiwork – this is really sad. This is what lockdown does to a chap.

I flick on the iPad and select Dua Lipa's 'Physical', connect to the speaker and crank up the volume. I feel more energised than I have in weeks. It must be the thought of crisps and nuts. I dance around the room, and I almost feel like breakdancing as a sudden wave of unexpected happiness washes over me. Perhaps I should take up some kind of exercise again. My old training rope lies across the back of the sofa, still attached to the Budweiser packet – I could start skipping again. Then again, Sophia might think someone's coming through the ceiling if I bang about like that. Perhaps I'll give it a go in the day, while she's out. I might even do some push-ups. I need to do something to keep fit.

I catch sight of myself in the mirror and want to laugh – my hair has gone crazy. I'm going to have to shave it sometime, given that a trip to the hairdresser isn't going to happen any time soon.

My phone buzzes round the table.

'Hi, mate,' I answer. It's Dan, my friend from school. Back in the day we used to have some right old laughs. I'm really pleased to hear from him. It's been a while and I haven't exactly had much contact from the outside world.

'Hi, Jack, how you doin'?'

'Yeah okay, you know . . . considering.'

'Matt said you're having to self-isolate. That's a right bummer. Mind you, sounds like you're having a party.'

I turn down Dua Lipa. 'Thought I'd liven things up a bit.'

'The party starts at home, right? Reminds me of that night at "Urban Reef" when we all went late-night surfing.'

'Yeah, Matt miraculously found he could super surf after several beers, until that huge wave totally took him out.'

'It was brilliant, happy days,' he says.

'Feels like another lifetime, mate.'

'I know. How are you coping on your own?' he asks.

'It's okay I suppose.' I pause a second. There's no point in pretending it's all great when it isn't. 'Well not really – it's boring to be honest and I never thought I'd say this, but I'm a bit lonely. How's tricks with you?'

'Complicated.'

'That doesn't sound too good. Work not going well?'

'No, the delivery job's all right. As long as people keep their distance, and most of them don't even come out the house. I had someone earlier today who just yelled out the upstairs window to leave the parcel on her car. Makes me feel like I've got the plague.'

'For all they know, you might have,' I joke.

'Yeah it's made everyone pretty fearful . . . Bad times, mate. Nah, it's not work that's the problem.' He sounds furtive and lowers his voice to a whisper. 'It's Rick.'

'What's up with him?' Rick is Dan's room-mate. We all worked together in the holidays in our first student job down at the local eatery. Rick is a nice enough guy, a real joker, but he can be full on when he gets going.

'He's not the problem, exactly. More his girlfriend. Wait a minute.' He breaks off for a moment. 'I'm shutting the door – I don't want them to hear.'

'I didn't know he had a girlfriend.' That's the other thing about Rick – he's a bit of a lad. I don't think he's ever stuck with anyone for more than a couple of dates. They usually run away and change their number, if not their whole identity by that stage.

'He didn't.'

'I'm confused now.' I shove in a mouthful of cake; perhaps the chocolate will help my addled brain.

'He has now, though, and that's the problem.'

'Don't you like her?' I'm also wondering how he even met someone in the current situation.

'No, I don't think anyone does. He must have been totally trashed when he met her.'

'Surely he can't see her at the moment anyway? We're all in lockdown.'

'That's the thing: she was a one-night stand and hasn't gone home since they got together, because the next day the lockdown started.'

This does not surprise me with Rick at all. 'That's classic. So you're all stuck with her.'

Dan sounds cross now. 'Yes, and she's the most hideous person ever. Totally obsessive.'

'Maybe she can't help that. Anyway, you are a bit of a slob.'

'But it's *my* flat! I didn't ask to live with her and I really can't do it. You know my new rugby kit?'

'Yeah.' Perhaps I'll finish that cake. I reach for the rest of it.

'She's dyed it.'

'Dyed it?'

'Dyed it. Pink.'

I laugh again; I can't help it. 'That's unfortunate.'

'Unfortunate! It's a flipping disaster. It cost over a hundred quid and now it's bright pink. All because she can't leave anything unwashed or not put away. I can't find anything. And she is the world's pickiest eater – except when it comes to *my* food. I went to the cupboard yesterday and she'd eaten all the Twix.'

'That is a serious offence, especially at the moment; snacks are like gold dust. Perhaps you should lock them away?'

'And my beers have all run out because they're her favourite.'

'I suppose at least you can go get some more.' I'm beginning to struggle here. It's tough having someone grumble about stuff running out when at least he's able to get out. It's a basic human right.

'Not the point though, is it.' There's a silence. 'It's no good, Jack. I'm going to have to move out.'

'But where would you go?' Dan is a bit of a drama queen. Only he could think of flouncing out of his flat in the middle of a lockdown.

'That's the thing, I was wondering . . .'

'Look, Dan, of course you could crash here if we weren't in the middle of a lockdown.'

'I was hoping it might be okay, just for a couple of nights.'

'It's not that. I just can't risk it – I'm meant to be

staying in. Can't even go out for a walk.' I feel really awkward now.

'I haven't really been in contact with many people.' I hate it when people say things like this. I know Dan has at least seen Rick and this new girl, whoever she is, and we don't know how many people she sees each day or anything else. The whole situation is so complicated; the risks are incalculable.

'What, on your delivery rounds?'

'Yeah, we stay at least a couple of metres away.'

'I know, mate, but I just can't risk it,' I repeat almost as though I'm convincing myself. It would be so nice to have Dan here. We could have a real laugh. It would be someone to watch TV with, help cook, and besides I miss him. I don't even know when I'm going to see him again. But no, it's too high a price to pay. 'I'm really sorry. What about Matt?'

'I could ask him I s'pose, but he's a terrible snorer.'

'Desperate times,' I say.

Dan has to go after a bit more chat. It's one of the horrible things about this virus – it puts you in awkward situations where you really want to help, especially people you care about, as well as do something that you know will help your own mental health, but you can't.

'Jack?' I hear a faint voice from outside.

'Hello?' I go out on the balcony.

'I thought you were having a party up there!' she says.

'Maybe a small one.' Okay this is slightly embar-rassing. I didn't know the walls are so thin.

'I love that song – it's terrific to dance to. I could hear you having a go.' I can hear laughter in her voice and I'm glad she can't see the state of my hair.

'No comment. The party's winding down though. I just had to let a good mate down who wanted to come crash here.'

'Is he being kicked out?'

'No, but his flatmate's one-night stand turned into a live-in girlfriend when she couldn't leave due to lockdown.'

She laughs, a bright bubbly sound. It's infectious.

'I guess it is kind of funny.'

'It's hilarious. And it's not like he's really homeless so you don't need to feel guilty.'

She's right actually. I don't, so I'm not going to.

'Have you got that list of stuff you'd like?'

'Sure thing.' Within minutes I'm lowering down the Budweiser box, my list of requests in it; carefully packaged and stowed away, hanging on to my yellow lifeline, which is swaying gently in the evening breeze.

'Got it,' she says.

'You don't need to get all of it.'

'I know,' she says, 'but I'll prioritise the crisps and beef noodles; they're total necessities.'

CHAPTER 5

Sophia

Carrying three heavy bags of shopping makes the stairs feel as though they are going on forever; I'm really glad I don't live on the third floor. Not that I mind doing this for Jack. It must be terrible not being able to go out and get the basic necessities we all take for granted. With a sigh of relief, I reach the top floor and rest for a moment. Only then do I realise I don't actually know what Jack's flat number is.

Okay, I tell myself, keep calm; it must be the one above me. I'm three along on the second floor so of course, he must be third flat on the right on the third floor. That makes sense. I think so, anyway, but I don't actually know. If I went back down to my flat I could call up to him, as I don't have his number, but that would be a right old faff. I'll just knock and then stand at an appropriate distance and see who comes to the door. This seems like a plan. I approach the third door along

69

the corridor and knock gently, then stand a couple of metres distant along the corridor and wait with a sense of heightened expectation. I can't wait to see this guy who I've been talking to for the past couple of days.

And wait. Nothing. The long row of depressingly brown doors all stare blankly back at me. I walk forward and knock again, much louder this time. I also call 'hello?' for good measure. I hope it is Jack's flat; what if it's some poor older person who needs food and thinks all these provisions are for them? I'd have to give them all Jack's food of course. I have nightmare visions of having to fight my way back into the supermarket, having already queued in a socially distanced manner and then go back round the one-way system all over again.

I really hate one-way systems. I know it's necessary in this case, but I think there must be, somewhere buried deep within me, a small but vital streak of anarchy, because I really don't like being told which way I should go round a shop. It feels sort of robotic and soulless somehow. At least in a food shop, they're not that much fun anyway and during this pandemic I can see the sense behind it. But in IKEA – that's something else. I've been so many times with Jess and insisted on going round the whole store against the direction of the arrows. 'What is your problem?' she always joked.

'I don't want to go that way,' I would remark. 'I need to go and look at the futons and then I must pop down to the Market Hall (who doesn't just love all the nick-nackadee noodles down there). But who wants to traipse

70

twenty miles extra with everyone in the wrong direction when you could just walk straight there?' Jess would laugh at me over this, but I've always liked to go my own way. Maybe that's why in the end I was never really cut out for a career in law; it was too predictable and logical. I needed something with more flexibility and creativity. With the kids in school, you simply never know what's going to happen next.

Speaking of which, I'm not getting anywhere at all, I'm still standing here like a spoon waiting for Jack, or someone, anyone, to open a door. My phone pings in the arrival of a new WhatsApp message.

Hi Sophia, Just wondered how you're getting on working in a school with all this hoo-ha going on. Marge

Typical Marge, she is obviously itching to hear some gossip about work. Marge is the local neighbourhood busybody who knows everything about everyone. If someone at number 32 dyes her hair, she knows what colour and exactly when they changed it. I'll never forget the time Erica's mum came to visit and within minutes Marge appeared asking whose yellow car was parked in the car park, because she didn't recognise it and thought it might be an intruder. Of course we didn't believe her for a minute; she spent so much time once she was at the door finding out who Erica's mum is, what her job is and where she lives. I can't think how she remembers all the information she accrues, but either way, she's the only person who might be able to help with my current dilemma.

After a moment's thought, I reply.

Hope you're well. (This seems to be obligatory on all messages currently, along with 'stay well' or 'stay safe', as though it will somehow magically ward off the virus.) *Yes, school is different but I'm enjoying working with the kids, they are all coping well. Funny question, but do you know what flat number a young guy called Jack lives at? I think he lives above me but I don't know the number.*

Thank goodness Marge is immediately on it like a car bonnet.

Hi Sophia. You mean the one who works at Soho? Used to live with his mate Chris until he moved out last month.

I told you: she knows everything about everyone.

Yes that's the one.

He lives in flat 89. The one above you.

Thanks, Marge, you're a star.

Why do you need to know?

I'm just dropping him off some shopping.

Yes he's in the vulnerable category because of his kidney. I'd have thought he'd be able to get delivery.

He can't, they're all booked. Thought I'd help him out as I was already going to the shop anyway.

Kind of you – how come you know him?

I don't, just trying to be neighbourly. Thanks again, Marge. Just going to drop it outside his door.

I get off the phone quickly before she asks any more questions. Marge is like the inquisition and has a way of winkling information out of the strongest of people.

I am totally hopeless at keeping things to myself; I have this habit of blurting things out before my brain has engaged with my mouth. Also I'm not sure if Jack will want Marge to know all his business, much as she seems to know a lot of it already.

I knock again more confidently this time and call 'hello' again for good measure, then stand well back but there's still no response. There's nothing else for it; I'll have to leave the bags on the doorstep. I can always give him a shout from the balcony to let him know I've dropped it off. Perhaps he's in the shower or something. Having placed the bags up against his door, carefully out of the way of the corridor (yes, I do like to worry about everything) I stand and stare momentarily at the plain brown door. It's kind of strange to think that such a lively outgoing guy is stuck behind this bland boring façade. I give myself a little shake and leg it back down the stairs.

My phone rings as I'm letting myself back in the flat. It's my mum.

'Hi, sweetheart, how's it going?'

'Fine thanks. I've got a day at home so a bit of time to sort some stuff out and prepare activities for the kids tomorrow. How about you?'

'The surgery has been quieter than usual, to be honest. I think people are more anxious about coming in, not surprisingly. They've all been told to stay at home if at all possible.'

'Maybe not a bad thing, as long as it's nothing urgent.'

'That's the problem,' she replies. 'We're having to keep an eye on our older patients, because they tend to follow the government advice to the letter, even when they need help. Not including Uncle Jim of course.'

'How is Uncle Jim?' I'm really fond of the old guy in spite of his idiosyncrasies; he is the last of a dying breed. He might be cantankerous and has always been a bit of a hypochondriac but my mum says he was one of the first to enlist in 1939 to work on oil tankers, one of the most dangerous jobs there was. He was only fifteen and lied about his age so he would be eligible. Pretty brave I think; so you never know about people really.

'He's fine, although Jess was worried as he keeps telling us all he has a bad stomach still and has been losing weight. So she phoned the surgery and asked one of my colleagues to call him.'

'Good idea,' I say.

'Well it *was*,' my mum says awkwardly. Oh no, what did he do this time?

'He picked up the phone to Dr Gregor, answered all his questions – did he feel dizzy, was he struggling to eat, et cetera? You know the sort of thing.'

'Yes,' I agree, 'basically all the symptoms Uncle Jim said he was having.'

'That's the one,' says my mum. 'Well of course Uncle Jim said he hadn't got any of those issues and was perfectly fine. Seemed surprised the doctor had phoned at all.'

'How typical!'

74

'It was. He's apparently decided he's not ill after all.'

'I don't understand. Did he just suddenly wake up and feel better?'

Mum laughs. 'I wish. No, it turns out it's all because of his neighbour Geoff.'

'Geoff? Has he become a doctor then?'

'No, it's because Geoff had an accident with the hoover and according to Uncle Jim, he hit his wall so hard with it that all his photos fell out of his picture frames and broke.'

'Uncle Jim's or Geoff's?' I ask.

'Uncle Jim's.'

'That's sad,' I say. I hate the idea of his losing his picture frames; his photos mean a great deal to him. 'Can we get them replaced?'

'He's already on it,' Mum says. 'Apparently he went down to the picture framers at nine o'clock this morning and was hammering on the door.'

'But they're shut,' I say confused.

'I know, but Uncle Jim thought they should be open as an essential service. Anyway, the upshot of it is that he's decided that Geoff shouldn't be left to do his own cooking and hoovering and has been on to social services and his MP.'

'Whoa – go Uncle Jim!'

'Yeah apparently it's given him a new lease of life and he feels much better. He doesn't need the doctor any more.'

We both laugh and after we work out how we can get some more picture frames sent to Uncle Jim, my mum rings off. Our conversation about Uncle Jim has made me think. Perhaps everyone's mental health is better when we have a purpose and feel needed. Especially someone like Uncle Jim who has been hard-working and much valued during his whole working life as an ambulance driver and now he's been left in a flat with no one needing him, his health has deteriorated.

'You all right?' asks Erica, emerging from the shower. She's been on an early shift today so is around for the evening, which is really nice. I'm hoping we can chill out and watch *Love is Blind*. We'll probably Zoom Jess afterwards – we are behind a couple of episodes and have loads of gossip to catch up on.

'Yeah, fine,' I say. 'Just thinking deep philosophical thoughts to myself.'

She laughs. 'Be careful with them – they're in a strange place.'

'Thanks a lot.' I wander out onto the balcony and listen for a moment. I can't hear anything up above.

'Hello?' I call. I've taken to leaving the balcony door open a lot of the time as it's quite warm for the time of year and in case Jack needs something.

'Sophia?'

'Hi, Jack?'

'Yep, I'm here.' He sounds a little flustered.

'Are you all right? I knocked on your door; well at least I think it was your door – I've left your shopping outside.'

'Thanks. Did you knock? I didn't hear you, I was on

the phone.' He definitely sounds dazed. 'Sorry, thanks. I mean . . . it's just that the baby's coming.'

'Right now?' I ask.

'Yeah. I was on the phone to Sam. He's popped out to the waiting room, but at least they've let him go in with Tina at the moment. Her contractions started to become regular about 10 p.m. last night. I think they were in the queue for Tesco.'

'Tesco? At 10 p.m.?'

'Yeah a bit weird I know, but apparently Tina had a craving for nachos and she was feeling uncomfortable so wanted to take her mind off it.'

'In the middle of a pandemic?'

'I know, poor Sam sounded beside himself; said there was no reasoning with her so he just gave in.'

'Probably the best way,' remarks Erica, who has joined me on the balcony. 'How long's she been in labour?'

Jack hesitates a moment. I call up to him, 'Jack, this is my friend Erica – she's a fully qualified midwife so you're in safe hands!'

'Hi, Erica!' he says, sounding more his usual self. 'I don't know. Apparently the contractions are every three to four minutes.' Jack recites this fact as though he has learnt it by heart.

'Okay, well that means she is probably about six centimetres dilated so she's still got a way to go until that baby's going to be born. You can never tell though.'

'How dilated does she need to be? Sounds horrible.' Jack is obviously totally traumatised. It almost makes me want to giggle – guys just have no idea what women have to go through. I have a sudden memory of a conversation I'd had with Ryan about having kids when he'd announced we would definitely have at least two, but there's no way he'd be in the delivery room because he would be too grossed out. What had started out as a lovely dinner in our favourite restaurant had left a very sour taste in my mouth that had nothing to do with the food.

'Once she's eight centimetres dilated, she will be ready to give birth,' Erica confirms.

'Excuse me,' an unknown voice floats from seemingly out of nowhere. 'Do you think you can talk about nice things like flowers or something? I'm trying to eat my dinner.'

'Oh, sorry,' I call guiltily. 'It's just we're in the middle of a baby being born.'

'How fabulous!' exclaims the voice. 'Do I need to shimmy across with hot water and towels?'

Erica laughs. 'Not these days – we've moved on a bit since then but thanks.'

'How very disappointing. Can't I do something? I've always wanted to say I've helped deliver a baby.'

'The baby's not here,' shouts Jack from above.

'I could help make tea or something?'

'No,' Jack says, laughing now, 'it's my brother's baby and his wife's at the hospital.'

'Shame,' says the voice, sounding rather crestfallen. 'And here I was thinking this was my big moment.'

'Thanks anyway though,' I say, feeling sorry for the guy. He sounds like a laugh. 'Where do you live?'

'In flat 29,' comes the voice.

'Hi, nice to meet you, we're Erica and Sophia – are you on the second floor?'

'Yeah that's me.'

'Well, you must be to the left of us then. Jack, whose brother's wife Tina is having a baby, is on the third floor. He's above us.' This is a bit random; I'm introducing someone I've never met to someone I don't know and have never met. This lockdown just gets weirder by the minute.

'How fabulous, I love the idea of having a socially distanced meet and greet. Hello, all, I'm Greg at number 29.'

'Great to nearly meet you, Greg at number 29,' Erica says.

'Yeah,' says Jack, 'sorry to ruin your tea, mate.'

'S'all right,' calls Greg. 'I'd much rather hear about the baby than most things. Beats the news at the moment anyway.'

'My phone's going again,' we hear, accompanied by a crash from above. 'I've dropped it.' This is followed by a lot of scuffling and general cursing.

'You all right up there?' Erica asks.

'Yes fine thanks, it's okay – not smashed.'

'What a relief,' comments Greg. 'I remember dropping my phone down the loo and it was never . . .'

'Just a mo, Greg, Jack's on the phone.'

'Sorry, guys.'

'Sam, hello? Yes I know, I dropped the phone.'

Erica and I exchange a smile; he's in such a tither.

'He's almost as bad as some of the dads I have to deal with,' she whispers.

'It's all okay,' calls down Jack. 'Sam just popped out to tell me she's in transition or something like that – sounds as though she's turning into something else.'

'In a way, mums do at that point.' Erica laughs. 'Women in transition can sometimes become a bit unreasonable because they're exhausted with the contractions and frustrated because at that point they can't push . . . Sorry, Greg!'

'You're all right, darlin',' he calls. 'I'm on dessert now and no one puts me off Rocky Road and ice cream.'

'Ooh I'm so jealous!' I realise I haven't had Rocky Road for ages. In fact I'd totally forgotten it existed. Now I come to think about it, I really need Rocky Road back in my life. It's definitely going on my list next time I have to do the weekly shop.

'I'd send some across, but I've pretty much eaten it all,' remarks Greg.

This guy is hilarious. I can't believe I haven't come across him before when he lives so near.

'So . . . basically won't be long now then?' asks Jack, bringing our attention back to the current issue.

'No – the baby might well be born in the next hour or so, although it's a first-born and they can be unpredictable.' Erica is matter-of-fact.

'But I don't know what to do with myself until then. I'm all over the place,' says Jack, sounding more restless than one of my reception students.

'Why don't you go and grab your shopping from outside the door and then come back and we'll all have a drink?' I suggest.

'Excellent idea.' We hear Jack walking inside his flat. 'What can I do to help?' calls Greg.

'We could put on some relaxation music, whale sounds or something,' suggests Erica, although she doesn't sound too enthused about it.

'Please don't.' I laugh. 'Whale sounds always make me ridiculously stressed.' I love relaxation music and have got quite into mindfulness when I get a minute, especially during the lockdown. I find I need it. But whale sounds, they're like a really horrible eerie shrieking; makes me feel really tense. Who on earth first thought they were relaxing in the first place? Thinking about it, who even discovered whales make a sound, as they're not discernible by the naked human ear? Even more puzzling, whoever that person was felt it was important to not only encourage other people to listen to the hideous sound, but worse still, that it was necessary to record it for innocent people going about their daily business who would never ordinarily listen to whale noises. It's worrying really.

Before we can discuss the choice of music any further, the dulcet tones of a saxophone lilt over the edge of the balcony and waft towards us on the afternoon breeze.

Erica and I both stand transfixed, wrapped in the chocolate velvetiness of the sound. For a moment we are transported far away into another place, another world where there isn't a pandemic. A perfect time and place – it's like a really mellow version of 'Perfect Day'. Now *this* is my kind of relaxation music.

'Is that Greg playing?' Erica asks peering over the balcony rather pointlessly. She can't possibly see anything of him, as his flat is to the side of another part of the building, which juts out obliterating the view.

'I guess it must be, unless he's put on a CD.'

The music ends and we both feel a sense of regret, bereft almost.

'Hey, Greg, was that a disc?'

'No, it was me,' he replies. 'I like a bit of a blast on the old sax.'

'Man, you are talented.' Jack has obviously returned.

'It's just a few notes all thrown together,' says Greg.

'Play us something else,' I urge throwing myself down in a chair and making myself comfortable.

'I've got the rest of the shopping to unpack – I could do with some accompaniment,' Jack adds. 'Thanks so much for this, Sophia,' he calls down. 'You're a lifesaver.'

'Don't worry; I was going to the shop anyway. You really need to give me a list each week and I'll sort it.'

'Yeah she loves shopping,' says Erica, sarcastically.

'I hate food shopping,' retorts Greg. 'You can go for me too.'

'Course I will,' I say.

82

'Nah you're okay.' He laughs. 'I'm allowed out – when I'm not at work.'

'You still working, then?' Erica asks.

'There's no rest for the wicked.'

'That good, huh?'

'Yeah, but I love my job, hard though it is sometimes.'

'Are you a medical worker then?'

'Not exactly. I'm a carer at the local autism residential college for young people.'

'Whoa, that's tough,' says Erica.

'It can be, but also really rewarding.'

'I can imagine,' I say. 'Why haven't they gone home to their families?'

'Many of them have, but for some it's just not possible. Either the family don't want them, or in some cases they desperately do, but can't cope with them.'

We are all silent for a moment. Lockdown is incredibly tough for so many people and makes difficult situations for many even more complicated. I think of all those who are struggling – those living on their own, people with health conditions, elderly people, the kids in the residential colleges, who already have anxiety and struggle with the complexities of life without a lockdown being thrown into the mix. I feel as though we should be able to do something to help them. I need to think of something, however small, to try to make a difference.

Whilst I stand there, Erica disappears inside to call her mum, and Greg's saxophone starts again, weaving its magic once more.

I think about the old guy who I often see walking through the courtyard, treading slowly as though he carries the weight of the world on his shoulders.

'That's it,' I say loudly.

'That's what?' I jump, as I hadn't realised Jack was back out up above.

'I've had an idea.'

'About what?'

'Helping people. I'm thinking I could get some messages around on WhatsApp to get in touch with anyone like you who's struggling with getting shopping, or who's lonely?'

'You really are a glutton for punishment.' He sounds impressed.

'I know, but I'd hate to be bored.'

'Like me.'

'I didn't mean it like that. You can't go out – you have an excuse.'

'That doesn't really help. I hate it. I feel so powerless.' His words pull at my heartstrings, but at the same time, I'm amazed how honest he is being about his feelings. Ryan convinced me that all men are emotionally unavailable, but it looks as though maybe he was wrong.

'There must be something you can do,' I muse.

'Like what?'

'Just give me time. Are you on WhatsApp?'

'Yeah of course.'

'What's your number? I'll add you.'

I feel kind of excited about this. I might get to see what

Jack looks like. I'm not shallow, I'm really not, but it would be nice to see him so I can put a face to the name.

Jack tells me his number and I pop it in, a feeling of exhilaration rising up in me, which I can't quite quash.

His number bings up. *Hi Sophia, thanks for inviting me to the group!*

I quickly press on his profile picture. It's of a flipping cocktail. I don't believe it. It's a very attractive one, but even so.

Give me some time and I'm going to think of some stuff you can do to get involved. Meanwhile, enjoy having a break! I message back and press send. This is kind of sad, messaging when we're able to call up or down to each other. But he can get hold of me when he needs to now, and somehow that's strangely reassuring.

'So you can message me any more shopping lists direct,' I say, pocketing my phone.

'Great. I've already started scoffing the crisps. They are just the best. Can I pass you some down?'

'No I'm good thanks. I'm on the hard stuff: Dairy Milk.'

'Sam's calling,' Jack says, suddenly sounding really tense.

'Go answer it!'

'Have I missed anything?' asks Greg, who has stopped playing and is obviously intrigued.

'That baby must be on its way by now,' Erica says, reappearing with a couple of glasses of ice-cold wine.

'I don't normally drink on a week night,' I protest.

85

'You have to celebrate,' calls Greg. 'Unless of course it's not born for another day or two.'

'He or she will be along before then,' Erica says. 'First babies may be late, but once they start coming there's no stopping them.'

'Thanks for that,' says Greg. 'In that case, I'm breaking out the scotch.'

'She's here!' Jack cries, interrupting our conflab on the ins and outs of childbirth, but his voice cracks and he breaks off, clearing his throat. 'The baby's here. It's a girl.'

'Wonderful,' I shout in delight, torn between tears and laughter. Jack is making it sound as though he's the father in the birthing room.

'Congratulations, Uncle Jack,' Erica tells him. 'What's her name?'

'Yes, we must know the name,' calls Greg, his enthusiasm for the whole situation makes me smile.

'Carrie Elizabeth,' Jack manages to say. It sounds suspiciously as though he's crying. 'Sorry, guys, I'm just a bit emotional.'

'Take your time,' Erica says. 'Babies can make you feel like that.'

'They don't usually.' Jack laughs. His voice sounds stronger now.

'I love her name. Carrie is gorgeous – it's unusual,' I say. 'How's Tina?'

'And Sam?' asks Erica. 'Dads are often totally exhausted by the whole process, as you can imagine!'

'I'm totally exhausted just hearing about it,' jokes Greg.

'They're all doing really well. He's sent some pictures. I must show you.'

Within minutes, thanks to the wonders of technology, we are all admiring a tiny pink-faced bundle, her eyes, two gossamer slender curved lines, edged by fairy-tale-long lashes and a tiny rosebud mouth.

Greg bursts into 'All That She Wants Is Another Baby,' on the sax.

'Have you got a drink, Jack?' I ask.

'You bet,' he says. 'Well . . . here's to Carrie.'

'To Carrie,' we all echo from our individual balconies. Toasting a tiny little miracle, born in the most trying of circumstances. We sip our drinks and bask momentarily in the warmth and happiness that only the hopeful joy of a new birth can create, along with a shared sense of feeling amongst those who otherwise must stay apart.

CHAPTER 6

Jack

Today is kind of a weird day. I feel randomly cheery and hum to myself whilst showering, which I haven't done for ages. I've printed out the picture of Carrie and put it on the notice board in the kitchen. Sam's been on the phone twice today, first to tell me that Carrie has got through three nappies already and that he's sure she has almost smiled, even though the midwife says it's wind. Google says babies can't smile until six weeks of age, but it's a nice thought and that's what matters.

I flick on the kettle and open the instant – and nicely caffeinated – coffee Sophia bought for me yesterday. I'm so grateful to her. I also have a fresh baguette and some strawberry jam – it feels very continental. As I sit to eat my breakfast with the balcony door open, I wonder what she's doing. I'm struggling to remember which day it is. I glance at my phone. It's Tuesday and lockdown has been going on two weeks already. The days are beginning to blur into one.

I've checked my phone a couple of times, in case she's had any more thoughts about the WhatsApp help in the community thing, but so far it's quiet. I click, not for the first time, on her profile picture. I'd like to know what she looks like, but unfortunately the photo is taken from miles away and I can't really see her properly. Frustrated, I try to enlarge the picture but it won't work. I can just about make out she's got dark hair, I think, or it could just be she's standing in the shadow. She's outside somewhere, maybe on holiday but I'm not sure where. It looks sunny and she's standing under a tree. For goodness' sake, I can tell more about the tree than her.

Why would she use a profile picture like this? I suppose she could be shy about her looks, perhaps self-conscious. I imagine she's pretty but it wouldn't matter – she's such a nice person and has a bubbly voice. And it's not like I need to think about it anyway, as I've had enough of women for the time being. Although Sophia seems different somehow. More straightforward. Perhaps that's just because I don't really know her.

My phone blasts out. I've changed the ringtone to Dua Lipa just because it makes me feel happy. I answer it. 'Hi, Sam, what's up.'

'Nothing, I'm about to set off to pick up Tina and little Carrie.'

'That sounds so nice: Tina and Carrie. Listen to you.'

'I know.' I can tell by his voice he's grinning from ear to ear.

'Seriously, I'm so happy for you.'

'I know, Uncle Jack – you have already been put at the top of the babysitting services list and you're down for our first Mummy and Daddy weekend trip away.'

'A whole weekend – when?'

'I thought in a couple of weeks; should give Carrie long enough to get into a routine.'

'Yeah right, you had me going there!' I hesitate for a moment, before adding, 'But seriously, I can't wait to see her.'

'I know, mate, we'll Zoom you later so you can get a look. Also Tina will want to say hi.'

'Bless her, I would think she'd rather sleep after all this.'

'Well, that too. She's fond of you though. Can't think why! And I mean it, when this rubbish is over we will need you to help out. We're going to need a break by then.'

'You're not even a day in yet!' I laugh, but I'm secretly really chuffed. It's so good Sam feels he can rely on me, even after everything that's happened in the past. 'Have you got everything you need?'

'Yep, I have a list.' I can hear Sam rustling his to-do list. I can picture him in his snug Victorian hall, papers everywhere, family photos all over the wall, and feel a wave of homesickness to be there with him and his little family. 'Baby seat, that's already in the car. You need a blinking degree to fit it as well.'

I laugh. 'I've heard that – complicated things. What about baby clothes and stuff?'

'Tina's had what she and Carrie are wearing planned for weeks; you'd think the media were going to turn up at the door, as though she's Princess Kate, she's put so much thought into it. She even had a blue baby suit ready in case the baby was a boy.'

'Brilliant.' I laugh. 'It's good she's got it all sorted.'

Sam goes and I smile to myself at the thought of him trying to bundle the list of necessities into their car, which is pretty compact. As I wander towards the balcony, the stack of plant pots Sophia left outside my door this morning attracts my notice, complete with various packets of seeds – tomatoes, chilli plants, cucumbers, mint rosemary and thyme (for cocktails of course) – and a bag of compost.

I haven't grown anything for years, not since living at home with Mum and Dad. I remember sowing seeds in the garden with Sam when we were kids; it was fun actually, maybe I'll give it a go. Three-quarters of an hour later, I stand back to look at my handiwork – the balcony now has several pots of flattened earth, bare as yet, but I have carefully labelled each and watered them, ready for the magic to begin. They make the balcony look more lived in somehow. I have made a satisfying amount of mess on the floor, but it's soon swept up.

As I meander across the room to make another coffee, my eye falls on my old guitar case, half hidden down the side of the sofa. Perhaps Sam's right; I should give it a go. I haven't really touched it since over a year ago, long before the lockdown started. Somehow it feels like part of my old life. I pull it out and cough from the piles of dust, which rise up and engulf me. Maybe I forgot to clean behind the sofa – will put that down on my to-do list for later . . . or never. Fortunately, tucked away in its case, my guitar is pristine, the dark chocolate brown rosewood reassuringly shiny.

I sit and tentatively pick out a couple of notes. It's really out of tune. I mess about with the tuning pegs and try again. Within moments my fingers, albeit a little rusty, find the familiar notes and I lose myself in the old tunes from summer in Crete. I thought these songs would make me sad, but actually they simply remind me of the exotic warmth, the gentle breeze, the misty islands shimmering on the horizon and I escape for a while, far away from my flat to the sandy shores of Agios Nikolaos. I can almost smell the bougainvillea.

CHAPTER 7

Sophia

'Who's Charlie Mackesy?' asks Milo, except he pronounces Mackesy as *Matesey*.

'Charlie Mackesy is a famous artist and writer. I don't know if any of you have heard of his beautiful book, *The Boy, the Mole, the Fox and the Horse*?' I hold up my copy for everyone to see.

'I've heard of it,' Lola says. 'Mum has that book.'

'Well my lovely sister Jess gave it to me for my birthday,' I tell them.

'My sister gave me some sweets for *my* birthday and then ate most of them,' Milo says sadly.

'That's a shame, but little sisters often do things like that.' I smile.

'Mum got me some more though,' he says.

'Well that was good.'

'Not really . . . my dad ate those ones.'

I laugh. 'Poor Milo. Okay, back to Charlie Mackesy.

He creates pictures showing the journey of a boy, a horse, a fox and a mole, which show us how we can be kind both to others and to ourselves.'

'I can't see, Miss Trent,' whispers Zane.

'That's okay, just come forward and kneel down here; make sure you leave enough room for a whole long brush handle between you and the others.'

'Is something bad going to happen if I don't?'

'No,' I say simply. Poor kid, he's anxious enough already. 'But it's important you leave a space around you so that you don't catch the virus from other children and they don't catch it from you.'

'But I don't have a wirus,' he says looking even more confused. Oh dear, we've been through this several times, but it's really tough for the little ones to understand.

'Imagine it's a game. Haven't your mum and dad got a Wii at home that you can play on?'

'Yes.' He nods.

'So there's a game on it where you have to make shapes to fit in the bubble, isn't there?'

He nods.

'And you have a big bubble round you and you just have to make sure you don't burst that bubble or the game's over.'

'I'm good at that,' says Zane with a small smile.

'Okay then, let's see if you can sit where you can see my book without bursting your bubble.'

Zane arrives at his allotted space and sits down, extremely pleased with himself.

'So, Zane, you have been kind to your friends by not bursting their bubbles and kind to yourself as you haven't burst your own. Charlie Mackesy is such a kind man that he gives away his beautiful drawings, which are now worth a lot of money, to people he doesn't even know.'

'How does he do that?' asks Freya.

'Before the lockdown started, he would leave his finished drawing on the train for the next passenger to find.'

'Like a present?' asks Milo.

'Yes, exactly like a present.'

'Even though he doesn't know the person.'

'Absolutely – it's a lovely thing to do, giving happy thoughts and drawings away to others. Also if we think about helping someone else, it can take our mind off how sad and worried we might be feeling about ourselves or our families and give us a warm sense of giving.'

'Can we do that?' asks Alfie.

'Yes it's a lovely idea, isn't it, Alfie?' I'm so pleased he's talking out loud in front of the class – there are only five others but this is still a huge breakthrough.

'Sometimes I feel lost,' he says sadly.

'I think we all do at times, especially at the moment when maybe we can't see our friends or our grandparents,' I say.

'I can't see my grandma and she gives me sweets and makes sure no one else eats them,' calls Milo.

'She sounds wonderful. Well the thing is, in one of the gorgeous pictures in the book, Mackesy says that the dark clouds may seem huge, but they will pass and the blue sky is always up there. You just can't always see it.'

'Like on an aeroplane,' says Lola. 'Last time we went to Spain, it was raining when we left the airport in England but then the plane got really high and the sky was all blue.'

'That's exactly how it is and just like the dark clouds, the virus will go away and we will all be able to see our families and loved ones again really soon.'

Everyone stares at me transfixed. 'In the meantime, it's quite normal to sometimes feel a little sad, or down in the dumps. So, that's exactly what we're going to do today. Let's all think of things we could do to help other people feel good – and ourselves too, when we're feeling down. Any ideas?'

'Read a book,' suggests Freya.

'Yes well done, read a lovely cheerful book. Anything else?'

'Do some Airfix?' suggests Alfie. He's really beginning to find his feet now.

'Yes that's a great idea. Do you like doing Airfix?'

'I love it,' he says, then adds shyly, 'I could bring some pictures in to show you of the things I've built.'

'That would be lovely, Alfie, please do – we would all love to see them.'

'I like to do cooking,' says Lola.

'Well maybe we could do some more here,' I say. I'll just have to think of some social distancing friendly recipes!

'Any other ideas? What about you, Zane?'

'I like cuddling my cat,' he says quietly.

'That's a lovely one – animals always have a way of making you feel better. And there's another thing you can always do: ask someone for help. It could be one of the adults in your life or a friend, or I'm always here if you want to talk about anything that's worrying you. Now I've photocopied some of these pictures and I'm going to place them round your desks and next to that a clean sheet or two so we are all going to think of some more slogans and drawings like Charlie Mackesy's to make people feel better – or you can simply copy some of his. It's up to you.'

I walk around the desks putting out the papers and making sure each child has their own pot of pencils and colours.

Within minutes the kids are all scribbling away and a contented silence falls on the room except the very slight scratching of pens and pencil on paper. The concept of being kind and thinking of others is already working like a charm, and it gives me the idea that there must be some way of helping both Jack and the rest of the people in our little community to feel less isolated. I just need to work out what it is . . .

CHAPTER 8

Jack

I peer at myself in the mirror. This hair has got to go – it's a disaster. Not that anyone's going to see me at the moment but *I* can see my hair whenever I walk past anything shiny, even the kettle. It's really bothering me now. It's strange how things don't get to you when you're busy going about your usual business, but when you're stuck in for days on end by yourself, you pick up on every little thing. That's fine when it's good things – like sometimes I can hear the faint drift of Greg's sax or I might notice a beautiful but lost seagull calling overhead – but when it's the water bubbling through the pipes when the boiler's heating, or the fact my hair looks crap, it suddenly feels like a problem of gargantuan proportions.

I wish Greg played his sax more often; he's a really talented musician. He's probably at work now. I don't envy him his job; I'd almost rather be stuck here all day. Almost. I had a chat with him yesterday. I can't believe how time is passing. We have already been in lockdown more than two weeks and he was telling me what he has to deal with. The kids who are stuck at the care home are really struggling with the restrictions.

'One girl,' he told me, 'likes her walk every day – it helps her cope with her anxiety, which is high at the best of times. But at the moment we often haven't got enough staff to cover taking her out. So she's got to walk on her own.'

'What does she do?' I asked.

'Sometimes she still walks, but she says it's lonely. Other times she's just too anxious to go out. She says having to worry about not getting near people in case she gets the virus, as well as managing her usual anxiety, is too much. Then she just lies in bed all day as she's too depressed to do anything else.'

'That's really upsetting. Isn't there something you can do?'

'We're not allowed to do drives, which used to help her so much before. The car's great because you're both looking forwards and there's less eye contact. This can really reduce anxiety for anyone with autism if they enjoy the car. There's more distraction and less pressure on them to feel they have to make conversation. The student I'm talking about loves the countryside, so I used to take her for drives to see the trees and fields. Being stuck in at the moment, she's trapped within the four walls, except for once a day when she can walk for hours, but even then she gets distressed as the parks and green spaces around here are busy on fine days and social distancing is practically impossible.'

'Surely these kids should be an exception to some of those restrictions.'

'In theory, yes, but in practice I understand the rules. Anyone could say they're autistic to pop out to the beach or something.'

'I s'pose, but it seems really hard.'

'It is, but I'm trying different strategies to try to help. Another guy, he likes going out to the pub and gaming at the café round the corner. Of course he can't do that right now so his anxiety is bad.'

'How do you cope?'

'Well, distraction is good, so we're trying to do stuff inside like workouts. Routine is key, so we've all been doing that first thing in the morning. We try movies, but if they're really stressed that doesn't work – exercise seems best.'

'Perhaps I should give it a go. I'm very unfit these days and a bit frustrated at having to stay in.'

'I can recommend it. Also, I'm going to take in my sax. One of the students is really gifted on the piano so it would be good to get jamming.'

After our chat, I wondered what I could do, whilst I'm here; if there's some way I can make a difference to other people who are struggling. I'm going to have to think of something. Meanwhile, talking of struggling, I need to do something with my hair.

I google 'cutting your own hair in lockdown' and

watch a couple of cool guys on YouTube who had trendy styles to start with, not like mine. They just razor some really great shapes and look quite decent at the end of it. I stand and examine my slightly, okay, *completely* scruffy hair, which has a habit of standing up towards the ceiling once it gets past a certain length. I'm not sure I should go with the shapes thing. I'll just try a straight and neat haircut. I could even film it and put it out on YouTube, do my own version of 'How to cut your ridiculously long and out of control hair during lockdown'.

I find a guy with a good, straightforward approach. He suggests a towel round your shoulders to avoid too much mess – and I take his advice as I really don't want to hoover again – and a pair of kitchen scissors. Has he seen the state of my kitchen scissors? No, fortunately, he hasn't. I'm really glad I decided not to film this. I scrape a piece of bacon out of the blades and give them a scrub with some antibac liquid. I open them a couple of times having dried them carefully. Hmmm they really are slow; the blades don't really meet properly and don't exactly look prepossessing.

Gingerly, I take a tiny piece of hair and try to snip it across in the way the guy on the video suggests. Nothing happens. Desperately I start to saw and hack. It's no use; I try to move the blade up the shaft of my hair because these scissors really aren't doing anything. Oh for goodness' sake. I fling the offending scissors down on the bed. They are crap and useless, although I guess they were quite good at cutting bacon. Wait a minute – how does that work, surely my hair's thinner than meat? Shaking off this disturbing thought, I decide I am not going to give up; I refuse to be beaten by my hair.

I pin the towel round my shoulders and secure it with an elastic band, then arm myself with my beard trimmers. I can do this.

'Start sooner rather than later. The longer you leave it, the harder your hair is to cut,' the man says. He's a bit annoying. It's all very well for him to stand there looking all cool saying that, when he's a fully qualified hairdresser and has perfectly sharp hairdressing scissors. He's smug too – very unappealing. Maybe he's right though – I've left it ages; I'm never going to be able to sort this awful wig hair out. Maybe if I comb it with some water it will be okay. I wet my comb and scrape it through my crazy barnet. Great, now I look like my grandad in the pre-war years. I just need a comedy stick-on moustache to complete the look.

This is ridiculous; it really can't be that hard. I grasp hold of the beard trimmer and gently prod at the side of my head. I hardly dare look, but something definitely came off. It's not bad. I have a neat line just above my ear.

With growing confidence I continue to clip one side of my head – it says to just do one bit at a time and then you can't go wrong. I take a look in the mirror. I am getting pretty good at this. Yeah, this could be a new sideline when all this is over; I could become the bartending barber – cocktails and clips. I can see it now.

My phone's going. I could leave it, but it might be Sam. I peer at the screen from the corner of my eye. Yep, it's him. I turn off the clippers and answer.

'What the . . .' exclaims Sam. Of course, he would keep calling on FaceTime. You'd think being here all alone at least I'd have some privacy.

'I'm cutting my hair,' I say. 'It was taking on a life of its own.'

'I'm not going to disagree with you there, mate, but isn't that a bit drastic?'

'I haven't finished yet, I was in the middle of the style transformation when you rang.'

'Saved by the bell I should think,' he jokes. 'It's all right, it can wait. I just wanted to show you how much Carrie has grown; but she can't see her Uncle Jack like that, it'll give her nightmares.'

'Harsh,' I reply. 'Okay, I'll phone you back in ten.'

I reassume my position at the mirror. This time I start at the left side above the ear, where the hairdresser bloke suggests. He must know, as he looks good, and I'm pretty pleased with the line. Hey I could even go round offering to do people's hair for them in lockdown. Although that would be risky. I wouldn't exactly be able to socially distance. Maybe I'll scrap that idea then.

Suddenly, the razor makes a funny little noise, halfway between a bee getting caught in a spider's web and a hoover sucking up a coin. Then it stops. I squint at it, dust off some hair with my little razor brush (why are they so small? It does barely anything) and flick the remaining hair off with my towel. I put the razor back to my hair and try again. Nope, nada, nothing. It's totally dead.

Now I'm beginning to panic. This can't be happening – it has to work. I turn it on and off again and shout at it in agitated tones, imploring it to work. It's always been a good trusty razor and has never let me down until now. I bash it on my hand for good measure, just in case I can somehow jolt it back into activity. But it won't . . . do . . . anything. I stand there staring dumbly at it as though somehow by sheer willpower I can make it work. I catch sight of myself in the mirror.

If I thought I looked bad before, this is something else. I have one side of my head trimmed quite neatly and the other, well one bit near my ear is short, then the rest rises up in one great big tuft, waving triumphantly at the ceiling. I look awful. It's not even like those cool hairdos people have where they shave one side and the other's long. This just looks wrong.

Dua Lipa blasts out again. 'Sam,' I answer.

'Hi, Jack. You've missed a bit, mate.'

CHAPTER 9

Sophia

'So what do you think of these?' Jess asks. We are currently on FaceTime and she is wafting gazebo designs at me.

'Erm, lovely?' I say.

'Sophia, are you concentrating? I need to know which one to pick.'

'I thought you liked the one with the swathed curtains?'

'Yes I do, but it's over £200 to hire and it seems a bit expensive.'

'What about the lacy-style one?'

'That looks too cheap, don't you think?'

'Not really, it's quite pretty and it is less money, isn't it?'

'Yes, but I don't like the colour. It looks off-white; I think it'll clash with my dress.'

'Then you'll have to stick with the one you like.'

'Oh I don't know, Zach is going to go mad about this.'

'Just don't tell him,' I suggest. 'It's not like he's going to look through every account is it?'

'Mad about what?' I hear Zach ask in the background.

'Nothing, darling, just didn't want you inundated with presents you might hate like, I don't know . . . doilies or something.'

'You are hilarious,' I laugh. 'Doilies? They went out at the end of the last century. He's never going to believe we were talking about wedding presents.'

'It's worked anyway; he seems to have gone. That's the trouble with this flipping lockdown, you can't get away from each other any more.'

'Here speaks the soon-to-be-married woman,' I joke. But inside I don't feel half so light-hearted about it. This could have been me if things had been different. I know I need to move on from the constant 'what ifs' but the way 2020 is working out, it doesn't look as though I'll be able to get out there again any time soon.

'You wait; you'll see when you find the next love of your life. Speaking of which . . .'

Here we go. Sometimes I wish Jess would just stop.

'No,' I say firmly, before changing the subject. 'Did I show you these beautiful pictures the kids did at school?'

'Yes they're very nice, but don't change the subject. I have a lush, I mean really decent guy from work who has said he would love to meet up with you.'

'No, definitely not.' To be honest I would like to meet someone, but not anyone Jess recommends. It's bad enough she tries to manage my life for me without picking

110

my boyfriends as well. 'Anyway as you pointed out, it's not possible during a lockdown,' I add.

'I meant on Zoom or FaceTime, silly. Come on, he's good-looking, single . . .'

'That always helps,' I remark drily.

'Good sense of humour . . .'

'Hmmm that's important.' I don't add any more because actually maybe he does sound okay, but you never know with Jess.

'. . . And seems really caring. I saw him with a lovely bunch of flowers for his mum the other week and it wasn't even her birthday.'

'He's probably a mummy's boy then,' I say, grabbing hold of the excuse.

'He is not,' Jess insists. 'I can spot those a mile off.' This makes me smile, because Zach is also a complete mummy's boy. 'Come on, Soph, you've got to give this one a go. It's hardly going to hurt just talking to him on Zoom. You don't even have to wear those painfully high but totally gorgeous new heels you bought last month.'

'True. They are stunning, but the blisters have only just healed. I suppose if I have to, I could always cut him off and say we got disconnected.'

'You couldn't. It says you've left the meeting. Besides you won't need to get rid of him; he's lovely.'

'Huh easy for you to say – you haven't got to meet some random guy who's practically a stranger on Zoom,' I say disgruntled.

'He's not random or a stranger, I know him. Glad

that's settled then – and I've decided, I'm going to go with the more expensive gazebo,' she says whipping the picture up in front of the screen with a flourish. 'Zach will never find out the price,' she whispers.

'Start as you mean to go on,' I joke and leave the call, relieved to have got off the line, then realise with a sinking feeling that Jess has taken this conversation as a yes to the Zoom date. Just great.

I look at the pages in front of me and ponder. The kids really have done a terrific job. Obviously these are photocopies of their original artwork as they wanted to take theirs home. I look at Alfie's, a beautifully drawn sketch. I had no idea he had this talent. He has used various animals, more like the characters in *The Wind in the Willows*, which he says is his favourite book. Each animal has a tiny face mask and little gloves and in the middle are tidy piles of fruit and foodstuffs, which they are putting into baskets. The slogan reads, *'If we work together, we can all make things better.'*

I wonder if we could use this, putting the number of our local WhatsApp group on the bottom. I could make loads of photocopies and we could get them out to all the flats. Of course the only thing is someone like Jack couldn't deliver them and I need to think of something he can do – he feels so helpless, I can tell. My eye goes down to Zane's little rendition of Charlie Mackesy's mole character – it's more of a splat, really, but he has drawn little feet and arms and painted over the top in painstakingly big letters, *'I may be small but I can make a difference.'* I wonder . . .

I walk out on the balcony. 'Hey, Jack, you around?'

There's a moment's silence, only one moment, I notice, then: 'Hi, how are you?' he calls. I'm inordinately pleased to hear his voice. It's strangely comforting to know he is just upstairs even though I can't see him.

'Good thanks,' I reply. 'Have you got the emergency supply rope?'

'Just a mo and I'll send it down.' There's a thump and a scraping sound and soon the trusty Budweiser box bumbles into view. 'Is it more crispy cakes?' he asks hopefully.

'Nope I'm afraid not, though I might be making flapjacks later if you fancy some.'

'Bit healthy,' he says, then laughs. 'Mind you, I really need to get a bit fitter after all this sitting around, so flapjacks would be amazing.'

I roll Zane's picture into a scroll, and tuck it into the Budweiser box to send up.

'I may be small but I can make a difference,' he reads out loud. 'Thanks . . . are you trying to tell me something?'

Oops, I didn't think of that. 'No, sorry, I mean . . .' Epic fail. 'What I mean is I've thought of something you can do from home that might help others. Although you're already doing your bit by staying in.'

'I know, my razor wit and bubbly personality is a danger to the public otherwise.'

113

'I wasn't saying that, though you're probably right.' I grin to myself. 'It was just that I had an idea. How are you at talking to people?'

'Not bad – I'm talking to you,' he says, and I can tell he's smiling.

'Absolutely, and you like working in a bar so you're perfect for this. How about you become our guy who chats to people who just want someone to phone them every so often? I thought we could create a support network of volunteers like you who could ring anyone who's stuck in on their own for regular chats.'

'Well yeah.' He pauses. 'Yeah I think it would be good. I'd be more than happy to do that and it might cheer some people up. In fact I'd quite like the chat as well; gets a bit quiet up here.' Aha – my idea seems to be working perfectly. I thought Jack might be too proud to admit he's lonely and needs some support, but this way I've hopefully solved it, without him losing face.

'That's brilliant. I just need to work out how we organise it, but I think if I use some photocopies of the sheet I gave you – with the WhatsApp group on it – I'm sure we can get them round to people.'

'Great,' says Jack. 'Count me in. Although, it's just a phone call isn't it, not FaceTime or Zoom?' He sounds anxious, which I find surprising. He's obviously worked in a job that takes oodles of confidence and yet he's worrying about a Zoom call. It seems odd.

'That's what I was thinking,' I reassure him. 'It might be less complicated, initially at least, especially for any older residents who can find technology daunting. Why do you ask, anyway? I didn't have you down as the shy or nervous type. Or have you grown two heads or a comedy beard or something?'

'No,' says Jack far too innocently. Something's definitely up. Either that, or he is totally lacking in self-confidence.

'Don't believe you. Come on – spill.'

'Well . . . I had an accident whilst cutting my hair.'

'What kind of accident?' I have horrible visions of him having cut himself and having to wear a large sticking plaster over half of his head like a character in one of those dodgy old black and white horror movies.

'One involving the razor giving up halfway through.'

'That's a nightmare,' I say, trying to sound sympathetic even though secretly, I just want to see how bad the damage is. Maybe he's really sensitive about his hair.

'Yes it is. One half of my head looks quite neat and the other half has Troll Doll hair.'

I can't help it – I laugh. 'It's only hair.'

'It's a disaster,' he insists. 'Anyway, I don't want to give any of these people I'm trying to help a terrible fright.'

'Is the razor totally broken or could I send up some batteries?'

'It's broken, but it's okay – good old Sam is on the case. He's ordered me another one like his own, but of course all of those kind of things are slow delivery at the moment, so for now I have to put up with my slightly deranged hairdo.'

'I wish I could get to see it. But at least you don't have to wait too long to get it fixed. That's kind of Sam to sort it out for you – he sounds like a fantastic brother.'

'Yep he is, when he's not being annoying.'

'How are Carrie and Tina?'

'Doing really well. I've managed to Zoom a few times and watch Carrie having her bedtime story.'

'That's lovely. I hope it was a good one.'

'Yes it was *That's Not My Puppy*.'

'Sounds really gripping.' I think I know this book off by heart – it's one of the pre-schoolers favourites and although it's enjoyable the first few times, it does become a little predictable on the twentieth reading.

'It was,' he assures me. 'The funny thing was that by the end Carrie was still awake, Tina was asleep and my head was nodding.'

'That's hilarious.'

'How's your sister – Jess, isn't it? How're the wedding plans going?' I'm touched by how much Jack remembers and it's surprisingly good to have someone outside the family to talk to about Jess's crazy antics.

'Full steam ahead of course. It's only a few weeks away. We've been discussing gazebos this morning.'

'Exciting times . . . but surely she doesn't need a gazebo, because everyone will still be in lockdown?'

'You would think. But it's a small one that she and Zach can stand under in the garden whilst the priest marries them.'

'There's simply no stopping Jess is there? You've got

to admire her organisational skills. Will he have to socially distance?' asks Jack.

'Yes. So much so, that he will be marrying them via Zoom.'

Jack pauses for a moment. 'That situation is fraught with interesting possibilities. Anything could go wrong!'

'Not if Jess has anything to do with it. She plans everything meticulously – nothing will dare go wrong. She's an organisational freak . . . including threatening to arrange me a virtual blind date this week. It's probably already all set up.'

There's a longer silence and I wonder if he's still there.

'Jack?'

'Yeah.'

'I thought you'd gone.'

'No.' Another pause. 'I was just looking inside as I thought I might have left the kettle on.'

'Oh.' That's strange – it's most likely an electric kettle surely so it wouldn't matter. 'And had you?'

'Had I what?'

'Left the kettle on?'

'No.'

'Oh.'

He clears his throat. 'So, you have a blind date. Lucky you. Will you actually meet the guy?'

'No, it'll be online.'

'Oh.'

Okay this is weird. Our usually flowing conversation has come to a screamingly obvious halt. 'I don't really

117

want to even do that,' I tell him. 'It's such a hassle. He's a colleague of Jess's – works at the same marketing company.'

'Well . . . he might be nice.' Jack sounds doubtful.

'Not if my dating history is anything to go by.'

'History of bad experiences, eh?'

'You could say that. I attempted to get back on the dating scene during my teacher training a year ago, after a messy break-up from a long-term relationship, and I had a fair few disasters.'

'I'm intrigued now.'

'Really, you don't want to know.' I'm regretting opening up this line of inquiry.

'I've got all evening; I could cancel all my other appointments and even send you down an Old-Fashioned. I'm a very good listener and obviously I need to get practising for my support line.'

I can't help smiling. Jack makes me want to open up, even about disasters I've long tried to bury in the hopes they haven't put me off dating forever. 'Okay, seeing as you're twisting my arm.'

Minutes later, I'm sitting on my balcony sipping at my cocktail, hoping it's enough to give me the strength to contemplate my recent bumbling efforts at dating.

'Well the first guy, John – he was really sweet. I met him in my English classes. He offered to take me out for a coffee, turned up with a red rose.'

'Sounds like a real smoothie.' Jack is trying not to laugh, I can tell.

118

'Yes he appeared promising, but only long enough to lure me into a second date. At that point he held my hand and his was quite, well . . . there's no word for it other than *slimy*.'

'Perhaps he was nervous,' Jack points out charitably.

'I could have forgiven him that of course, but when he was walking me home he swooped in for a kiss and his lips were kind of yeuch – too wet, so I moved my head and he sort of missed.' I'm cringing just remembering it. 'Then he said, "Oops, maybe next time".'

'Ah. So no spark.'

'Nope, none at all. He was really nice but I just didn't like him in that way. Then I had a real job to get rid of him because he became a bit of a cling-on. I had to call in all the girls to get him to move on by mentioning my fictitious new relationship with another guy.'

'Sounds effective. Your friends are probably quite intimidating if they're all training to be schoolteachers.'

'Rude! But to be fair, you wouldn't want to mess with my teacher-training gang. They're used to dealing with a class of disruptive primary school kids, so one slightly weak and wimpy young man didn't stand much of a chance.'

'I almost feel sorry for him now.'

'The next one,' I continue swiftly, 'was Fossil Guy.'

'Fossil Guy,' Jack repeats, sounding mystified.

'Yep, he was a crazy boffin, an expert in palaeontology and scaphites.'

'Sounds like a disease.'

'Yeah.' I laugh. 'With him it was like one. He was training to teach geography – to senior kids. He loved to talk in great scientific depth about everything, so he would probably have bored them to tears. The first date fossil hunting on Cramley Beach was interesting, but two more fossil hunting trips later, I realised that was enough to last a lifetime. When I went back to his place, he painstakingly went through his fossil collection, one by one – and he had over a thousand. I don't know how I got out of there before reaching premature old age!'

'Still, look on the bright side,' Jack says seriously, 'at least now you know the difference between an ammonite and dinosaur poo.'

'Not you too!' I squeak.

'Nope,' he admits, 'I just noticed them in the gift shop when I went to the National Trust Shop once.'

'You'd better watch out, if it gets around to your Soho customers that you've been frequenting National Trust Shops your reputation is going to be in serious trouble.'

'Oh no, my secret's out,' exclaims Jack in mock horror. 'Please don't tell them about my obsession with fossils; I've always hidden it so well.'

'Well now it sounds as though you have the mad professor hair to match.'

'How rude.' Jack is still laughing. 'But I don't think you can top that date.'

'I bet I can,' I tell him, though I wish I couldn't. 'The last, but definitely not least awful, was Mick. He was good-looking, funny . . . ticked all the boxes. He was in

120

several of my classes, seemed really patient and good with kids.'

'Sounds perfect. What was wrong with this one? Was he a secret prank caller – or no, I've got it, he was a fraudster and cheated people out of their money in his spare time?'

'Idiot!' I laugh. 'That would be a bit of an escalation from a fossil fancier. No, nothing as dramatic as that. But it was pretty weird and stressful at the time.'

'I can't stand the suspense,' Jack says.

'Mick wasn't bad in himself; his annoying rugby-playing friend Pete was the problem.'

'Ah, the toxic friend situation.'

'Yep, that's the one. Wherever Mick and I went, Pete had to come too. It was kind of weird. I sort of accepted it at first as I thought maybe he was lonely or something. I even suggested one of my friends came along too so we could go out as a group.'

'Did that work?'

'No, Pete was such a loud, irritating chauvinist pig, with views he seemed to have borrowed from the Victorian era, my friend ended up leaving early.'

'So when did you realise it just wasn't going to work?'

'I stuck it out for a few months.'

'You're very patient.'

'Yep, perhaps *too* patient. In the end when Pete was on yet another date with us, in which he upset the waitress for the umpteenth time, he added insult to injury by putting his hand on my thigh during dinner. I just snapped.'

'Cheeky sod!'

'Yes and to make things even worse, when I confronted Mick about it, he said I was "lying, because Pete would never do such a thing"! I ended up suggesting that as Mick was so fond of Pete he should date him instead of me, and I stormed out of the restaurant.'

'Sounds very dramatic, but well done you!'

'Yes it was.' I laugh a little at the recollection. 'Now I'm telling you about it I just can't understand why I ever went out with him in the first place, but he was kind of subtle and there was always what seemed to be a valid reason why Pete needed to come along.'

'You can't blame yourself for being too nice,' says Jack.

'I guess not, but I feel such an idiot.' Maybe that's why I put up with Ryan for so long. I think I had always known there was another side to him that might be kind of shallow, but it had taken my illness to force it to the surface where I could no longer ignore it. Although I'm not surprised I was fooled; at times he had been really considerate. I just don't know – I'm so confused.

'Don't say that, because you're not. Besides . . .'

He's quiet for a moment, and I wait, wondering what he's going to say. 'I think any guy would be very lucky to go out with someone like you.'

That means a lot. I don't know what to say. 'But you haven't even really met me.'

'True, but I've had enough experience to know how to recognise a kind and genuine person when I hear one.'

122

'Don't – you'll make me big-headed,' I say, embarrassed. But secretly I'm singing inside. Because in the damaged and cynical world we are living in, which seems to be totally falling apart, it's really good to have someone who thinks you're doing something right somewhere along the line.

CHAPTER 10

Jack

A couple of days later I'm quite upbeat, waiting for Sophia to drop some more food at my door. I'm confident that this time I'll get to actually see her. Whilst socially distancing of course. I don't need loads of stuff because she was so kind getting me extras last time, but I've asked for some essentials like Ambrosia rice pudding. I must confess it isn't as good as Mum's, but with her living over a hundred miles away and us being in the middle of a lockdown, it's the closest I can get.

My phone shouts out and I grab it, wondering if it's Sophia. It isn't, it's my dad. 'Hi, Dad, how are you?'

'Good thanks, though your mother's driving me mad.'

'Oh – bit too cooped up, eh?'

Dad lowers his voice to a whisper. 'There's no getting away from her at the moment, son.'

'Well no, we are in the middle of a lockdown.'

'I know but she seems to be *everywhere*. Just when I

think I'm going to have a sit-down and watch a bit of the match, she's got the next thing on her to-do list for me to get stuck into.'

'I thought there wasn't any sport on at the moment.'

'There isn't. These are old ones I've recorded.' My dad is a complete sports nut; he loves watching football. My mum had satellite television installed a while ago, as she's really into languages, but my dad had it permanently tuned into sport. Now he can watch football matches live every day of the week, all over the world. Except not at the moment of course as we're in lockdown. As you can imagine the switch-off of sport is a bit of a result for Mum, so she is making the most of it.

'Anyway, are you busy?' Dad asks.

'No, although I was just about to . . .' I gesture aimlessly to the door, which is pointless as my dad is hardly going to see me.

'Good – of course you can't be, can you, stuck in all day?'

'No, but I was just waiting for . . .'

'It'll only take a couple of minutes. I wondered if you could talk me through this email I tried to send.'

That's the thing with this lockdown. If only we had had suitable warning, we could have all taken some time to enrol our boomer parents on a social media course at the local library, or given them a crash course ourselves, so that they were ready for this from a technical point of view. As it is, they are trapped in a world where their only means of seeing us is through technology they have little or no knowledge of. Trying to help them involves attempting to explain over the phone, which is about as easy as a game of Twister in the dark with directions given in Morse code, without any instructions for how to work or understand Morse code, or Twister either for that matter.

'It's difficult to tell you without seeing it, Dad,' I explain gently.

'The thing is, I sent an email to your mother's Italian teacher – and it took her ages to write it as well, because it was partly in Italian.' Oh no, this just gets worse. 'I wrote it all out for her, not the Italian, she managed to type that in, although it kept autocorrecting the Italian words to English.'

'I suppose it would,' I say, then add without thinking: 'You need to change the settings to autocorrect Italian . . . but then it would struggle and keep auto-correcting the English.'

'How do I do that?' asks Dad enthusiastically. 'I'm sure I can give it a go.'

'I think we'd better leave that for now,' I say hastily, 'and have a try at that when you're more advanced. First of all, where's the email?'

'I sent it.'

'Well that's what you wanted, isn't it?'

'No, not really because there's now an email saying "message undeliverable".'

'Oh, so it hasn't gone.'

'No presumably not.' I can hear a whole lot of talking

in the background – my mum is obviously really stressed out about the whereabouts of her email.

'I think it would be best if you write it again,' I start.

'Sorry, your mother's talking at the same time. I can't hear you.

'Can you write it again dear?' I hear my mum getting agitated now. 'Your mother spent hours writing that email,' Dad adds gloomily.

'We'll find it. I know, I'll FaceTime you.'

'How do you do that?'

I count to ten before I reply. 'We've done it before. Put the phone down and pick up when I call you on the FaceTime App.'

He does actually manage to accept the call, but all I can see is their kitchen ceiling. It's strangely nostalgic, seeing the yellow swirly plaster and a homely looking little cobweb in the corner, along with the resident spider my dad calls Horace.

'Hi, Dad?'

'I can hear you but I can't see you,' he says.

'Yeah that's because the phone's pointed at the ceiling. I can see Horace but not you.'

'No that isn't Horace, he left; felt a need for further social distancing. This is his son Harry.'

'Oh right.' I can't believe we are discussing the spiders who live on my parents' ceiling. 'Yep okay, turn your phone round so the screen is facing you.' The image spins around and shows me the floor and the dog, Max.

'Hi Max,' I say, pleased to see him. He wags his frondy tail and then runs to the door and scratches it with his paw, obviously expecting me to arrive. Even the dog's confused. 'Dad, can you hear me?' I try.

'Yes,' he says, but he sounds distant. I now have a close-up of his ear.

'Dad – you need to hold it out in front of you. Yes that's it.' I can now see him. He looks well, I'm relieved to see. 'Now I can see you.'

'Good grief; what on earth have you done to yourself?'

My hand involuntarily goes to the tufty half of my head. 'Shaving malfunction.'

'You should borrow mine. Don't want one of these new-fangled things.'

'Very kind but Sam's ordered me a new one.'

'Thank goodness someone's got some sense. Reminds me of that time your mother decided I should cut your hair because we hadn't had a chance to take you to the barber's.' He studies me on the screen. 'I suppose it's got a certain *je ne sais quoi*.'

'Yeah ha-ha.' I start to try to explain how he can show me the computer, so that we can end this madness, when the line goes dead. I decide to take the opportunity to check if Sophia's outside with the shopping. I'm on my way to the door when the phone goes again. I ignore it. I can phone him back in a second. But now the landline is going too. Oh, for goodness' sake.

I answer the landline, thinking it could be the hospital. 'There you are! Your mother was worried.'

'But I was only talking to you a moment ago,' I protest. 'Why were you ringing my mobile as well?'

'That was your mother. We thought if we both phoned you, you'd have to answer one of them.'

My parents. I love them, but honestly they are a nightmare. I painstakingly sort out the problem with the email and Dad manages to send it to the right address, thus ending a simple issue that just swallowed ten minutes of both our lives.

As soon as we're done, I rush to the door, hoping Sophia hasn't dropped the shopping yet. How ironic. I've gone from desperately wanting food at all costs, to hoping it isn't there because I want to catch a glimpse of the girl I've been talking to. Just to put a face to a name, of course. Weird, but right now company has become more important than food. It's just nice to have someone to talk to, other than Sam and my parents, that is. There's nothing more to it than that. I've also hidden my extremely dodgy haircut under a beanie. I really can't face Sophia seeing how bad it looks in reality.

Holding my breath, I open the door to see three bags full of shopping. I sigh and wander back into the flat for my attractive plastic gloves before returning suitably armed to bring the shopping in. The door downstairs squeaks provocatively and I wait a moment, ever hopeful, but the silence confirms no one is coming up. I must have just missed her.

Later, having checked the balcony a few times, I hear Sophia downstairs laughing at something and I peer over, in case she is on her way out for one of our now-regular evening chats. 'Hello?' I call softly.

There's no reply but I can still hear Sophia talking so I assume she must be with Erica. I'd like to thank her for doing the shopping. She's even included Haribo Starmix, which I didn't order, but she knows I really like. I wonder if she might like to try the new cocktail I've been working on, as a thank you, and I hover around in the hope she appears.

Then I remember – she said tonight was her date with that guy. Ben, I think his name was. I wonder how it's going. Not that it matters; it's just that I'd really like her to meet someone nice. She deserves it, and it doesn't sound as though she has had much luck with guys. I also get the impression the guy she broke up with after a long-term relationship really hurt her, though she noticeably hasn't talked about him at all.

I can just make out a couple of words. She's doing that thing people do on Zoom where they semi-shout, as though it somehow helps the other person hear what you're trying to say over long distance. She sounds really happy and bubbly and even though we've had a lot of fun during our evening chats, I don't think I've ever made her laugh like that.

Perhaps I'll just go back inside. I feel awkward hanging around now. Dates are private things and it's none of my business. He had better be a good one though. I hope he realises how lucky he is.

CHAPTER 11

Sophia

'Soph?'

'Hi, Jess, did you get my messages?'

'Well yes, but I couldn't make head or tail of half of them. You were laughing so much.'

'I think I was getting hysterical by then.'

'It went well with Ben then? I told you, he's a great guy.'

I pause. 'Didn't you hear *any* of my messages?'

'Well I heard something about someone at the door, and a takeaway, but that was about it.'

'Oh my God. Well in that case, I'm going to have to give you the whole story from the beginning. I am telling you now, this guy – even though he was up against a good deal of competition – has managed to bag the award for World's Worst Date.'

'What? I don't believe it, he can't have. He's really lovely. And anyway,' Jess adds as an afterthought, 'no one can be worse than Fossil Guy.'

'He was. He quite simply cast Fossil Guy and even Pervert Pete into the shade.'

'You're having me on.' Jess sounds genuinely perplexed. 'He's one of the nicest men I've ever met.'

'Wait 'til you hear this then. He FaceTimed earlier today and was really nice, said he's been your colleague for some time now and liked the sound of me when you were talking about our family.'

'I *told you* – he's really nice.'

'Nice? He's good-looking, I'll give him that – nice jawline. Anyway, we got chatting about our favourite foods and stuff and how he's into the beach and late-night picnics and it was going really well.'

'Sounds perfect,' Jess says, still desperately clinging to hope.

'Then he told me about his last trip skiing in Switzerland.'

'Uh-huh, I told you, *he's a catch*.' My sister seems to have forgotten how this will end already.

'Mm. It all sounded very nice, although the only time I've got on any skis, at the dry slope, I fell straight on my behind.'

'I'll admit you weren't a natural.' We had gone for Jess's thirtieth and it had been enjoyable, apart from the skiing, at which I was a total disaster area.

'No, I wasn't. I think ice skating is more my thing.'

'Maybe,' she snorts. 'Anyway, what happened next?'

'Well he was in the middle of telling me about the après ski in Zermatt, when he broke off and said, "Oh sorry, my Indian's just arrived".'

'That's fair enough,' Jess exclaims, as if this is my only objection to Ben. 'He was probably hungry.'

'I get that, but he cut me off.'

'What do you mean, cut you off?'

'Literally one minute he was there and next he'd gone.'

'Maybe you lost signal.'

'I would have thought that, but then he sent me this text saying, *"Sorry babe had to go"*.'

'That's okay then.'

'*Babe* – I mean, please? I hardly know him.'

'Your problem is that you're far too uptight,' Jells tells me, seizing on what she believes is his only crime.

I let it go. 'I thought it was weird so I gave it half an hour or so for him to eat his Indian and then I FaceTimed him back.'

'Ooh, bit keen, but understandable. He is fit.'

'Jess, you are a soon-to-be-married woman.'

'I know, but I'm not about to take the veil.' She smirks.

'Okay, fair enough. Anyway, I messaged him and he cut me off several times.'

'Maybe he was still eating his takeaway.'

'That's what I thought . . . so I phoned him again half an hour later.'

'Soph, that's really embarrassing. You're turning into a complete stalker.'

'No, I just had intuition. He picks up and whispers "hi", then goes running into the bathroom. I could see the sink and toilet.'

'Bit unusual.'

'Yeah and the tiles were horrible, orange and black. He was acting really oddly and was sat talking to me on the loo.'

'What, he was *on* the loo?'

'Just sitting on it fully clothed,' I reassure her. 'He wasn't actually using it. He wasn't a total psycho.'

'Glad to hear it. Maybe there's a perfectly reasonable explanation for it, like he's got a nosy flatmate or something, so he went in to bathroom for privacy.'

'Funny you should say that, because he *has* got a flatmate. I could see all her things strewn around the bathroom: perfume, hair mousse and her pink razor.'

'She could just be a friend.' Jess tuts. 'You're always so paranoid.'

'Yeah that's what I thought, until he suddenly says, "Just a minute, babe," to me, then I hear him shout, "I'll be out in a mo, just finding you a surprise; make sure you're ready for me".'

'Okay . . . that is kind of weird, but maybe it was some kind of joke. I can ask him about it at work.'

'I wouldn't do that,' I say quickly. 'I would have thought it was a joke too, but then he adds, "Make sure you wear the black and red thong. Benny's getting down and dirty tonight".'

For once, Jess is completely silent at the other end of the line. 'What?' she says after a moment.

'Yeah quite.' I start giggling. I really can't help it.

'Benny?'

'Yep, Benny!' This time we both dissolve into laughter.

'What did you say? Did he get back on the phone to you?' splutters Jess.

I can barely answer – I'm nearly crying with laughter. 'Yep, he came back on, and he must have taken one look at my expression – you know I can never hide what I'm feeling.'

'No, you can't. I can always read you like a book.'

'And he went, "You just heard that, didn't you?" I just said, "Maybe next time you should make sure you've pressed mute before you call out your sex plans to your girlfriend in front of another girl you're try-ing to chat up".'

Jess chuckles. 'Oh my, I am not going to let him live this down at work. *Benny*. What a complete moron.'

'I'm good at finding those.'

'I found this one for you,' Jess admits. 'I am so sorry.'

'Maybe just give up the whole matchmaking thing?' I ask, seeing my opportunity and seizing it with both hands.

'Okay I will.'

Thank goodness, at least the message is finally getting through.

'*Although* there's Ollie – he's a mate of Zach's. He's really nice, and he's coming to the wedding. It would be really nice for you to have a virtual wedding date on the day.'

Oh, for goodness' sake.

CHAPTER 12

Jack

Nothing feels right today at all. Worse than that, it all feels completely wrong. Even the arrival of a new shaver in the post doesn't cheer me up. Having carried out the usual rigmarole of opening the parcel with gloves and using disinfectant wipes on the shaver (let's hope it still works in spite of this), I'm ready to rumble. I've given up with watching YouTube. Today I'm going to wing it. After all, it's only hair and it surely it can't look any worse than it already does.

Without further ado, I trim across the shaggy offending part of my hair and soon it looks reasonably similar to the other side. Sort of. Near enough, anyway. It doesn't matter in any case. No one's going to see it.

Dua Lipa bursts out on my phone. I'm going to have to change that ring tone – it's getting on my nerves now. It's Sam.

'Hi, mate, you all right?'

'Yeah,' I grunt.

'Oh my, you're like Austin Powers when his mojo gets stolen by Dr Evil.'

'Ha blimmin' ha.'

'Seriously, what's up? Your hair does look better by the way, not half so scary. The shaver turned up then?'

'Yeah it did, thanks. I'm sorry I don't mean to be grouchy. I just feel a bit crap today.'

'We all get off days. You need to speak to your favourite niece.' He gets up and reaches over to the pink lacy crib I can see in the background and lifts out little Carrie, looking rosy and snug in a fluffy pink rabbit romper suit.

'It fits then?' I ask.

'Yeah she loves it. You have surprisingly good taste considering you don't know any kids.'

'Hello, Carrie,' I say. 'Is your daddy being rude about Uncle Jack?'

She is an alert little baby. Her slate, bluey-grey eyes peer at the phone with surprising intensity. 'Wow, she is so with it,' I say.

'Of course, she's just like her mummy; nothing gets past her. Anyway come on, out with it, what's up?'

'It's Sophia,' I say, surprising myself because I haven't been able to admit even to myself exactly why I'm feeling so fed up.

'Who?' He wipes up some dribble from the corner or Carrie's mouth with a pink cloth. Everything is pink in his house at the moment. 'Oh, the girl downstairs.'

140

'Yes, that's the one.'

'But you haven't even met; you can't be stressing about her surely? I thought you had forsworn all women in any case, after the last one.'

'It's crept up on me.'

'The girl downstairs?'

'Ha-ha, no these feelings I s'pose. We've been talking a lot.'

'At a distance, I hope.'

'Yes,' I snap, and instantly feel bad for it. 'We've just been chatting over the balcony.'

'It's flipping *Romeo and Juliet*.' He puts on a mock high, fluting voice. '"But soft! What light through yonder window breaks? It is the east and Juliet is the sun"!'

'I didn't think you knew any Shakespeare,' I retort.

'It's Tina – she made me watch the version with Leonardo DiCaprio about ten times. She's got a real thing about him. And I did *Macbeth* at school. It was much better; everyone was murdered.'

'Cheerful. Anyway, we haven't been serenading each other from the balcony. She's much more real than that. But yesterday evening she went on this virtual date.'

'Who goes on virtual dates?'

'I s'pose lots of people do during a lockdown.'

'Maybe you should consider it, now you've sorted your hair out.'

'I don't need a date. I can't cope with it, not after Laura. I thought I gave her what she wanted, but I just made her miserable instead. I'd rather steer clear. Besides,

I'm obviously not suited to making any girl happy at the moment. Look at me, stuck in, because of my cruddy health condition – no social life, nothing. I'm a total wreck. I don't want to be feeling like this about anyone.'

'But?'

'I just do. We've been chatting each evening and I've lowered down some Old-Fashioneds and she's sent me up some cakes.'

'No wonder you like her – the way to your heart is definitely through your stomach.'

'And she's been doing my shopping.'

'She's obviously very kind. It's no surprise you're thinking you're falling for her. You're bound to feel a bit strange when you're stuck in all the time and then this nice kind girl comes along, sorts your food out, talks to you in the evenings when you're bored. It's the whole being-rescued thing. Don't worry about it. Once you're back out in the real world again, you'll look back on this little episode and laugh.'

'It's not like that,' I say, shaking my head. 'She's different.'

'Yeah but you're not exactly meeting many people to compare her with, are you? You don't even know what she looks like.' He awkwardly shifts Carrie who has fallen asleep on his arm. 'Do you know, for someone so small, she gets really heavy.'

'I can't wait to have a cuddle with her,' I say.

'I know. It won't be long hopefully, by then she'll be waving her arms and trying to talk to you. Look, if you really like this girl why don't you try to find out more about her? She's bound to have a Facebook account or Instagram or something.'

'I don't like to. It's weird I know, but I feel like we've got this unspoken agreement that we're just going to keep it like this. Neither of us knows what the other looks like. Anyway, I don't want her to think I'm a stalker.'

'I don't see why you can't just look each other up.'

'For a start, I don't know her surname and she doesn't know mine. I have her WhatsApp now but the picture's taken so far away I can't really tell what she looks like.'

'I thought you said she brings you shopping.'

'She does, but I've missed her both times. Yesterday was so close. I was waiting just so I could get a glimpse and then Dad rang about this problem with his emails.'

Sam sighs heavily. 'Don't mention the dreaded emails. He and Mum are being a nightmare with the whole thing. They phoned last night to ask about setting up a Facebook account amongst other things.'

'Facebook! What do they want with that?'

'Apparently Mum's friends are all on Facebook and she thought it would be easier.'

'Not considering they can't send emails properly yet.'

'She was also checking you're all right,' Sam adds.

'Of course I'm all right. I only spoke to Dad yesterday!'

'I know, but she worries. Apparently she's sent you a parcel with some of your favourite things in it.'

Now I feel bad for being impatient. 'That's really kind

143

of her. It's just, you know, I don't want to go back to the whole overstressing thing she does.'

'She's your mum, it goes with her job description. Give her a chance. She's bound to worry about you on your own.' Sam is always the voice of reason.

'Okay I'll give her a call later. I miss them actually.'

'I know, mate.'

We chat for a little longer before Sam promptly disappears as he reckons Carrie has sneakily filled her nappy whilst asleep. 'Just ask Sophia what her surname is and put yourself out of your misery,' is his parting shot.

I'm glad we don't have smellovision. Babies are all very cute but the nappy thing gives me the heebie-jeebies.

I could ask Sophia for her full name I suppose, but I don't really like to. I can tell Sam thinks I've gone a bit strange during the lockdown, but there's a part of me that doesn't want to break the spell of this unusual thing – whatever it is we have going on. Not that it is even a relationship, but it is a kind of friendship. Maybe I'll catch a glimpse of Sophia one day by chance. We certainly can't risk meeting each other; she works in a school. Besides, even if I like her, what am I going to do about it?

The home phone goes. It's my dad. 'Hi, Jack, we've got a problem.'

I'm instantly alert. 'Is everything all right? You're not ill are you?'

'No, son, nothing like that,' my dad says in an exasperated tone. 'It's your mother's emails.'

'Oh.' That's a relief. I really wish he wouldn't do that; thanks to the incessant daily news updates, we're all constantly wired for imminent disaster. I could certainly do without Dad ringing up with a tone of impending doom. 'What's up? You were sending them out with no problem yesterday.'

'I know, that's the flaming annoying thing. There's no rhyme or reason with these computers. Your mother wanted another email sent out to her friends from her Italian group.'

'Yes.'

'So I put in all the email addresses one after the other, as you've told me.'

'So far so good. Did they ping back? Maybe you put a couple of the addresses down wrong.'

'No they sent.'

'Well that's great. By Jove, I think you've got it.'

'They sent,' he says again, 'but for some reason at the end of the email there was a photo of your mum and me in Cornwall!'

'A photo of you on holiday?'

'Yes but she *didn't* attach a photo. In fact she says she doesn't know how to and besides, she couldn't remember ever having seen it and was horrified about her hairstyle.'

'Why?' I ask, thinking it can't be worse than my recent one.

'It was frizzy, she said. But it looked like it always does to me, not that I told her that.'

'No, that is a bit random. I didn't think you could attach photos by mistake.'

'It's worse than random. She's had several very angry emails from people telling her she shouldn't be travelling and worse still, one from her friend – who lives in Cornwall by the way – saying it's people like us who are not only setting a bad example by moving about during lockdown, but also that going on holiday to Cornwall is unforgivable. Of course your mother said a few things in return and now I don't think we'll be going to stay again.'

For the first time today, I have to laugh. I really can't help it. I've heard of communication issues due to language barriers, but during this lockdown it's the language of computers that's proving far more tricky.

CHAPTER 13

Sophia

I've gone from not even knowing there's a guy living above me, to worrying because I haven't heard anything from him for a while. Well, not since the day before yesterday anyway. It's really unusual because our evening chat whilst chilling out on the balcony has become a bit of a thing. I now leave the door open all the time when I'm home, as the weather's still warm and sunny and we sit on our own individual tiny pieces of outdoor space whilst he tells me about a funny incident from his day and I tell him about the kids at school. There's something comforting and companionable about it.

I've been at school this morning but since I've been back it's horribly quiet. Erica is in bed as she was on late shift and came in at silly o'clock completely exhausted. I didn't tell her the amusing Benny story, just popped her into bed with a mug of hot chocolate. She had barely managed to spoon down the spag bol I had made for her, she was so tired. 'So many babies all at once,' she said, 'including a set of twins, and one was breach.'

'Don't even go there,' I said. 'Just get some rest.'

She needs to feel lively for later, because tonight it's Jess's virtual hen do. It should be a laugh as it's an ABBA night and I've ordered a dodgy set of L plates and a T-shirt saying 'I was quarantined on my hen party'. And some Team Bride sashes of course. Jess's has Bride to Be on it and stickers for all the hens saying, 'Jess's Lockdown Hen Party'. As well as that I ordered some cute little sparkly pink hats and glasses, which are hilarious. I look like something out of a panto. Sending them out to all thirty of us took some doing but it should be fun.

My phone bings to announce the arrival of yet another message about the wedding.

Have you got any further with the bridesmaid's dress? Thought it would have arrived by now?

I haven't broken it to her yet that the one we ordered arrived yesterday, but it doesn't fit. She is going to go completely nuts. I tried it on last night after my hideous non-date with Benny (am going to have to think of a suitable nickname for him – currently all that springs to mind is dirty Benny, which doesn't really have much of a ring to it) and the zip didn't do up more than halfway. I don't quite know what's going on in this area, because Erica had helped me do the measurements with the old tape measure from my trusty childhood sewing box and I double-checked the number she wrote down made sense. For some reason or other, my boobs seem to have grown.

I think Erica must have made a mistake with the measuring, but she reckons it's all the lockdown binge eating mixed with Jack's cocktails (sadly, she could have a point). Either way, unless I put a large panel of matching fabric in the gap, this dress is a no-go. I am going to tell Jess, honestly, but I'm just waiting for the right occasion. For now, I text back:

Trying it on, will let you know how it goes.

Great, send me a pic.

Okay, will do.

This is a disaster. I can't send her a photo; she'll see it doesn't fit at all. Unless I send a picture taken from the front and leave the back undone? No, it's no good, I'll have to tell her or risk it falling off halfway through the wedding ceremony. It reminds me of the time I wore a dress that was too small for me, for dinner out with Ryan. I had managed to squeeze into it and thought I'd got away with it. That is, until I sat down in the restaurant and heard a sickening ripping sound. The whole of the back of my dress had split. It meant at the end of the evening I had to reverse out of the restaurant backwards. Afterwards I had seen the funny side, but Ryan was horrified as we had been meeting with some of our fellow lawyers and in his words, the whole incident was *most embarrassing*.

No it's no good, first I need to think of an alternative so she doesn't panic too much. I mooch into my room and start rummaging in the cupboard for a long dress, which might just do. It's funny how your wardrobe can

149

be full of stuff but when it comes to it you still haven't got anything to wear that's vaguely suitable. Normally this is an excuse to go on a good old shopping spree in the cheapie shops but in lockdown this is hardly possible.

I don't fancy mail ordering anything – the sizes vary so much and I don't want to have to send more hideous packages back at the moment; it's not exactly an easy process. I'm notoriously bad about returning packages at the best of times. I actually have a couple of old parcels in the bottom of my cupboard, which I have never returned and I won't ever wear. One contains about three pairs of Spanx. I know, three pairs – I don't know what I was thinking. I don't think anyone had warned me how horribly tight they are and that my stomach would have to go *somewhere*, and ended up in places it shouldn't in an extra layer, like a rubber ring. Most unflattering.

I give up; I have no contenders in the bridesmaid dress stakes. Most of my dresses are too short or too long or too just not right.

I am disturbed from my musings by the dulcet tones of a guitar. It's good, actually. It seems to be coming from outside so I wander out onto the balcony. The old chap I've seen meandering through the courtyard with his head down has stopped and is looking up towards me. I smile down at him – I've so often wondered who he is and if he is okay during this pandemic. He always looks so solitary.

'Beautiful playing, isn't it?' he says to me.

'Yes, I'm really enjoying it.'

'Not surprised – I'd like to have a neighbour play to me in the day.'

'I bet. Do you live across the way?'

'Yes number 23 Fairmile Drive, on the other side of the block. Used to live with my wife Elsie but she's gone now.'

'I'm sorry. That must be tough.'

'That's the way it is, love,' he says pragmatically. 'Nothing much you can do about it. People come and people go. But she was the love of my life. Most days I feel like I've lost my right arm.'

'I can believe it.'

'If you'll take my advice you'll make the most of every minute, girl; you never know when it's going to be snatched away.'

I know this. I have become painfully aware of it since the start of my epilepsy. Before that, I never really thought about life in general or the meaning of it all. But in that moment everything changed. I changed. I no longer wanted to be a top lawyer, cracking cases, wearing sharp suits, getting married to Ryan. I'd had it all mapped out but that first seizure made me realise something was missing . . . and that something was meaning. That's what made me change everything. To train as a teacher, try to give something back, make a difference, even though it's small. It matters.

At first I had hoped Ryan would come along with me. But he made it very clear he had wanted to marry a fellow lawyer. Both his parents were lawyers, he had it all planned for goodness' sake, so he got left behind too even though he was the one who dumped me. Major stuff happening in your life makes you change your perspective on things.

'You're right,' I say smiling at him, although if he were nearer he would see the traitorous tears glinting at the corners of my eyes. That's the other thing with serious issues. You figure you have them all neatly packaged away at the back of your mind, carefully labelled 'dealt with' and then out of the blue some little thing that you least expect jolts it back to reality. It might just be a tiny word someone says, maybe a stranger, something seemingly unrelated or something you read casually and before you know what's hit you, the wound is open again, raw and painful as it was before. I believe in time it will get less and less but sometimes it still takes me by surprise.

'He's a good looker too and such a nice lad,' the man says.

'Who?' I'm confused now.

'Jack.'

'Jack? Is he the one playing?'

'Of course – didn't you know? Was always playing the guitar on his nights off at Soho.'

'Are you taking my name in vain?'

It's Jack. I'm ridiculously pleased to hear his voice.

'Hi, mate, how's it going? Giving the old guitar an airing?' the man asks.

'Thought I'd give it a go. Miss having an audience though.'

'I miss the old place too. Having a pint on your own isn't the same.'

'That's for sure. Still, hopefully won't be for much longer and we'll be back with the regulars,' Jack assures him.

'That's what we're hoping. And at least I get my constitutional once a day.'

'Seen any of the other boys recently?'

'Nah they're all staying in. Place is like a ghost town. You're lucky though, mate, you've got this beautiful young woman living below you.'

I smile and blush. Perhaps he should have gone to Specsavers, but it's a nice compliment. I haven't been called beautiful before – pretty, yes, but never beautiful.

'Sophia?' Jack asks. He obviously hadn't realised I'm here and I'm embarrassingly glad he didn't say someone else.

'That's me,' I say with an awkward smile. 'And you are?' I ask, peering down at the man.

'I'm Bertie. Pleased to meet you, love.'

'Bertie and I have known each other for a few years,' Jack says.

'Yep, I'm renowned in this area for my quick wit and ability to eat fish and chips at any time of day or night,' Bertie jokes.

I laugh. 'Sounds good. I really miss fish and chips.'

'Yeah it's funny the things you want when you can't have them,' says Jack. 'I miss KFC Bargain Buckets. Though I've been very well looked after by Sophia here.'

'Lucky you,' says Bertie. 'Well must be going. *Countdown* is on and I need to have my lunch first. Got to stick to my routine. Lovely to meet you, Sophia, and keep smiling, mate.' He nods to us both and walks on steadily, head bowed again and vanishes from sight as he leaves the courtyard.

'What a lovely guy,' I say.

'Yeah he's the best,' replies Jack.

'He must be very lonely on his own.'

'I think so. His wife died a year ago and this lockdown on top of everything else – it's terrible really. He was always down at Soho, him and a lot of other great people.' He sighs and I realise how much Jack must miss his old life. It must be really tough for him staying in all the time.

'I didn't know you play the guitar?' I ask.

'I'm a bit rusty.'

'I genuinely loved listening. You should play more often.' I pause for a moment. 'Didn't hear you playing last night.' In fact it had been unusually silent, as he hadn't come out at all.

'No I just got an early night. I was tired.'

'Oh.'

'Yeah sometimes it's tiring doing nothing.' There's an awkward pause. 'How did your virtual date go?'

'Best not to talk about it.'

'Oh . . . it went well then?' He sounds flat, disheartened even, or am I imagining it?

'Well it was very funny.'

154

'It's important he makes you laugh,' Jack says, misunderstanding.

'Yes although it would have been better if I could have laughed *with* him rather than *at* him.'

'Oh. You mean it wasn't in a good way.' I could swear he suddenly sounds more cheerful.

'Not at all. He was a complete loser. Rivalled the last two guys to be honest if that's even possible.'

'Surely not – they sounded bad enough!' He laughs.

'Yep, put them totally in the shade. Whilst he was talking to me his current girlfriend walked in.'

'Oh no – classic! What did he say?'

'At first he pretended it was the Indian takeaway.'

Jack snorts. 'You've got to give him points for trying.'

'Yeah right.' I tell him the rest.

'So will you be seeing him again?' Jack asks when I'm done.

We both laugh hysterically and somehow the bad date doesn't really matter any more. I really missed our chat last night. Jack always helps put stuff in perspective.

'Are you busy?' I ask.

'Well I'm waiting for the latest instalment of *The Little Red Hen*, but other than that I'm all yours for the evening.'

'I could do with some fashion advice. How is little Carrie anyway?'

'Doing just fine. Even though I'm her uncle and a little bit biased, she's really cute. What do you mean, fashion advice?'

155

'Well I just need to run some outfit ideas for this wedding past you. Not visually of course, but I could put them on and describe them to you. I know that's a bit weird, but I've really messed up – I ordered the bridesmaid's dress Jess wanted and it's arrived but is far too small.'

'Oops, don't you just hate it when they undersize stuff.'

'Happens all the time.' I laugh.

'Can't you order the size up and whilst you're doing that I can whip you up a Margarita? The fresh limes you bought are perfect for it.'

'Well it's a definite yes to the Margarita but you don't get out of the fashion decisions I'm afraid – a bigger size won't come in time.'

'Okay, I'll make the cocktails and send one down. Let's get this over with.' I can tell by his tone he's laughing and doesn't really mind, so I pop inside to grab the few dresses I've already discarded.

Having sent up some crisps and pretty much devoured the cocktail, which was a very generous measure, we are still no further ahead in the bridesmaid dress situation. I have just been describing my turquoise cocktail dress with a large purple flower at the top.

'No good – you might outshine the bride and that's never a good thing,' Jack says matter-of-factly.

'Fair point. Her dress is very delicate; I'm not sure I should wear anything too bright. It's no good.' I slump down on the corner seat on my balcony. 'I give up.'

'Wait a minute,' says Jack. 'What about your flatmate Erica? Hasn't she got any dresses you could borrow?'

'Maybe,' I say doubtfully. 'She isn't really into going out much, but I could ask her. She might be asleep, but I guess I could sneak in and have a quick look in her wardrobe.'

'Does she sleep heavily? I don't want to hear any screaming and shouting if she gets aggressive when you wake her up.'

I laugh. 'She can be pretty grumpy and she has had a tough shift, but she usually sleeps quite well.' I take a final slurp of my Margarita. 'I'm going in.'

'Good luck. If you get caught, I'm going to pretend I'm out.'

'Yeah right, thanks a lot.' I smile and go back into the flat and stand outside Erica's door. I feel a bit furtive actually; I really don't want to wake her as that would be mean, but I do have to get back to Jess and she is going to be mad unless I can think of a suitable alternative.

Slowly, delicately with the tip of one finger, I push open Erica's bedroom door. Thank goodness it isn't old so doesn't creak. Nothing. There's no noise other than her steady breathing. Okay, I can just creep across the room to the wardrobe and have a quick look. I did lend her my grey jumper the other day when she had lost hers.

I tiptoe across the bedroom slowly and quietly and go to open the wardrobe door. Erica gives a grunt and I freeze where I am, feeling ridiculous. Of course I'm going to tell her afterwards but this does look a tad weird. To my great relief, she turns over and settles down again. For some reason I have been holding my breath and I take a moment to get myself back together.

The wardrobe door opens smoothly and I peer inside. Unlike mine it's fairly neat and Erica's clothes are all stacked tidily in drawers or hung up. Typically though, she mainly wears tops and trousers. There's barely even any skirts. It's no good – I'm going to have to give up. Just as I'm about to close the wardrobe door, I notice a scrap of pale pink fabric squashed in the corner of the cupboard. I touch it; it seems to be a long draped skirt or something. I pull it out and shut the door and leg it back to my room. I unfold the fabric, confused. I remember this; it's mine. It's a long flowing tie-neck dress that you can wear in different styles. If it still fits, it might just do.

I put it on and try tying the straps up around my neck. The dress looks good. It always was flattering, fitting tightly under the chest and falling nicely to the ground. With a pair of heels it will be perfect. I don't like the neckline though, it's not quite right. I wander out to the balcony, feeling overdressed and slightly chilled in the early evening air.

'Jack?'

'Any good?'

'Yes actually, I found an old dress I'd completely forgotten about. Not surprising really though, as for some reason it was in Erica's wardrobe.'

'Oh no, not a clothes-stealing room-mate!'

'I think there might need to be an inquiry into this.'

'What's the dress like?'

'Long, light pink with tie-neck straps, but they don't look quite right.'

'Why not?'

'I don't know – it just looks wrong.'

'Can they tie elsewhere?'

'Yes, they can. That's the good thing about this dress. I'm going to try one shoulder.'

'Go for it.'

I dash inside and fiddle about in front of the mirror, tying the strap behind one shoulder and draping it over the other. This dress always was pretty clever. Yep, it's perfect. I leg it back out onto the balcony.

'Problem solved.'

'Just call me Heidi Klum.'

My phone goes . . . It's Jess. 'Oh God, I need to get ready for her hen do.'

'You'd better go then.'

'I'm going. If you hear some strange goings-on, it's only us.'

'Nothing new there then,' he says, and I can hear the smile in his voice.

'Thanks. If you want to join in with the singing feel free.'

'I'll tune my guitar.'

CHAPTER 14

Jack

'How's it going then, Jack? You sound pretty upbeat this morning.' It's Sam on the phone and he's right, I feel on top of the world today.

'Pretty good actually. Although a bit tired. Sophia and Erica had a hen do last night downstairs, so it was late by the time I got to bed.'

'You went to a hen night?' Sam asks incredulously.

'Not exactly.' I think back to the raucous singing, the loud renditions of 'Dancing Queen' and the shaving foam that seemed to land like falling rainbow clouds on the courtyard below, and anywhere else it came into contact with. The moonlight had been amazing, lighting up the city skyline and the dim outline of the flats. Somehow it had all felt like a wonderful distraction, but I'm not going to even try to explain this to Sam; he'll think I had one too many again. 'At one point I might have played my guitar whilst everyone on the Zoom call downstairs sang along.'

'So you're an honorary girl now?'

'I did help out with a clothes crisis.'

'I don't know what's come over you; we need to get you back out with the lads. Mind you, it will make you an even better godfather to Carrie.'

I laugh. 'I can be in touch with my feminine side. Wait a minute, godfather? Are you serious?'

'Course, who else could we find to do the job? Only kidding – you'll be the best.'

I'm feeling emotional now. 'I will honestly look out for her to the best of my ability.'

'I know you will.'

'Speaking of looking out for people, I'm in demand. You know old Bertie, from Soho?'

'Yes, great bloke. How's he coping?'

'Bit lonely I reckon on his own, but Sophia and her trusty team of volunteers are out delivering flyers so we can help people like him.'

'That's kind but . . .'

'Wait, I have a message already.' I look down at my WhatsApp.

Hey Jack, it was good to see you yesterday. Thanks for the offer of help. I found Sophia's leaflet this morning in my letterbox. If you don't find it a nuisance, it would be lovely if you don't mind phoning occasionally. Be nice to hear a friendly voice. Thanks, Bertie

'I have my first client,' I say.

'Client? What are you doing, consultancy on creating the best lockdown cocktails?'

'No,' I laugh, 'although that's not a bad idea. I'm phoning people who just want a chat, because they're stuck in lockdown on their own. Bertie's my first client but I reckon there'll be more.'

'You'll be so good at it. Whose idea was that?'

'Sophia's.'

Sam's silent for a moment. 'She sounds quite something.'

'Yes she really is. We've got some other ideas as well. Sophia's going to pick up shopping for people who can't go out and I was even thinking we could get a crowd of residents and Soho regulars together to do Zoom quiz nights.'

'Great idea – count me in.'

'As long as Carrie comes too. She might be able to help you with the answers.'

'Think I might leave her in another room with Tina and have a night off.'

'Getting to you, is it?'

'Babies are lovely but exhausting. Anyway, Tina has a couple of nights off a week at the mo to chat to her old work friends on Zoom, so it would be nice for me to have a break too.'

'Sounds a good idea.'

'Anyway, what are you going to do about Sophia? Have you found out her last name yet?'

'No, I don't want to ask. I've got a better idea.'

'Mysterious.' There's a loud wailing. 'I'm going to have to go. Carrie's due her next feed.' He holds the phone up. 'Can you hear your gorgeous niece summoning me?'

'She's starting as she means to go on.'

'Yeah right, with us all wrapped around her little finger.'

Sam rushes off and I glance at the picture of me stuck on the fridge. I'm in front of the taverna in Agios Nikolaos. I look the picture of health and happiness; the tan suits my dark colouring. I expect to feel the familiar wash of complicated feelings swamp over me, but strangely they don't.

I settle down to look at my WhatsApp, which is binging at the arrival of more messages by the minute. I can't believe I was bored and not sure what to do with myself. This little lot is going to keep me busy.

I read the latest. *Hi my name's Derek. I know Sophia has kindly set up this support group.* (Everyone seems to know Sophia, she's that kind of girl.) *I saw this flyer and wondered if any dog lovers out there could give me some advice. Benson, my Alsatian pup I adopted just before all this hoo-ha, is extremely bouncy and eating my whole flat during this lockdown (quite literally). Obviously I can walk him once a day but he's driving me mad the rest of the time. Any dog lovers out there with some ideas, I'd be really grateful.*

I smile to myself. That must be challenging – poor old Derek. A large bouncy dog shut in for most of the day is a bit of a disaster, to put it mildly. I start flicking through the messages; some woman called Anna suggests Derek could hide treats behind the sofa so Benson can try to find them. That's not a bad idea actually – it would

164

keep him busy, but he might chew his way through the sofa to get to them! Then some bloke, Nick, says he's never done that again since trying it with his dog, who didn't find half the treats and his room eventually smelt like mouldy food and he had to throw away his sofa.

My phone bings again. It's someone called Marge. *Derek, do you really think you should be keeping a big dog in a flat? It's hardly a sensible arrangement. Maybe you should consider rehoming him.*

Just great, that's really helpful then. It's not exactly good advice when it's too late, for goodness' sake; he's already got the dog. I hate it on these groups when people use every opportunity to have a go at others.

But we've got a couple more people who would like a regular call. Mavis at number 23 would love a chat every other day. *What a lovely idea. I would so enjoy talking to someone other than my budgie, Sunny. I like gardening and have always played the piano as well as singing.*

Greg downstairs has put: *If anyone likes the sound of the sax I'm happy to play any time when I'm not at work.*

Sounds great, Greg, I send back. *Anyone else fancy a jamming session – we could all do some singing and play whatever instruments you have?*

Count me in; Mondays or Wednesdays are good with me, say 6 p.m.? Greg.

Okay then, I type, *anyone fancying a musical session, it can be playing the saucepan or the spoons, singing or any instrument. Out on your balcony 6 p.m. Wednesday week, as it will take me a while to get some music together for us all to practise.*

I'll sing if you play. I hear you were really something at Soho.

That's a bit disturbing. Who sent this message? I squint at the screen. It's the woman called Anna. I wonder where she heard that from? I don't know what to put now. Perhaps I'll just say: *Or if no balcony you are welcome to sit in the courtyard whilst socially distancing of course.*

Can't wait, Anna xx

I am going to have to keep this one at arm's length. For the first time ever I'm actually grateful for social distancing.

Be along with my deckchair then as long as it's not raining. Looking forward to a sing-song. Be like old times. Bertie.

As long as it's a pleasant sound. I don't want any loud disturbance. It will upset my Minnie. Marge.

Who is Minnie? I have no idea but I'd better reassure Marge we won't upset Minnie whoever she is.

That's fine – it will only last half an hour at the most so we don't disturb anyone's peaceful evening.

I'll take your word for it, but any unpleasant ruckus and I'll be complaining to the residents' association. Marge.

This Marge sounds a right one. Shame she can't befriend Anna and let the rest of us get on with things. Still, this is an amazing start and I actually feel busy and useful for the first time in ages.

'Hey, Sophia?' I wander out onto the balcony.

'Hello?' she calls.

She was quick responding. I wonder if she was waiting to hear from me.

'You okay?'

'Yes, you?'

'Brilliant thanks; your flyers are already getting an incredible response. I've had loads of replies.'

'I hadn't seen yet. Who got back to you?'

'Well Bertie obviously – he's really looking forward to a regular chat and a nice old lady called Mavis.'

'You'll be really good at this.'

'There's some bloke called Derek who has a large dog called Benson who's eating the contents of his entire flat.'

Sophia laughs. 'It's a shame they don't do dog TV.'

'Great idea. I'll try and set up a dog channel on YouTube in my spare time.'

'Even though you don't have a dog?'

'That's only a small point. Anyway, the best thing is we're going to set up a musical evening on Wednesdays at 6 p.m. Anyone can join in and sing or play whatever instrument they fancy.'

'That is amazing. You've done a fantastic job already.'

'It was your idea. There are a couple of slightly bizarre members of this group though.'

'You bet there are. Who in particular?'

'Some woman called Anna who seems slightly over keen. And a right old busybody called Marge who's going to report us all for troublemaking if we make too much noise.'

'Marge is all right, but yes she does have to be involved in everything. She'll be fine as long as we can convince her somehow it was her own idea. Anna I don't know.'

'Both seem a bit scary. Anna wants me to serenade her with my guitar.' I pull my hand nervously through my slowly regrowing hair.

'She'd better join the queue.'

'Yeah right.' I shrug the compliment off, even though I'm pleased. 'And who's Minnie?'

'Oh, she's Marge's cat. She won't be singing or playing the triangle will she?'

'No, but apparently she's easily disturbed by uncouth noise.'

'That's warned us then.'

I laugh. 'But seriously, I can't thank you enough.'

'For what?' she says innocently.

'For giving me a purpose. Something to do. I feel better than I have for ages.' I stretch myself luxuriously out on the chair and gaze at the view.

'That's all the cakes you've been eating.'

'I was wondering if there is anything I can do in return to thank you.' I know before she answers, she isn't going to take me seriously, but I've already thought of something, which she might appreciate.

'Honestly it was nothing. You really don't owe me.'

'No but this might help you out.'

'Okay I'm intrigued now,' she says and I smile.

'Well, you know your sister Jess won't stop trying to set you up with dodgy dates for this wedding of hers?'

'Tell me about it – the latest one sounds worse than ever.'

'I thought of a way to get you off the hook.'

'Nothing will get Jess to stop. It's never going to happen. I admire your optimism though!'

'It's only, I thought maybe this might be a solution . . .' I hesitate, then force myself to continue. It's now or never. 'Maybe you'd like me to be your virtual date for the wedding. If Jess thinks you have someone, she might stop being so persistent.'

'You?'

Oh no, she sounds surprised. What was I thinking? I've completely misjudged this.

'Well yeah, I mean not *with* you obviously. I don't need to be on the call but I could be up here offering moral support throughout the service. I could wear my suit and everything. I mean it doesn't matter, it's just an idea . . .' I mumble, my voice catching.

'Jack.' She stops me. 'I think it's a great idea. You're on, it's a date.'

I can't believe it. She's said yes; she wants me to go with her to her sister's wedding (well sort of anyway) and I'm her date. I'm on top of the world. Although – wait a minute, she wasn't taking me very seriously a moment ago. Maybe she just thinks it's a joke. Darn it, how do I know?

CHAPTER 15

Sophia

'Jess, are you all right?' Okay, this is a really stupid question. She's obviously not all right; her face is streaked with tears and her mascara's slightly smudged. All of which is totally unheard of for Jess; she usually looks immaculate.

'Not really,' she sniffs.

'This is so hard. I wish I could give you a hug.'

'I know, it's all so tough.' She wipes her eyes with a tissue. 'That's the thing, when I heard the planned wedding was going to be cancelled, I was just so upset; then it was brilliant we could go ahead with it online.'

'I know,' I say soothingly. 'It's going to be wonderful.'

'Then this morning I just woke up feeling terrible about it all.'

'To be fair it was quite a heavy night of partying and you're not as young as you were.'

'Ha-ha.' She attempts a watery smile. 'It's not that – it just suddenly hit me that you're not going to be there

171

or Mum, or any of my posse. You're all my support team and I need you.'

'But of course we're going to be there; we'll be more "there" than we would be if this were a normal wedding. This virtual ceremony means Mum and I can be with you from first thing in the morning, right through. We'll be with you every step of the way.'

'I guess.' She perks up a little. 'Still no hugs though.'

'I know. It will have to be a virtual hug, whatever that is. You'll get enough hugs from Zach to make up for all of us put together anyway.'

'True.' She smiles.

'How's he doing after the stag do?'

'A bit worse for wear. I've hardly seen him today. But Henry has posted some very entertaining pics of him wearing a veil, a blonde wig and someone's hideous purple bra (goodness knows who it belongs to) on social media. I've suggested he wears them on Saturday!' Henry is Zach's older brother who is currently out in New Zealand. He's a marine biologist but is obviously having to stay in at the moment, leaving him plenty of time for sending dodgy outfits to his brother.

'Classic – you'll have to ping some across to me. I could do with a laugh.'

'Be prepared, they're eye-popping. And Henry says he has some other plans for the day itself. He's making me really stressed to be honest. I've threatened him with some serious repercussions if he does anything awful.'

'Yeah I can understand that. Henry's idea of entertainment would be to get Zach's ex-girlfriend to give a speech or something ridiculous.'

'Don't! He won't, will he?' She's really agitated now.

'Of course not – I'm only kidding. Are you sure you're happy with my dress?' I had plucked up my courage and shown Jess yesterday and she really liked it; in fact she took it all remarkably well.

'Yes it's beautiful; you look amazing in it. I'm so glad you're going to be my bridesmaid.'

'I know. It's really exciting now. It's going to be the most amazing wedding ever.'

'I hope so.'

'Seriously, it's not often I say stuff like this, so put it in your diary, but you have done an incredible job and worked really hard. You're pretty amazing.'

'Thanks, hon,' she says, glowing. 'You've been helping me all the way.'

'I've loved it.' I wave a couple of bridal magazines at her.

'Your turn next!' She laughs, but her words hit home. The old hurts lurk ever near the surface. I can't help thinking that in another perfect world where there really are happy ever afters, I would be marrying Ryan now.

'Definitely not,' I reply, shutting that line of conversation down at once.

'I wish you would let Ollie be your virtual date for the wedding.'

'I think I can do better than that, although I'm sure he's a nice guy. I might even have a better option than Benny!'

'I'm never going to live that down, am I?'

'Absolutely not! Never.'

'So who's the guy?' Jess asks, obviously dying from a mixture of curiosity and disbelief. 'Am I going to get to see him?'

'No he's not going to be on the call but he'll be really close.'

'Don't go all mysterious on me, Soph. Come on, spill.'

'Okay, it's Jack.'

'Jack?' She sounds really shocked.

'From the flat upstairs.'

'Oh my gosh, he's your date? Sophia, there is a whole load of subplot I've missed here.'

'There is, but you'll have to wait. I've got some stuff to prepare for the kids tomorrow.' There's no way I want to give Jess a sniff of the fact this is kind of a fake date.

'You can't leave me like this . . .'

'Bye, Jess, sorry – got to go. And stop worrying, it's going to be amazing.'

I get off the call smiling to myself. Sometimes I quite like the fact Jack hasn't met Jess, or anyone else for that matter. It's easier somehow, less complicated.

I am really busy as in spite of Jess's micromanaging of the perfect ceremony, there are a few things she doesn't know about this wedding. I've been in touch with Zach and Henry and we have managed to collect some pre-recorded messages from people who mean a lot to her. She knows our dad is giving a speech from the States, where he now lives with his family, but she doesn't know her godmother is playing her favourite song on the violin, along with the other musicians in her quartet who are all going to join together on the video call. She wasn't actually going to be able to make the original physical ceremony, so I'm hoping this will be even more special. I'm really excited about this wedding. There's going to be surprises all round.

Another part of my plan takes place the next day.

'Can I paint whatever I like?' asks Alfie.

'Of course, as long as it's something nice. The idea is to wish my sister Jess and her fiancé Zach a happy wedding day,' I say. 'And you've all worked so hard at your maths this morning, you deserve some fun time doing arts and crafts.'

'I've got an idea,' Alfie says dipping his brush in the paint and starting to make bold brushstrokes on the paper. I watch him, fascinated. I can't believe how he's come out of his shell the last few weeks; he really isn't the same lad as he was as part of a class of thirty-two.

'I'm going to paint some roses. Everyone loves flowers at a wedding,' announces Freya.

'Can't we do something more interesting like cars, or my cat?' Milo asks, looking disconsolately at Freya's brightly coloured page.

'Yes of course – you can do anything you like.' I walk

at a distance round Zane's chair. 'That's nice, Zane, what are they?'

'Chocolate cakes,' he says.

'Of course.' I peer at the monstrous brown mountains. 'They're lovely and big aren't they?'

'That's how I like them,' he states. You can't argue with that.

'My goodness, these are lovely, Pritti.' I stop transfixed and admire Pritti's page, on which she's created intricate flowers, which twirl artistically into a forest of swirls and scrolls.

'I got the idea from henna tattoos – the bride normally has them painted on her hands but I thought I could do them as part of a picture,' Pritti says.

'They're so elaborate – well done.'

'Mum has sent my best dress for the filming,' Freya says.

'I'm going to wear my Spider-Man outfit,' Milo adds, not to be beaten.

'Sounds awesome – every wedding needs a visit from Spider-Man for luck and I'm really looking forward to seeing your dress, Freya.' That's the great thing about a virtual wedding: it really doesn't matter what these kids wear. They had the idea of doing a big picture for Jess, so I suggested that – as it has to be done whilst staying two metres apart – they each paint their own picture and I'll join them all together. Part of my surprise for Jess is to make a video of the kids presenting their paintings and they are so excited.

176

'Just like on the Zoom screen, all the wedding guests will be apart but their images will all come together to make one big audience,' I had explained to the kids. And that's how I like to think of it. We may all be socially distanced but tomorrow on the screen and in spirit, we are all going to be together.

CHAPTER 16

Jack

It's strange to be wearing a suit again. Having slobbed around the flat in tracksuit bottoms and comfortable T-shirts until now, I'm actually looking quite smart. Even the hair's not bad. Well, not *that* bad anyway. I rummage about in the bottom of the cupboard for my best shoes. I don't remember the last time I wore them. I've been in for three weeks and four days now. This lockdown definitely plays with your brain. It feels like a time bubble, which in some ways has gone on for ages; in others, time feels like it's going really quickly. Maybe time is playing tricks with my brain, or what's left of it.

I saw this psychiatrist on television the other day who said it was because if you do the same thing every day, time feels as though it's going quicker because there's nothing to distinguish the days. That's a depressing thought, but not for me any more, somehow I now have a purpose and it feels good.

I check my WhatsApp. *Thanks so much for the call today, mate; it was like old times. Next time I'll make sure I have a beer at the ready and we'll go through some song suggestions for next Wednesday. Bertie*

I enjoyed it, I reply. *Have some ideas already. Let us know what shopping you need. Sophia's got a team of people to pick stuff up.*

As I'm typing another message bings in:

Let me know if you need anything from the shop. I'm also making you some meringues. I heard you have a sweet tooth. Anna xx

This is definitely getting disturbing. I *do* have a sweet tooth, but how does she know that? I ignore her for now.

Nice talking to you yesterday. I have the sheet music for Elton John's 'I'm Still Standing'. Any good? Mavis

I loved chatting too – yes that's a great song. Everyone's bound to know that, I reply. *Looking forward to it!*

My phone rings suddenly, making me jump as I'm staring at it. It's Sam on FaceTime. I answer.

'Hey, I was looking for Jack. Is he in?' Sam asks, his face deadpan.

'Ha blimming ha, I don't look that different.'

'You look like a different guy and you're acting like one too. What's with the suit?'

'I'm helping Sophia out with her sister's virtual wedding,' I reply.

'With that hair cut?' He grins.

'No it's okay. I'm not going on screen.'

'So why bother with the suit?'

180

'Helps me play the part,' I say, brushing a couple of stray bits of fluff off my jacket.

'You look good. Have you got some champers at the ready?'

'Actually I have. Sophia bought me a bottle of fizz.'

'I was joking. Blimey, does this girl think of everything?'

'Do you know, I really think she does. Anyway I'd better go. I don't want to be late for her.' Whilst talking I've been rushing round the flat, grabbing my comb and running it through my hair one last time before I go back out.

'Mate, you've really got it bad.' He puts me on to Carrie who's happily kicking while lying on her baby mat. 'Carrie and I wish you luck, and Tina does too.'

Tina comes into view. 'Hi, Jack, hey you look good!' She's a little too surprised for the compliment to be flattering. 'Are you off somewhere?'

'No – long story.'

'By the way, I like the sound of this Sophia.' She raises her eyebrows suggestively. 'She sounds fab.'

'I know,' I say. She is too. It doesn't matter how much I try to deny it to myself, I am totally smitten with her.

CHAPTER 17

Sophia

This is it! The day of Jess's wedding and I can't believe it's here already. From all that time ago, when we started looking at dresses and venues, flowers and music choices, it's all gone so quickly. Yet in other ways it seems another lifetime we were in the bridal shop trying on dresses. This world we live in now is totally different. I give myself a little shake; today is not the day to be brooding about things. Jess needs me to be on top form, helping her to have the best wedding ever.

I dial her number on FaceTime. 'Sophia!' she answers, raising a glass of bubbly to the screen.

'Hey, looks like you're having a good start to the day!' I laugh. 'Where's mine?'

'You've got to join me – come on, open some, it's not that early.' I meander to the fridge and pull out a bottle I'd put there ready yesterday. It's a funny thing, but I love the way we don't usually drink at certain times in normal life (whatever that is, I can't actually remember any more) and then when it comes to Christmas, weddings, christenings and other special occasions, suddenly it's perfectly fine to drink champagne at eight o'clock in the morning.

'Cheers,' I say raising my glass. 'Happy Wedding Day to my favourite sister!'

'I'm your only sister!' she remarks. 'Cheers, here's to it!' She takes a sip. 'I can't believe it, it's actually sunny. The weather's been dry for so long, I was so worried today it would finally rain.'

I peer out the window. 'Blue sky, hardly any clouds – it looks perfect. How's the gazebo looking?'

Jess takes the phone to the window and shows me the view. I can see down into her small city garden, where a white gazebo with intricate lace design topped with sheer white swathes of fabric sweeps back to reveal a couple of big screens, on either side are pots of sweet peas, lilies and roses, a mass of stunning blooms on a long table, which also has photos on it.

'Wow, Jess, that looks incredible!' It really does, I never imagined anything so lovely.

'I know, didn't the team do a tremendous job!'

'They did. I'm so amazed; I had no idea there were people out there who set up tech for virtual weddings.'

'I guess it's become a thing now.'

'You always were a trendsetter! Is Zach safely out of the way?'

'Yes I haven't seen him since yesterday, which has been

really difficult to pull off in our house as you can imagine. He slept in the spare room and then this morning I said I'd eat first thing and then be up here out of the way, getting ready.'

'I don't know how you do it, Jess. You think of everything.'

Over much giggling, more champagne and plenty of banter, I help Jess with her make-up. Luckily she is pretty good by herself; I'm acting in more of an advisory capacity.

A couple of hours fly past and it is nearly time for the ceremony. Jess has her computer in the corner with me on Zoom so I can see a full-length view of her in her wedding dress. 'You look simply gorgeous,' I say. 'That dress fits you to perfection.'

'I do feel pretty good.' She twirls in front of the mirror.

'Okay, I'm going to join the ceremony now – and, Jess?'

'Yeah?' She turns and looks at me, her tiara sparkling in the midday sunlight.

'Enjoy it. This is your moment.'

'Thanks, Soph, for everything.' I touch the screen as does she, our fingers meeting but not meeting and that has to be the best we can do for now.

I log out and then try to log into the Zoom ceremony. Oh for goodness' sake. I try to copy and paste the password and the whole computer jams.

'Jack?' I call. The balcony door has been open all morning so we can easily talk to each other. 'How are you doing?'

'Hey,' he replies. 'Everything okay? You all set?'

'No, I can't log into the ceremony.'

'Oh no, that's a nightmare! Haven't you got the password?'

'Yes, but it's all jammed.'

'Just log out the whole thing and turn your laptop off for a minute. And take a breath.'

'Yeah I am a bit stressed.' I turn off the computer and take another sip of champagne. 'Have you got a drink ready for the toast?'

'Yep I've opened my Cava ready and checked it for quality control.'

'It's pretty good isn't it?'

'Is it working?'

'Just a minute, I'm logging back in . . . yes, oh thank goodness, I'm in.'

'Well done.'

'I'm glad you're here, Jack, or I'd be totally panicking.'

I turn back to the screen. 'Oh, here's Sophia. What kept you? We thought you weren't going to make it!' It's my dad, lounging on a very nice outdoor sofa in the California sun, next to his new wife and stepdaughter, all looking sickeningly tanned.

'Thanks, Dad, had some technical issues. Hi, Karen and Sarah! Wow you have some serious sunshine out there.' I notice Zach on the main screen, waiting nervously in the gazebo. 'Hey, Zach, you're looking really smart.'

He smiles shyly, fiddling with his tie. 'Is she nearly ready? I'm getting so nervous.'

Everyone laughs; I just can't believe all the tiny screens, which are filled with smiling and familiar faces. It's moving actually, a chequerboard of supportive people. Mum is gorgeous in a floral dress and an amazing hat. 'Mum, you look beautiful!'

'So do you,' she comments, coming far too close to the screen and bashing her nose. 'Oops, I can't ever get used to these things. That dress is perfect on you. Just a minute, Uncle Jim's having trouble getting on the screen.' She's got the mobile attached to her ear. 'Look, Jim, if you press on the screen it should work. Didn't Fern sort it for you?' Fern is Uncle Jim's long-suffering carer who pops in a couple of times a week to help. I think she deserves a medal; she's such a lovely person and seems really fond of him. 'What do you mean she did it and now it's gone?'

Zoom works really well when it's just one or two of you, but I'm finding when there's a few people – and in this case I think there must be about a hundred of us – it's really awkward. For a start, you never know when to speak and end up either talking at the same time as someone else, or not saying anything and sitting mute throughout the whole thing, which kind of defeats the purpose of being on the call at all. Also, it is meant to pick up the person who's talking and zoom in on them (in fact, good point, is this why it's called Zoom?) which is fine when that makes sense but not when it goes onto someone totally random. Which it does right now. Without warning the whole screen goes to Uncle Jim's flat. I can kind of tell it is because no one else has net curtains like that and cushions with clowns on. But oh no, we're getting a close-up view of an old lady who's adjusting her skirt and pants in the bathroom.

'Uncle Jim,' I call, 'where've you got the computer screen set up?'

'What eh? You sound like my niece, Sophia.'

'Yes I am Sophia. Uncle Jim, you need to move the screen. We can see, well I'm not sure what really. Have you got a woman in your bathroom?'

By this time the screen is focused on a close-up of a woman whose voluminous skirt seems to have got caught up in her knickers. It is not a flattering view to put it mildly.

'Good grief,' shrieks someone – I think it might be Zach's Auntie Val. 'Somebody turn off that screen, it's positively indecent!'

'What did you say?' bawls Jim. I don't know why he's shouting when it's him who can't hear us. There doesn't seem to be any logic in it.

'Move the screen,' hollers my mum at top volume.

'All right, all right, no need to shout,' he says, calmly now, as if we're the ones being unreasonable. Suddenly, thank goodness, the woman disappears from view – but then the screen goes black.

'He's gone,' says Mum to my stepdad, Mark, who is now sitting with her.

'Probably a good thing,' says Mark under his breath but we all rather ironically hear him as clear as a bell.

'No I haven't, and I heard that,' comes Uncle Jim's voice, but we still can't see him.

'Are you all right down there?' calls Jack.

I mute my microphone. 'I guess, apart from the fact my Uncle Jim's got some strange woman in the bathroom flashing her knickers at the entire wedding congregation.'

'Sounds more entertaining already than the average wedding.' Jack laughs.

'Oh no.' I can't help it, I yell with laughter. 'The vicar has just come up on the screen. He's got St Paul's Cathedral as his background.'

'That sort of goes with the wedding theme, I suppose.'

'It's not that, he's brushing his hair with a toothbrush.' He is too; it's sort of slicked in a long comb-over, nicely damped down as though he's used an entire tub of Brylcreem.

Jack chuckles. 'Doesn't he know he's on?'

'Obviously not, just a minute, I'm going to unmute myself. Zach!' I say to the groom, who's clearly oblivious and is staring nervously at the door, waiting for Jess to appear. 'Zach! The vicar doesn't seem to realise he's on!'

Zach looks at the screen, where by now the vicar is trying to pluck a couple of stray nose hairs with some tweezers, which we have an excellent view of as he has the screen positioned so we can practically see his entire nasal cavity. To be honest, his task seems entirely point-less as he has what seems like bushes sprouting from his nostrils. I hardly think plucking one or two stray hairs at this point before the ceremony is quite going to cut it.

'Reverend Bumble!' Zach is saying. 'Er, excuse me, Reverend Bumble?' You've got to give Jess's future husband points for politeness. 'Reverend!' He raises his voice to a shout now. 'Your camera is turned on!'

The vicar jumps as though he has been shot, dropping his trusty tweezers and next thing his screen goes black and he's apparently left the meeting.

'We've lost the vicar!' laments Zach. 'Where's he gone?'

'It's okay I'm sure he'll be back,' I say more optimistically than I feel. I wonder if it's too late to recruit another vicar. This one seems slightly faulty.

Before anyone can do anything else, gentle music starts playing and Jess, resplendent in her dress, comes through the doorway of her townhouse and walks down the short stone path to stand by Zach. She looks so calm and radiant with happiness. I don't think she even noticed the previous goings-on at all.

You can see Zach is totally blown away and tears start coming to my eyes already. 'You look incredible,' he tells her.

'How's it going?' calls down Jack.

'She looks beautiful,' I say, back on mute. 'We have temporarily lost the vicar and my Uncle Jim but apart from that . . .'

'Only a minor point.' Jack chuckles.

As if by magic, the vicar's screen reappears, rather comically at the same time as Uncle Jim's. The vicar is now standing in front of an attractive cottage garden with foxgloves and roses – it's all beautifully picturesque.

Uncle Jim is now on his sofa, huddled into one end, whilst the voluminous woman who was revealing too much of her anatomy earlier is at the other end. I presume they think this is social distancing. I still don't even know who she is – probably some random passer-by knowing Uncle Jim.

The vicar seems totally oblivious to the fact we were all party to his earlier hair and nose preparations and welcomes us to the wedding in hearty tones.

'We are virtually gathered here today, to witness the marriage of Jessica and Zach.'

'Have they found the vicar?' asks Jack.

I check I'm on mute. 'Yes but he's awfully funny, like a comedian dressed up. I've never seen anyone with more protruding teeth and uncontrollable facial hair, which seems to beetle all over his face like caterpillars – you know the kind with spikes, which you're not supposed to touch because they're poisonous?' Not that I was thinking of touching the vicar's face, but Jack will know what I mean.

The vicar continues in a sonorous, booming voice. 'Does any man know of any just cause or impediment why they should not be . . .'

'Wait!' calls Uncle Jim.

'Oh no, I was worried this would happen,' my mum laments. 'Shh, Uncle Jim, you're not supposed to join in this bit.'

'There's a mouse,' he says.

Everyone peers at the screen, which happens to be

191

trained on the Reverend Bumble as he's the one speaking and sure enough, in the scene behind him there's a tiny little mouse, running so fast in the grass it looks as though it's on wheels. But before the vicar can do anything a ginger cat legs it onto the scene and grabs it in his mouth and then tries to exit the garden by the nearest fence.

'Oh,' gasp various people.

'Tiddles, leave that mouse alone!' shouts the vicar.

Cats usually hang on to a mouse they've caught if they can, but I think this one is somewhat surprised (I can't blame him, as the vicar is waving his cassock at him, which is a pretty scary sight), because the cat immediately drops the mouse. It proceeds to run across the lawn again, where it's snapped up by a dog. Rather than running off with its prize, the spaniel sits holding the poor little mouse in its mouth. This mouse must be thinking it's having a really bad day. Meanwhile on the screens it's total pandemonium: kids are laughing, people are offering helpful advice. Mum's yelling, 'Tell the dog to leave it!'

The bride and groom are doubled up with laughter.

'Nell, leave!' bellows the vicar. Fortunately Nell is obviously of a biddable disposition and promptly drops the mouse, which seemingly perfectly unharmed, scurries off into a nearby bush and relative safety.

The vicar looks a bit shaken by all of this. 'Sorry about that,' he says casually, as though this sort of thing is commonplace. His face looms ridiculously close to the screen. 'I will be having a serious word with my pets after the service. Now . . . where were we?'

Both Jessica and Zach say their vows clearly and thank goodness the screen only freezes slightly once, which is good going for a Zoom call. I notice Mum wiping a tear from her eye and even Henry the best man looks quite emotional for him, either that or he suffers from hay fever.

Thank goodness and, I think, truly miraculously, the rest of the service goes without a hitch and the vicar looking eminently relieved pronounces Jess and Zach man and wife. As he does so, a great cheering comes from all the screens. Jack and I cheer madly too and round Jess and Zach's courtyard garden, the neighbours in balconies either side of their house, throw down confetti, in a shower of rainbow pastel colours. It's all really emotional and not for the first time today I'm really glad I've worn waterproof mascara.

Dad gives his speech and tells Jess how important she has always been to him and how he looks forward to welcoming Zach as part of the family. Zach's mum also gives a speech saying how fond she is of Jess and I feel a flash of envy. Ryan's mum was always horrible, making little snipey comments. Even when I had passed all my legal exams, she had nothing nice to say about it and I wonder randomly what Jack's mum is like.

The Reverend Bumble returns to the screen. 'Now Jess's godmother Steph is going to play the bride's favourite song, "All You Need Is Love", with the Quatrani string quartet!'

Jess's face is a picture, she obviously did not see this coming and I have to say I am also in tears as the strings group play her favourite piece of music. It's so touching, all the musicians creating a completely united and beautiful piece of music from their separate homes.

'Thank you so much, Steph, Mum and Sophia, who I think might have organised this. You're the best!' Jess says through her tears.

All the relations on the screens clap and whoop.

'And now,' says the Reverend Bumble, 'we have a montage created by Jess with the aid of a few little helpers.'

The screen fills with photos of Jess as a child and of Zach when he was little, followed by lots of romantic shots of them both and then pictures of all of us as families, both ours and Zach's. It all ends with a close-up of the paintings created by my class at school, which have come together to make an amazing big picture. It all works surprisingly well, with a large message in the middle, entwined with painted roses, saying, 'Happy Wedding Day to Jess and Zach!'

'Thanks so much,' Zach says. 'This painting is brilliant, thanks to Freya, Pritti, Lola, Milo, Alfie and Zane! We will be sending them all thank you cards with a piece of the wedding cake.'

'Okay, so there's someone watching this who is going to get a surprise of their own,' says Jess, grinning.

Whilst I am watching and wondering what she's talking about, out of the corner of my eye, I notice a deliveryman walk through the courtyard's archway to stand under my balcony. 'Sophia Trent?'

'Yes,' I say, surprised.

'Delivery for you – catch!' With that, he throws a stunning bouquet of flowers. I realise it's Jess's bouquet as it sails towards me and in spite of my shock and usual ineptitude at sports, I somehow manage to catch it. Everyone on the screen cheers and I wave the bouquet at them.

'Jess, you are unbelievable!' I laugh at her. She's just phoned me on FaceTime.

'Ah, it's my wedding day, I'm allowed to create a few surprises of my own!'

'Seriously thank you so much – it's gorgeous. I am so proud of you, Jess. You are the most beautiful bride I ever saw and I think I cried during half the service.'

'No, thank you – look what you've done to make this day so special. I'm really proud of you, especially after all you have been through.' I surreptitiously brush back the tears. I can't cry at Jess on her special day, but her words mean so much. She might not understand exactly how I'm feeling some of the time, but she knows it's been tough and that counts for a lot.

'Jess?'

'Oh Zach's calling me. I've got to go and speak to a couple of our guests I haven't had a chance to catch up with yet, but seriously, Sophia, thanks for everything.'

She rings off and I stare at the bouquet for a second, lost in thought.

'Hey,' calls down Jack, 'was that the bride's bouquet you were given or is some random delivery man trying to chat you up?'

'Yeah.' I try to sniff quietly whilst wiping my face carefully with a tissue, so Jack doesn't hear I've been crying. Weddings are meant to be happy. 'I wish he'd brought me chocolates like the Milk Tray ad,' I quip.

'Meant to be good luck though. Is it all over?'

'Yes.' I smile. 'It was such a beautiful ceremony, even with everyone watching from their living rooms. Made me feel so lucky that even though we all feel isolated at times, for so many different reasons, we aren't alone, we're all surrounded by people who love us. And at the end of the day, love conquers all.'

Jack's silent for a moment. 'Wow, you're quite philosophical when you get going.'

'Sorry,' I say, blushing. I hope I haven't scared him off. 'I probably shouldn't drink any more; it's gone straight to my head and now here I am rambling away.'

'It's nice,' he assures me. 'I like talking to you. Also I think it's the first wedding I've ever been to that I've actually enjoyed.'

'But you weren't even at the actual wedding,' I protest.

'That's probably why!' He laughs.

'You are totally impossible.'

'I know, Sam's always telling me that. Like another drink? I can make the next one a mocktail.'

'Good idea.' I sigh contentedly after he's lowered it down on the rope. The Budweiser packet apparently came to a bad end, so Jack's replaced it with a cardboard wine carrier. He's covered it with sparkly dark blue paper with stars on, I notice. The thought of him painstakingly cutting up wrapping paper and sticking it on the cardboard makes me smile. It makes me wonder if . . . well I don't know, it's probably nothing, but maybe Jack is trying to impress me? Or perhaps it's my imagination? I'm never very good at reading the signals. Look at what happened with Ryan. I had no idea my change of career was going to be such a disappointment to him. Or the epilepsy, although I know it was a shock. Now I worry what any future boyfriend would feel about my condition. I'd love to have half of Erica's certainty round men and relationships.

'I'm so pleased today went well,' I continue. 'The last wedding I went to was with Ryan, my ex, so I thought I'd never enjoy one again. But this was great. Then again Jess and I have always been close.'

'You didn't mention Ryan amongst the dodgy line-up of exes,' he says tentatively. I wonder if he's trying not to intrude.

'No I s'pose I didn't. Anyway, how about you – I haven't heard about any of yours at all.'

'Not much to tell to be honest. I dated a few girls in Agios Nikolaos.'

'I can imagine. Being a barman in Greece must have been like one big party.'

'Maybe. I had a few dodgy experiences though.'

'Oh, anything you care to share?'

197

'I went out with a Greek girl. She was bubbly and fun – Xanthe, her name was.'

'She sounds lovely.'

'She was, but not lovely enough for me to cope with her family.'

'Well,' I say, thinking of my own, 'families can be tricky.'

'You're telling me. This little lot were something else. Within two dates, I had to go to meet her mother and was questioned by not only her father, but also by her three brothers – who were huge by the way; I wouldn't have wanted to take them on in a fight – as to what my intentions were.'

'Slightly awkward.'

'Yes very. I'm afraid a couple of dates were enough. I was too scared.'

I laugh. 'Fair enough.'

'Then there was "Alexa".'

'You dated the app?'

'No, ha-ha, very funny. She was a nice girl but very blunt, had a habit of saying exactly what she thought.'

'I guess at least you knew where you stood.' I don't add that I would have given anything for Ryan to have some similar traits. Honesty is important in any relationship. It had turned out I obviously didn't know Ryan at all.

'A bit too much so. I remember one time she told me I was quite good-looking for a British guy.'

'Ooh, that's a burn.'

'Yep, you'd think I'd have had the sense to run away then, but after the third date, she turned up with another fit Greek god on her arm and told me I was dumped and she was going out with him.'

'Her loss.'

'I don't know about that; he was really very good-looking.'

'What happened after that?'

'There were a couple of girls who I just went on a few dates with, but nothing serious.' He pauses and I feel as though he has perhaps been holding something back. 'And then I met Laura.'

There's something in the way he says Laura, something final. As though maybe she changed something. 'Laura?' I echo.

'We went out a few times, then it got serious quite quickly. She was different somehow. There was something fascinating and incredibly attractive about her, but we argued like cat and dog. We were more on and off than a bride's nightgown.'

I would laugh but somehow it doesn't seem right to. 'I guess some relationships are like that. But it sounds as though you had a connection, lots of sparks?'

'Yes we did,' he says thoughtfully. 'Laura was one of those girls who attracts people like a moth to a flame. She sparkled when she was on good form and I fell for it like the idiot I am.'

'What happened?'

He sounds distracted, far away somehow, even though

his voice stays steady. 'I was really keen on her, yet . . .' I wait patiently for him to continue. 'Yet even then, I had some small niggling doubts that maybe there was more to her than I was seeing. Just sometimes, she would let her mask slip slightly and I would think, *did you really just say that*? But then within minutes, she would be lovely again and I would wonder if I imagined it all. She made me doubt myself and what I was doing. We rowed like anything as sometimes I would confront her about it and she would laugh at me.'

I'm silent for a moment. 'That must have been hard to deal with.'

'Yes, I think people change – or maybe sometimes they're good at hiding their real colours and you find you never really knew them in the first place.'

'That's true,' I agree. 'Sometimes it feels as though you never really know someone, however much time you spend with them. And other people you've hardly met feel as though you've known them all your life.'

'Yeah,' he says contemplatively, 'it's strange but I feel like I've known you forever.'

'That's because you've been stuck in and had no one else to talk to!' I feel ridiculously pleased and yet . . . something makes me deflect the compliment. Ryan would say nice things all the time, but in the end it didn't count for anything, not after things changed.

'Maybe, but I don't think so.' He breaks off. 'Anyway, what are you missing most during this lockdown?'

His abrupt change of topic takes me by surprise, but

200

I'm kind of relieved. This feels like safer territory. I still don't feel able to discuss relationships. Even after all this time, it feels too painful. 'That's easy, contact, with the people I care about, my family, my sister. I would do anything just to give her a hug right now. You must miss your brother right?'

'Definitely. I'd love to see him and Tina and have a cuddle with my new little niece. Did I tell you I'm going to be Carrie's godfather?'

'You'll make a great godparent,' I tell him. Even though I haven't met him properly, I can tell he would be brilliant with kids – his sense of fun, his understanding of different issues, the way he reacted to Carrie's birth. And he never forgets to ask about the kids at school.

'What's the first thing you'll do when you get out of here?' he asks.

'Well other than hugging my family, I'll probably go for a walk on Sparrow Hill and just enjoy the quiet and stillness of the fresh air whilst gazing at the patchwork fields, the birds, butterflies and fresh green tree-lined lanes of the countryside. You feel on top of the world there and can see for miles.' I then realise maybe I'm being a bit insensitive. 'Sorry, that's not very helpful saying that when you can't go out at all. I guess at least I can take a short walk now. How about you?'

He pauses. 'Well I would love a walk, maybe not so much in the town, but Sparrow Hill is lovely. But there's something I'd want to do before anything else, if I could get out of here.'

He says this quietly. His voice is slightly husky and I'm almost too nervous to ask him. 'Really, what?'

'I'd love to walk down those stairs, through your front door – if you'll let me in of course – and sit watching the sunset with you, whilst we have one of our chats, as we could have done before all this . . .' my heart is in my mouth '. . . except . . .' He gives a dry laugh.

'Except?'

'That would be awkward because I'm still married to Laura.'

CHAPTER 18

Jack

The picture of a beach hanging on the wall looks kind of funny, upside down and round the wrong way. In fact everything's a bit fragmented and I seem to be cuddling my dressing gown, which is wrapped around the table leg. Where the heck am I and what's going on? I shut my eyes; it's far too bright to be looking at anything for long. Cautiously I open them again. Okay I'm on the floor in my flat. Why did I sleep here? I put out my arm and touch the sofa. Must have crashed out on there and fallen off. It's cold too, and where's that awful brightness coming from? I peer blearily round, through squinty eyes, towards the source of light. I've left the balcony doors open.

I remember I was talking to Sophia but I think I might have said something wrong. Was it the wedding? No, that went well. Yet I have that horrible feeling you get when you've had the opportunity for something wonderful to happen and suddenly it's been taken away. Then, like a tidal wave, realisation comes rushing back and crashes over my head, leaving me cold. I can't believe I told Sophia about Laura.

I hold my head in my hands, drawing my legs up in the foetal position. Shutting my eyes doesn't help. I remember it all, with hideous technicolour clarity. Like a total bastard, I said to Sophia that I wanted to be with her and then told her I'm married. Just like that, out of the blue. I am such a loser. I know I had to tell her sometime but not then, not like that.

My mouth is so dry I can barely move my lips at all. I need to get myself off the floor and find cold water, and lots of it. After a fight with the overwhelming wooziness, I struggle to my feet and stagger to the kitchen. This is why the specialist said no alcohol binges, with dodgy renal function the normal hangover is amplified by about a hundred. As I sip water, having downed a couple of painkillers, I try to piece together the events of last night. Only I could mess up like this. Sophia and I had been chatting away as we always do, yet last night it felt different, somehow much more intimate. I wanted to be close to her, to feel her mouth on mine, even though I don't know what she looks like. Yet I've blown it.

I shower with the cold tap on full jet for the first few seconds in a ridiculous attempt to punish myself for my idiocy. I feel a blimming mess. I hear my mum's voice: 'You need to pull yourself together, Jack. What did you want before all this rubbish? You're not a child any more. It's time for you to grow up and get on.'

It's strange but I don't even need to speak to my mum to know what she would say and she would be right. She's said enough before. I was too busy to hear her or take any notice. Too busy running away. Running away from a history of medical stuff, hospital visits, all of which I wanted to draw a veil over, block out. It was like I was trying to prove something to myself: *I can party; this disease isn't going to define me.*

There's an irony to the fact that it's taken a pandemic and a random friendship with someone I've never met, to make me stop and think about things. Make me listen to sense. From today on, I am going to be different. No more Jack the joker, the charming barman who everyone likes but no one really respects.

I check my phone. Last night I sent a desperate text to Sophia, trying to explain that I hadn't meant for it to come out like that. Trying to tell her that I haven't seen Laura for a year. I've been trying to get her to agree to a divorce. The message shows as still unread.

As I'm staring blankly at the screen, a reminder pings up. I'm due to phone Mavis at eleven-thirty. I'm just about on time. I dial her number.

'Mavis?'

'Hello, Jack, how nice to hear from you. How's tricks?'

'Not too bad, bit tired today after a late night.'

'Oh dear, been partying again have you?'

'Yes something like that.' I smile in spite of my muzzy head. 'And how are you?'

'Good thanks; I've been up and had my exercise round

the estate. Popped into Newsie to get my fresh bread. Early on a Sunday, there's hardly anyone around but I wore my mask just to be sure.'

'Organised as ever!' I comment.

'Ooh yes I can't bear hanging around in the morning. Wastes the day! I bumped into Bertie and had a socially distanced chat. I'm worried about him though,' she confides.

'What was up?'

'He just seems quiet. I think this lockdown's getting to him.'

'I can imagine.' Although I can't really, as it must be especially awful for Bertie – he's lost his wife; his life partner of over half a century. 'I suppose at least he gets out for his walk once a day.'

'I know, but it's lonely for him after Elsie died. He hasn't even got Cooper to walk any more.'

'Cooper?'

'His little Jack Russell. He loved that dog, he went everywhere with him but he died a couple of years ago. He was a good age though – sixteen.'

'Yes I remember now; I'd forgotten his name. That's a pretty good innings. But it's a shame – having a dog at a time like this would give Bertie some company and he could meet people, well, at a distance anyway.'

'Yes it's important, gives you someone to talk to. My budgie Sunny and I have whole conversations about all sorts of things. He chats with me all day and understands everything I say. Can't get him to be quiet during the church service though.'

'You take him to church?' I must admit I'm struggling not to laugh at this image.

'No I have an online service every Sunday.'

'And how was it today?'

'Very uplifting. It's not the same as being in the actual church of course, but the vicars share out the prayers and service from their homes and gardens. Makes it feel like having a family for me.'

'That's so nice.'

'Yes, Rev Bates has asked me to do a reading next week.'

'Go you!'

'I know, but to tell you the truth, Jack, I'm not sure how to record myself on my iPad. I'm still scared of it to be honest.'

'That's okay. I'll help you by telling you how to do it. It's quite simple really. Or if you find it too difficult, I'm sure Sophia will record it for you. She could stand in the courtyard at a distance and film outside.'

'What a lovely idea, Jack. Sophia is a dear, I'm sure she would do that. Why didn't I think of it?'

'Well that's why it's good to run things past other people. It can help.'

'You're so right, dear; problems often seem insurmountable on one's own. That's what today's sermon was about. Helping one another and how this crisis has made people realise what is important to them. Friendship and companionship rather than money and things we think we need but we don't.'

'Sounds about right.' And I've lost perhaps one of the best friends I've ever had, because I was so stupid. I try to concentrate on the conversation. 'He must be a wise man your vicar,' I comment.

'He certainly is and the sermon really cheered me up. He said we shouldn't be afraid of the new normal that will follow this lockdown.'

'I guess.' I have my doubts: I think we all feel pretty uncertain.

'He's not saying we aren't afraid of it because of course we all are; we just want things to go back to how they were. But maybe they can't. Maybe things need to change and we have to move forward, learn from what's happened and embrace new things.'

'Wow – that's positive.' I guess change can be a good thing, and I know we need to learn from our mistakes. But I can't believe falling out with Sophia is part of anything positive at all, I might have lost her altogether and she has become such a positive part of my life. Maybe I haven't realised until now just how much.

'That's what I thought, but perhaps a little heavy for a Sunday morning if you've had a bad night! How is Sophia anyway? I hear you've become good friends.'

I'm silent for a moment.

'Oh dear have I said something wrong,' she says. 'I'm always putting my foot in it.'

'No, you haven't. Not at all. Everything's fine. It's just we had a bit of a misunderstanding and the thing is, I really like her.'

'Then tell her,' she says, like it's that simple after what I did. 'That's the best way: be honest and open. Sophia's a lovely girl. She'll understand.'

'I've messaged her but she's not replying at the moment. I think I've really upset her.'

'Keep trying, dear. As Anne of Green Gables said, "Tomorrow is a new day with no mistakes in it . . . yet".'

'Anne who?'

'She was the heroine of a book by L. M. Montgomery and a very good one too, except like all of us, she kept making mistakes. It all turned out well in the end and she's right – every day is a new start.'

'It is, I guess, with no mistakes in it yet,' I repeat. 'Do you know what, you're right. Thanks so much, Mavis. I'm going to go and sort some things out.'

'You do that and thanks for the chat, Jack. I really enjoyed it.'

'I should be thanking you – you've just really helped more than you will know.' I leave the call.

She has as well. It's time for a new beginning.

I fry up a large pan of bacon and eggs, fried bread and baked beans. Okay so I'll start the healthy diet another day. Don't want to change too many things at once. The greasy breakfast is delicious, just what I needed, and I scroll down my phone. There's her number. I press on it firmly before I can change my mind. It rings for several seconds and I desperately hope she answers.

'Hello?'

209

'Laura, it's Jack.'

'Oh.' Her voice changes, the tone dropping away from the cheery note it had when she first answered.

'How are you?' I ask, determined to be civil, as though we are just regular friends calling for a catch-up. No remnants of a failed and deeply acrimonious relationship to be seen here.

'Fine,' she says guardedly. To be fair, it's a stupid question in the middle of a pandemic and a loaded one. There's always a slight hesitation these days after asking how someone is, a hidden worry that maybe the person might not be all right, or someone they know might be really ill or worse. The virus has ensured that the usual daily assumption that someone is likely to be perfectly okay when you phone them has been removed along with all our other comfortable and routine safety nets that we have always taken for granted.

'I just wanted a quick chat, if you're not busy,' I say.

'Well I'm about to do the shop,' she says tersely.

'That's fine; don't let me stop you. I'll phone later if you like.' I try to keep my tone light. I am determined this is going to work. I can't change anything else in my life during this lockdown but I can get this off my chest.

'No,' she sighs, 'it's fine. I can go in a while. Apart from anything else I suppose I should be grateful that you've phoned. You haven't returned any of my calls before.'

'I know – well it's been difficult.' What's been most difficult is the fact Laura is convinced that I'm still going to go back to her. 'But the thing is, Laura, things have changed. I've changed.' There's silence on the end of the line and I hope she's still there. 'Have you received the papers?'

'Papers?' she echoes as though I am speaking in a different language and she has never heard of divorce papers, let alone received any. This is what makes her so darned difficult to deal with. She's as slippery as those things in arcade machines that you pay money to try to win.

Okay, keep calm, Jack. Count to ten. 'The divorce petition.'

'I don't think I . . .'

'Because Malcolm Peterson says he delivered it to you at 12.20 on 16th March.'

'I don't remember – maybe it was my neighbour Kev.'

'It was definitely you. You signed for it.' Wow, nothing about this girl changes. It somehow strengthens my resolve. I'm doing the right thing.

There's a silence as she digests the information. 'He was sent from Fraser Symonds. As you apparently didn't receive the last two copies, I paid for this one to be delivered by hand to you.'

'You really mean business don't you?'

'To be honest yes.'

'You only ever phone when you want something. Did you ever care for me?'

I'm not going to fall for this. Not this time, even though her tone has changed and she's plaintive, pleading almost. 'Yes. I did. You know what we had was really special and meant a lot to us both and we had some amazing times but it wasn't healthy. We weren't suited at all. In the end all that was left was toxicity.'

'We could have tried again.'

'It still wouldn't have worked. Look, Laura, when I met you I was angry. I was running away from years of childhood illness, failed medical procedures. I just wasn't in a good space. I went to Greece to get away from reality, to actually live a life away from hospitals, meds, my parents who have helicoptered around me for ever. Wanting the best for me, but I found it all so stifling. I just wanted to be normal, have a laugh, be relaxed like my mates.'

She remains silent so I continue, 'I did love you. Who wouldn't? You were sparky and fun, full of zest for life. We had a ball together. I'm never going to forget that, but we should never have married. I'm not the guy for you and you aren't the girl for me. I've changed now; I'm not that carefree bloke you thought you were marrying. He was just a knee-jerk reaction to a life I wasn't happy with. The Jack you married doesn't exist.'

'But I could have changed, too.' She's making me feel really bad now, but this happens every time. I need to stay strong; I know I'm not the right guy for her. We are so completely and utterly different but she doesn't understand that. I'm not the person she thinks she wants.

'You *did* change. Into this clingy person who I don't even recognise. And that was my fault. You're so much better than that, Laura, and somewhere you will find a guy who makes you happy, who wants that adrenaline ride for real, that constant spark you can get from each other.'

'You might find that part of yourself again. We could go back to Greece, start over.'

'But I don't want to. I've decided to study. Do that college course I always wanted to take.' I've surprised myself, but now I've said it, I'm realising how determined I am to do it.

'What college course?' Typical Laura – I told her all about my ideas for this course last year. She had been totally against the idea, said it was a waste of time and I would be bored.

'The one I was going to do before all this kicked in. At the Chiropractic College. It's what I wanted for years before . . . before I got so darned angry and sick of everything.' My God I'm surprising myself with what I'm coming out with. It's all true, but seems to have been buried somewhere ridiculously deep until now. I still want to do this course. I'd love to be a sports physio – really help people with back issues, sports injuries. 'You know I was inspired by the physio at the hospital; he changed so many lives for the better,' I say. 'I've got loads of ideas.'

'Is that really what you want?' asks Laura.

'Yes, it is. But what do *you* really want, like really want to do more than anything?' I'm desperate for her to do what she really loves, instead of hanging on for me to become something I never will. She's a free spirit. Settling down is not for her, I know it isn't.

She hesitates a moment. 'I'd really like to go travelling again, see more of the world. I don't want to stay here. This pandemic has just made me want to go even more desperately.'

'That's good. I think it's made us all have a rethink, change our priorities.'

'I guess you're right. I don't want to give up travelling; I had no idea you wouldn't have wanted to come.'

'Not any more,' I say gently.

'Are you sure there isn't someone else?' She sounds suspicious all of a sudden.

I wait a moment before replying, 'Yes, there is.'

'I knew it,' she spits triumphantly.

It had been going pretty well until now, but I don't want to lie to her. We need to be honest with each other. 'Not like that. I mean I don't even know if she likes me – we've never met face to face – but it's made me realise.'

'Realise what? That doesn't sound like a proper relationship.'

Of course it doesn't. She must think I'm mad and, honestly, to be dumped for someone I haven't even met does sound crazy, although it's not like that. Laura and I were finished a long time ago. 'Maybe it isn't, but either way, it's made me want to change myself, or rather, find my old self for the better,' I try to explain.

There's a long silence at the other end of the line. 'If you really feel like that, I understand. Maybe I'm trying to hang on to something that never was.'

'I don't know. We were younger then; maybe we just

didn't really know what we wanted. I think we both deserve better than an unhappy marriage and that's before all the other pressures life can throw our way.'

'I know.' There's another silence. 'I'll think about it . . . and, Jack?'

'Yeah.'

'I hope it works out for you.'

For a moment I can't trust myself to speak and end up gulping instead. 'Thanks, Laura. As soon as this is over, do that travelling. You only get one shot.'

'I might just do that.' She pauses a moment. 'Whoever this girl is, she must be quite something. Before, you could never even talk to me about how you felt about your operations let alone admit as much to me as you have today. Goodbye, Jack.'

'Bye, Laura.'

I hang up and stare at the screen. At least that's progress. Somehow I do feel sad. Right now a lot of my pent-up anger at Laura has ebbed away. She's no easy person, an understatement really, but I was an idiot. I genuinely hope she finds happiness. We just jumped in too fast.

I check my phone again but Sophia still hasn't read my text. I peer over the balcony as earlier I sent down the wine box and a bacon butty. But it's still there, resting outside the railings, untouched; I don't think she's even opened her door.

CHAPTER 19

Sophia

I need to concentrate on today's lessons. The busier I am the less I can think about things like pandemics, the number of people who are sick, lonely people stuck in the flats, the daily update and Jack. It's best to just block it all out. Like it never happened. Like our friendship never existed. After all, it might as well not have happened. As it turns out, I don't know him at all. I don't even think we're friends. Friends don't leave out vital details like the fact that they're married. There are no secrets between good mates.

This relationship, whatever it is, was all in my head, the result of being in my flat too much and my usual way of feeling sorry for people. I can't help it, I'm just one of those people who always worries about the underdog. Whenever I'm watching movies with the girls and someone gets their just desserts, I still feel kind of bad for them. The others always say, 'You're too soft,

Sophia,' and I probably am. So no more Miss Nice, hello Miss Reality Check. This is how it is from now on.

'So,' I say to the neatly spaced expectant faces, sitting carefully at two metres distant from each other and in front of me. 'Today I've asked you to bring in something that's special to you and I've brought some things that mean a great deal to me too.'

'I've brought my Spider-Man,' shouts out Milo waving a vivid red figure dressed in a spider-web-covered suit.

'I thought you might.' I smile. 'Now you can each have a turn – one at a time, Milo! Wait a moment please. Each person can have a go at showing the rest of us their favourite thing and explaining why it means so much to them. So who wants to go first? Zane? Hold on, Milo, you can go second.' Milo sits down again, but I'm worried he might burst if he has to wait much longer.

'I've brought my bunny,' says Zane, lifting a white toy bunny up in the air the wrong way up, so his long floppy ears hang down in a comical fashion.

'How lovely – is he a he or a she?'

'He's a he.'

'Okay and what's he called?'

'Bunny.'

'Of course! He's very special and looks really fluffy.'

'Yes he is.' Zane nods his head vigorously. 'He is fluffy, except when he falls into the drain outside our house.'

'Oh,' I say, taken aback. 'Does he often fall into the drain?'

'No, just the once.'

'I should think that was enough. So how is he so lovely and snowy white now?'

'Mummy washed him in the sink and then put him in the washing machine.'

'Sensible Mummy. Well at least he's nice and clean now and he has a unique talent – he obviously likes exploring drains. Let's hope he doesn't make a habit of it at the moment though.' And let's hope this all happened before the virus outbreak.

'No, my mummy says I have to keep hold of him, especially when passing anything wet.'

'Very sensible.'

The children each go through showing their beloved toys or objects. Milo does a very lively impression of how his Spider-Man can climb walls; Freya has a jewellery box which her parents gave her, with a dancing ballerina; Pritti has a lucky stone with a Hindi message meaning 'peace and love' on it; Alfie has an airfix model of a Red Arrow Hawk, Ben has his first paint box chock full of a myriad of colours; and Lola brings out her Winnie-the-Pooh, who is looking a little shabby but much loved.

'Okay, so we have all talked about what is special to us and why. Now there's a couple of friends I'd like you to meet. One is Mr Ted, who was mine when I was little, so he's a tiny bit tatty round the edges.' I lift up Mr Ted who looks decidedly worse for wear. His fur has been pushed the wrong way, his nose has totally gone, leaving a solitary piece of thread, and his ear looks suspiciously as though it might fall off.

219

'He looks like he's been through some troubles,' remarks Milo.

I smile at Milo's oddly mature way of putting it. 'Yes, he does and I guess in a way he has been through some stressful times. He was my best friend through growing up. I would hug him when I was afraid or upset and he always made me feel better.'

'That's what friends are for,' says Freya.

'Absolutely,' I say. 'Now here I have another special item of mine for you to see.' I hold up a brand-new teddy with fluffy fawn-coloured fur from the shop. 'This teddy is really new. I saw him when I was in a gift shop a while ago and couldn't resist. I thought I might give him to someone else.' Actually he had been for Ryan. Looking back I don't know what I was thinking. He would have considered it overly sentimental; it was hardly his thing. 'But I ended up keeping him. I just couldn't part with him so he sits on my desk at home and watches me work.'

'I like his eyes. They're like little buttons,' says Pritti.

'Yes he is cute isn't he? Now if I had to choose which bear I liked the most or that was most important to me, which one do you think it would be?'

'The new one!' shouts Milo.

'The old one,' says Lola.

'Yes, Lola, well done, you're right. I like both of them, but in spite of how tatty my old bear is – and I know his ear is in need of urgent attention – he's especially important to me because of what we have been through together.'

'Did he make you feel better when you were sad?' asks Zane. 'My bunny does that too. He gives the best cuddles.'

'Yes, Mr Ted made me feel better and now just seeing him makes me happy. He brings back lots of great memories. So in spite of the fact he's tatty and his ear's nearly coming off, it doesn't matter. Does anyone know why that is?'

'Because it's what's underneath that counts,' Alfie answers.

'Well done, Alfie, it is. So it isn't about how smart things are, or how much money we have or how much things cost, what makes them precious is what they mean to us. I think this virus has made us all change our priorities hasn't it? Do you think the same things matter to you now as they did before lockdown?'

'No, before lockdown all I wanted was riding lessons, but now I just want my mum to come home safe from work every day,' Freya says. Her words make me swallow involuntarily. I know just how she feels. Each and every day I've been offering up prayers that Mum will be okay, that she will escape this virus. We all know it can be especially risky for those on the front line.

'Absolutely – that's really what matters,' I say in what I hope is an upbeat manner.

'Although I would still like riding lessons.' She gives a shy smile.

I laugh. 'Fair enough, I don't blame you. I always wanted a horse when I was a child.'

'Did you ever get one?'

'No, but I guess I just didn't want one so much when I was older.' That's the thing, our priorities change. I wish my disagreements with my mum were still as simple now as they were when I was a child. She had been upset at my change of career direction and heartbroken over Ryan. *Such a nice lad with impeccable manners. Charming parents and all so successful.*

'I still want my brother to stop eating my sweets,' Milo says, jolting me back to reality.

'I can understand that, Milo,' I reply, 'but is there anything else that's important?'

'Yes, because we don't have so many sweets now, I do share and he gives me some of his chocolate.'

'That's perfect,' I say, relieved that I've managed to make a teaching moment out of Milo's obsession with sugar. 'So maybe in spite of the fact things are tough right now, we are all learning what really matters to us.'

Freya puts her hand up. 'Miss Trent.'

'Yes, Freya?'

'Isn't it people who are the most important thing? And how we help each other through things? That's what really counts.'

'Yes, Freya, you're right, that is what means most, especially at the moment – we all really need each other now more than ever.'

* * *

222

As I drive back to the flat, I ponder on the fact that kids, for some reason, often get to the real heart of the matter so much better than adults. Why don't we keep the simple, accepting and honest outlook on life we had as children?

As I pull up into the car park my phone bings the arrival of a text. It's from Jess. *Hey Soph, hope you're well and everything's okay. Zach and I are having a great time on our virtual honeymoon. No work, no stressful phone calls (not meaning you of course) just chilling out and watching old romantic movies and lazing in the garden. Absolute bliss. Hope you and Erica are okay and the kids at school are happy. Loved the pictures they did for our wedding, they're so cute xx*

Yes we're all fine, don't be fooled though, they really aren't that cute normally, but they are good kids. How's married life? xx

Zach's managed to get some fresh shellfish delivered so he's creating a special dinner tonight. I'd better make the most of it – we'll be back on stuff from the freezer next week! xx

Sounds like here then! I'm hoping Erica will have cooked tonight; I'm shattered! xx

Well don't overdo it. Make sure you get some down time. Are you still looking after all those neighbours of yours? xx

Just a few of them, but Jack's been doing loads xx

I type his name without thinking, and then it all comes crashing back and I wish I hadn't.

Ah and how is Jack? xx

Sorry, must go. Erica will be wondering where I am xx
Okay, send my love to Jack and look after yourself xx
Enjoy your time off xx
Will do! xx Don't think you're getting away with it
about Jack. I'm going to need to know all the details
when I'm back from my virtual honeymoon.

I send her a picture of the raised-eyebrow emoji and click my phone off before trudging up to the flat. I wish she were usually as easy to dismiss, although there's a part of me that misses our regular chats.

'There you are,' says Erica opening the door with a flourish. 'I thought you must have got lost.'

'No, just a busy day. Had to do some planning for the next few lessons and you know how it is.' I stumble into the flat, dump my bags in the decontaminating corner and wash my hands thoroughly. We have this rule in our flat that any bags or parcels or things from the currently potentially toxic outside world are left in the corner for anything from a few hours to a couple of days to get rid of any potential germs. I also wipe things off at regular intervals with sprays and cloths. Disinfectant wipes are simply impossible to get hold of now, along with yeast and flour. It's as though this pandemic has made everyone into cleanliness freaks, germophobes and wannabe bakers. I have an old bread machine, which was Mum's back in the day. It probably still works but I haven't been able to try it out as you can't get yeast at any price.

Fortunately for everyone, the general population seems to have realised that toilet rolls are not going to run out any time soon and there are plenty available in the shops now. Shame I ordered fifty rolls on the internet, but I expect we'll get through them eventually.

'Cup of tea?' I offer Erica, as I flick the kettle on.

'I'd love one thanks.'

I bumble about making the tea and eating biscuits at the same time. I always come in from work super hungry. 'Good shift at the hospital last night?'

'Yeah it was okay. We had a dad who got angry about the social distancing thing, but he settled down in the end after the baby was born. Got a bit hairy at one point though.'

'Sounds stressful. That's ridiculous – you're only trying to protect his family.'

'I know. It was. I came in, drank a large brandy and went straight to sleep.'

'Don't blame you.'

'I found this on the balcony.' She holds up the wine box and the remnants of what looks like a bacon bap with a letter tucked in next to it.

'Oh? That's random.' I buzz round the kitchen nonchalantly.

'It's from Jack. I thought you'd want to read it.'

'Not really.' I busy myself adding sugar to Erica's tea, spending an inordinate amount of time stirring it.

'You're going to wear the pattern off the inside of the mug in a minute. Come on spill – something happened with Jack didn't it?'

'Not really.' I take a bite of custard cream.

'You can't fool me. Come on, Soph, you'll feel better talking about it.'

I fling myself down on the sofa and take a revitalising sip of tea. 'I s'pose. It's just I really liked him. I still do, but I can't stand people who hold stuff back. It's really not okay in a relationship.'

'But you're not really in a relationship are you? You're just mates. You haven't even seen each other.'

'I know, but I guess I felt there was more than that, like he really understood stuff. It was as though there was a connection.'

'And?'

'And he just suddenly announces he's got a wife.'

Erica almost drops the wine box she's still holding. 'Oh okay that's bad. I didn't see that coming.'

'No one saw that coming.' I've since been wondering if maybe I should have, replaying our conversations, trying to work out if I'm overreacting or if he's just another disappointment.

'But didn't he mention anything about her before?'

'No, yes. Well no not really, but I guess it never came up.'

'So maybe he didn't deliberately hide her from you.'

'I can't believe we're having this conversation. You know I have issues with this sort of thing after Ryan was the most emotionally unavailable man on the planet. I vowed I would never go out with or confide in anyone like that again.'

'Has Jack tried explaining?'

226

'He sent a text but I haven't read it.'

'Why not? At least give him a chance. He seemed really decent and I just can't imagine from what you've said about him he's the sort of guy to keep a hidden wife.'

I laugh. 'You make him sound like Rochester in *Jane Eyre*.'

'Ha-ha, no idea who you're talking about. Anyway, if you're not going to look at his text, I'm going to read you this.' She takes the folded piece of paper out of the wine box.

Dear Sophia,

I've got so many things I want to say to you but now I have a pen in my hand I don't know what to write. The thing is, over the past few weeks I've come to look forward to our chats and our evenings sharing balcony cocktails. You're so easy to talk to and, without realising it, you've become part of my life.

I know it sounds crap, but while I find it easy to be positive, maybe even fun when I'm chatting, when it comes to talking about the things that really matter, the stressful subjects, I just seem to stick my head in the sand. My life has been full of serious conversations and well-meaning medical professionals talking at me, wanting to ask me if I'm okay, how I'm feeling about my transplant, how I feel about having a chronic illness, how I'm feeling about the meds and I just haven't wanted to talk about it. I didn't know how I felt and I sure as heck didn't want to talk about it!

For the last few years I've been running away, from

227

my diagnosis, from my parents, from serious stuff and I spent some time drowning my sorrows, pretending I was fit and well and just, well normal, in Crete. Then Laura came along. As I told you, she was different, feisty, didn't give a darn about anyone or anything and that's what I thought I needed. But as I've already said, we were more on and off than the British weather.

What I didn't tell you was stupidly we decided to get married a couple of years ago. In my defence I can only say I was young and I felt like rebelling about everything and Laura was really pushy about getting hitched straight away. So we got married abroad, without my family (yes, they were hurt too). I feel terrible about it now, but I guess I just wanted to hit out at everything. I know, I sound like a complete idiot and I was.

It soon became really obvious we weren't going to work as a couple. Sam and his partner Tina were getting married, I missed my parents, my health started to deteriorate again. I realised running away wasn't the answer; my kidney disease is a part of me, of who I am. I tried to explain to Laura, offered for her to come back to the UK with me, but she wouldn't. She said I was being boring, giving in. She wanted to travel, she needed excitement and fun, the spontaneous barman she'd met in Agios Nikolaos, but that guy wasn't really me.

All I can say is, this lockdown, meeting you, the whole situation has given me time to think and realise I need to grow up. Stop running, accept how I am, who I am, what I am.

For nearly a year I've been trying to divorce Laura. I knew the relationship wasn't working. We are totally wrong for each other. But Laura refused to accept it. It's made things so difficult. I've been constantly on to the solicitors, served her the divorce papers, but she just ignored them. In desperation I paid for them to be delivered and signed for. But still nothing from her and I figured I'd leave it until we had been separated long enough for a divorce to be granted naturally as we had been apart for a couple of years.

But now I realise yet again I was just hiding from reality. It's you I need to thank for helping me see this. You've helped me understand how I feel. I'm just sorry I came out with all that stuff the other night and in the wrong way. No wonder you aren't talking to me. I hate thinking of you sitting in your flat, going about your daily life angry with me, believing I'm a total waste of space. I hope you might forgive me and just be my friend again, because to be honest you're the best mate I've ever had. I've never nearly met anyone like you . . . and you do make the best chocolate crispy cakes ever.

With very best wishes,

Your upstairs neighbour Jack

Erica gives me one of those looks, which shout loud and clear whose side she's on. I'm silent for a moment, digesting Jack's words, ruminating on them, whilst anxiously scoffing biscuits. I just can't help it, I always stress-eat. I often drive everyone nuts in the cinema because as the film gets more tense, I munch more and more popcorn until whoever's sitting next to me gives me an annoyed nudge and I realise what I've been doing.

'You've eaten half the pack, Soph!' Erica picks up the crumpled and seriously depleted packet of custard creams.

'I feel sick now.'

'So . . .' Erica watches me put the remaining biscuits back in the cupboard.

'So?'

'What did you think of what he said?'

'I don't know. It's so hard. I mean I kind of feel sorry for him. I know how it feels to have a health condition and at least mine's only been recent. On the other hand my new resolve to stop being a pushover is already clearly wavering. The trouble is I can always see the other person's point of view.'

'Yeah but on the other hand, I can understand why he didn't say more about Laura. It sounds as though it was a pretty messed-up relationship.'

'I guess, it's just that after Ryan and his repressed, "I can't talk about how I'm feeling" issues, until suddenly he just couldn't deal with my health or my change of career or anything, I've found it really hard to trust any guy again and I felt as though Jack was different. Maybe I was wrong.'

I put my head down on my knees, trying to block out the memory of the day Ryan had dropped the bombshell that he was finishing with me, totally out of the blue. We had been walking out in the forest, just like any other walk and he'd just turned to me and out of nowhere said, 'Soph . . . I think we should delay the wedding.'

'Delay it? Why?' I'd asked, shocked.

'Because I think this condition . . .'

'Epilepsy. It has a name.'

'Yes, your epilepsy,' he continued, saying it as though it was something only I have, and as disdainfully as if it were leprosy. 'Because of your epilepsy I think maybe we should delay the wedding until you feel better.' He couldn't have chosen a more volatile topic or rubbish use of words. Uncontrolled epilepsy is a stealer of freedom, of your independence, of any kind of social life at all. After my first seizure, there was concern but it was soon forgotten, swept under the carpet in the hope it was an isolated incident. Within days of my second, I was completely and utterly relegated to the status of toddler. By my mother and sister at least. Ryan coped by pretending it didn't exist. If we didn't talk about it, it wasn't there.

'Feel better?' I'd asked incredulously.

'You know what I mean.' He hadn't met my eyes, choosing instead to stare randomly at a tree branch hanging overhead.

'No, I don't.' I had stopped in the middle of the path; everything around us had seemed to come to a screaming halt too. 'I feel fine, Ryan, most of the time. At least the meds work, at least I don't have seizures any more and can go out and actually do things. I'm the same person you've been going out with for the past five years.'

'Yes, but *are* you?' he had asked, his dark eyes boring into mine. 'You've thrown away all those years of work. You chucked it all in. I don't understand – you've thrown

231

away everything you studied for. Then you announce you want to teach, to do something more meaningful for goodness' sake. How am I supposed to feel? You make it sound as though being a lawyer is worthless. Thanks a lot.'

I'd been silent for a moment. I really hadn't meant to make him feel that way. 'I didn't mean it like that, just that I needed to do something where I felt I was giving something back.'

But he had carried on oblivious. 'I went along with you training to be a teacher, hoping it was just a phase. You might have tried teaching and hated it. How was I to know you'd love your new life and would leave me behind with your old one? We had so many plans. We were going to have kids soon for goodness' sake. I thought maybe you've overdone it. Perhaps you needed a break, to sort your head out.'

I'd wanted to push him off the path we were standing on. He had wanted to have kids soon, I hadn't been so sure. He'd had it all so neatly worked out: we would be the perfect team of lawyers, as his mum and dad had been before. Although it was fine for me to give up my law career to have his kids, but not to do what I wanted to do; he wasn't interested in my feelings. As I stood looking at him, I began to wonder if I ever knew him at all. 'There's nothing wrong with my head, thank you. Lots of people have seizures. It's quite common. It's just made me rethink things and change my priorities.' I'd looked at him pleadingly. 'I hoped you might understand.'

'I do understand. I just think you shouldn't be too hasty. Maybe this . . .' he had hesitated a fraction too long, then continued as he met my steely glare '. . . epilepsy is making you feel different but once you've got used to it, you'll go back to being your old self.'

'Maybe I don't want to be my old self. Perhaps I want more than that now. I want to be someone who does something that matters.'

'Being a lawyer does matter,' he'd said defensively.

'Yes.' I'd realised I was still offending him, so I'd struggled to try to explain. 'Being a lawyer is a fantastic job, but I want to give something back, work with kids. Change something about this tired, jaded old world.'

'But you never mentioned this when I met you.' Looking at his puzzled face I had felt a little sorry for him. He'd been genuinely shocked at what happened. He just couldn't keep up.

'No because I didn't feel that way then, but now I do.'

After a long pause, Ryan had said quietly, 'Maybe you don't even want to marry me any more.'

'I did,' I'd said sadly. 'I do, but you have to accept me for who I am.'

He'd shaken his head. 'I'm just not sure who you are any more, Sophia.'

And in that moment it had ended, along with my job and everything else that I thought had been sorted so perfectly.

* * *

'I'm no expert on men,' says Erica, putting her arm round me, 'but I suspect Jack is totally different from Ryan. To be honest, I always felt Ryan was the sort of guy for whom appearances mattered more than reality. I mean . . . look at his mother.'

I chuckle. 'I know what you mean. The old-school – can't talk about our feelings or emotions; illness is a weakness.' I remember him once telling me about the time the family cat died and it was as though he had never even existed. He was just never mentioned again. There was certainly no talking about it. Ryan's family are worryingly repressed when it comes to emotions.

'That's the one. But Jack has been so kind: sending down drinks; he's regularly phoning Bertie, Mavis and several more otherwise very lonely people pretty much every day.'

'I know. He's a decent guy.' I dry my eyes with the tissue she gives me. 'It's just all been too much lately, this whole lockdown thing. Mum, you, the kids at school – I worry about everything. And much as I like Jack, I just don't think I can put myself out there again.'

'I know it's hard, Miss Worrywart, and that's why we all love you so much, because you care. But for just one moment let yourself enjoy something for what it is. Jack's just a friend and right now a fairly lonely one who has been through a lot and thinks he's really upset you. Give him and yourself a chance. Otherwise you'll regret it.'

CHAPTER 20

Jack

For the first time in a couple of weeks I can't be bothered to get out of bed. I've got a whole load of stuff to do, but no real inclination to do any of it. I switch on my phone, hoping there might be something from Sophia. I flick onto the message I sent her a couple of days ago and it says 'read', yesterday evening at 8 p.m. I'm not sure whether that's a good thing or not. Surely if she'd forgiven me she would have replied.

Yesterday evening had gone on forever. I'd wandered about the flat aimlessly picking things up and putting them down again. I'd half-heartedly played the guitar, ready for our balcony music night this week, but it hadn't really felt right. Some days, however hard you try, the notes don't sing out and the melody doesn't flow.

I kept the balcony door open and at one point, pulled up my trusty wine box, full of hope that there might be a reply. The note and the bacon butty had gone but the box was sadly empty. It felt symbolic of my current life without Sophia. I've had to put the box on top of the cupboard because even the sight of it reminds me of what an idiot I've been.

Whilst I'm staring at my phone screen, a message pings up. Is it her? No it's Marge.

A little bird told me about you and Sophia. Just know this, matey, if you upset that girl, you'll have me and the rest of the block to deal with. She's an exceptional young woman and has been through enough crap lately without jerks with wives they've kept hidden in the woodwork. Watch your step, sonny. Marge.

What the heck? She's even put an emoji with eyes peering to one side as though they're looking at me. Is she for real? In any case who is this little bird? I haven't told anyone except maybe Mavis but she's a kind old soul. She would never tell Marge and in any case she's been sympathetic. This is all I need, the vengeance of the neighbourhood. It's not like I can even run away at the moment. As I'm fretting about this threatening message from Marge, another text comes in; loudly announcing its arrival and making me jump.

Hear you might not have anyone to do your shopping now. Do let me know if you'd like any extras. I'm only just across the way. I can be right there in seconds, Anna xx

For goodness' sake, with neighbours like these, I think the prime minister should increase the social distancing rules to twenty metres just to be on the safe side.

I look at myself in the mirror, to see tufts of hair beginning to grow back and dark shadows under my eyes. Man, I need to pull myself together and sort my life out. Grabbing a banana and some soya yoghurt with honey (it's natural so must be healthy) I sit at my laptop and start to trawl through college courses simultaneously spooning in a large mouthful. Erm yeah, I'd rather eat my sugar-laden bad-for-you box of cereal. Manfully I swallow down as much of my healthy breakfast as I can.

The course I've found at the local college, only half an hour away, looks great. The college is renowned for its 'pioneering work in chiropractic and sports massage' and has a course I would love. If only I can get in, that is. I'm going to have to give my CV an overhaul. I'm just reading a hideously outdated version I did before I went to Greece when my phone rings.

'Hi, Sam,' I say.

'It isn't Sam, it's Tina. I was just calling for a chat.'

'Oh – hi, Tina.' I am surprised I must admit, as although I get on well with her and we often might have a quick chat on one of Sam's FaceTime calls, I don't remember the last time she actually phoned me. 'How's Carrie?'

'Gorgeous, she's really smiling now and she's so aware of what's going on all the time. It's a bit sad, but sometimes I just sit and gaze at her because I can't believe she's here.'

'I can understand that,' I say. 'It is miraculous.'

'She is exhausting though! But now she's nearly going four hours between feeds at night some of the time.' This

237

still sounds like some kind of torture to me, but I decide it's probably best not to say anything.

'Wow I knew you'd soon get her trained, all those episodes of *Supernanny* you watched paid off!'

'She's a bit young for that yet.' Tina laughs. 'But she loves singing and music. You'll have to play your guitar to her again later – she went straight to sleep during your performance the other night.'

'Doesn't bode well for our balcony music night coming up – mind you, it might help people who are struggling with insomnia!'

Tina laughs again. 'Speaking of balconies, is everything okay with you and Sophia?'

Oh for goodness' sake, I might as well put out a press release or get a megaphone and shout it from my balcony. 'Does everyone know about this?' I ask.

'I don't know. Just Sam said you had been really down and I wondered if it was to do with Sophia.'

'You don't miss anything do you? Is that what you call feminine intuition?'

'Yep, that's the one and it's usually pretty accurate. Am I right or am I right?'

I sigh heavily. 'Okay, I give up, you're right. I messed things up with Sophia.'

'I can't believe you have. What did you do? Hang on, wait a minute.' I can hear little Carrie crying in the background. 'Sam?' she calls. 'Can you pick her up please?' There's crackling on the other end of the line. 'Okay, I'm back. Sam is pretty good at cuddles and she's

238

not due a feed until twelve. Where were we? Sorry, I still need to majorly catch up on sleep.'

'I was telling you where I messed up with Sophia. I think it was the point where I got very tipsy and having told her I just want to be near her, when she was probably thinking I'm some weird creep, I announced I'm still married to Laura.'

Tina lets out a breath. 'Oops. You really know how to woo a girl don't you?'

'Yep that's me. A total expert on dating,' I say sarcastically.

'Don't be so hard on yourself. The main thing is, have you explained how you feel? Or have you gone all I-don't-want-to-talk-about-it.'

'I wrote her a letter.'

'Good start.' Tina sounds impressed. 'Has she replied?'

'No not yet,' I admit, 'but maybe she will.'

'Hmm,' she says, 'unlikely.' I feel unexpectedly crushed. If Tina thinks I've even gone about fixing things the wrong way, what hope do I have? 'It will have helped,' she goes on, easing the discomfort in my chest, 'but you're going to have to do a whole lot more work, Jack Stanton, if you want to dig yourself out of this mess.'

'I don't know.' That letter was the only move I had. 'What else can I do? I could get some flowers delivered.'

'No, it needs something more inventive than that,' Tina replies, unimpressed. 'What does she want more than anything else?'

'I don't know and even if I did, I wouldn't be able to

get it for her,' I point out. 'I'm pretty broke on furlough and can't go anywhere anyway.'

'Well, if you want to give up so easily . . .'

'No I don't – I really like this girl, Tina. I know it sounds strange when we haven't even met but . . .'

'It's okay, I get it, but you're going to have to think outside the box, something really special – and above all be open and honest with her . . .'

'Okay I'll think of something,' I promise. 'And thanks, Tina. Whatever Sam says about you, you're the best.'

She laughs. 'I like to try. Bye, Jack.'

She's right. I do need to think of something amazing and different, just to convince Sophia I'm not some idiot who will let her down. I finish the application form for the Chiropractic College and press send, then sit staring at a piece of paper hoping for an idea to come to me. I don't know why anyone sits looking at a blank piece of paper hoping an idea will come to them as if by magic. It really doesn't work. What did Sophia say she likes? I'm not really sure other than children, food, alcohol, music . . . There must be loads of possibilities with this. But there's nothing special in any of my ideas – they're all really mundane. What did she say she really missed? Hugs, her family – well I can't do much about that – she obviously misses the countryside as she said the first thing she'd do after lockdown was go to Sparrow Hill. Can't do anything about that either.

I draw a line through my page and turn it over. By now it's getting to dusk. The shadows on the walls are lengthening. I look up as a pigeon flies past the window, but all I see is its shadow, an outline of a bird flying to a nearby rooftop with a fine twig in its beak. It must be nesting.

'That's it!' I exclaim to myself and then laugh as I really have lost it, shouting out loud to no one in particular. I need to phone Bertie, who is due his regular call, but after that I have some friends from Greece who might just be able to help me create an amazing surprise for Sophia.

I dial the number for Bertie.

'Hello,' he answers, but sounds quite unlike his usual self, really down and flat, instantly dampening my own buoyant mood.

'Hi, Bertie, how's it going?'

'Oh hello, young man . . . Well, it's going I'll give it that.'

'One of those days?' I ask.

'You could say that. I have managed to have a little amble round the block.'

'The daily constitutional?'

'That's the one. But my back is painful – it's a real nuisance and stops me doing as much as I'd like. I managed to get some tomatoes potted up and a few geranium cuttings started but I feel tired today.'

'I'm sorry to hear that. I think that's the effect of lockdown. You can feel exhausted at the slightest thing.'

'I don't know. I've been doing all right. But these updates, the sheer numbers of people dying. It's a bad business.' He sighs heavily.

241

'I know. I'm afraid I've stopped watching it, which feels selfish. But right now it's a bit like self-preservation; it's about protecting my mental health. Maybe you should turn it off.'

'Perhaps you're right, Jack. I can't do much about it, that's for sure.'

'But it sounds as though you've got a lot done in that garden of yours. I'd love to see some pictures if you fancy sending them over. I miss seeing flowers and greenery in this flat, although I do have some tomato seedlings coming up and a couple of cucumbers.' The cheery little plants gently waving in the breeze catch my eye out on the balcony. The sight of them makes me feel slightly sad as they remind me of Sophia. I miss the sound of her voice.

'That's a good start!' Bertie continues. 'Of course, I'll email you some photos across. Garden's not doing too badly even though I say so myself. The spring has been the most beautiful I've seen for years. Just a shame about what's going on.'

'True – and I bet you miss the old cricket.'

'Yes, nothing to watch on the television. Thought I'd do some tidying up today and I found Elsie's old writing case.'

'That's really nice,' I say hesitantly. I have no idea how it must feel to suddenly discover your wife's favourite things after she's died.

'Yes it was,' Bertie assures me. 'Brought back so many memories. I opened it up, just to peek inside. I haven't looked since she went; I couldn't face it you know. But as I managed to get the top open, it overbalanced and fell on the hard floor, breaking the hinges totally, papers and half-finished letters scattered everywhere.'

'Oh, Bertie, that's terrible. Is it fixable?'

'I don't know, Jack. I don't mind telling you I felt so fed up; I just left it there. For the first time in ages I just sat down and cried whilst holding a letter she had been writing to her niece. The way the writing stopped, it's as though she has just popped out of the room to grab a cup of tea and the letter's still waiting there for her to return. Just like me.'

I stay quiet for a minute, sensing that he needs to breathe. 'That's tough, Bertie,' I tell him at last. 'I'm sorry. You must really miss her, especially at the moment. Did crying make you feel any better?'

'Not really, but I've managed to pick up the writing box. Badly damaged though.'

'I'll think on it. There must be something we can do.'

'It might be easier to fix than me, eh?' He chuckles.

My heart fills with tenderness for my old friend. 'You're doing pretty well really, Bertie. You're like a rubber ball – there's no keeping you down.'

'Not usually, mate, but this has knocked me a bit. This whole lockdown thing is a curve ball.'

'I'm not surprised. How's the practising going for "I'm Still Standing"? That should be a good evening; something to take your mind off things.'

'I've nearly learnt all the lyrics. Could be ready to rumble by Wednesday.'

'Great, we're all looking forward to it!'

'Yep I'm not sure how a balcony choir is going to work but hey ho!'

'The balcony choir, that's it – that's what we'll call ourselves.'

'Whatever floats your boat,' he says and with that wry comment, he rings off.

CHAPTER 21

Sophia

I can't believe how quickly human beings can get used to something, even something you would never imagine being normal, such as a lockdown. We adjust to it as though this is how it's always been, like moles or solitary beings who live alongside rather than with their fellow creatures. Not at first – of course there was that strange period of adjustment, that unreal feeling, the silence, the quietness. It was all so surreal, the daily briefing, the feeling of quiet camaraderie; we're all in this together.

I remember the first evenings whilst Erica was at work were filled with uneasy busyness, phone calls to Jess to discuss the latest developments on *Love is Blind*. Calls to Mum to check she was okay. In spite of this, every moment seemed to have lasted for hours, yet as time has gone on, after the first few weeks of lockdown, a routine has built up and I feel in some strange way this is our new way of life.

When I had first gone out of the house to work in the mornings, the streets were deserted, apocalyptic, with queues of people waiting to get into the shops, all at an orderly two metres apart. It was like something out of a sci-fi movie titled *The Germ*. The masks, which we were used to seeing in hospitals, or other countries, are now commonplace. If someone had told me last year, that in 2020 we would be living like this, each in our own sterilised, antibacced world, I would never have believed them.

Yet conversely, even though somehow it feels like it's gone on forever, in other ways I don't know where the time's gone. It's already nearly the end of April and I can't even pinpoint what I've been doing except existing. The days and hours have become short chunks of activity, each day simply putting one foot in front of the other. I catch sight of my 2020 diary, which sits mostly blank. I haven't filled anything in since February. I flick back through the last few weeks and except for Jess's wedding, it's as though they haven't even happened.

Weirdly when I passed the local pub, The Greyhound, on my way to school yesterday, the front billboard had 'Book now for Mother's Day,' all over it. Mother's Day was back in March, yet no one was able to go out except for essentials, let alone to a pub. It all sits derelict, ghostlike, abandoned, the sign for potential Mother's Day celebrations that could never happen swinging sadly in the breeze.

Perhaps I'll phone Mum. The evenings seem so quiet

when Erica is on shift, Jess is on her virtual honeymoon and I miss Jack and his banter. I look at the door to the balcony, which still stays shut. Somehow it feels like a safety barrier for the things I can't deal with right now and sadly Jack is one of them.

I dial Mum's number. I don't think she's working this evening. 'Hey, Mum! How are things?'

'Sophia! I'm glad it's you.'

'You answered quickly. Were you expecting a call?'

'Not really, I just thought it might be Uncle Jim again.'

'Oh no, is he okay?' I ask.

'Well I wouldn't go *quite* as far as "okay", but he's reasonably well, which is the main thing.'

'Definitely, but I expect he feels lonely in his flat.'

'I think he must do, but he has two carers coming in as much as they can and I phone him most days.'

'I guess that helps. Is he any less confused?'

'Not really, that's the problem. He doesn't really understand why I can't visit him even though I've explained so many times,' she sighs.

'I guess it is hard if he forgets what's going on.'

'That's partly why I bought him the talking clock.'

'A talking clock?' I say with a smile. 'Sounds like something out of an Enid Blyton book.'

'Didn't I tell you about it?'

'No, I'm sure I'd have remembered.'

'Well it's one of my bright ideas . . . Which, of course, turned out to be not so bright.'

'Couldn't he work it?'

'Oh yes, he could work it. It announces the day and time every hour and I'd thought it would be a good plan for him so he could remember what day it is and what time.'

'Sounds ingenious.'

'That was the idea, but he got rid of it.'

I roll my eyes. 'Did he give it away?'

'No, it's worse than that. He actually phoned me up and said, "Don't you like me?" Totally took me aback because he didn't even say hello first or anything. I didn't even know who it was for the first few minutes.'

'That must have been a bit unnerving.'

'You're telling me. Then I said, "Of course I like you, Jim. We're all very fond of you. Why do you ask?" And he responded, "I thought you must be trying to punish me – giving me this clock. It's enough to drive anyone mad. Figured you'd only give such a hideous thing to someone you really dislike." Just like that!'

'That's a bit much,' I say, starting to laugh. Poor Mum, she always tries so hard with Jim and whatever she does, he always manages to find a way to ruin it.

'Wait until you hear what he did with it. Apparently he went on his usual walk on the cliff top and put it under the bench on the Sandy Ledge Viewpoint.'

'What?' I laugh. 'He left it at the top of the cliff?'

'I know.' She laughs too. 'Can you imagine, hidden behind the bench, it'll make people jump out of their skin hearing, "It is now 2 p.m. on Wednesday 22nd April".'

'Enough to make them fall off into the water! They

won't know who is speaking to them either. That's hilarious.'

'I know, if it's one thing you can say at least Uncle Jim still has a sense of humour.'

'True. And surprisingly you have too, after a day's work. How's it going?' I ask her.

'Busier now, but still much quieter than it was before this outbreak. Lots of disinfecting and rules to be followed. At least we can do most of our work on the phone and online. Makes me glad the surgery is ahead of its time and had organised online accounts for many patients.'

'I guess, for those who can work it.'

'Yes, that's the only thing,' she agrees. 'The older generation tend to phone and in any case they like the personal approach. I don't blame them. We all need to keep talking or we'll end up forgetting how to interact. That reminds me, is that neighbour of yours still phoning vulnerable people for a chat each week?'

'Yes I believe he is,' I say shortly. I really don't want to talk about Jack right now.

'Such a great idea and so important. I've asked for people to volunteer at the surgery to do the same to support isolated patients. It's all about making people feel they matter.'

'What about you, Mum? I hope you're looking after yourself.' I constantly worry about her working in a doctor's surgery. It must be one of the highest risk places to be right now.

'Yes, I'm about to sit down and watch something relaxing, probably about gardening, with a glass of chilled white wine.'

'Sounds like bliss.' I smile. 'I'll let you get on then.'

'Aren't you having your usual chat with Jack upstairs?' she asks, just as I thought I'd got away without discussing him.

'Maybe. We've kind of not been doing that at the moment.'

'That's a shame. He sounds such a nice lad.'

'Maybe,' I hedge. Then I come out with it, even though I know my mum will worry about me. 'I just feel men are perhaps all the same.'

'Sophia, that's a terrible thing to say,' she scolds. 'They are most definitely not. Much as I couldn't stay married to your dad, I did love him. And it all led me to Mark in the end.'

'I suppose – it's just I don't want to get hurt again. Ryan was my everything, yet look how he behaved.'

'I know it was hard. But Ryan was confused. It was a terrible shock to him – your illness,' she says, softening. I try to breathe calmly and count to ten. Mum always defends Ryan; she absolutely loved him. 'But if you don't ever trust anyone again, how are you going to move on? Besides, Jack's just a friendly neighbour. You've been much more cheerful since you've been speaking to him. Give him a chance to at least explain himself. We're all in lockdown for goodness' sake; don't shut yourself off to deal with everything alone. No man or woman is an island. There's a reason why they say that. Ooh . . .' She breaks off, distracted. 'It's eight o'clock and *Gardener's World* is starting. Love you, bye.'

'Bye, Mum.'

'Remember what I said.'

'Yes, Mum, bye!'

As I'm pondering over Mum's words, I meander towards the balcony doors. Perhaps I should let some air in. Jack probably isn't there anyway and the flat's stuffy as it's a suntrap. The sun has been peeping through the venetian blinds all day.

Something outside catches my eye, a movement out in the courtyard. Intrigued, I open the door and step out onto the balcony. Down below, a van is parked. That's odd. I wonder how it got there; nothing usually comes through the archway into the courtyard. I watch as a couple of people in black leggings and black tops with ballet pumps get out. For a fleeting moment, I wonder if they're going to come and burgle someone by walking on a tightrope. I've never seen delivery drivers dressed like this. As I watch, another person with a dark bun gets out and with the help of a guy unclips something at the top and bottom of the van. I watch amazed as they pull out a vast screen.

As I stand there watching, more figures wheel lights in front of the screen and efficiently they all disappear behind the van. Romantic music comes on, the lights dim and then to my amazement, a shadowy figure of a man appears behind the screen sitting on a sofa surrounded by other bits of furniture and a window, all created by the shapes of shadowy dancers. The man moves from side to side, as though he is lost. He peers out of the window but is totally alone.

The image transforms to two balconies – there's a girl in the lower one, sitting reading a book and the man stands in the top looking out. I can tell the shapes are formed by the movement of the shadowy figures, but they are so quick and move so adeptly it is hard to tell. Then all the shadow hands start clapping and the girl leans across the balcony, her head in her hands. The man calls to her and sends down a shadowy box on a rope. She then puts something in it and sends it back up. He dances happily and so does she. But then another woman within a photo frame at the back of the screen puts her arms out to the man – the girl below walks inside and her balcony is empty.

I am spellbound.

The man above sends away the woman in the frame sitting with his head in his hands, then he writes a letter and lowers it down to the balcony below, but it remains empty. He comes down the rope himself, dances outside her balcony, with his hands to his chest, then outstretched towards her as if to say he's sorry. The girl comes back out and puts her hands out to him and all around there are lots of hands clapping.

Then the music stops and a group of eight men and women come running out from behind the screen and take a bow. Everyone is clapping. All the neighbours who have gradually filtered out onto their balconies cheer and wave at the performers.

'Woo!' shouts Greg from his balcony on the side.

Down in the courtyard I can see Bertie waving his cap and Mavis is there at two metres' distance in a deckchair. All round the edge there are little clusters of people, all socially distanced.

'Good evening!' shouts one of the dancers. He has a thick Greek accent. The clapping and cheering dies down. 'Thank you so much everyone for your wonderful applause. It has been an absolute pleasure to perform for you this evening. Of course I must thank Jack who lives in the flat up there – hi, Jack – for inviting us to come and perform for you all. And most of all hey to Sophia – to whom this performance is dedicated, with thanks from Jack for all her support over the last few weeks. Are you there, Sophia?'

Totally embarrassed I step forward a few steps to the edge of the balcony and give a little wave.

He waves back. 'I must add,' he continues, 'that we are a group of performers, called The Shadow Dancers. We are originally from Greece and we all live together in one student house in Braxton, so no social distancing necessary for us. If you would like to see us perform again, we have a variety of routines. I have left a pile of leaflets for you in the courtyard to take. We are not able to perform in the usual way at the moment, but are hoping when the lockdown eases a little, we may be able to tour and perform to people outside their communal buildings and hospitals, retirement homes and those sorts of places.'

'Hear hear! We all want more!' shouts Bertie.

Everyone claps.

'Encore!' shouts someone.

'Okay, one more!' calls the man.

The figures all run back behind the screen and within minutes they have merged together to form a new scene of a hillside, with trees and plants and a bird flying across the top. The man and the woman come from either side of the screen and run to each other – embracing and dancing together until they both form a heart with their arms. I stand completely motionless, transfixed by what I have seen. There's another great cheer from all the balconies.

'Thank you for watching and goodnight!' The group all bow and with graceful moves, retreat behind the screen to more applause. I am still completely stunned at what I have just seen; it all feels surreal and almost as though I've walked out into a different planet.

'Man, that was something,' says Greg. 'The kids at my college would love this. I wonder if they can set up the screen anywhere?'

'I guess,' I reply. I'm still dazed.

'Hey, Jack, that was really something, mate,' calls up Bertie, 'and all for your Sophia. You must be an exceptional young lady.'

'She is,' calls Jack and I blush.

'Hey, Jack,' I squeak.

'Hey,' he answers, tentatively.

'Thank you,' I tell him. 'It was beautiful. I can't believe you did that for me. How did you arrange something so amazing in the middle of lockdown?'

'I met the group in Greece, and we've kept in touch. I persuaded them to give a special performance. I know it's not strictly shopping or an important trip as the rules dictate, but I thought it would really lift everyone's spirits so it counts as a vital service. Also Georgio did bring Bertie some milk, so it's technically a food delivery.' I watch amused as one of the figures places a bag of shopping on the ground a couple of metres from Bertie.

'Do you always think of everything?' I ask.

'No,' he admits, 'usually I'm hopeless, but since I've nearly met you I think anything's possible.'

'I don't think I've ever had that effect on anyone.'

I watch as the figures down below pack up as quickly as they had unpacked and the van starts to amble on its way. The neighbours including Bertie have all melted away and it's just the two of us out in the fast-cooling evening air.

'I've never seen a performance like that,' I comment.

'They are pretty talented aren't they? I just wanted to find a way to let you know how much you've inspired me and I hope maybe they can soon get out and about to perform to people again. They don't usually use the van but had to improvise and it's given them the idea they could maybe go outside nursing homes, hospices – that kind of thing. They can still socially distance.'

'Jack, that's a beautiful idea; I love it.'

'I just really wanted to say I'm sorry.' I hear his voice break slightly.

'You don't need to. You didn't do anything wrong. It's good you told me – it was just a terrible moment.' I speak more flippantly than I feel. To be honest I'm still smarting a little from his not telling me sooner. Trust once broken is a hard thing to regain.

'I should have told you before. It's just that sometimes the most obvious things are the hardest to say.'

'I know what you mean. I've had stuff it's been hard to talk about too. I've struggled enough with my diagnosis of epilepsy.' I wait for him to change, to say something about how horrified he is.

'You have epilepsy? I had no idea.' He doesn't sound shocked, just concerned.

'I didn't want to tell you. It's just that my epilepsy has a way of changing my life, my relationships. I haven't been able to talk about it to anyone really and yet it's only been a couple of years. I can't imagine what it's like for you to have been in and out of hospitals all your life. I was totally depressed about how it ruined so many things for me, but at least I had all those years without seizures – and it's not all bad, I love my new career.'

'I've had time to come to terms with my diagnosis. You probably haven't yet, you're still processing it.'

'I guess.' I take a sip of drink. 'Do you ever really come to terms with it?'

Jack pauses a moment. 'You do. It's taken me years but I guess sometimes it bothers me more than at others.'

I nod, even though he can't see me. 'When I first found out I have epilepsy, I couldn't stop thinking about it. It felt at times like I was done, finished, nothing was going to be the same again. For ages I couldn't go out on my own, couldn't stay in on my own. People always had to be with me and I was afraid. That's the thing with seizures, or mine at least, I never knew when they were going to happen. Then as the meds began to work slowly, gradually, I forgot about it for several hours at a time, then hours became days. I'm one of the lucky ones, though, for some they can't forget it; it's something that is a part of their everyday lives.'

'Eventually you'll forget for longer,' he tells me, 'until it's just normal for you; taking the daily meds, the hospital check-ups. It's part of your life and it's not all bad. There's some lovely people I've met along the way. I've had a couple who maybe haven't understood, but that's just how it is. Why would they when it's not them?'

'It changes your perspective on things,' I agree. 'I've become less tolerant somehow. After the incredible people you meet grappling with this kind of diagnosis in hospital, the amazing hospital staff, then somehow it makes it harder to tolerate the people who just don't get it. And then there's how it affects your relationships.' I pause, thinking of Ryan and how it changed things irrevocably for us. What we had was good until then, or at least it seemed as though it was.

'It does change your relationships,' he says. 'I would never have met Laura if I hadn't been running away from my condition, if I hadn't been trying to be someone I'm not; good old fun-loving, comedian Jack. In the end the result was, it hurt us both and I feel really bad about that. And now here I am, just an ordinary guy stuck in my flat.' He goes silent for a moment and I don't know what to say. 'The thing is,' he continues, 'you don't have to tolerate the people who don't understand. If I can find one good thing to come out of having a long-term condition, it's that it makes you sort out what really matters to you. Cut the crap. People either accept and change with you or you leave them behind.'

'That's true, being sick meant I changed my career and a lot of other things . . .' I tail off, not wanting to elaborate.

'What did you do before?'

'A lawyer.'

'Wow – I didn't see that one coming. But I can imagine you'd be good. You see what you want or what needs doing and you get it done.'

I smile at his words. 'I guess I was successful, but I don't think I was fulfilled. Teaching every day is exhausting but I never get bored. I never think, *I really don't want to be doing this*.'

'I can imagine you're perfect at it. How are the kids? I've missed hearing about them.'

'A couple of them have really come out of themselves since the class has been so small. Both Alfie and Zane have come on leaps and bounds.'

258

'Thanks to their teacher, I should think.' He sounds proud; actually it's kind of cute.

'Maybe a little,' I concede, 'but having so few in the class has given them confidence too.'

'You're so inspirational I've just enrolled for a college course.'

'Really? Jack, that's fantastic. What is it?'

'I always wanted to be a sports therapist as you know and I've just filled out the application form and pressed send. So watch this space.'

'I'm so pleased for you.' I can hear the excitement in his voice. It makes me smile. It's so lovely to feel his passion for something he's going to be doing. This lockdown has taken away any certainty. It's great to have some potentially coming back.

'I got side-tracked with the whole Greece thing. I was running away really, then got caught up with Laura and, well, you know the rest. But now I'm back on track.'

'Good for you,' I say. 'When would you start?'

'September, hopefully, if I get in . . . and if we're out of lockdown.'

'Oh I reckon we will be before then.'

'I can't imagine it now. It feels weird somehow.'

'I guess it must. At least I've been going out. But the whole social distancing thing, it's made me realise how important being with people is.'

'Yep, I must admit I feel like I'm in some kind of bubble.'

'It will end,' I say. 'It can't go on forever.'

'Maybe when we get out of this, you and I could go to Sparrow Hill for a walk together. If you'd like to that is?' he asks hesitantly.

'That would be lovely,' I reply more confidently than I feel. I'm just not sure how I feel about Jack after all this. His initial failure to reveal the facts of his marriage to Laura still bothers me after what happened with Ryan. The wound of unpredictability in a relationship, when touched, is still raw. I still don't know if I can trust Jack and yet he understands what I've been going through better than anyone, almost better than myself. I just don't know what to think.

CHAPTER 22

Jack

'So you've kissed and made up?' asks Sam, whilst Carrie burbles in his ear.

'Not exactly, but yeah.' I smile as I think of my conversation with Sophia last night.

'Fair play, mate, you don't do things by halves – shadow dancers! No wonder she was blown away. Tina was well impressed and asked what went wrong with my share of the romantic-gesture gene pool.'

'She really enjoyed it. And Georgio has done okay out of it. Greg, one of the other neighbours here, has booked for them to go and perform to the kids at his college.'

'Surely no one's allowed to mix?'

'There's a patch of grass opposite the college where the van can park and the screen just pulls out.'

'Still sounds risky to me,' Sam points out. 'Police were stopping people whilst they were driving up Valence Road at the end of our street yesterday. Not that we go out except for our once-a-day walk with Carrie and once-a-week shop. But I make sure I put the shopping bags on show in the front seat in case I get stopped.'

'They're taking it seriously then,' I reply. 'It's weird, I haven't been out for so long. I don't even know what's happening out there.'

'Trouble is there's confusion about exactly what the rules are and where you can go and how far. I mean one form of exercise a day is fine, but then for how long? In theory you could walk for three hours and go to the next town, which you shouldn't be visiting.'

'Not many people are going to do that though are they? Although,' I add, 'Greg says his kids are struggling at the college. Several of them find exercise and being able to get out is their main way of managing anxiety and once a day isn't enough.'

'It must be really tough. Let's hope it won't be for too much longer.'

'I think it will be, at least for us people shielding.'

'You've done a month already – you can do this,' Sam says bracingly.

'I know. It's okay. I'm busy now – in fact, speaking of which, I need to sort some messages. I'll speak to you later.'

'All right, busy busy! Bye, mate. Say hi to Sophia for me.'

'Yeah, even though she doesn't know you.'

'Sounds like she soon will though.' And with that he's gone.

His words make me think. I hadn't really figured out

what was going to happen when this lockdown is over, but the thought of being with Sophia and introducing her to Sam and his little family is one of most amazing things ever. It's made me really reconsider what is important in my life.

I check my WhatsApp. There's a new message from Derek:

Total disaster. I've gone and hurt my back and Benson is climbing the walls even more than usual. I'm worried I'm going to have nothing left in one piece. Is there some kind and energetic soul out there who might consider giving him a walk as part of their daily exercise? I would be very grateful – might even be a beer or two in it.

There's no replies to this so far. I immediately text Sophia.

Hey Sophia, how are you doing? It was great to catch up last night. Have you checked out Derek's message on WhatsApp? I'd love to walk Benson if I were allowed out. My parents used to have an Alsatian. They're such beautiful dogs, but strong on the lead! Any ideas?

Hi Jack, thanks so much again for the show. Just spectacular. I still can't believe it happened. It was like a bit of magic coming into my pretty dreary routine. Don't worry about Derek. I love dogs so I'll take Benson on my daily walk x

Oh wow. She's put a kiss. She's never done that before. Okay, Jack, don't get overexcited it could just be a typo; maybe she forgot it was me and did it by accident. I'll see if she does it again.

Thanks, Sophia. I wish I could come with you x

Okay so I've put a kiss, I couldn't resist.

Me too x

It wasn't a mistake. She's put another kiss. Either that or she only did it because I put a kiss. Okay I've got to stop doubting myself; I'm so happy I strum out several bars on the guitar, whilst singing at the top of my lungs.

'Nice singing, Jack,' comes Sophia's voice from below. I forgot, she can hear, but I wasn't even sure she was in. Darn it, in an ideal world your crush can't hear that weird crazy dancing thing you do around the room because you're so happy they texted.

'Thanks.' I peer down into the courtyard.

'I've messaged Derek. He's really pleased,' she calls. 'I'm picking Benson up tomorrow and will be walking him every day this week, round work of course.'

'That's terrific. He looks gorgeous. Did you see the picture Derek posted of him?'

'Yes he's so fluffy. I just want to cuddle him, like a big bear.'

'You talking about me again?' asks Greg. I had no idea he was there – that's the thing with the angle of these balconies – and he has this entirely bizarre habit of appearing every so often, well not literally of course, but we suddenly hear his voice floating from nowhere, or his saxophone.

'No, didn't know you looked like a bear, mate. She's talking about Derek's Alsatian.'

'Fair enough, I can take the rejection. Are you walking him, did you say, Sophia?'

'Yeah why?'

'I just had an idea. I wondered, if Derek agrees, if you might walk him down to the college sometime? The kids would just love to see him. They're really into animals, well apart from Stan, but he can stand back and I think he quite likes them really at a distance. You'd be amazed how responsive autistic kids are to animals. They are less complicated than people and accept the kids for who they are.'

'I think that's why we all love animals. I would so like a dog,' I say. 'Maybe one day.'

'I reckon Derek would be fine with that, but message him on the group chat. Just let me know and I'll walk him past.' Sophia is on board as always. I just love how easy-going she is. Laura always took every opportunity to have an Academy-Award-winning performance or major strop over the slightest things. It was totally exhausting.

'That'd be great. As long as it's scheduled; they don't like surprises,' Greg comments.

'That's okay – I understand. We'll arrange a time so they know when to expect us.'

'What time are you walking tomorrow?' I ask casually.

'I don't know. About four, I should think. Why?'

'Oh no reason,' I reply. Except of course there is a reason, a really huge, tantalisingly exciting one. If I know what time Sophia is going out she will have to walk through the courtyard and I might finally catch a glimpse of her and discover what she looks like. Not that it matters of course, but still I really want to see her. I can't wait.

CHAPTER 23

Sophia

'Five minutes,' I call to Erica. 'Are you going to be ready?'

'Yeah, I'm just checking the veg.'

'It's done – I looked at it just now. We'll be ready to eat afterwards.' I look inside. As I thought, Erica is actually picking at the cold chicken left over from yesterday. 'Oy leave that alone – there'll be none left!'

'It's just so tasty, I can't resist!' Erica meanders out, still scoffing a chicken wing.

'Could have brought me some,' I comment.

It's 7.58 and as usual the neighbours are making their way onto their balconies or onto the courtyard below ready for the weekly clap.

Like everything else, it has become a part of our new life. Every Thursday at 8 p.m. we all stop whatever we're doing and clap for those heroes who are out there facing an unseen, terrifying, unthinkable battle.

In some of the flats opposite, the windows are filled

with rainbows, or *Thank You NHS* signs in vibrant colours. I've been fascinated by a chalk drawing on the road on my way to school, where a thanks to the NHS is etched in beautifully crisp blue and white lettering. It has been there for weeks, as though held by some kind of indelible magic. I know it hasn't rained for such a long time, but still. It must have had so many cars driving over it in spite of the quieter roads. I often wonder as I pass it who stood in the road and decorated it with chalk. I have a suspicion it might be the owners of the New Agey shop nearby, which has dream catchers and unicorns in the window. Somehow that makes me even happier, passing the chalk message each day, as though it may bring us all luck.

I love watching how people behave during the clap. I don't often have the opportunity to people-watch any more; the courtyard has been so quiet. But on clap nights, slowly, hesitantly, almost as though they've forgotten how to do it, everyone comes out of the woodwork, like mice timidly venturing forth from the shed for crumbs. Some neighbours are already chatting across the way, calling to each other across balconies, one or two standing in the courtyard below, in neatly socially distanced clusters.

It's a strange thing but I've lived here a couple of years and I don't remember many people ever actually talking to each other, and then often only on WhatsApp. They were all too busy I guess, too wrapped up in their own lives to even pass the time of day. All like battery hens crammed into our tiny pens, living day in and day out in our own neat, compartmentalised bubbles of work and play, physically within a few metres of each other but mentally miles away. Ironically it's taken a world pandemic and the isolation of lockdown to make us reach out to each other. To look around us and notice we aren't desert islands marooned in the middle of an ocean, separated by miles of sea; we're an archipelago of people, joined together by crisis, all working together to help those who can't get out or who live alone to cope with this unprecedented situation.

Bertie is down below talking to Mavis, who is perched on the edge of the raised flower border a couple of metres away. He looks up and I call to him. 'Hey, Bertie?'

'Hello, young lady, how's it going? Bet everything's a bit of a let-down after that performance of Jack's the other night?'

'Maybe,' I agree. 'But I always look forward to seeing everyone at the clap.'

'Become a right little social hasn't it?' he replies.

Jack has obviously just come out on the balcony. 'Hi, Bertie, how's tricks?' I hear him ask.

'Better for being out and about. Wish I could have walked that crazy dog of Derek's though. Does you good to have a fellow creature around you.'

'I know, it's a shame; would be nice for you to have a bit of company.'

'You could ask Derek?' I suggest.

'No, love, he's far too boisterous for me – not Derek, I mean, but Benson.' He laughs uproariously at his joke.

'Not with my dodgy back. Never cope with a big dog. Much as I love them. Can't walk as far as I used to.'

I am about to reply when someone starts clapping. There's always one I've noticed who likes to be the first to start it. Lately it's almost become a competition, with a couple of contenders at the top of the league table, consisting of Marge of course – she always has to be first into everything – closely followed by her equally nosy friend Vic, who is just as keen to be both seen and heard preferably at the same time. My bet is on Marge though. I look across the courtyard and yes, sure enough, there she is in the corner, a self-satisfied kind of smile sprawled across her face.

I nudge Erica who is clapping beside me and she follows my gaze and laughs. 'Marge wins first prize this week again,' she comments in a loud whisper.

Inside we've left the television on and the room flashes blue and white as paramedics, police and emergency service workers in the car park of the local hospital put on their emergency lights to pay their respect to workers. I glance in briefly and have to swallow back tears; it really is an incredible sight. Everyone everywhere is working together to try to keep spirits up and thank those who are so selflessly risking all to help others.

Erica notices and smiles. 'You big softy, you off again?'

'I can't help it.' I can't. It's a fact I cry at loads of things, at happy films, sad films and even those in between. It's one of those things I just have to put up with.

As the clap draws to a close, the majority of people drift away and back into their own separate lives until eight o'clock next Thursday when we'll do the same thing all over again. There are some elements of this lockdown that really remind me of that movie *Groundhog Day*. I never liked it to be honest.

Bertie remains below chatting to Mavis who is obviously just as happy to have a long catch-up, putting the world to rights.

Mavis looks up and notices me peering over the balcony. 'Hi, Sophia, thanks so much for helping me with my iPad the other day.'

'That's okay. Let me know if you have any other problems.'

'Well I could do with some help getting more people to make scrubs with me.' Every afternoon Mavis has been sewing scrubs for medical staff, whipping them up with an ease that would frighten even the most accomplished needleworkers on *The Great British Sewing Bee*.

'Mavis, I've got some photos of my colleagues at the hospital wearing the results of some of your hard work!' Erica calls out.

Mavis's face breaks into a huge grin. 'How lovely, I didn't expect that.'

'They're all super pleased with them. I could upload the photos to the WhatsApp group and see if anyone else is interested in making them.'

'Thanks, dear, that sounds good – and I'll keep sewing.'

'Please do, we can always do with more, Mavis.'

'Did you have any luck fixing Elsie's writing case?' I hear Jack ask Bertie.

'No, lad, worse luck. I think it's completely broken. I had a try but it just made me feel sad, as the hinges are totally broken. I've put it to one side as a bad job.'

'I'm sure someone could fix it,' Jack says. 'We just need to find the right person.'

'What is it?' I ask.

'A box of my late wife Elsie's writing bits and bobs. I dropped it on the floor the other day, daft old bugger that I am, and it's broken.'

'That's really sad,' I say. 'But my stepdad is a whiz at fixing things – he has a business, doing odd jobs and stuff like that. He might not be able to fix something so delicate and old, but I think he has a mate who specialises in restoration. I could ask him?'

Bertie looks touched. 'That would be grand; I'd be so chuffed. It's sad seeing it smashed and broken on the shelf.'

'I'll send him a text,' I promise.

Soon Bertie wanders off, realising it's time for his evening crossword puzzle, and Mavis meanders along at a safe distance behind him, homeward bound to feed her beloved budgie Sunny.

I hear Jack's voice from above. 'That was kind of you.'

'Not a problem, anyone would do the same.'

'Fancy a mocktail?' Jack asks me. 'I'm eating healthy in the week but I'm experimenting with wicked shrub mixers at the moment.'

'Shrub? Sounds like something my grandma would have made!' I laugh.

Jack sounds outraged. 'It's spicier than your gran would have liked it. Well, it's just a syrup blending fruit, sugar and vinegar. But I like to add cardamom to give it a kick.'

'Erm I'm not really sure about cardamom in a drink. I mean, it's fine in a hot toddy in the winter.'

'I'll make you some different ones and you can decide which is your favourite,' Jack says, obviously put out at my lack of enthusiasm for his spicy shrub.

'Okay well I'm happy to be your guinea pig. What's first up?' I reply.

'Lemon lavender mocktail. Very summery, with a hint of refreshing citrus.'

'Sounds perfect.'

'I'll send one down.'

'I've missed the visits of your wine carrier.'

'More than our chats?' His voice has a teasing note.

'Definitely. But I like those too.'

Erica drifts out onto the balcony. 'Have you seen my scrubs?' she asks.

'They're in the cupboard, neatly folded,' I reply with an eye roll that I want her to see.

'I didn't see them there,' she huffs.

'That's probably because you weren't looking.'

'Hi, Erica,' calls Jack, 'would you like a mocktail?'

'No thanks, I'm off to work in a mo . . . and anyway, I prefer my cocktails with plenty of alcohol.'

'Fair enough, I'll make you one of my margaritas when you have an evening off.'

'Deal.' She smirks at me and adds in an undertone, 'I'll leave you two balcony lovebirds to it then.'

'Shhh!' I retort, half ushering, half shoving her back into the flat. Irrepressibly she grins and scarpers, no doubt still in search of her uniform, which is where I always put it when I've washed and ironed it.

I make myself comfortable on the corner seat on the balcony and within minutes a very elegant glass appears with a piece of lemon and a delicate strand of lavender. 'It's a very pretty colour,' I announce, carefully taking it out of the box. I take a sip and try not to cough. 'It's very nice. The only thing is . . . I mean, it's very pleasant but . . .'

Jack tuts. 'Come on, be honest – I need truthful feedback.'

'Well the lavender is quite *lavendery*. I don't dislike it but it actually does remind me of my gran.'

Jack lets out an exasperated laugh. 'Oh great, that's really hip and current if it reminds you of your gran. Turns out you were right in your earlier judgement then.'

'I don't mean it in a bad way.' I laugh too.

'It's okay. That's the point of experimenting. Perhaps I'll make the next a lemon and lime mocktail.'

'Ooh that sounds perfect. Let me just finish this one first. Do you know, it grows on you after the first few sips. Very calming.'

'I'll make it on the over sixties nights.'

I laugh before turning more serious. 'Speaking of over sixties . . . I'm worried about Bertie.'

'Bertie? Yeah I guess he is a bit down at the moment.'

'I just wish he could come out with me to walk Benson. It would be so lovely for him to spend some time with a pup – they're so cheerful.'

'If a little crazy, by the sound of it!'

'Yes, that too. I wonder . . .' I break off for a moment.

'Sounds like you have one of your ideas brewing,' Jack observes.

'Well, yes, I was just thinking maybe we could get Bertie a dog. Of his own.'

Jack snorts but it sounds as though he's drunk a load of his mocktail down the wrong way as there's a lot of coughing going on. He finally manages to recover. 'Nice idea, but how are you going to find and adopt a dog in the current situation?'

'Leave it with me, I'll find a way,' I say as I finish my drink. 'Any chance of that lemon and lime mocktail? I might even have a packet of Pringles I could split with you.'

'Coming right up. But I don't think even you, with your super skills, are going to be able to find a dog for Bertie during a pandemic.'

CHAPTER 24

Jack

I am sitting and staring at the email from the Chiropractic College. It's been there ready and waiting in my inbox for a few minutes but I daren't open it. I really want this. It would be awful if they just rejected me. The idea of having a course starting in September has lifted me through this lockdown. Well that and Sophia. Okay . . . so, mostly Sophia. But that's going to change. I know lockdown won't last forever and I just don't know what will happen with her afterwards. When we finally meet, will she like me? Is this all just the result of a strange situation and as things go back to normal – or the new normal they're talking about, whatever and whenever that is – will we just drift apart, back into our own busy lives we lived for years without knowing of each other's existence? Somehow this thought makes me feel lonely, empty even. I almost don't want things to go back to how they were before, if it means losing Sophia.

It's no good, I'm going to have to open this email.

Dear Mr Stanton,

Thank you for your application to study on our Sports Therapy Course. We enjoyed reading your CV and forms and would be delighted to invite you to take part in an interview with Lee Brockenhurst on Wednesday 29th April at 2 p.m.

Kind regards,

Diane Reeves

This is the best news. Before I stop to think, I message Sophia.

Guess what? I've been given an interview for the Chiropractic College. Can you believe it?

To my delight, she immediately messages back.

That's amazing. Well done, Jack! She follows the message with a cheery face and an exploding whatever it is, that looks like a party popper coming out of an ice cream cone. *I knew you could do it!*

Thanks. I'm so excited. But dreading the interview. Haven't done one for years.

That's okay, you'll walk it. But I can go over some questions with you later on the balcony if you like?

That would be helpful. In return, I won't subject you to another lavender mocktail.

Done! Maybe see you when I'm back from my walk with Benson? I've got one more lesson then I'll pick him up from Derek's.

Hope you have a good time – make sure you keep a firm grip. He could pull a sleigh better than a team of huskies according to Derek!

Probably why he put his back out.

I expect so. Look after yourself and I'll speak to you on the balcony later.

Sure thing x

She's put a kiss again. It can't be an accident.

Looking forward to it x

I just had to put a kiss too otherwise it would have looked unfriendly.

I tidy away my lunch things; today I made a real effort and created a salad with cold chicken and brown bread. All delivered by Sophia of course, although now I have got a regular delivery slot at the supermarket as well. It's finally got a bit easier as they have given me priority due to my health condition.

Each week the shop has become a major project and I'm beginning to feel as though I'm taking a degree in shopping. I collect everyone's wish list, including Bertie's and Mavis's well before the cut-off time the night before it's delivered. Then I bag everyone's separately after it's delivered and lower stuff down to Sophia or Erica on their balcony to distribute.

The guys who deliver stand well back so I don't feel awkward social distancing. Even better, it means I can order ingredients for cocktails when they're available and surprise Sophia as well as being able to order her some shopping, which I leave outside my door for her to collect. I don't know how but we still haven't managed to see each other, but with one thing and another, we always miss that opportunity. Perhaps it's not meant to be.

Maybe someone somewhere is trying to tell us that this relationship only works when we aren't together. Perhaps that's what makes it so exciting. I brush that awkward thought away like a sticky piece of spider's web you get stuck in your hair when walking through woods in autumn. I really don't want to think about it right now.

I pick up the phone and dial Sam.

'Hey, Sam, how's it going?'

'Someone is sounding on top of the heap today,' he observes with a smile in his voice. 'I've got Mum and Dad here on Zoom – hey, guys, here's Jack.'

'Hello, son,' says Dad.

'I can't see him,' says Mum. 'Where is he? Is he next to Sam?'

'No, dear, he's on the phone, not on our computer screen.'

'Are you all okay?' I ask. These days you can never be sure with anyone; even if they're feeling physically okay there's a high chance they might be struggling mentally during this lockdown – because quite honestly, who isn't?

'We're all fine thanks. Been doing the garden. Watching some television. Your mum's got quite into her iPad now she knows how to use it,' my dad says proudly.

'It's wonderful,' she chips in. 'I love it. You can type stuff in and it will tell you all about anything you want.'

I love Mum. She's about twenty years behind everyone else but is super thrilled about everything and her enthusiasm is infectious.

'Oh, I can hear Carrie,' Sam says. 'She must have woken up. Who wants to say hello?'

'Oh definitely,' says Mum.

'If we must,' says Dad at the same time.

'Ken, that's hardly very nice,' she reproaches him. 'This is your granddaughter you're talking about.'

'You know Dad's joking,' Sam intervenes. 'I bet he's the first trying to teach her about football.'

'Probably true,' I add.

Twenty minutes later when everyone has finished admiring the baby, I decide to announce my news.

'Anyway, I have something to tell you. Do you remember that college course, the one on Sports Therapy?'

'The one you were going to do years ago, but decided to run away to the beautiful Grecian Isles instead?' Dad replies.

'Yes that's the one.' I grit my teeth so I don't make a hasty response I might regret. It's all in the past and I know I did the wrong thing; I don't need Dad to remind me of it.

'I have an interview this week at the Chiropractic College.'

I am bombarded with noise. 'Well done, Jack!' Mum bellows. 'I knew you'd come back to it.'

'Eventually,' adds Dad. He just can't help himself.

'Good work, mate! I knew you could do it. Hey, Tina, Sam's got an interview for the Sports Therapy Course! She says well done, that's amazing,' Sam relays.

I eventually manage to get off the phone after all my

281

family's congratulations – which might be somewhat premature, as I might not get through the interview. But it's a start. This return of optimism won't be quashed now that I've taken steps in the right direction; I could even apply for a different college or something. Starting is always the hardest part; whoever said that is right.

I decide to spend my time reading up about the course and thinking about questions I could ask in the interview. I'm already looking forward to practising with Sophia later. She's had loads of interview practice for her teaching jobs.

As the afternoon goes on, a feeling of anticipation, of tightly muted excitement, grows in the pit of my stomach until I can barely sit still. It's ridiculous really. I mean it doesn't even matter what Sophia looks like, but somehow I need to know. I have this overwhelming curiosity, which has been building and like an itchy mosquito bite you've been trying not to scratch, I desperately want to just catch a tiny glimpse of her. Just to see if she looks as I imagine she does.

Four o'clock draws nearer and I stake out the balcony, trying to read the latest Lee Child book, which Sam kindly posted to me. You know you've got it bad when you've read and reread the same paragraph four times and still have absolutely no idea what it says. Especially when you discover it's upside down. I chuckle to myself and then stop, realising maybe I've been alone too long. It's a good job no one can see me. They'd think I was totally crazy.

Four o'clock comes and goes and still no sign of Sophia. I peer at my phone for the hundredth time and wonder if I made a mistake. It's nearly quarter past and I give up any pretence of reading the book and cast it to one side. It's no good; I can't concentrate at all. I was like this right at the start of lockdown too. Twitchy. I couldn't focus on reading a book or settling to any task for any length of time. It was as though I was subtly but seriously switched on to high alert. Yet for the last few weeks that feeling has settled and I've been able to read a few thrillers, which really take my mind off things.

Not this time though, I am like a contestant on *Blind Date*, excited but anxious. Except this isn't even a date. I really need to get a grip, seeing as getting out more is hardly an option.

From below, there's the sound of a door banging in the courtyard, and someone walks into view. It's her, it *has* to be. I crane my neck and am rewarded by the sight of a willowy figure in a long white top, jeans and pumps walking briskly across the grey stones. But her face and hair are totally obscured by a huge wide-brimmed sun hat. As I watch, she disappears round the corner, along with my hopes of finally seeing what she looks like.

CHAPTER 25

Sophia

The first part of my walk with Benson is totally taken up with trying to keep a firm grip on his lead; this dog has the strength of a horse.

'Are you sure you'll be all right, love?' Derek had asked, almost cowering away from the large boisterous dog as he barged towards me and out of the front door. Benson that is, not Derek.

'He'll be fine. I'm sure he'll calm down after some exercise,' I say more positively than I feel. He is super wired. I've seen working Border collies with less energy than this thunderbolt of long limbs, fluff and vitality.

'I hope so. He has been very cooped up,' Derek said, hovering like an overanxious parent about to leave their child at nursery for the first time.

Fortunately I was out of view as soon as I left the courtyard – he had been making me nervous. I had already planned my route, as the only stretches of green around us have become a hive of activity. The whole town has only one place to visit for their daily exercise, making it increasingly difficult to socially distance. Mind you, Benson would soon clear a space if I let him off his lead right now. He would have knocked people over like skittles.

I have to choose somewhere that isn't so appealing to the crowds trying to get their daily exercise, whilst I check out how much I can control this super bouncy pup. Instead of heading towards the park, I make for the back of the local industrial estate, where there is a patch of waste grassland that backs on to what looks a bit like swamp. I'll have to hope Benson doesn't like water.

We pass Mavis on the other side of the street at top speed and I can barely shout, 'Hi, Mavis, lovely day,' and she can barely reply, 'Looking after that livewire! Good luck!' before I am off again. We manage to reach our destination without too much trouble, considering. I find my pace has quickened dramatically as Alsatians have a long loping stride, which requires a fast walk/half run to keep up. And then of course there's the whole social distancing rigmarole.

I find myself smiling apologetically as I take a wide berth round a couple coming towards me on the main road. It seems to work. They smile and nod back; it kind of takes the sting out of the physical rejection of the action. At least the roads are quiet; it makes it easier to walk round people safely. I have never known the streets be so silent. The main road near us is usually a nightmare to cross but today as every other day at the moment, it is deserted and I cross with ease, which is a relief, as I don't really want to touch the button at the pedestrian crossing.

I walk round another corner and an old couple leap into the road abruptly as though I have the plague, crossing with a distressing urgency. I don't blame them at all, but it brings home the weirdness of the situation. We have been cannoned into a strange new apocalyptic world of physical and for some mental isolation. One where hugs, a friendly pat on the shoulder or any contact at all is forbidden. Sometimes I feel as though I'm in some film, one that I didn't audition for, and at any time now all the crew will come out from behind the scenes saying, 'Okay, folks, that's a wrap,' and we'll all go back to normal, whatever that was.

As I walk past the sheltered housing flats near the industrial estate, I find myself wondering how the people shut inside, not even able to take daily exercise, are coping. They must be barely able to see the sky from here, cooped up in their little boxes. I fervently hope they get to spend time socially distanced in the dining room or something so at least they get to see a friendly face once each day. As I continue walking past, I notice it actually looks deserted apart from a colourful smattering of cheerful posters, probably done by young relatives, consisting of rainbows and flowers and *thank you NHS* displays. It lifts my spirits just seeing them, those and the cuddly teddies and rabbits carefully arranged in the windows.

In fact I feel super cheerful, as I continue to ride the recent rollercoaster of emotions, sad one minute, jubilant the next over the triumph of the indomitable human spirit over adversity. I start to hum as Benson and I cross the final road and he leaps up at me, catching my sudden lift in mood.

The wasteland behind the deserted estate is a great idea. There's no one else here and having checked the coast is clear of cars or unwitting passers-by, I let Benson off for a run. He's off with one huge bound, charging towards the shrubland and bushes beyond. Maybe I should have kept him on a lead, but a long line would have hampered him. He needs to run; he's been so cooped up.

'Benson! Benson, here, boy!' I yell, hoping he will listen. At first he doesn't and I momentarily panic. How on earth would I explain to Derek I've lost his dog, but then he comes to a full emergency stop, all four long legs ridiculously splayed under him. Then he turns sharply and comes running back to me at full tilt. For a second I feel pretty stressed, as I'm half worried he might not stop and completely take me out, but he doesn't. Miraculously he skids to a halt by my side. 'Clever dog.' I reward him with one of his liver treats.

After a play with the ball, which Derek kindly provided, I start to meander home. Thank goodness. Though I haven't managed to wear him out – I know the warnings of not overexercising young Shepherds – he walks nicely alongside me. I pass some neat little bungalows, with their tiny pebble gardens or their pretty little display pots, and for the first time in weeks, I drink in the beauty of my surroundings. It may be suburban but everywhere there are small splashes of colour, a rockery with miniature pink flowers and tiny blue harebells here, a pot of vivid geraniums there. I duck under a couple of pink blossom trees, which are early this year, but are a sure sign May is on its way. The birds, emboldened by the quietness of the streets, flit to pick up grubs not far from my feet and I feel reassured by the fact that in spite of our troubles, Mother Nature is just keeping right on going regardless and there is great comfort in that.

One of the things that fascinates me since this lockdown is the abundant life unexpectedly growing on the verges of the roads. I have never thought about verges before as I drove or walked past, unless there are poppies or wild flowers growing by the side of the road making a particularly beautiful display. Road edges were just there, a normal part of life. I never thought about people needing to maintain them. But since lockdown, the neglected verges have become jungles of long grasses, stretching triffid-like towards the sky. The secret anarchist in me takes a delight in this rebellion against our human need to control every space, as a whole variety of flowers are growing in places you don't expect to see them. Our human loss has been nature's gain.

Benson is ridiculously pleased to see his owner again and Derek is thrilled to have had a break. 'I don't know how to thank you, Sophia, I really don't!'

'Honestly you don't need to,' I assure him. 'I loved every minute of it. I enjoyed getting out for a walk and it's lovely to have some doggy company. Jack and I were thinking of maybe trying to find a rescue dog for Bertie. He seems so down lately and it must be really tough since Elsie died.'

'That would be marvellous. A dog would do him the world of good. But you don't want anything too lively. Take it from me!'

'Definitely not,' I agree. 'I was thinking a small dog, maybe a Jack Russell or a Cavalier King Charles; they're always really sweet and happy to have a walk but just as pleased to have a nap!'

'That's what I think he needs . . . and maybe a bit older, not a pup?' Derek lovingly pats Benson on his head as he tries to shove his soggy and bedraggled squeaky duck into his hand. 'Look at this guy, still lots of energy!'

'You're right, any breed is going to be lively when they're young. Maybe an older dog who just wants someone to give them a fuss, lots of company and a nice ramble every day.'

'You could put an advert out on WhatsApp?' Derek suggests.

'That's an idea, but I was trying to make it a surprise.'

Derek starts to laugh. 'Not sure surprises are a good thing where animals are concerned! Anyway it's the sort of thing that's nice to plan.'

I feel foolish. 'Yes, fair point. Of course, Bertie might

not want another dog. I'll talk to Jack about it. He knows him better than me. Anyway – got to dash, I have to get dinner on. Erica's on late shift again tonight.'

'Bye, love, and thanks again. Say thank you, Benson! Speak!'

'Woof!' Benson happily joins in and Derek gives him a treat.

'Been practising that all week he has – there's a good lad!'

Benson gives another loud woof and I wave. I don't know why but I always wave at dogs. Jess used to tell me it was perfectly normal as long as they didn't ever wave back.

My phone rings as I'm on the way back to my flat. 'Hey, Jess,' I answer it.

'How's it going? Seems ages since I spoke to you.'

'I know, it does.' It's only been a week or so, but then Jess and I usually speak nearly every day. 'How's loved-up married life?'

'Can't complain.' She laughs. 'Okay, so it's been wonderful. I really didn't expect much from a honeymoon in the middle of a lockdown. I mean it's not exactly romantic, or so you would think.'

'Well yeah. I mean no, not really.'

'It was fab though. Just being able to not have to go and do anything. We enjoyed romantic movies in bed, ordered takeaway, sat in our gazebo in the sun and watched our wedding all over again.' I've never heard Jess so relaxed and chilled.

'Sounds perfect.' I smile. 'It's like you're in your own little romantic bubble.'

'I guess it is . . . though it's almost made me feel guilty.'

'Why?'

'I don't know,' she muses. 'I suppose it's because we're in the middle of a pandemic. Things are stressful for so many people, and we've just switched it all off.'

'I don't think that's selfish; you're allowed your honeymoon. Besides, looking after your mental health in lockdown is important. At first I watched all the briefings, but I was getting so upset, I've given myself a social media and news break.'

'Sensible,' Jess agrees. 'I guess it's about being aware, but not depressing yourself totally. Speaking of which, that's the only thing with taking a break from reality . . . the return to work is a bit of a shock!'

'Wouldn't know – I haven't had a break from it yet!'

'How's things going with Jack?' Jess changes the conversation with all the subtlety of a rhino in full charge.

'Good, he's a nice guy and got his friends to do the most amazing shadow acrobatics in the courtyard to say sorry.'

'Sorry.' I hear a rustling in the background. 'I had to put down my packet of crisps. I thought you said he put on *shadow acrobatics*.'

'Yep, he did.'

'Oh my gosh, Soph, this guy is a keeper.' She lowers her voice. 'Even Zach has never done anything like that, though he can be pretty thoughtful. Although wait a minute.' Jess snaps back to her usual whippet sharpness. 'You said it was to say sorry. What did he have to apologise for?'

I sigh. 'It's a long story.'

'I have plenty of time.'

'Well it's nothing really. He just forgot to tell me he's still married.'

'Oh.' Her tone becomes serious. 'That's not good. Why didn't he mention it before?'

'He didn't want to talk about it. Anyway, we're only friends so why would it matter?'

'Because friends don't keep things from each other.' Annoyingly, she has voiced the anxieties I had thought I had put to bed. 'Hmm he sounds immature to me. You had enough problems with Ryan being unsure of what he wanted in life. Sounds like you've found another one.'

'Maybe.' I try not to feel disappointed at Jess's words. 'It doesn't matter in any case, I've forgiven him as a friend and that's all he is.'

'But . . .'

'Sorry, I've just arrived back at the flat. Speak to you later, bye, bye . . .'

And with that, I flick the red button. Ha, I'm quite proud of myself. For the first time ever, I have managed to stop Jess's inquisition. Besides I don't want to think about exactly how I feel about Jack right now; it's easier not to.

* * *

293

Later that evening, I'm sitting on my balcony sipping a rose lemon spritzer mocktail. It's one of Jack's latest creations. 'This is delicious. You have totally nailed it . . . this time,' I tease.

'Uh-huh,' he agrees from above. 'I have to say this is one of my better ones.'

'Hope you've made a note of the recipe?'

'Of course, it's all in my little book.'

'Not your little black book?' I joke. Oops, where the heck did that come from? I'm not drinking alcohol so I don't even have that as an excuse.

'Nope, I don't have one of those. It's an old scrappy notebook that I've had for about a hundred years. It's embarrassing-looking really.'

'I'll have to order you another one,' I say making a mental note although I've already ordered a few too many things online lately. It's far too easy to do, even if the delivery times are longer due to priority quite rightly being given to essentials, and there's loads of things you still can't get. Like disinfectant wipes – apparently they've been requisitioned or something.

'So are we ready for the Balcony Ensemble?' asks Greg.

'Yes it is that time I think,' Jack says. 'Thanks for the interview help, Soph, I think it hopefully went quite well.'

I smile at his use of the abbreviation of my name. Only my close friends and family call me that. It sounds perfect and somewhere inside there's a warm fuzzy feeling in my stomach, a feeling I thought I'd forgotten.

I lean out over the balcony as slowly the courtyard

begins to show signs of life. Mavis arrives with her cavernous bag of stuff, the one she's never seen without, from which she unpacks a mac and an unfolding chair. Bertie comes round the corner with his usual precise small steps and on the balconies opposite, usually deserted except for during the clap, faces start appearing.

'Okay,' calls Jack, after a pause whilst he waits for everyone to settle. It's hard for everyone to hear as the courtyard is echoey and Bertie puts his hand to his ear.

'Are you all ready?' shouts Jack loudly.

Bertie and Mavis give the thumbs up and the couple with a young child in the flat opposite smile and wave.

'Right, "I'm Still Standing", we'll have a run-through from the start and see how we go. Apologies in advance for the sound quality but this speaker is as good as we've got at the moment and it will be on high volume.'

I hear Jack moving about above.

'Bear with me a second, there's a problem with the wire.'

'Just a minute, Jack?' I call.

'Yeah?' he replies.

'Mavis is trying to get your attention.'

She is, she's waving her mac and what looks like a shoe in the air.

'What is it, Mavis?'

'Anyone lost a sandal?' she asks, waving a blue shoe, which looks a bit worse for wear, in the air. It's muddy and has a half-broken strap.

'What are you doing with my best blue sandals?' Marge

appears from under the archway. 'That's mine and what *on earth* has happened to it?'

Mavis stands her ground but is rather flustered. 'I just found it in the raised bed here; I think I must have sat on it. It was half buried.' Ever observant of social distancing, she advances a few steps and places it gingerly on the ground a few metres away from Marge's feet. It looks rather pathetic all alone on the floor in the middle of the courtyard. It's so dirty and bedraggled.

'How did it get like that for crying out loud?' Marge is outraged.

Bertie starts a great chuckle, which makes his sides heave with mirth. 'I reckon it's those young foxes that have been raiding the bins round here. Cheeky rascals! Either that, or someone thought they could grow shoes if they planted them in the ground.'

There's a ripple of laughter round the courtyard. Marge does not share in this humour. 'My sandal was not in the bin. They're my best pair.'

'Not any more,' remarks Greg and I have a job not to snort.

'These foxes have been taking stuff from my garden too,' says Bert, trying to placate Marge. 'They're young and will play with anything. Did you leave your sandals outside?'

Marge deflates, holding the sandal, or what's left of it, delicately between her fingers. 'Well I suppose I could have done . . . but only for a short while.'

'That's all it takes,' says Bertie, 'cheeky little things they are.'

'Well I don't know what they want with my sandal,' remarks Marge. She looks round at all the people gathered, and seems to remember that she's a woman not to be trifled with. 'And if there's too much noise-making with this singing I shall be on to the council!'

'She'll be lucky to get hold of anyone there at the moment,' mutters Greg.

'We'll keep it down, dear,' says Mavis soothingly. 'And we'll let you know if we find your other sandal!'

CHAPTER 26

Jack

Marge, although evidently still not happy, has conceded defeat and disappeared back through the archway still carrying what's left of her blue sandal. Who knew that foxes would take a sandal, chew it up and bury it in a flower border? I guess they're more like dogs than we thought, unless it was Benson all along and Derek is staying quiet for health and safety reasons.

Since Marge's stroppy exit, the courtyard echoes with talk and laughter. 'Hey guys!' I call. 'Shall we get back to the music?'

There's general agreement. 'Ready when you are, Jack!' says Bertie waving the sheets aloft in his hand.

I manage to successfully connect the right lead to the phone this time and the opening piano chords of Elton John's iconic tune start to play.

I rush to the balcony and frantically start to conduct to bring everyone in, but it's disaster. Some have already started whilst some have got left behind because they can't see me due to the design of the building. The verse is so quick, and to be fair any piece of music isn't going to work without everyone starting together. I wave my hands for everyone to stop. I just don't know how Gareth Malone, the great choirmaster himself, does it!

'Okay, okay. That was lovely and enthusiastic, but we all need to start together. I've worked out how to press play on my phone, so let's start again. From the top.'

I press play and miraculously everyone starts immediately. Mavis's fluting voice echoes high above Bertie's deep baritone on the chorus and everyone else seems to be somewhere else in between, pretty randomly in fact. This is going to take some work.

After half an hour or so, I've managed to split everyone into groups and it's sounding vaguely okay. 'Well done, this is really beginning to shape up! Okay time for the musicians to have a go if they'd like.'

A mellow hush comes over the courtyard as Greg and I play – he is on the sax and I'm on the guitar. Even more of a shock is that someone on a balcony opposite, I think it's a young woman, joins in on the oboe. The melody is beautiful and the sound reverberates around the courtyard and into the air, spiralling out to the streets beyond.

A burst of applause rings out after as we all clap and cheer each other's efforts. A small group of children opposite play a cheery tune on their recorders. One of them is holding a large tenor recorder, which is nearly as big as she is! The atmosphere is electric, almost cosmopolitan.

There's people coming out on their balconies I've never even seen before. The festivities carry on long into the evening, until the ever-lengthening evening light fades and people drift back indoors.

Thank goodness Marge seems to have stayed out of the way; maybe we haven't been too loud or maybe she's still looking for her other sandal. Who knows?

'Phew,' I say to no one in particular but hoping Sophia might still be there.

'That was brilliant, Jack! Everyone loved it.' Sophia is there. Of course.

'I hope so – they certainly seemed to enjoy it and so did I.'

'I had no idea half of these people live in this block! It's crazy it takes a pandemic to get everyone to meet each other.'

'True enough, and the same is true of us.'

'Maybe,' she says, and I can almost hear the smile in her voice, 'but we haven't exactly met each other yet.'

'No. But I would like to ask you something.' There's a silence and I hope she isn't put off after the last time.

'Fire away.'

'I just wondered if you would come out with me . . . or rather, stay in with me, on a virtual date?' I hold my breath momentarily. It's said, I can't take it back now.

'Oh.'

Well she hasn't started screaming and yelling, which is a good start I guess. This silence is awkward though; I have no idea how to interpret it.

'That would be great,' she says slowly, 'but I don't think I can date a married man. It's against my principles.'

Oh crikey. Is she joking now or being serious? It's difficult to read people's tone or meaning without seeing their body language. What is it they say? That eighty per cent of our communication is through visual cues? No wonder I'm struggling here. 'Then I guess I'll just have to wait until my divorce comes through. It shouldn't be long.' I hope it won't be anyway, but with Laura it may be forever. I'm still relying on her to do the right thing and I'm not sure she will.

'I guess I'll have to wait then.'

How am I supposed to take that? I suppose I'll just have to be grateful she says she'll wait. That's got to be a good thing hasn't it?

CHAPTER 27

Sophia

'Okay so is everyone sitting comfortably? Reasonably comfortably anyway?' I've always wanted to say that. It's such a storytelling stereotype – *are you sitting comfortably? Then I'll begin.*

The children are sitting cross-legged in front of me, each on a picnic rug they have brought from home. It's a funny thing, sitting cross-legged. I mean why is it easy when you're a child, then as you get older, you're unable to do it any longer? Well – you can, but at the very real risk of not being able to get up again. The kids are all spread out at two metres' distance from me, and from each other of course. This wonderful sunny day at the beginning of May is perfect for outdoor education day.

'So first of all I want to thank you all for sending me such wonderful videos and pictures of the things you found in your garden. Zane, that stag beetle was a giant.'

Zane grins. 'It was very big. My mum and sister started yelling and running away. But I thought he was mega.'

'Yes he was beautiful, although I don't think I would have wanted to pick him up.'

'Neither did Mum or Lana – they refused to go out again 'til he had gone!'

I laugh. 'To be fair, not everyone is into creepy-crawlies. I loved your picture of the hedgehog who lives in your garden, Lola. Have you seen her again?'

'Yes.' Lola nods. 'She crosses quite often; we think she squeezes under the fence. We've started putting cat food out at night and it's always all gone in the morning.'

'That's because a cat ate it,' says Milo categorically, picking up pieces of grass and throwing them down again.

'It wasn't! We don't have a cat,' Lola protests, looking unhappy at the thought.

'I expect it was the hedgehog,' I placate her. 'But you can always make a hedgehog feeding station and then a cat or another animal can't get at the food,' I suggest.

'What's a hedgehog feeding station?' asked Milo, interested now, his piles of freshly plucked grass forgotten.

I hold up a picture. 'They're easy to make out of an old box or a storage unit – you'll need a grown-up to help you though.'

'I'm going to ask my brother to do it with me.' Milo is definitely keen on this idea.

'Well I've taken some copies of the design and instructions and at the end of the lesson I'll put them down for you to help yourself to. Then if you get a chance to make a station, I'd love to see some pictures.'

'Cool,' says Zane, 'I want a hedgehog in my garden.'

'Me too,' says Freya. 'I could call it Mrs Tiggy-Winkle.'

'What if it's a boy?' asks Alfie.

'How do you tell the difference between boy and girl hedgehogs?' asks Milo innocently.

Oh no, I always dread these kind of questions. 'Best to ask them,' I reply without really thinking. Oops, this kind of gets worse. They never teach you how to handle things like this at teacher training. They really should.

'Wouldn't they just run away?' asks Freya.

'I would.' I laugh. Everyone looks a bit fazed. 'I was just joking,' I clarify. 'But in all seriousness, male hedgehogs are a little bigger than females. Interestingly they all have slightly different markings.' I show some pictures of hedgehogs on my laptop before I bring up today's main event. 'Okay so I'm going to show you all a short film, "What happened when we all stopped" by Jane Goodall. Can you all see?' Everyone nods and I click on play.

The animation bursts into life and the children watch transfixed. As always when I see this poem and beautiful animation, I wipe away a tear.

'Are you crying, Miss Trent?' asks Lola.

'No, although it is a very moving film – what did you think of it?'

'I liked the animals,' says Milo, 'but it was sad at the beginning when the people saw that they had damaged all the earth.'

'There were no plants or animals. Not even any hedge-hogs,' says Zane plaintively.

'No you're right, because people haven't been looking after the earth. But at the end of the video, what happens?'

'It's all happy again because the people all work together to plant things, even in flats and in small places.'

'Yes, well done, Freya. I've been growing things on my balcony, even though I only live in a flat.' I bring up a picture of my tomato and cucumber plants. 'My neigh-bour Jack has been more adventurous than me. He's grown chillies. Look, aren't they colourful?' I don't add the fact that he's planning to use them in a cocktail.

'I love chillies.' Pritti smiles. 'My mum uses them all the time in her cooking and it's tasty, although I don't like the really hot ones. They make my dad go bright red in the face.'

'I'm not surprised. So this film shows us it's impor-tant to remember we need to look after our world. It's the only one we've got. And since we've all been home much more than usual, it's given us all a chance to stop, think and notice. Notice the things around us and how important they are to us. To discover what effect we have on the world. Did you hear that all the dolphins have come back to the water near Venice because there have been fewer visitors?' I show the kids a clip on the screen. 'And do you know what I saw in the playground the other day when I was getting ready to go home?'

They all shake their heads. 'A hedgehog?' asks Zane.

'No, although that would have been nice. I saw this lovely animal.'

I press a button on the screen, which reveals a picture of a deer. An extremely startled deer, who looks as surprised to see me as I was to see her. Her head is turned towards me as she stands motionless like a statue.

'Wow!' says Milo. 'I wish I could have seen her.'

'Me too,' says Alfie.

'Well if you're quiet, you might just be lucky. She might come back. As we live in town, it's really unusual to see deer but they're obviously about now there are fewer people. They must live on the bits of heath and wasteland left free from buildings. So over the next couple of weeks we're going to do two things. First I'd like you to take some photos of any unusual birds or bugs or animals you see that you don't normally. It can be anything, doesn't matter how big or small.' I'm expecting to see a whole load of pictures of their cats and dogs despite this instruction. 'And secondly we're going to grow some seeds in the little pots I have here, so we can start to grow our own veg to help the planet.'

I dish out the recycled plastic pots to the kids and each comes up one at a time to put in some compost. Then I show them how to push the bean seeds into the pots. Finally a little water and they all look very pleased with themselves. Only Zane has managed to spill his earth in his shoe, but he's tipped it out and refilled the pot so it's all good. 'Okay, so don't forget to water these little guys, and speak to them often.'

307

'Talk to plants?' asks Milo, obviously perturbed that his teacher is losing her mind.

If it's good enough for Prince Charles, it's good enough for me. 'Yep a lot of gardeners do it. The plants like it – it makes them grow better.' Goodness knows what parents are going to be saying about me. Never mind, the kids have enjoyed it and that's the main thing.

As I arrive back at the flats, parking carefully by the bins, a message pings up on my phone. *Did you mean it when you said your stepdad's friend would look at my wife's old writing box? It's looking very forlorn all broken in the corner.*

I quickly type back. *Yes of course. He said he would have a look this weekend.*

That's wonderful. I don't suppose you could pick it up soon? It makes me feel so sad seeing it sitting in bits on the dresser like that.

I could come and get it now if you like. I will look after it for you very carefully.

You are a treasure! Please do drop by – I'll put it outside the door.

No problem!

I wander up to the flat, put my bits away on the table and wash my hands.

'Do you fancy chips tonight?' Erica shouts from the shower.

'Definitely.'

'I'll pick some up on the way home then.'

'Sounds perfect. Get an extra portion for Jack, would you?'

There's a brief silence. 'All right. He might as well move in here. You're always feeding him.'

'I'm not,' I reply indignantly. Except I am actually; all the time. Perhaps I'm a feeder, or whatever they call it. He seems to like it though, and I love our chats on the balcony. They're the highlight of my day. Our next project is operation find Bertie a dog. Once I've checked with him that he wants one of course.

CHAPTER 28

Jack

'Do you think we should have looked to see if we can find Bertie a dog before asking him if he wants one?' I ask, smiling at Sophia's enthusiastic tone. I'm lying out on my balcony, the May sunshine warm on my skin. I've even got my shorts on. My ridiculously pale legs are reflecting horribly in the sunshine. I've noticed there's fewer pigeons and crows about than usual; perhaps my legs are scaring them away. At least there's no one to see them. There's got to be some advantages to lockdown.

'No,' Sophia answers, 'there's bound to be someone out there who has a dog who needs a home. Fancy some more Twiglets?'

'Thought you'd never ask.' I send down the new basket, which Sophia had left outside my door. It came at the right time as my trusty wine carrier came to an unfortunate early demise last week.

'Oops,' Sophia had exclaimed loudly and then started laughing.

'Have I missed something?' I had been hanging over the balcony aimlessly peering over at the courtyard below and hoping somehow I could magically see her, but of course I couldn't. I never can.

'I've ripped off the handle, I'm so sorry.' She had gone off into fits of laughter, not sounding sorry at all.

Her laughter was infectious. 'Don't know your own strength? At least I know now not to take you on at arm wrestling when this is all over.'

'I'm useless at it,' she had said with a laugh.

'Don't believe you now. Send it back up and I'll assess the damage,' I had said and within minutes I was in hysterical laughter as well, as I hauled what was left of the carrier back up. Sophia, ever resourceful, had tied a hasty knot, which she had fastened with an array of paperclips and something that appeared to be an old pair of tights attached to a bit of the sparkly wrapping and it looked decidedly sad and skew-whiff. 'What the heck have you done to it? It's all mangled!'

She was still laughing. 'I don't know how that happened; it just kind of fell apart, and after all your hard work too.'

'It's all right, I'll make another one,' I had said, 'and I'll make it out of wood or something so it's tamper-proof.'

I hadn't needed to as the next day, outside my door along with my shopping had been a very posh basket with holders for two drinks and a small bowl. With Sophia I've begun to think anything is possible. Maybe she can get Bertie a dog whilst in lockdown too.

I bring up the new basket, now complete with Twiglets. 'So at least we know Bertie likes the idea,' I say.

'Well generally yes.'

'Are you sure he really wants a dog?'

'He didn't actually say it in so many words. But he *would* like a dog – he admitted he misses Cooper and he would like one now, but he said lockdown isn't the right time.'

'Oh,' I say scratching my head, 'maybe we should wait then. Do you think he means it's not the right time for him or because of the virus?'

'He means because of the virus of course,' Sophia says without missing a beat.

I wish I shared her confidence. It's a terrible thought to turn up to someone's house with a dog that they don't want.

'Maybe it would be an idea to find the dog and then ask him,' I suggest cautiously.

'Of course, that's exactly what we'd do. I wouldn't turn up on his doorstep randomly with a dog,' she assures me, though I'm not so sure, as I suspect she had liked the idea of surprising Bertie.

I smile to myself. 'So in my spare time today I did have a quick look online but some of the rescues are closed.'

'The one over at Summertown isn't; so now I've checked with Bertie, I thought we could ask there.'

'Great idea – so are you happy to do that? I wondered about asking on WhatsApp too? Just a general enquiry – without making it obvious that I'm asking for Bertie,' I say.

'Definitely, I'll put a message out. There must be people who are struggling to look after or cope with their pets in lockdown, sadly.'

'I read something about it the other day. Someone who was ill and their friend had to take the dog on. Makes you feel sad just thinking about it.'

'Talking of sad,' Sophia replies, 'I picked up Elsie's writing case from Bertie at the same time as broaching the subject of the dog.'

'Oh I bet he was pleased. Your stepdad's friend is going to have a look at it, isn't he? Do you get along well with your stepdad?'

'Yeah, he's nice, really.'

'Really?' I ask hesitantly, not wanting to pry.

She's silent for a moment. 'Yeah well, I haven't always liked him. It's tough; someone trying to replace your dad.'

'Yeah, I can imagine that.' I think of my dad with his greying temples, his lightly balding patch and his dodgy glasses with multicoloured lenses that he thinks are really cool but went out of fashion years ago. 'Mine can be annoying, but I can't imagine him and my mum not together. I mean, sorry . . .' I realise my foot is now firmly in mouth.

'No it's okay,' Sophia says. 'I know it was the right thing. My dad was a bit of an idiot. Much as I love him

– because he's my dad – he and Mum were like completely different people. I don't understand why couples stay together for the sake of the kids; their constant rowing was awful. And Mum needed her career and Dad, well, he just wanted her to revolve her life around him. He met his new wife quickly and that was it.'

'I'm sorry, that must have been difficult to cope with.'

'Yeah it was. But Mum was so much happier – no more rows over her late shifts and Mark is really supportive. To him, it's just part of the deal and he's more than happy to cook as well. His own business means he's able to be pretty flexible.'

'That's good. He sounds like a decent guy.' I pause, reflecting on my parents' marriage in a way that I very rarely do. 'To be fair my parents row quite a lot. Especially at the moment, in lockdown. I think it's driving them to the edge of tolerance. They were arguing about the way my dad eats his peas the other day.'

Sophia laughs. 'I suppose if you're together twenty-four seven you are going to row about pretty much everything . . . You've got me wondering now. How *does* he eat his peas?'

'I have no idea.' I shrug. 'I think he scoops them up and Mum says he should prod them with the end of his fork.'

'Oh my gosh, I'm really worried now. I'm trying to remember how I eat my peas. I'll have a look next time.'

I laugh. 'How could it ever matter to anyone but my mum?'

'It does, if I ever come round to dinner with your parents.'

There's a silence.

'Not that I, er . . .' She breaks off awkwardly. 'Hey look, Jack, I'm sorry – I mean, I sound like some kind of stalker. You'll probably want to get well away from me after this. Back to Greece or somewhere far away.'

Is that what she thinks? Or does she want to get away from me and doesn't know how to say so? 'Not at all,' I say lightly, not wanting to come on too strong since she turned down my offer of a date. 'I love our chats. I can't imagine being without them now or you.' I hope I haven't overstepped the mark. My feelings just tumbled out in spite of my best intentions.

'Me neither,' she says quietly, so quietly I can't pick out the words but they are there hanging in the air between us like beautiful crystal rainbows and I hold on to them because they make me feel so happy, even if I have only imagined them.

'That's it then,' I say after clearing my throat. I never could do anxious pauses, and anyway who on earth makes out on separate balconies apart from Romeo and Juliet? And that was rather a long time ago. And I bet they could see each other. Or maybe they couldn't. Perhaps I should have paid more attention at school. 'It's settled – when this is over you are invited round to meet my crazy family and I'm sure my mum will not mind at all how you scoop your peas. If you do, that is.'

'I think I probably do,' she says guiltily.

'Do you know, I was hoping you'd say that!' I laugh, but then wonder if I'm taking all this too seriously. She's probably only joking. When this is all over, she will be able to find someone far more interesting than some random guy she's been having a laugh with. Good old Jack, I've always been great at the banter, but when it comes to making someone happy in a serious relationship, I'm just not sure I'm much of a catch.

CHAPTER 29

Sophia

As I'm getting ready to go to bed, I ponder Jack's words. Not about the peas, but just generally. Lately I've begun to realise I can't imagine life without him now. I can't remember what it was like not knowing him. He's changed the way I see things. The balcony has morphed from someplace I barely even went – in fact I used to forget it was there for weeks at a time – to an extension not only of my living space, but the centre of my whole social life.

There's a strange part of me that doesn't want this lockdown to end although I long for normality. I'm frightened it might end this almost-relationship we have going on. There's a peacefulness, a restfulness to the routine of it, each day I work and come home, cook dinner for Erica and sometimes Jack too. We all sit out on the balconies eating our dinners, plates precariously balanced on laps. The weather has continued to be bizarrely clement, granting us all some slack from the current situation that rages invisibly out there beyond the streets, beyond these buildings where individuals carry out their own routines, their own coping strategies to simply get through this.

One evening Jack cooks me a lentil dahl and lowers it down and we talk and laugh, whilst Erica is out on shift, about everything and nothing whilst eating our dahl and scooping up the delicious remnants with some slightly charred naan that he'd forgotten to remove from the grill.

As I'm going through my usual night-time routine, i.e. feel too tired to remove make-up, wonder momentarily whether I can get away with leaving it on, decide I can't unless I want to look like some kind of nightmarish monster in the morning, which will terrify my school kids, blunder back out of bed, find cotton wool pads, remove make-up, haphazardly slather moisturiser over my face and then decide actually now I'm wide awake.

My eye travels to where I had carefully stored the separate sides of Elsie's writing box, which Bertie had placed gently on the doorstep for me to pick up, wrapped in tissue and then enshrined in a reusable Save the Planet bag for some reason. I lift it down, holding the two sides and placing them on the bed, one at a time. It's an incredible piece of workmanship. One of the corners is split where the box would have been joined, but the hinges are still there, a little tarnished perhaps, but I am hopeful my stepdad's friend will be able to fix it.

I run my fingers along the slightly tarnished wood, through which tiny glimmers of the beauty it used to have shine tantalisingly, offering a hint of how precious it must have been. I wonder if it was originally a present from a new husband to his beloved wife, or a gift between close friends. I have a fascination for vintage things and love seeing them restored and imagining the stories such objects could tell if only they could talk. This box has seen several generations I'm sure and I wonder as I gaze at it how many female writers have used it to pen the story of their everyday lives or even love letters.

I turn the box over carefully. It obviously once opened to remove the papers and envelopes within, closing neatly to make a base to write the letter on. It could then have been quickly opened and the letter speedily hidden if someone came into the room.

As I examine the box more carefully, I notice it's a lot shallower than it would seem from the outside. It's as though the bottom is thicker than it needs to be for such an ornate and delicate object. I've seen things like this before on restoration programmes. The exciting part where the presenter or at least the restoration person, I can't think of another name for them, maybe it's restorateur? Anyway, I've seen items like this where the expert reveals that there is a secret compartment at the bottom of the box. I remember one was a puzzle box, which had a certain clever way of opening, but the puzzle needed solving first.

I study the base of Elsie's box, but there are no buttons, or gaps to push my finger in. No hinges or obvious things to press. How disappointing, although Bertie would have told me if there had been any secret compartments.

I sit on the bed and stare at the case. I touch just inside the edge, near the corner, inside the box, enjoying the feel of the smooth walnut when suddenly the wood moves under my hand and a small square drawer pops out. I gape at it in surprise for a moment and then put out my hand gingerly. I don't know what I'm expecting, but I can see a corner of paper neatly and compactly folded peeking out from the edge of the recently revealed space. Carefully so as not to tear it – the paper looks old and a little fragile – I pull out a letter that has been folded over many times. I unfold the pieces of paper. The writing is in fountain pen, beautifully scrolled in an old-fashioned style, carefully etched out across the slightly faded cream paper.

To my darling Bertie,

I am aware that if you're reading this, I've probably gone to the great stomping ground in the sky and you are having the awful task of having to go through all my stuff, which is probably a right old nuisance as I know I've always been a terrible hoarder. I remember you saying that you would manage to help me become tidier if it was the last thing you ever did, but you obviously didn't succeed, though you did in everything else. You've been an amazing life partner and I couldn't ask for a better friend and companion. You are my everything.

I stop reading for a moment as my eyes are blurring with tears and I realise with a start I shouldn't be reading this. I find myself looking furtively over my shoulder as though I'm doing something wrong, which I am because this isn't my letter, it's Bertie's.

I start to fold it back up but as I do so, a stray sheet floats to the floor in a zigzag trajectory, which is odd really as there's no window open or a breeze. I shiver. I need to get to bed. I always did have an overactive imagination. I bend quickly and pick up the paper but as I do so, its words catch my eye. *I know I should have told you and now I realise it was the wrong thing. We never did have any secrets, but I was worried if you had discovered I had a daughter you would have judged me. Please believe that I was young and inexperienced and it was never meant to happen. The lad in question was passing through and I guess one thing led to another.*

I stop reading and sink onto the bed. Elsie had a daughter and Bertie didn't even know? That's terrible. But why didn't she give him this letter? Did she mean to and maybe didn't get a chance? Perhaps she thought Bertie would find it in her box, or maybe she died before she could move it from its secret compartment? I don't know what to do. I need to give this letter to Bertie but somehow I feel bad about it. Did Elsie change her mind and decide to keep it secret? Should I keep her secret too?

I fold the letter together quickly and carefully, pushing it back into the small hidden compartment and shut it as if somehow this will solve the problem. But a secret can't be unlearned; this Pandora's box has shared its inner knowledge with me and now I am in a quandary because I just don't know what to do.

CHAPTER 30

Jack

'Jack?' I wonder if I am dreaming someone calling my name. I look up and the stars are twinkling and I'm lying on my back on the balcony lounger. I must have fallen asleep out here and it's cold now. I shiver involuntarily. 'Jack!' Okay, I definitely heard that.

'Sophia?' I reply groggily.

'Yes it's me. I was hoping you might still be outside although I thought you'd probably gone to bed.'

'No I fell asleep out here – must be all the fresh air! Is everything all right? I mean are you okay?' I'm instantly awake, worrying maybe she isn't feeling well or something.

'Yeah, I'm fine. It's just I don't know what to do. I've found something and it's made me really stressed because I don't know what to do with it.'

'Sounds intriguing.'

'Yes it is, but I don't know where to begin. Are you

sure you're not too tired now to listen to me blathering on?'

'Of course not. How about a whisky chaser to warm you up? It's chilly out here now.'

'Ooh yes that would be amazing. I do feel a bit shivery.' I can tell from her voice that whatever it is, it's shaken her up.

While Sophia goes back inside to grab a jumper and a rug, I hurry in and pour a generous measure into a glass and warm some nuts in the grill. 'Okay are you ready for your drink, madam?' I ask, back on the balcony.

'You bet. I thought you'd never come back,' she says.

'Coming right up – or down, if we're going to be technical. Stand by!' I lower down the precious cargo, which is met by a 'yay' of approval from Sophia. As I pull the basket back up, I notice she's popped in some little hot sausages.

'Thanks, these are perfect!' I say appreciatively biting into one.

'No probs,' she replies. 'This whisky is pretty spot on.'

'I try my best,' I say. 'Feeling better now?'

'I am a bit thanks, although I'm not sure if it's the drink or just talking to you.'

'I can take credit for both,' I say glibly and we both laugh. 'So?' I prompt her, not wanting to rush her, but wanting Sophia to know I care.

'So . . . how well do you know Bertie?'

I wasn't expecting that but it sounds ominous. 'Fairly well, why?'

'It's just . . . oh gosh, I'm making a right mess of this,' she says, and I half worry she'll clam up and leave me in suspense.

'You're not, but just start at the beginning and I'll pick it up as you go along.'

'Well I've found this letter, whilst picking up Elsie's writing case. And I was just looking at it, and maybe exploring it too, wondering if something that old would have a secret compartment . . . and then whilst I was running my fingers along the base, a button popped up, revealing a small drawer that came out.'

'Sounds like something out of a movie.'

'I know and of course when I saw the corner of a piece of paper, I couldn't resist pulling it out.'

My heart goes out to her – she sounds so ashamed of herself. 'You'd need superhuman self-restraint not to.'

'I couldn't help reading the first few pages. I didn't mean to. Now you're going to think I'm as bad as Marge.'

'No one's that bad, Soph!' I laugh. 'Anyway, I would have done the same.'

'That makes me feel a bit better,' she admits.

'So, what did it say?'

'It says something about Elsie having a daughter before she met Bertie.'

'Wow that's heavy. I only met her a couple of times before she died. She was a wonderful woman.'

He sounds rather emotional, so I give him a moment. 'I know, I mean I may have got the wrong end of the stick as I haven't read the whole letter.'

327

'So you think he doesn't know anything about this?'

'That's the thing; I think Elsie meant to tell Bertie, but I presume she didn't as the letter was concealed. Maybe she decided she wouldn't.'

'Maybe she died before she could give it to him,' I suggest.

We're both silent for a moment. 'That's an awful thought,' Sophia says at last. 'Do you think we should tell him?'

'We have to,' I decide. 'He needs to know. I mean he might have a stepdaughter somewhere out there he doesn't even know exists. And when he's such a lonely guy, I just don't think we should keep that from him, do you?'

'No, I don't think we should.' Sophia sounds relieved. I'm guessing she wouldn't relish keeping a secret from someone she cares about, and I'm hit with guilt all over again that I took so long to tell her about Laura. 'So how am I going to tell him? Maybe you should, as you know him best?'

I pause for a moment. 'I don't think I should tell him just randomly over the phone, do you? He's probably going to be really shocked and upset. He might need support.'

'Okay, well you could tell him over the phone that I've found something he might want to see in Elsie's case and I will drop it over to him if he would like to read it?'

'I guess.' I'm not sure how we should handle this to be honest; it's such a difficult situation without adding a pandemic and the need for social distancing into the mix. 'I think you should be with him whilst he reads it or at least nearby. In case he takes it really badly. What about the dog thing?'

'I think maybe we should leave it for now,' Sophia says sadly. 'There's so much going on and it complicates things.'

'As if they're not complicated enough already,' I mutter. 'I'm just not sure how Bertie's going to take the news that Elsie had a child. He and Elsie were never able to have kids and this is going to be an almighty shock, especially as she potentially never confessed to him.'

'I know, but I guess she must have had her reasons?' Sophia always sees the best in people. 'And you never know, it might help Bertie to know he has a little part of Elsie left.'

CHAPTER 31

Sophia

You would have thought Jack's whisky chaser would have given me a good sleep, but instead it just seemed to give me weird dreams. I wake with a start, having had a restless night with writing cases and letters swirling round my head, Alice in Wonderland like, and I am relieved to find myself in my own bed. The writing case on the edge of my dressing table catches my eye and the events of last night crowd back into my head. Poor Bertie, I wish that had all been a dream.

I think the plan I agreed with Jack will have to do, but it seems a little flawed in that Bertie is going to be left to deal with this upset on his own due to the whole social distancing thing.

'Soph!' Erica bangs on my door and walks in unceremoniously. 'I've made vegan banana pancakes if you fancy them?'

'Ooh sounds good,' I say, before pausing, confused.

'Have you become vegan then?' It seems a sudden change from the chicken-thieving Erica of just weeks ago.

'No,' she scoffs, 'it's only because we're out of milk and I found a recipe on the internet. It's nice actually, if you add enough maple syrup.'

'Anything tastes good if you add enough maple syrup,' I point out.

'Anyway,' Erica says, flopping down on the end of my bed on top of my feet, 'what's up with you? Been up partying with Jack all night?'

'Something like that. I do feel tired.'

'Well at least it's no work for you today. By the way, the hospital phoned.'

'Maybe I forgot an appointment,' I worry, 'or they've cancelled one.' I start rummaging about the bed for my T-shirt and leggings so that I can start getting ready.

'Anyway,' Erica says again, not to be derailed, 'I have news and I know how you like news!'

'I'm not sure about anything today,' I mutter.

'Oh, well I won't tell you then. I shall keep it to myself.'

'Oh stop playing hard to get.' I laugh. 'What is it?'

'I thought you said something about Bertie,' she starts, and I jump at his name like a scared rabbit. Honestly this espionage, secret letter thing is making me a nervous wreck. 'Are you all right, Soph? You look a bit pale.'

'No I'm fine,' I wave my hand.

'I thought he was looking for a dog and I've got this colleague, Jan – you know the one with the husband with the ridiculous amount of body hair and none on his head?'

'Erm . . .' I can't remember actually. I get confused with who's who amongst all Erica's friends, though you'd think I'd remember a description like that.

'Well he's busy at the moment as he's working two jobs – taken one as a delivery driver as well as his other job, because they're desperate for delivery staff. You know all the supermarkets and stuff – and besides they need the money.'

'Yeah.' I'm still confused as to what Erica's on about.

'And Jan is having to work long shifts at the hospital as always, so their dog, Tilly, is being left long periods of time and she's begun to get separation anxiety.'

'Oh that's a shame. Dogs hate being left alone all the time – they're social creatures.'

'Well this one certainly is and she's started getting really distressed – the dog that is, not Jan although she is upset about it as she loves Tilly. Anyway the long and short of it is that they're looking for a home for her.'

'Oh.' I stop my rummaging and pay attention. 'What breed of dog is she?'

'A small spaniel I think – you know one of those King Charles?'

'Cavalier King Charles?'

'Yeah something like that. Anyway she's red and white. With a cute little face, lively little thing from what I remember. I only met her once when I went over to Jan's for dinner. Jumped all over me, which was annoying.'

'You're not really a dog person though are you?'

'Not really. Give me a cat any day; you know where you are with a cat. But she's quite sweet – has a thing for socks, carries them round in her mouth.'

'She sounds lovely. How old is she?'

'I don't know. I haven't asked Jan. I wasn't sure if you were still looking or not. But I told her you've got an old friend who lives on his own who would never leave the dog for long and she would get loads of attention.'

'She would – it would be perfect. Have you got a photo?'

'Yes somewhere on my phone. Give me a mo.' She scrolls through her photos.

'How many have you got on there?'

'Millions,' she replies drily. 'Oh here she is. She's very cute.'

She holds the phone up to reveal a photo of a small Blenheim-coloured Cavalier King Charles spaniel, looking up at the camera with the breed's trademark beseeching eyes.

'Oh my gosh, she is gorgeous,' I say admiringly. 'You have to text her now that we're interested. Bertie would love her. Absolutely.' I throw my agreement with Jack to the wind, excited that I'll have something positive to bolster Bertie with after we give him such difficult news.

'Ow!' I realise I've been clutching Erica's arm and I've totally creased the clean freshly ironed shirt she's got on. Having said that, to be fair it's always me who irons it.

'All right, all right, I'll text her. Don't forget to have the pancakes,' she orders as she leaves my room.

Once I'm dressed, I wander out into the kitchen to discover the bowls and the pan, all left in the sink. That's the thing about Erica: she might occasionally cook, but likes to use every single pan in the cupboard and seems to forget they all need washing up. The banana pancake tastes delicious anyway and I enjoy the sugar hit whilst texting Jack.

Hey, are you awake? Thanks for last night.

Hey, nice to hear from you so early, he replies.

It's 10 a.m.

I know; that is early.

Okay, I put a laughing face emoji, *anyway I think we might have found Bertie a dog!*

That's great, but weren't we waiting 'til we'd dealt with the other thing?

Yes we were, but I don't think we can pass up this opportunity. Erica's work colleague is having to rehome her dog because of their working hours and she looks perfect for Bertie. Look! I post the pic of Tilly with a smiley face and puppy faces and hearts next to it.

I can see you're sold then.

She'd be going to a perfect home with Bertie.

She would – he would make such a fuss of her, he writes back. *So what are we going to do about the other thing?*

What do you think we should do? I don't want to lose this dog so maybe I'll speak to Jan first and see if Bertie wants to meet her.

Good plan. The letter can wait. It's been hidden for

however many years; a few more days won't make any difference.

Erica comes bouncing into the kitchen. 'Jan was pleased to hear about Bertie. She's going to be really upset of course, but she loves the idea that Tilly will go to a home where she's given all the love she needs. She says she's a right little cuddle monster.'

'Can I go round soon?' I ask.

'She wants you and Bertie to meet Tilly this weekend if at all possible. She says she'd rather get it out of the way if it has to be done.'

'That's understandable. Okay I'll just check with Jack and see if he thinks I should message Bertie or if he should?'

'Jack this and Jack that. You two are like an old married couple already.' Erica laughs.

'We aren't,' I say, feeling flustered. I don't know *what* we are. 'I mean I like to ask him about stuff, but you know, only important things . . .' I look up and see Erica's expression. 'Oh right, you're joking . . . ha-ha.'

'You are seriously joined at the hip.'

'We do have a bit of a connection but we haven't even met, so we're not exactly an item.'

'You so are.' Erica laughs, going out and shutting the door before I can stick my tongue out at her.

Okay so are you going to tell Bertie about this dog or am I? I text Jack.

You can and send him the pic, see what he says.

Hey Bertie, I type on WhatsApp. *Hope you're well, I*

336

know we were talking about you maybe having a dog one day and I know you were only thinking about it after this lockdown. But here's the thing. Oops I've pressed send before I meant to.

It's very kind of you, love, he comes back to me before I can get the next part written, *but no it doesn't seem the right time and I've been feeling very low lately. I'd be pretty rubbish company for any dog. Maybe after the lockdown.* Oh, no.

That's the thing, Bertie, this little dog needs a home now. Her owner is having to work long shifts and the dog is miserable. Please at least look at her photo. She's very sweet. I attach the photo of Tilly that Erica has just airdropped to me and sit and look at the screen, waiting anxiously. No one could resist that face. No reply. Okay maybe he can resist that face.

Ping, another message comes in.

Poor little soul, it's gorgeous. The shame of some people. Why on earth do they get a dog if they can't be bothered to look after it?

Oh great, Marge is on the case. I didn't realise I'd sent my message on the group chat. I seem to have lost brain cells during this pandemic.

It's okay, Marge, I type back. *The dog has been really well looked after and the owner has just had a change of circumstances. It could happen to anyone.*

Happens all the time. People just don't think. In any case she should put her on a rescue site. They check who might be adopting, much more sensible. Otherwise you get all sorts of weirdos. *Puppy farmers and stuff, they might breed from her poor little mite.*

She's spayed so I don't think that's going to happen, I respond. *And of course I'm sure Jan will keep looking until she finds the right home for her.*

She doesn't have to. Oh it's Bertie; he's back. *She's a grand little dog. I'd love to have her. Sort me out a meeting – socially distanced of course, Sophia love. I would do anything to look after such a sweet little girl. She won't have to worry about being left alone with me around.*

Before I can reply, Marge is back on the case. *You want to be careful, Bert, you never know what the dog's like. She could have all sorts of vices. I knew someone in Granthorpe who rescued a little white dog, looked like butter wouldn't melt. I never saw such a sweet little dog. She'd only had it three days and it bit her hand. She ended up with four stitches and it went septic.*

Marge is something else. If she can find a problem with something, she will.

I'll be fine, Marge, thank you for your concern. I grit my teeth as I write back. *Cavaliers have very sweet natures. More likely to lick you to death than anything else.*

Well don't say I didn't warn you. I can imagine her sanctimonious expression as she types this.

I put Marge to one side and go back to the matter at hand. *Okay, Bertie, I'll organise a time with Jan to meet Tilly, although I'll meet her first, just to make sure she's friendly (to stop Marge from worrying) and then I'll sort*

*out a meeting for you – outside of course – and we'll go
from there. As long as you're sure.*

*Sure? I think it's meant to be. This little dog needs a
home and a warm lap and I need some company. It's a
match made in heaven.*

I make the arrangements through Erica and tell Jack the
happy news, well, as long as it all works out anyway.
My phone bings and announces I'm due on the video
call with the hospital at 3 p.m. I sit myself in front of
the screen having checked the view behind me is not
offensive. I mean you don't want left-over washing up,
or anything embarrassing like *Fifty Shades of Grey* on
your shelf when talking to the doctor. Mind you, they've
probably seen it all. Whilst I'm checking the image, I
accidentally press a button and for some reason my
forehead becomes enormous and my cheeks puff out like
a hamster. I look hilarious.

Erica wanders past casually and glances at the screen.
'What are you doing? You look like a chipmunk.'

She peers at the screen and immediately her face changes
too and we both roar with laughter. 'Try this image,' she
snorts and our eyes swell up like comedy googly eyeballs
and our teeth chatter like frenzied rabbits. We are in the
middle of making stupid faces and laughing uncontrol-
lably when my epilepsy specialist hoves into view.

Erica, still doubled up with laughter, rushes off into
the kitchen and I am sobered up immediately by the sight
of my doctor's earnest and concerned face in front of me.

339

'Just a second.' I fiddle with the screen and after a couple of false starts, during which my face stretches as wide as the screen and my eyes become just two straight stretchy lines, the image goes back to normal. 'Sorry about that,' I say breezily as though I had just had some interference on the line or something.

'No problem at all, computers can be tricky things.' He twinkles at me and I relax. This is nice actually, sitting at home with a coffee instead of having to drive all the way to the hospital, struggle with parking, park three streets away, run all the way into the hospital, realise you need the toilet because you really shouldn't have had that last coffee. Then rush to your appointment, worried you're going to be late, panic at the length of the queue at the desk because you know you're *really* late, then be shown into the waiting room to discover you've got a fifty-minute wait and you could have taken things a bit more steady on the way and not got half so stressed after all. But you never know; that's the problem.

'This is very civilised,' I say to Mr Zivan, 'and the clinic is on time.'

'I know,' he says cheerfully. 'I haven't had to step out of my home and I've managed to complete half my afternoon patients without overrunning.'

After our discussion I wander across to the balcony, stunned. 'After more than two years seizure-free, if you are unhappy with the side effects of your medicine, you can always try coming off them,' Dr Zivan had told me.

I had assumed I would have to stay on them for life. Of course, as the specialist has pointed out, if the seizures return as I reduce the meds, I will have to stay on them permanently, or I might even have an increase in seizures, which are harder to control, although there might be a faint possibility that, if the electrical activity in my brain is in one place, I could have an op that could make me seizure-free for the rest of my life.

'This is a really personal decision,' he said, 'and because of the pandemic, I wouldn't come off the meds until that has settled, whenever that is.'

'What about my kids at school?' I whispered. 'I can't risk having a seizure in front of them.'

'You could lower the dose in the summer holidays,' he suggested.

It all sounds so simple in theory, but as he had pointed out, there is always the risk I could have a seizure even in several years' time and that thought will always lurk in the back of my mind like a marauding shark, silent, deadly and constantly there. I wouldn't be able to drive for two years if I have a breakthrough seizure. My freedom, everything I've now built up slowly, painstakingly again from the beginning – that would all go and what about my family and friends? How will it affect them?

The thought of coming off my meds is a wonderful one, but at what cost? This has become my normal, this new existence on epilepsy meds – not one I've chosen admittedly, but now just like the idea of leaving lockdown, I'm not sure if I'm ready to leave the security of what I know to move forward into the unknown.

CHAPTER 32

Jack

I hear a noise from below, whilst I'm hovering restlessly on my balcony. I feel so trapped by this wretched lockdown, I want to be with Sophia to support Bertie when he reads that letter – he's an old mate after all. I so badly want to go and meet Tilly with her, just walk to the park. It's a simple enough request in ordinary circumstances. I look out over the rooftops and the scene below in the courtyard and wonder if this is what prisoners feel like. Although probably not; even they're allowed outside for exercise every day.

As I observe the suburban mass in front of me I imagine what it would be like if we could see this virus, as though it were visible in blue and red clouds, spiky round shapes suspended in the air like in the images on the news on the television, like in some weird sci-fi video. I guess at least if we could see it, we would know what we were avoiding; as it is, we all see suspicion in each other's presence, in everyday objects, in the very air we breathe.

I hear the noise again, suspiciously like a sob.

'Sophia?'

There's no response, but another muffled sniff.

'I know you're there.' I suddenly realise if Greg or anyone is out on their balcony, they're going to think I'm mad out here talking – for all I know – to myself. But I know she's there, I can sense it.

'Yes?' she finally answers.

'What's wrong? Are you okay? I mean obviously you're not because I can hear you're crying.' *Oh shut up, Jack, you're babbling now.*

'No I am okay, it's just I had to talk to the specialist at the hospital and . . .' She breaks off. 'You know how it is.'

Her words bring back a flood of memories. A stream of well-meaning specialists and doctors, one after the other, throughout my childhood and teenage years, telling me my life wasn't going to be how I planned, that it would be full of restrictions, then asking me how I felt about it. 'I know exactly. Many a time I've come away from the hospital wanting to cry or shout and break a few things. Mind you I've only had one doctor who really wasn't too understanding.'

'No,' she sniffs again, 'although I know what you mean. I had one like that too, but mine's lovely. It's just he's said I can maybe come off my meds.'

'But that's amazing . . . isn't it?' Then I feel stupid for

saying that. I know how it is; I've been there. You just get used to one thing, which takes goodness knows how long, and then things change and you have to readjust all over again. 'I don't mean that, Soph, I mean it's positive you maybe could come off the meds if you want, but I'm sure you have a choice.'

'Yes I do, but it all feels a bit much at the moment. I just want to shut my epilepsy in a closet and forget about it.'

'I know how you feel. Just give me two minutes.' I rush inside, grab some Dairy Milk and a wad of clean tissues, go back out on the balcony and pop them in the basket, carefully lowering it down to her. 'Watch out, incoming.'

'Oh, Jack!' She's laughing and crying now. 'I've got the mixed emotions!'

'Just have a good old nose-blow and some chocolate and you'll feel better, I promise.'

I can hear her trying to blow her nose, but it sounds more like a mewing cat and we both burst into laughter. When we manage to stop, I call down again, 'I thought maybe you'd rescued a cat for Bertie rather than a dog.'

She laughs. 'No, although speaking of which, I'd better get ready. I'm meant to be going to see this little dog. I just don't feel like facing anything. Somehow talking about my epilepsy brings it all back again.'

'That's okay,' I say brightly. 'Look, the specialist said you can't do anything about it for a while anyway, didn't he?'

'Yes,' she replies.

'So I know it's tough and easier said than done, but try dismissing it as much as you can for now. You don't need to make a decision yet. Just mull it over and in time, over the next few weeks, how you feel will become clearer.'

'I guess.'

'Of course the other option is, like my mum says, do a "for and against" list. Sometimes, though I won't admit this to my mum, it does help you work through your thoughts.'

'That's just the sort of thing my mum suggests,' Sophia says.

'Did it work?' I ask.

'Last time I tried it I was deciding whether to stay with an ex-boyfriend at teacher training college, and yes I think it did kind of work.'

'There you go then.'

'I'm sorry, Jack.'

'For what?'

'Bleating on, about my meds when you probably can't . . .' She breaks off.

'Can't what?'

'You probably can't stop taking yours.'

'It's okay, I didn't even think of that.' It dawns on me that for once I wasn't thinking about myself. Sophia matters to me more than anything. 'My meds are a fact of life. I'm so used to them I don't even remember what it was like before I started taking them. Anyway as you

346

know, I've done my fair share of running away and rebelling against them. As a teenager once I didn't tell my parents but I hid my meds and didn't take them for two days.'

'Oh my gosh, that's terrible . . . but I guess I can understand why.' The fact she gets this makes me feel ridiculously happy.

'Yeah, I was angry. Angry with why I had to take them and angry with everyone, really.'

'What happened?' she asks.

'I felt ill and stupid. My mum found out and was upset, but she was cool. She just sat me down and said I didn't have to take them but if I wanted to stay well it was pretty necessary.'

'She sounds a sensible mum. I'd like to meet her.'

'You know the invitation is there,' I tell her. 'She would adore you.' She would too; I just know it. She didn't ever really like Laura; I think she knew right from the start it was a mistake. Though she had tried very hard with her. Of course I was so determined to be independent, to go my own way, that I wouldn't listen to her warnings. 'Does your mum understand?' I ask, biting into a piece of chocolate.

'Not really,' Sophia admits. 'Because she's a GP, she can be quite matter-of-fact. If you need meds, take them – she doesn't always understand why you might not want to. She's studied the whole science of it and is frustrated that anyone might refuse to take something that can make them better.'

'Fair enough – she's right really,' I say.

'She is, but it doesn't take into account the emotions that go alongside, of wanting to drink, to go out partying, be like your friends.'

'True but then no one really understands unless they've been through it,' I reply.

'I've never met anyone like you, Jack,' she says softly, and my heart flips. 'You just totally get it. I felt so alone before with this diagnosis, but not any more.'

I can't believe she's just said that. 'Me too,' I tell her. 'I mean I've felt alone too. Even Sam doesn't really understand, but you do.'

'Well . . . we can be alone together,' she says.

'Deal, well – almost together, anyway.'

CHAPTER 33

Sophia

'So soon things might be changing,' I say to the kids, who are busy making May Day pictures out of wrapped-up tissue paper.

'I don't want them to,' says Alfie. 'I've got used to this now.'

'I think we all feel like that and that's normal, but all the kids at home are going to want to gradually start coming back to school. Businesses need to open and parents have to go back to work.'

'It's nicer without the other kids,' says Freya categorically, folding some purple paper with terrifying precision.

'I don't want things to change,' says Zane. 'I have a whole table to myself,' he sweeps his arm all over his desk for emphasis.

'Change can be a good thing. We might be scared of it, but sometimes it can be lovely and we don't want to be separated from our friends all the time do we? Now speaking of a positive change, who would like to see a photo of a little dog I am helping my neighbour Bertie to adopt?'

'Yes, yes please!'

I hold up a photo of Tilly, which I've printed out especially to show everyone. She's looking really regal with her long ears dangling down either side of her face, and she's sitting on a very nice tartan cushion.

'Oh she's so cute,' shrieks Lola.

As I'm driving home, I consider how quickly things are moving. Bertie's going to have a new friend and hopefully he won't be so lonely any more, and there are announcements on the news that by the 1st of June schools might start having children back a year at a time, the youngest first.

I'm so excited for Bertie about the dog, but apprehensive how everything's going to work out. The thought of the letter is loud in the back of my mind. I've given my stepdad the writing case for his friend to fix, having removed the letter for safekeeping and put it in my old jewellery box. But no matter how far down in my drawers it's carefully buried, its contents and the effect they're going to have on Bertie worry me, along with the decision I need to make at some point about my meds.

I've tried talking to Jess about it but like everything else: it's all totally simple in her mind.

'Well of course you'll stop taking them,' she says, rustling her bag of crisps at the other end of the line.

'Not necessarily.'

'But you've been saying to me they're making you feel awful.'

'Well yes they do, but the thing is, I don't want a seizure.'

'But you've had them before and you were fine.' She has the grace to adjust this a little. 'Well I know they're not nice things to have but maybe you won't have them now. Like the doctor said, sometimes the meds reset the brain signals and you won't ever have another seizure.'

'No one can guarantee that, though.'

'No one can guarantee anything, love. You could walk out of the house and get run over by a bus.'

'Not so likely at the moment,' I point out. 'There aren't any running. I've never known our road so quiet.'

'I just don't know, Soph, but I always thought your seizures were caused by stress and that you might just stop having them. I mean you had twenty-five years without them. Maybe they've gone.'

'But what if they haven't?'

'You'll deal with it,' she says confidently, 'like you deal with everything because you are an incredible person. I know it's tough but if you don't try coming off the meds, you'll never know.'

Back at home, I make a cup of tea and pop a couple of chocolate cakes and a picture of a rainbow Lola made for Jack in the basket, which he has just lowered down.

'Is this for me?' he asks sounding really surprised.

'Yes of course. It's for your window.'

'But Lola doesn't know me.'

'No but she knows about you – they all do. I told them how you're having to stay in all the time and she felt sorry, so made you a tissue rainbow.'

'It's very vibrant. I've just stuck it on my window. I think I might have scattered your balcony with falling bits of tissue paper though.' He pauses. 'I feel embarrassed you've been talking to the kids at school about me.'

'You don't need to be,' I reassure him, wondering if I talk too much about Jack when he's someone I've never even met. 'You're quite a celebrity. Well – you and Tilly the dog.'

'So that went well?'

'Yes, she's so sweet and super friendly, jumped all over my legs and washed my face whenever she could get near enough.'

'Bertie will love her; she sounds perfect.'

'Perfect as long as she has someone with her. I think she's got some antisocial behaviours if she's left on her own for any length of time.'

'Bertie won't leave her much at all,' Jack answers. 'I can imagine he'll take her everywhere.'

'Yes and there's a difference between him needing to pop out to the shop for a second and going to work for hours. She'll soon get used to the idea he's coming back soon if he just leaves her for a short amount of time.'

'When are you taking her to Bertie?'

'Next weekend. Jan is working most of this week and wants to be there to say goodbye.'

'I can understand that. It must be heartbreaking.'

'She's totally devastated as she loves Tilly, but she knows it's the right thing. I felt terrible because she started crying today but all I could do was reassure her that she's going to a wonderful home and Bertie will send her updates.'

'He will. He's a good bloke. I wish I could meet Tilly. I'd love a dog. Mum and Dad always wanted one but couldn't since Sam and I were born, because they were too busy working.'

'I know, same with us. One day it would be great to have one.'

'What breed would you choose?' Jack asks me.

'I don't know, I'm not too fussed. I love Benson but Tilly is gorgeous too. I think I'd rescue definitely. How about you?'

'I love big dogs, who you can have a good old walk and game of ball with, but I like all dogs.' Jack sighs. 'Right now, the thought of a walk is the most exciting thing ever.' I can imagine. He's been in for over six weeks now.

'I wish you could come with me. I took Benson to meet Greg's college kids yesterday.'

'How did it go? I bet they loved it.'

'It was incredible,' I tell him. 'Benson is usually the biggest loon ever, jumping and bounding all over the place. I have a job to keep hold of him on a walk usually. But with these kids, he seemed to be on his best behaviour. He went up to Lally, the student Greg was telling

353

us about. She's been stuck in lockdown away from her parents for more than six weeks now and he just wagged his tail, gave her one of his ridiculously huge paws and leaned against her with his head on her knee.'

'I think dogs sense, don't they, whether someone's scared or lonely?' Jack observes.

'Yes, having seen this, I truly believe they do. Lally would hardly come out of the residential college at first. She just shrank back into the doorway when I approached, but once I let Benson off such a short lead, she squatted down with him and started telling me how she has a dog at home, who she really misses. She was chatting away.'

'Animals are a good leveller, aren't they? They don't care if you're different for whatever reason; they like you anyway.'

'Shame people aren't a bit more like that.'

'Maybe some of them are,' says Jack.

CHAPTER 34

Jack

For the first time in ages, I hear the rattle of the front letterbox and I wander blearily towards it, armed with the obligatory disposable gloves, whilst tripping over my dressing gown belt. I must get myself a new one; this old thing got trapped in the door near the beginning of lockdown and has disintegrated and unravelled into nothing more than a long threaded piece of string.

There are a couple of bits of post; one uninspiring-looking envelope, obviously from the bank – it has that kind of bleak, formal look about it. The other one I pick up immediately as it has printed at the top right: *Chiropractic College*. I stare at it, willing it to have good news inside. Or it could just be some course information, nothing more.

The call had gone well the other day – I think it had, anyway. It's always so hard to judge with interviews. I had somehow managed to get myself into a shirt and tie – I was worried the shirt wouldn't fit after the combination of my sedentary lockdown lifestyle and the delicious treats Sophia sends up. It was a little snug, but the tie covered the straining buttons I think. I have now started to do Joe Wicks' YouTube workout every day in a desperate attempt to keep myself vaguely fit. That and a strange kickboxing video I found, which is kind of weird but works and is great for stress relief.

It's strange to think I didn't even know what Zoom was a few months ago, yet now I'm getting quite good at it. Calls to Sam and his little family as well as Mum and Dad have become a regular occurrence. I had even arranged an Easter Day Zoom call with the whole family, which was dominated totally by little Carrie of course, with Mum and her Blue Toothpaste episode threatening to overshadow the whole proceedings.

'The picture is flickering,' she had complained, tapping the screen as though somehow this would help.

'It's probably a bad connection,' Sam had said. He and Tina and Carrie were all looking the picture-perfect family on their screen. Carrie's gorgeous beaming smile could now hold the attention of the whole room. It was a smile that would melt even the strictest non-baby-admiring fraternity.

'Dad says it's something to do with Blue Toothpaste,' she announced. 'They keep sending me information on it and saying I can get a better deal if I go with Blue Toothpaste.'

I could see out the corner of my eye that Sam, Tina,

and even Carrie looked confused. We couldn't work out what Mum was talking about. She just wasn't making any sense.

'Blue Toothpaste?' exclaimed Sam scratching his head. 'Oh you mean Bluetooth?'

We had all snorted and laughed hysterically and even Mum had looked amused. They should really give her a job to check out technology for user friendliness – if my mum can work it anyone can. I'm sure she would be invaluable working for a technology giant somewhere.

I eye the envelope now and quickly tear it open before I can change my mind.

Dear Mr. Stanton,

We are delighted to inform you that after your Zoom interview on 29th April, we are offering you a place to study Sports Science starting on 7th September 2020.

Please find enclosed your acceptance form, which we would be grateful if you could sign and return by 1st June. We have also attached an information booklet on reading for the course and other important details. Congratulations and please do not hesitate to contact me if you have any other questions.

Yours sincerely,

Diane Reeves

I've done it! I fist-punch the air and do a ridiculous little dance that I'm glad no one is here to see. That's one of the few good things about shielding; no one is around to witness my strange dancing, my dodgy trackie bottom and Donald Duck T-shirt combination (I know, I should have got rid of that old T-shirt years ago). I feel a glimmer of hope in spite of everything. Soon I can get on with the rest of my life.

My phone sings out and I snatch it up immediately, hoping it's Sam or Sophia or even Mum and Dad. I have to tell someone the news. But it isn't, it's Laura.

'Oh hi,' I say feeling a wave of disappointment. I really don't want my good mood quashed. Come on, life; just give me a chance to feel more upbeat for a moment.

'Have I phoned at a bad time?' she asks, obviously sensing my mood.

'No, it's fine,' I reply, squashing down my feelings with an effort. 'How are you?'

'Fine thanks – look, I won't keep you.' She sounds unusually businesslike.

I'm sort of stunned because I'm mostly used to her trying to persuade me to have her back, or moaning about the fact that I haven't returned her calls. 'Okay,' is all I can manage.

'I've decided to sign the divorce papers.'

I'm flabbergasted. I thought this was never going to happen. 'Do you . . .' I clear my throat nervously, hoping I've heard and understood her correctly. 'Do you really mean it?'

'Yes. I've signed them and I'll stick them in the post box this afternoon.'

'Really?'

'Yes really.' Laura laughs wryly. 'You don't have to

358

be that surprised. I know I've been a bit of a bitch about it all, but I've thought a lot about it since we last spoke and you're right. We're just not right for each other. I was hoping you might turn back into the fun-loving, wacky guy I fell in love with in Crete and you've made me realise it's never gonna happen.'

Alleluia, she finally understands. 'No, I'm pretty boring really,' I say, more than happy to admit to this short-coming if it means Laura and I can get on with our separate lives. 'Although,' I add, because I'm just so excited about it, 'I've just been accepted to study at the Chiropractic College. Start later this year.'

'That's . . . er, great? If that's what you want. It is, isn't it?' she asks uncertainly.

'Yeah,' I tell her, smiling because Laura has definitely forgotten this ambition of mine, 'it's what I planned before – well before I got in a terrible stress and went off the rails, really.'

'I'm pleased for you, Jack. I really am. And guess what? As soon as this lockdown is over, Kimi and I are going travelling.' Kimi is one of the many friends Laura made in Agios Nikolaos.

'That's amazing. Where will you go?' I ask, genuinely interested.

'Thought we'd start in Ghana and move on round the coast. If travel restrictions allow. If not, we'll go wherever we are able to. The tents are packed and ready and my kit's all stocked up. As soon as this mess is over, I'm out of here.'

'Good for you. You'll have an amazing time – make sure you make the most of every minute.'

'I will.'

'And, Laura?' I add.

'Yeah?'

'Thanks.'

'It's okay,' she says. 'I'm doing it for me too. Stay safe.'

'And you . . .' I start, but she's gone. Just like that, it's over. She's out of my life and I feel . . . relief, mainly, and a hint of sadness at what we did to each other, what a waste it was. But this is the right thing; I could hear the passion in her voice when she talked of travelling.

And my passion? It's here with my family and a young woman who lives downstairs who I've never met, but I have fallen head over heels in love with nevertheless. I have to tell her, to plan the most amazing virtual date. For the first time in months I feel elated, on top of the world.

Speaking of which, I can hear Sophia on the phone, or maybe talking to Erica, and she sounds pretty excited. I wander out onto the balcony, ready to talk to her when she hangs up, but . . . 'Ryan,' I hear her say, along with something else I can't catch. Shocked, the wind well and truly taken out of my sails, I sink down onto the lounger on my balcony. Maybe I've misheard.

'I'm glad you're okay,' she's saying. 'Yes, it's been a difficult time for everyone. I've been busy working though and yeah Jess is fine. She had a lockdown wedding. Yes,

I'll say hi to her for you when we next speak. How's your mum?'

I can't believe what I'm hearing. Why are they back in touch? And surely this conversation should sound more awkward if they truly haven't spoken since the break-up? She's probably just being polite, though. Sophia is like a friendly puppy with everyone she meets – that's why we all love her. And when I think about it, I can hear a hint of reserve in her voice. She's *not* comfortable during this conversation, of course she's not, and I have to admit that I wouldn't want anyone listening to my phone calls with Laura, or drawing any conclusions from them. Half the time I don't know what I'm saying. I stand up to move back inside. I'm eavesdropping for goodness' sake.

'You told me it was over. What was I supposed to think?' she's saying in an urgent undertone. 'You couldn't even bring yourself to mention the word epilepsy. The seizures are under control at the moment but I'm still the same person . . .'

There's a pause and I can imagine he's trying to persuade her at the other end of the phone. 'I know, this lockdown has made us all reconsider things; it's given us time to think.' There's another silence. 'Of course I missed some of the things we had together. Yes it would be good to see you when lockdown's over. It's been so . . .'

This is too much for me. I don't want to hear what she's about to say. I rush back inside my flat, shutting the balcony doors with a bang on the outside world, firmly closing them on any hopes I may have had that Sophia considers me as anything more than some random guy in the flat upstairs, whom she feels sorry for because he can't go out.

CHAPTER 35

Sophia

I press the red button on my phone and throw myself down on the sofa. On second thoughts, I switch it off totally in a useless gesture, as though it's going to shut Ryan out. Why does he have to do this now? If he'd phoned a few months ago, I would have been so happy, overjoyed to go back to where we were. The wedding, everything could have been back on. But now? I just don't know. Ironically, although lockdown has given Ryan 'time to reconsider how he feels' as he puts it, it has given me time too. I'm not sure what to think. Things are so different now. I don't think I'm even the same person.

'I've realised I just can't be without you, Soph,' Ryan told me, after the preliminary pleasantries about how I am and how he is and how terrible the whole pandemic thing is. I hadn't known what to say. 'I won't go as far as saying I get why you changed your job,' he had explained, 'but I'm happy to go with it. As long as you don't give me lines for not finishing my homework on time.'

I know he was joking, but somehow there's a sting in the tail of his sentence and I can't help but feel resentful about his choice of words. I don't know why, but just speaking to him has opened up the same old nagging wounds and yet, paradoxically, it was good to hear his voice. You simply can't be with someone for five years and not feel anything for them. It would be great if you could just switch it all off and forget everything with copious amounts of chocolate and large doses of vodka but their effects are only a transient numbing.

Still, I decide nevertheless to drag myself off the sofa and grab a bar of chocolate. I take a bite and contemplate phoning Jess, but immediately dismiss the idea. She will just go crazy with excitement and have both of us married off by Christmas. She adores Ryan and seems totally impervious to his imperfections. She just doesn't understand that I was never able to discuss my meds or their side effects with Ryan; to him they were an inconvenience, an irritation. Yet Jack seemed to understand well before I'd even started trying to explain.

'How's Ryan supposed to understand what it's like to have epilepsy?' she had said when we first split. 'I know he's been insensitive, but it's a big shock to those around you.'

'But, Jess, you've been able to accept how it's changed me. Mum has too, albeit with a bit of a discussion around things,' I had protested.

'Oh come on, Soph, Mum went nuts initially; you know she did.'

'Yeah okay, she did,' I had admitted reluctantly. 'But I can understand that. To be fair she'd helped fund law school, so it's hardly surprising it was a shock that I suddenly wanted to throw it all away and train to be a teacher.'

'Bottom line is, she's your mum and she pretty much forgives you anything. It's a mum thing. Totally different with guys – look how Zach didn't get it that time I wanted to go to Spain rather than the trip he planned to Holland.'

'That's hardly the same thing,' I point out wearily.

'Yeah but they just don't get it at first.'

'I'm sure some do,' I had said.

'Not many,' she'd replied.

Jack does, my heart points out now. *But you don't even really know him, you've never met,* the voice of reason chimes in. *I know he's nice,* my heart insists, *you can just tell these things.* Reason gives voice to my worst fear, the one I've been burying for weeks now: *What if it's just that part of him you've seen? You don't know the whole Jack. If you actually met him, you might find that this whole relationship doesn't even exist. It's all in your head.* Besides, the reasonable voice continues, *the guy's still married, he's made mistakes before and he probably doesn't feel the same way about you, even if he thinks he might. Look at what happened with Laura. And worse, look at Elsie and Bertie – she kept a huge secret from him and they'd been married for sixty years. Maybe he didn't know her at all.*

The doubts rumble on, feeding into my insecurities and loss of trust. How do I know if whatever I have with Jack is real? I haven't even met him. Our relationship could be like a holiday romance, intense and wonderful at the time, but fizzles out under the glare of reality.

It's no good, I can't think about it any more now. Ryan's going to have to wait. I have to collect Tilly to take her to Bertie's, and Jack and I still haven't decided what we're going to do about the letter. It sits in my wardrobe drawer, waves of guilt crashing over my head every time I inadvertently think about it. I've spoken to Chris, my stepdad's friend who says the box is a wonderful item and it will be a pleasure to restore it. It will take at least a week's work, but I know that Bertie will be so pleased to have it back to its old self, so Jack and I are clubbing together to pay and Chris will do it for slightly reduced mate's rates.

Just as I'm leaving the house, my mum phones. 'Hi, sorry, Mum, I'm just off to pick up a dog,' I answer. 'I'll put you on hands-free.'

'Why a dog?' asks my mum, confused.

'Not for me, for my neighbour Bertie. He's lonely and one of Erica's friends can't look after hers so . . .'

'Sounds like a win-win situation then.'

'Pretty much. Speaking of which,' I add, 'I need your advice.'

'Fire away.'

'If you found out a secret about someone in a letter, but you thought the truth of it might hurt them, would you keep the letter from them, or would you give it to them regardless?'

'Give it to them regardless,' says Mum, without missing a beat. 'Just a minute; my bleep's going . . . Okay don't worry, it's nothing urgent. I'll phone them in a second. This isn't something about me, is it?' she asks with sudden concern.

'No.' I laugh. 'No, I'd just tell you if it were. It's Bertie. I found a letter from his wife, who sadly died last year. I inadvertently saw something in it that he needs to know.'

'Then you must tell him,' she says decisively.

'Yeah I know. I just felt bad about it as he's on his own and I was worried about the shock, then this dog came up and you know . . .'

'No, you just need to tell him. Give him the dog as well by all means, but it's important you let him know. People are stronger than you think. He'll be fine as long as you all support him.'

'Thanks, Mum. I know I should have done it straight away,' I say guiltily. 'I'm just in such a mess with everything. I thought I was doing really well and now it feels like it's all falling apart.' I try to stifle a sob. This is ridiculous. How old am I to be crying on the phone to my mum? Somehow everything's built up and I haven't wanted to worry Jess with it.

'Well, you do tend to take a lot on all at once,' Mum comforts me. 'I can't think who you take after!'

'I know, I like to be busy.' I sniff. 'It's just . . . Ryan's got back in touch and it's thrown me totally.'

She pauses. 'I'm not surprised that's thrown you, love.' Her voice becomes muffled as she turns to someone in her office. 'Just a minute, I'm going to field this call.'

'Do you need to go? I don't want to stop you working?'

'No, I'm on a break. I was told to get some fresh air. It's been a full-on morning.'

'I'm sorry, and here I am offloading my worries on you.'

'Don't be silly, that's what mums are for. So, Ryan's come crawling back has he?'

'Something like that.' I take a bite of chocolate, hoping it will make me feel better. It doesn't actually; now I just feel slightly sick, as I've eaten it too fast.

'What did he say?'

'Oh just that he'd made a mistake, and can we start again?'

She's quiet for a moment, then she asks, 'Do you want to? He's such a nice, steady chap.'

'I just don't know – that's the problem. I'm confused. This could be my opportunity to get my life back on track. Now I love my career and Ryan and I could give it another go.' I pause for a second. 'But then there's Jack.' I can't even bring myself to suggest to my mum that I'm considering gambling my entire love life on a stranger.

'The lad you've been looking after upstairs? But you've

never met him, Soph. That's not really a relationship is it? You don't even know him.'

I sigh. 'I know I don't. But somehow it feels as though I do.'

'Bit different when you were with Ryan for five years though – you've got a whole lot of history. What does Jess say?'

'I haven't told her. You know what she's like!' I exclaim.

'Yes, to be fair she does get a bit . . . enthusiastic, but it's only because she cares,' Mum acknowledges. 'She's always so thoughtful and quite brilliant with Uncle Jim. She's been dropping supplies to his front door every week, except during her honeymoon when I did it.'

'I didn't know – that's so good of her,' I admit. Then I smile. 'I hope the neighbour didn't run off with it again.'

'No, that seems to have settled down, although there's a new hoo-ha now,' Mum says, forgetting that we were talking about Ryan and me. 'Apparently he's been watering the flowers on his balcony so exuberantly it's been raining down on the woman below!'

There's a beeping noise in the background. 'Sorry, love,' she tells me, 'I really do have to go. Anyway look after yourself. Cheer up and just let things lie for now with Ryan. Time will tell and after all if you still really love him, you'll know it's the right thing for you to get back together.'

'Thanks, Mum. I'll let it simmer for a while.'

* * *

I ponder my mum's words as I drive to collect Tilly. She's right; I don't need to make a decision about anything for a moment. I'll just park it all – Ryan, Jack, epilepsy meds. It can all wait.

Picking up Tilly from Jan is every bit as traumatic as I thought it would be. We try to keep it as business-like as possible so as not to prolong the agony and I give her Bertie's details so they can stay in touch and she can hear how Tilly has settled in. Tilly is full of beans and as her owner wipes away a tear at the front door, Tilly thinks it's all an adventure and leaps into my car enthusiastically.

It's only a short drive home before I arrive in the little parking lot, call Tilly out and take her rather touchingly stashed pink bag of goodies and belongings Jan has packed for her. We walk the few minutes round to Bertie's little terraced place, with its garden chock full of holly-hocks and delphiniums.

Mavis is walking along the other side of the pavement. 'Oh my goodness,' she calls, 'what a dear little dog! Is this the new inmate for Bertie?'

'Yes,' I reply. 'Little Tilly is going to keep him company.'

'She's perfect.' She smiles. 'I won't stop you. I can see Tilly's on a mission, but I'll come by Bertie's tomorrow on my way to the shop and see if he wants anything.'

'Thanks, Mavis, you've been a star checking in on him every time you go out.'

'It's a pleasure. I'm fond of him and to be honest, it's

nice to have a quick catch-up; otherwise days can go by in this lockdown and you don't ever see a soul. Speaking of which . . .' She gets a beady look in her eye that almost reminds me of Marge. 'How's things with you and Jack?'

'He's good thanks,' I say, deliberately misunderstanding her. 'I've got pretty used to him being upstairs. I can't really remember what it was like without him.'

'Yes it's strange how that can happen and often when you least expect it.' She gives me a funny little wink and wanders off towards the small parade of shops at the end of the street.

Tilly seems to have some kind of sixth sense and drags me to Bertie's gate. His front garden earns her approval as she sniffs round the small mossy patch of lawn. The door opens and Bertie squats down on the doorstep with some difficulty, his arms stretched wide. I grab my phone from my pocket and get ready to film, before shutting the gate behind me and letting Tilly's lead go. As I press play, she runs forward to Bertie, her tail so full of wags, it's become a blur and she leaps with both her front paws on his chest and covers his face with kisses.

He laughs, and putting his arms round her he slowly topples backwards so that he's sprawling on the pathway, still chuckling, which Tilly seems to take as a signal to jump on his face.

'What a lovely dog she is then,' he says, once he can recover himself. 'Yes, yes plenty of fuss – that's what you like isn't it? Don't like being on your own do you? Don't blame you. Well you'll have plenty of love and cuddles in this house, my love.'

Tilly seems to understand every word he says, wagging her brown and white tail in big swirls, effectively sweeping the path with its movement. I take some more pictures of both of them, as Bertie leads Tilly round the front little patch of garden, talking to her all the time and introducing her to everything. It doesn't matter what he's saying; Tilly obviously just thinks he is great.

I give them a few moments whilst I lean on the wall and send the videos and pictures to Jack. *Look at this – pretty successful don't you think? x*

Within minutes, he's replied, *Brilliant! Brought a tear to my eye x*

Me too, speak later? x

Looking forward to it. Maybe a drink and some nibbles as well? x

Perfect, on the balcony at 7 p.m.? x

Done, looking forward to it already x

I look up at Bertie and Tilly, a smile on my face. There's something about Jack that just makes me feel like that, in spite of all the issues I've had going on – my meds, Ryan, Jess – I'm more settled somehow, as though I can take on the world and things will still be okay. He's such an upbeat kind of guy.

'I don't know how to thank you, Sophia,' says Bertie. 'I'd give you a hug if I could. Just know this: you have done more than you'll ever know.'

I look at his weathered face, with his laughter lines

and sparse grey hair and I am assailed by guilt over the secret I'm keeping. 'It was no trouble,' I tell him. 'I've loved every minute of it.' I bend to stroke Tilly's head. She's scratching at my leg, tail a-wag all the time. 'I'd better leave you two to get acquainted with each other.' I need to leave before I blurt something out. It's not the right moment.

Bertie strokes the dog, who has come and sat down by his side, as though she knows who she belongs to. 'Before you go, Sophia, I just wondered . . .'

I pause, my hand on the gate. 'Anything you need?'

'No it's just, I had the strangest thing happen today,' he tells me, hesitating. 'I had an email from someone.'

'Not one of those scammers?' I ask, feeling immediately protective.

'No, at least I don't think so, it was from a Flora Bird.'

I look at him questioningly.

'She says she's Elsie's daughter.'

CHAPTER 36

Jack

I sit and watch the video of Bertie and Tilly for the umpteenth time. I can hear Sophia in the background of one of them and I play it again a couple of times, just enjoying the sound of her voice. This is really sad; I'm totally obsessed with a girl I've never met. But then, perhaps like someone who is missing their vision, my other senses have become sharpened. I can tell that Sophia is the one. I can't be wrong – I know somewhere inside that we connect on a deeper level, something I didn't think I'd ever say.

My phone starts buzzing – Sam is calling, requesting FaceTime. 'Hey how's it going?' he asks.

'Good thanks. I'm just sitting here watching a clip of Bertie and his new dog.'

'Did Sophia manage to sort it then? Is there nothing this girl can't do?'

'Obviously not,' I say, feeling somehow proud. 'She is pretty amazing. How're Carrie and Tina?'

'We took Carrie out in the buggy again today for our daily exercise, though the city parks were pretty full so it was hard to distance and Tina got a bit anxious. We just made sure we walked round people. Carrie loved it; she had a huge beam on her face. I think she's going to be an animal lover. She's fascinated by the ducks on the pond; the birds in the garden and anything that moves really. She's such a bright little thing.'

'Takes after her Uncle Jack then.' I feel a little sad, disappointed that she's already developing into a little person and I haven't even met her yet.

'So, how's Sophia?'

'I don't know. I think I heard her on the phone to her ex last night. He wants her back.' Even the words make my heart sink further; somehow saying them makes it all feel more real.

'Has she told you that?'

'No,' I admit.

'Then how do you know? You're just guessing, and you don't even know what she thinks about the whole thing. Why don't you ask her?'

'I can't do that,' I protest. 'Then she'd know I've been ear-wigging.'

'Well . . . you kind of have been.'

'True, though I didn't mean to. No, I've got a better idea than that,' I say.

'Always have a plan,' Sam approves.

'I'm going to tell her how I feel.'

'That's original,' Sam says, sounding genuinely surprised. 'How *do* you feel?'

'I don't know exactly.'

He laughs. 'Great start.'

'Yeah right, thanks a lot. But I know I care a lot for her and I can't imagine being without her.'

'Sounds a bit needy?'

My confidence feels shaken. This is already so far outside my comfort zone. 'Okay that wouldn't be good. Do you think I should change how I put it? I don't want to sound desperate. I'm worried she just thinks I'm the sad guy who lives upstairs who she feels sorry for. Of course she'll want to go back to this successful ex who she was going to marry.'

'Well you're going the right way about showing her that,' Sam points out.

'I don't want to. I just don't think he's the right man for her – he dumped her when she got sick and changed her job because he simply couldn't deal with it. What sort of person does that?'

'Hmm yeah sounds like an idiot . . . but some women like bad men,' he says with a shrug. 'I've heard it's a thing.'

There's a noise in the background and I can hear Tina talking. 'She says "what do I know about women"?' he repeats with a snort.

'Tell Tina I agree; you are the last person to get women, Sam.'

'I'm not talking to either of you if you're going to

gang up on me. Anyway I'm married so it's obviously worked,' he says.

'Okay back to my thing. I'll just tell her I love her.'

Sam looks stunned. 'You actually love her? How do you know? You've never met this girl. I mean *truly* love her, not just think you do or the idea of her?'

I try not to let the doubts creep in. This is Sophia we're talking about – if anything, I know her better because all I've done is listen to her, and share my deepest worries with her. 'I do. Even if she still likes this Ryan guy, I'll wait. I'll do anything, I just want to carry on talking to her in the evenings, hear her laugh, her stories about the kids at school. I feel I know them, that I know her. I've even shouted hello to her mum on the phone. God, I feel I know her better than Laura, even though I was married to her for over a year.'

There's a pause as Sam digests this information. 'Do you know, Jack, if you really feel like that, good on you. But you're gonna have to tell her. Are you just going to shout down from your balcony?'

'I've got a plan,' I reply.

'Come on, out with it then.'

'Nope,' I tell him, 'you're just going to have to wait and see.'

'Oh man, you're rotten.'

'That way, if it fails you don't need to know, and if it succeeds I'll tell you.'

A text announces itself on my screen. 'Gotta go, Sam, I've had an urgent message from Soph.'

'Bye then, good luck – hope she gives you a chance. Write a poem – she'll love that.'

'Thanks, relationship guru.' I cut him off and finish reading Sophia's message.

Can I talk to you on the balcony when you're free? It's about Bertie – he's found out about Elsie's daughter x

No? That's bizarre, how? x

Long story, I'll tell you on the balcony in ten x

I'll prepare a couple of stiff drinks. Fancy a whisky chaser? x

Perfect x

Fifteen minutes later, I'm on my balcony sipping a whisky and leaning slightly over the parapet so I don't have to shout.

'How's the drink?' I ask.

'Spot on – just what I needed,' Sophia replies.

'So what happened?'

'That's the thing, I'm not at all sure. I was just leaving Bertie to get to know Tilly, obviously I sent you the videos.'

'Yeah,' I say, smiling. 'I'm happy for him.'

'I know, it was like it was meant to be or something. But then just as I was going, he came out with it. That he's had this email from a girl, Flora Bird, who says she's Elsie's daughter.'

I'm puzzled. 'But how did that happen, when we didn't give him the letter?'

'Apparently he just got this email from her. She was going to write to him, a proper letter, but was worried it wouldn't get to him because of the lockdown. So she sent him an email. Apparently Flora received a letter in the post a couple of months ago, from Elsie.'

'But that's not possible,' I say. 'How can she have been sent a letter from Elsie when she's been dead for over a year?'

'That's what none of us can understand.'

'Strange.' I shiver in spite of the warmth of the whisky. The thought is slightly creepy. 'So is Bertie okay? How has he taken the news?'

'He seems okay considering. I mean he's bemused and was wondering if it was some kind of scam, but what she knew about Elsie added up, and she sent him a screenshot of the letter that was written in Elsie's handwriting.'

'So he believes it's really her. What did she say to him? Is she nice?'

'He said it's a really lovely, friendly message; obviously it's been a shock for her as well, because she had no idea. Apparently Elsie originally decided it was best to just leave things as they were, but when she knew she was sick, she felt she had to try to find Flora.'

'Strange, you'd have thought she'd have done that before.'

'Yes you would. I can't imagine how awful it must have been to give up a child.'

'Things were different then though weren't they?' I ask. 'Maybe she had to, maybe her family didn't approve.'

'That's what Flora wrote in her email. She believed

until fairly recently her adopted parents were her real mum and dad.'

'Phew that's heavy,' I say. 'So what's Bertie going to do?'

'Well, Flora lives in France with her French husband, but she wants to set up a Zoom call to speak to him.'

'Is he going to?'

'Apparently he's up for it.'

'But before that we need to give him the letter. Have you told him about it?'

'Yes, I did. I felt terrible that we've kept this a secret. I said we'd only just found it and hadn't wanted to upset him. He seemed to understand but obviously I felt awkward about the whole thing.'

'Yeah it is pretty bad, but we did only just find the letter and we were going to tell him; we were just waiting for the right time. So have you given it to him?'

'No not yet, but I wanted to surprise him with the box and I thought I'd put the letter in, so he could read it himself as it was meant to be seen.'

'You think Elsie wanted him to read it then?'

'I do, otherwise she would never have written it.'

'But she never gave it to him,' he points out, 'although someone sent Flora a letter and it can't have been Elsie.'

'Yes.' Her voice sounds a bit anxious. 'Even though it was in Elsie's handwriting, she can't have sent it. It can't have taken that long in the post. I think I'll have another whisky.'

This seems a good idea and I pour another measure.

Just as I thought things couldn't get any more confusing, they have, and it's not just with Bertie's dilemma. Sophia hasn't mentioned Ryan once since her conversation with him the other day and neither have I, but his presence hovers in the air, as unfathomable and unspoken between us as the puzzle over who sent Elsie's letter.

CHAPTER 37

Sophia

'What about this one? Don't you think it's a brilliant one of Mum and Mark?' enthuses Jess. We're on a Zoom call, looking through pictures of her wedding.

'Yes, they look so happy. I can't believe how many great images you've got,' I say.

'I know. That's the good thing about it all being online – there's plenty of opportunity for photos to save.'

'Your dress was beautiful,' I say.

'Be your turn next,' says Jess matter-of-factly. 'You caught the bouquet, so there's no escaping it.'

'You sent the bouquet. Who else could have caught it? And anyway who believes in that stuff?'

'I do, actually,' she sniffs, 'and I happen to know a certain someone might be missing you and hoping you feel the same way too.'

'I can't imagine who you mean. Uncle Jim looks smart in this one doesn't he?'

'Don't change the subject, Soph.' Man, Jess can be persistent when she gets going.

'If you mean Ryan, I know. He phoned the other night,' I say.

'Oh that's wonderful, Soph, I'm so happy for you,' she gushes. 'He messaged me the other day and said he just can't live without you. Isn't that the most romantic thing you ever heard?'

'It would have been if he had said that a year ago,' I say.

'Well I know,' Jess says, brushing this off, 'but maybe he needed this lockdown to really think about how he feels. Perhaps it's done us all good to have time at home, to work stuff out.'

'Whatever his reasons, I'm confused, Jess. I just don't know whether I want to give him another chance.'

'It's not exactly starting again is it? You've been together for years. It will be like riding a bike,' she says confidently.

'Even though you remember how to pedal, you can still fall off,' I point out.

'That's a bit cynical for you, Sophia.'

'Maybe I'm having to toughen up.' I shrug. 'We've been apart now for quite a while. It's been hard.' My voice catches, annoyingly.

'I know, Soph,' she says, softening, 'and you've done amazingly. I don't know anyone else who would cope with what you have, and look at you. You've totally changed careers, the kids love you, you've kept going, you've helped me with the wedding, been helping everyone out during this lockdown. But maybe it's time for you to think of you and no one else. This is your life. You deserve to be happy.'

'I know and I think I've come to a decision.'

'That's wonderful! So have you told Ryan?'

'No, not yet. He said he'd give me some time to think about everything.'

'Phone him now,' she encourages. 'We can finish the pics another time. I thought I'd do a slideshow of some of them. Also, I was thinking . . .'

'Yeah?'

'I don't know what you think, but I was planning a wedding do after lockdown.'

'What? Another wedding?' I'm filled with horror.

'No not another *wedding*; just a post wedding, wedding celebration.'

'Jess,' I shriek.

'What?' she asks innocently.

'You really are something else!'

Once I've finally finished the Zoom call with Jess I wander bemusedly out onto the balcony. 'Jack?' I call as I can feel he might be up there. It's a beautiful day and he often sits on the balcony in the middle of the day and when I'm not working we sit and chat over lunch.

'Hey, Sophia,' he answers. 'How's it going?'

'It's going!' I groan. 'You're never going to guess what?'

'What?'

'Jess is planning another wedding celebration for after lockdown.'

'Just one more?' Jack teases.

'I'm not sure I can cope.'

'What does Zach say?'

'I expect he'll try to talk her out of it . . . and then give in gracefully!'

'He sounds a wise man.'

'Yeah right!' I laugh. 'Anyway, I do have some good news. Elsie's writing box is ready so I'm picking it up on my way back from the shopping trip this afternoon and I've arranged to take it round to Bertie, with the letter back where it should be.'

'That's great. Does it look good?'

'Chris says he's pretty pleased with it. I can't wait to see Bertie's face, although I'm not sure how to best support him with the letter. He's still not sure whether to call Flora or not.'

'No.' Jack pauses for a moment. 'How about I text Mavis to come along?'

'Mavis?' I ask. 'Why?'

'I don't know, I just feel as though she could be someone to have around as he opens it.'

'I was thinking of being there.'

'Oh – what time will you be back?' He sounds disappointed.

'I don't know,' I say, 'probably by eight. Why?'

'I've got something I wanted to talk to you about this evening.'

'Sounds serious.'

'No, well at least I hope it's a good thing. Say about 9 p.m.?'

'Okay, that's fine. We normally chat then anyway.'

'I know, I was just checking you were available.'

'Oh. I'm feeling nervous now,' I say, trying to laugh it off.

'You don't need to be.'

'I'll take your word for it.'

''Til later then,' Jack says.

'Okay . . . bye.'

'Bye.'

There's a pause.

'Are you still there?' he asks.

'Yes are you?' I answer.

'Yes.'

'Okay I'm going now then.'

'Me too.' I listen and can tell he's listening too.

'Okay, let's go in at the same time,' I tell him, laughing at the absurdity of it.

'On the count of three.'

'Okay, one, two . . .'

'Three . . .' he says, and I hear him pull the door shut upstairs at the same time as me. I smile and wander into the flat. What on earth is he up to this time?

I don't have much time to think on it any more as I have to go and pick up Elsie's case on the way back from the weekly shop so I don't break any rules by going out on an unnecessary trip. The supermarket is a complete nightmare as I was obediently following the one-way system, as always, then realised I had forgotten something on the shelf a few metres back. With a woman and her trolley right behind me I had no choice but to go all round the shop again and by that time, I'd forgotten what it was I was trying to buy.

Finally after this shopping ordeal (when did it ever get so complicated?), I manage to get to Chris's house – thank goodness he's all ready for me, bringing the case out and placing it on the seat outside his house and stepping back for me to look at it. It's tiny and he's quite a big guy, but he must be delicate with his movements as he handles the case as though it's made of glass.

'Wow,' I say staring at it disbelievingly. 'It's beautiful.'

It is; he's polished it until the walnut is shining like glass. It looks as though it has just been newly crafted rather than restored to its former glory. Gingerly, with bated breath, I lift the lid and inside the small sections are revealed, all fitted neatly back together.

'That compartment at the back is most unusual. Has a secret door.' I step back as he carefully presses on the bottom of the case and the panel slides back. 'It's not unheard of for these nineteenth-century cases to have a hidden compartment in them. Shame there wasn't something in there.'

'Maybe there was,' I say with a smile.

* * *

Bertie is waiting out the front of his house as I arrive at 7 p.m. as planned. Tilly appears at his feet, her tail wagging like a banner. She is totally at home here already, and she gives me an ecstatic welcome. By the front gate, Mavis is perching at an acceptable distance, on the wall. Jack is obviously really efficient when he gets going. I smile at her. 'Hello, Mavis, did Tilly give you a welcome?'

'Yes she's a darling,' she says, 'gave me a paw very politely.'

Bertie looks at the carefully wrapped package in my arms. 'Is it mended?' he asks eyeing it impatiently.

'Yes it is,' I say, 'and I think Chris has done an incredible job.' Delicately I unwrap the case and place it gently down on a small table Bertie has put out ready. 'What do you think?'

Bertie stands and stares at the writing case for a moment. 'My gosh, Sophia, it's as though you've turned back the clock.' He walks forward and reverently touches the shiny wood, feeling with his roughened fingers along the new but carefully matched hinges. He opens it and peers with pleasure at the fixed compartments ready for letters and envelopes. 'I shall put them back in there,' he says. 'It will be a pleasure to restock the letters and stamps, just as it was when Elsie was using it.' He looks at me with shining eyes. 'She would be as pleased as punch to see this restored to its old beauty.'

'She'll be looking down,' says Mavis with certainty.

'That she will,' he agrees. 'Now . . .' He brushes away a couple of stray tears that have trickled down his wind-roughened cheeks. 'Show me where this little hidey hole is then, love.'

I wait for him to step back a couple of metres, then press on the small panel at the base of the case and obediently the panel slips back to reveal Elsie's letter just as it was when I had discovered it.

Bertie puts out a shaking hand and slides out the letter, gazes at it for a second and then opens it up, the sight of the familiar handwriting bringing more tears to his eyes. 'It's as though she's just finished writing it,' he says.

'You go in, love, and read it. We'll wait,' says Mavis kindly.

As though in a dream Bertie walks in, Tilly at his heels, and he shuts the door. I'm so glad he's got such a lovely little dog; she'll look after him.

For a moment we both look at each other. 'I hope he's okay with this and it doesn't upset him too much,' I say at last.

'It'll be the making of him,' Mavis says with much more confidence than I feel. 'You'll see. I knew that – and so did Elsie, when she asked me to send the other letter to Flora.'

It takes me a moment to register what she's said. 'You? But why? When did you send it?'

Mavis laughs. 'All these questions. When she knew she was becoming more unwell, Elsie gave me the letter for safekeeping. She said she'd written one for Bertie, but she was in two minds about giving it to him. So she gave me one, which she asked me to send to Flora when the time was right.'

'So what made you send it now?'

'Elsie died sooner than we all expected. So I kept the letter as she asked – Bertie was in no state to read it then. I bided my time and then during this lockdown, knowing how lonely Bertie has been, I realised it was now he needed to hear about Flora. I had no idea you had found the other letter.'

'No, that was just sheer chance. But you were so right to send the letter to Flora now and she must have answered immediately.'

'It's almost as though it's meant to be,' Mavis says. 'He won't be alone any more – now he has a dog and a stepdaughter, he's got everything he needs.'

'Should I wait until he comes back out?' I ask. 'He's bound to be upset.'

'Don't worry, love; you need to get back. I'll wait and talk to him. I have all the time in the world.'

'Thanks, Mavis. Maybe you're right.' I wish I could give her a hug. She's such a dear. 'This whole situation has really surprised me you know, how everyone in this little community has looked out for each other. You're all like family now.'

She laughs. 'Well there'll be good things and bad things, ups and downs – there always are in life you know. But as long as we've got each other, somehow we'll all find our way through. Wartime spirit you know.'

I ponder her words as I wander back to the flats. Why

does she think I need to get back? Although Jack did say 9 p.m. It's even quieter than usual. I think I see a glimmer of one of the children opposite on the balconies, but when I look again she's vanished. Perhaps everyone's busy getting dinner, although it's a beautifully still evening.

Back at the flat, Erica and I eat watching something rubbish; tonight we're on fish and chips from the freezer. 'When are we going to go back to more takeaways?' asks Erica, peering disparagingly at an oven chip perched precariously on the end of her fork.

'Perhaps when lockdown's over. Anyway, we had takeaway chips last week.'

'They taste so much better.'

'I guess. It's always such a hassle though, putting it in the oven when you've got it home. You might as well cook it yourself rather than queue at the shop.'

'That's only because you're stressed out it might have the virus on it. Most people would just eat it straightaway.'

'Well you can't be too careful, not for Jack especially. Anyway, there's talk the lockdown's going to ease next month.'

'I know, but I don't think it will be back to normal.' She finishes her mouthful and replaces her knife and fork in the middle of the plate with a clatter. 'I'm off then. I'll be back in the morning.'

'Okay.' I smile at her. 'Are you sure you've had enough? And have you got your scrubs?'

'Yes, Mum!' Erica jests. 'Have a nice evening.' She stacks her plate in the sink, which makes a change, and there's a certain something in her manner as she's going out the door.

I bumble about clearing the table and getting the washing up out of the way.

My phone announces the arrival of a text from Jack. *No going outside until 9 p.m. x*

That's very mysterious and is making me want to go outside immediately x

Trust you (he's put a laughing face). *No peeking, speak in a while x*

I can't imagine what he's up to, but when nine o'clock comes, with some trepidation, I pull back the blinds and open the balcony doors. Without my realising the sun has gone down and it was actually slightly overcast today for the first time in a while. As the end of the restrictions hove into view it's almost as though the weather has dictated, *Okay, chaps, back to normal, cloud and rain are fine – we've got the people through.*

Darkness has mostly fallen in the courtyard but as I step out onto the balcony, a sea of lights twinkle at me. The effect is incredible; tiny candles glowing from each and every corner of the outside space. I am surrounded by tiny dots of light bobbing hearteningly in the darkness. This incredible light effect is mirrored in the sky, as up and beyond and above the rooftops, the moon is bright and full, paired with the twinkling wishing star next to it.

'It's beautiful,' I say, because it really is.

'I hoped it would be,' Jack answers from above.

'How did you manage it? Are you a magician?'

'No.' He laughs. 'But I had a little help from some friends.'

'I don't think I've ever seen anything like it.' My voice breaks as tears start to roll down my cheeks.

'Hey,' he says softly, 'are you okay?'

'Yes.' I laugh and sniff. 'This crying on the balcony seems to have become our thing.'

'In a good way this time I hope, though?' he asks.

'Definitely – no one has ever done anything like this for me, Jack. It's magical.'

'I just wanted to, well, I wanted to show you how much—' He breaks off. I can hear the emotion in his voice.

I wait quietly.

'How much . . .' His voice is stronger now. 'I wanted to tell you how much you mean to me and what a wonderful person you are. Not just because I'm grateful for what you've done to get me through this lockdown, which I am, but quite simply you are the most beautiful person I've ever nearly-but-not-actually-met . . . and I love you, Soph. I know you probably don't feel that way about me, because you've got an ex who you're still in love with and you probably want to marry and in any case we haven't even met, so you might hate me or find me annoying or . . .'

'Jack!' I interrupt.

'Sorry, I'm blithering aren't I?'

'No,' I say, 'I just wanted to put you out of your misery. I wanted to say *me too*. I mean; I love you too.' I stop for a moment, memories of our lockdown together rushing over me. 'You're thanking me for looking after you, but you're the one who rescued *me*. I was a complete mess, feeling lonely in the crowd even before that and now, thanks to you, I've realised it's okay. I can accept what's going on. I can just be me. You've helped with so many things and I don't need to know what you look like; I feel as if I've known you forever so it just doesn't matter.' I stop for a moment, as I can't believe all this has come out, but it's true. 'And in any case, I can't imagine life without you now.'

'Me neither,' Jack says, sounding ecstatic.

'Looks like we're stuck with each other then.' I laugh.

'Definitely,' he agrees. 'Fancy a glass of bubbly to celebrate?' Without waiting for my answer, he lowers down a glass of icy champagne and next to it are two heart chocolates. 'Incoming,' he says.

'One's for you.' I place one of the chocolates back in for him and he pulls it up. 'Not that you were sure of yourself or anything,' I quip.

'Not at all.' He laughs. 'But I thought if you said no I could just drink all the champagne myself.'

'Rude!' I chuckle.

'Cheers! Here's to us!' he says.

'To us.' I take a sip of the cold sparkling liquid.

'Thank goodness for that,' says Greg and as a round

of applause breaks out around the balconies. Greg starts up the sultry tones of 'Invisible Love' on the saxophone and I look out and see all the balconies have people and families gathered on them, raising their glasses to us, the little ones with squash in their cups I'm guessing. They're smiling, clapping, happy in spite of everything we've all been going through.

I look down into the courtyard where Bertie is perched on the corner of the raised beds, Tilly sitting on his lap and Mavis a short distance away. 'Cheers!' he says raising his glass. 'To Sophia and Jack, the perfect couple!'

I can see Erica down below in the courtyard holding up a lantern. She smiles and waves and gives a big thumbs up.

'Hear hear!' says Mavis, raising her glass too. Even Marge is smiling and clapping from the corner of the courtyard and everywhere I look, I am surrounded by love and community and most importantly of all Jack, who I would never have nearly met if it hadn't been for lockdown.

EPILOGUE

The courtyard is ostensibly unchanged: the flowers continue to bloom vibrantly, the earth is a little dry as it has been ridiculously hot and rain-free for a British summer. The balconies are the same. The pots of vegetables now sport tiny tomatoes and a couple of cucumbers are poking their heads from the yellow flowers. Yet there is a difference; something has changed. It is no longer quiet and still. Outside in suburbia, beyond the rooftops, beyond the flats, signs of the usual hustle and bustle, the background noise has begun its familiar hum. It's not quite back to normal – it's quieter than before – but tentatively, steadily, life is returning to the streets.

The builders were the first back, the noise of construction, concrete lorries, the cranes and diggers manoeuvring in the distance. Then bit by bit, more cars on the road, only a few at first, but gradually there is the steady stream and rumble, the noises that no one noticed before this lockdown, but after the silence we welcome back like old friends. The familiar – it's what everyone knows and there is a comfort in it.

The chalky white marks of distant jets once again adorn the sky, which today is a gorgeous intense blue. Some people are still anxious, venturing forth from their homes like cautious deer, vigilant, armed with masks and antibac, happy to return inside as soon as they can. Others are determined to get out and enjoy it whilst they can flock to tourist spots, living out every moment of life with a desperation born from the frustrations of temporary captivity.

This is the new normal. Whether it is better than the old one still waits to be seen, like everything in life, a story waiting to be told – it's in the hands of people to decide how it unfolds.

In the courtyard, there are signs of life. A young man, dressed in shorts and a blue T-shirt makes his way over to the raised flowerbeds. His brown hair has begun to grow back from its shortened crop. Even to the casual observer, he appears a little anxious but this is blended with an alertness, an appreciation for his surroundings, the flowers, a passing butterfly all attract his notice. Even the very air he breathes and the feeling of the sun on his back. He perches and waits for someone, his eyes closed in the sunlight, recharging his batteries after weeks of being inside.

Sensing he's not alone, he slowly opens his eyes. It's her, of course it is, he can sense her when she's near.

'Sophia?' It comes out as a question, but it isn't one.

'Jack.' She smiles and her whole face lights up, especially

her eyes, as he knew they would because although he felt he knew her anyway, he *had* met her before, all those months ago, and not even realised.

They stand for a moment, holding hands, just looking into each other's eyes, simply because they can.

'Jack, I . . .'

'Soph . . .'

They both laugh and stop, awkward as it always is when you first meet someone who you've only nearly met before. In their own time, they make their way side by side to Sophia's car, because now they've found each other, they don't want to let go. They talk and laugh as though they've known each other a long time, which in a way they have. Once they arrive at Sparrow Hill, Sophia parks and having unloaded the basket – which Jack has already filled with a bottle, glasses and sushi; requested by Sophia because it was the one thing she couldn't get during lockdown – they walk hand in hand to the brow of the hill.

Jack makes himself busy with the picnic rug, flattening out the wrinkles and placing cushions in all the right places.

'Have you done this before?' she asks, her laughing eyes crinkling at the corners.

'Not recently,' he quips. 'What's it to be? I thought you might like the lavender mocktail?'

She laughs. 'Maybe save it for my gran.'

'I thought you might say that,' he replies, 'so I brought some Pimm's. Just a bit, as you're driving.'

'Sounds perfect.' She smiles. They lie propped on the cushions, looking out over the view, Sophia cradled in against Jack's outstretched but protective body, both drinking in the vista of hills and patchwork fields, horses grazing the grass and birds flitting in the trees.

'When did you know?' she asks, munching on some smoked salmon. 'These are really good you know. Did you make them?'

'I could say yes, but I won't because you won't believe me,' he tells her.

'Well, they taste lovely either way. You haven't answered the question.'

'Just now,' he says.

'So you didn't realise before?' she asks.

'No – did you?'

'No, I had no idea,' she replies.

'Me neither, but then when I saw you, it all made sense – that rainy day in the street. You were lost in that huge mac but your eyes, they attracted me from the start.'

'With their lustrous beauty?'

'No, although they are very pretty!'

'Thanks.' She laughs.

'It was the way they crinkle at the corners,' he tells her. 'They're smiley eyes.' He stops and looks inquiringly at her, making her blush.

'Where were you going? You were in a real rush.'

'To meet Sam at the hospital for my check-up.'

'No wonder you were in a hurry,' she says.

'I'm always late,' he admits.

'Why doesn't that surprise me? Poor Sam.'

'Poor *Jess* – I knocked all her magazines onto the wet pavement.'

Sophia giggles. 'That was unfortunate.'

'Do you think she'll always hate me?'

'No.' She looks at him for a moment speculatively. 'I think she'll really like you. What about Sam?'

'He already loves you. He can't believe anyone could get me to sort my life out. He'll be forever in your debt.'

'You were already sorting yourself out,' she says, shaking her head. 'It was nothing to do with me. Maybe it was just having some time to think about things. Perhaps this lockdown has given us all a chance to think about stuff and what really matters. I was telling my school kids that.'

'How are they?'

'Good, even Alfie and Zane are enjoying having the whole class back together now.'

'I bet – more kids to play with.'

'True, although I'll always remember the times we had as a small group. It gave me a great chance to get to know them better and for them to grow in confidence.'

'It's weird but this lockdown has had a few upsides.'

'Like me?' she asks with a cheeky smile.

'Definitely you,' he replies.

Sophia's phone beeps. It's from Bertie. Sophia reads the message aloud. *Flora's flight gets in tomorrow at 4 p.m. I'd be really honoured if you and Jack would come for tea to meet her. Mavis is coming too. Tilly has a new red bandana especially for the occasion.*

'That's wonderful,' says Jack, lazily picking at long stalks of grass and tickling Sophia's arm with them. 'Shall we go?'

'You bet,' says Sophia. 'It's funny, you know, but I can't imagine Bertie without Tilly now.'

'No, neither can I. She's transformed his life. As well as Mavis and now Flora.'

'He says they've Zoomed each other several times and he can't remember the last time he laughed so much.'

'It's like it's meant to be. Speaking of dogs helping people, Greg says there's a local charity who work with dogs for the disabled. They're fundraising to train a therapy dog to work at the autism college.'

'That would be amazing,' says Sophia enthusiastically. 'I can't imagine anything helping the kids more. We'll have to see what we can do to organise some fundraising events.'

'Knowing you, you'll have it all sorted by this evening.'

'I'm good, but not that good.' She laughs, throwing bits of grass down his neck.

'Yuk, I'm going to be getting that out for days.' He throws a load back at her and long seeded strands land in her wavy hair.

The phone pings again. It's from Jess. *Hey, I've arranged a post-wedding organisational meeting for next week. Bring Jack; I'd love to meet him before the big day.*

'Are you up for a pre-wedding date next week?' Sophia asks.

'Ours?' he looks at her speculatively.

'No, steady on a bit! I mean Jess's. Will you be my official date this time?'

'You bet,' he says, 'on both counts.'

'I think I love you,' she says lightly touching his slightly stubbly cheek.

'I *know* I love you, and believe me lockdown gives a guy time to think about these things,' he says, gazing at her.

She laughs and instinctively they move closer to each other, their lips meeting, their whole beings connecting, as they hold each other, revelling in the joy of their basic human need for contact and warmth of touch. A luxury, which before they always took for granted, yet lockdown changed all that. In lockdown nothing was definite, nothing was certain except the strength and resilience of love and community.

But the reality is that when everything else stops, love is all that's left. It counts for everything as it always does, in the key workers, the nurses, the hospital staff, the shop assistants, the bus and delivery drivers – everyone braving a common enemy for the sake of others.

As they lie entwined in a tangle of limbs and love, it all feels so new, yet so familiar as the sparrows chatter overhead, a dragonfly rests momentarily on a nearby leaf and the sun beats down warm on their backs.

But Jack and Sophia are oblivious; they're immersed in each other. In the distance, but nevertheless all around them, the world inevitably begins to go about its business, slowly but surely discovering its new normal as they discover theirs.

ACKNOWLEDGEMENTS

I am so incredibly grateful to have been able to write this story about rather extraordinary happenings set within unprecedented times. In many ways, writing this book has carried me through what has been a difficult period and I hope reading it might help others who may have also been struggling, to try to make sense of this year's events in some small way.

Lockdown was an extraordinary experience, totally different for each and every one of us but I have tried to give a few tiny snapshots of how some things were, within a fictional framework. Jack and Sophia's story is set within the timeframe of actual lockdown, they virtually meet in a more than imperfect situation where everything around them is crumbling, all the familiar has become unfamiliar and yet in spite of their setbacks, both emotionally and physically they make it out the other side, still smiling. The idea of love conquering all is pretty universal and particularly pertinent right now in a world divided by a pandemic and disagreement, climate change and destruction. I really hope *Love in Lockdown* might give everyone a much-needed shot of optimism and a chance to believe that in the end if we all pull together, everything will be okay.

The minor characters in the book just came along as they so often do, making themselves known in their own unique ways. Gradually, a sense of community arose and I think that's one of the things to take away from lockdown, at times it brought out the best in so many people. There was a real wartime spirit, wonderful stories of how far people went to help others, delivering food to elderly neighbours or those who were shielding and you cannot fail to be uplifted by these amazing selfless acts of kindness.

The children also invited themselves to the story and I hope their scenes might bring a lighter note and emphasise the importance of talking about feelings and emotions with young people, as well as practising mindfulness and taking time out to enjoy the small shiny things in life.

I would not have been able to create this book, especially in so short a time, without the help of some total superwomen, especially Tilda McDonald, my editor. It has been an absolute privilege working with her, having the same vision for the story. Thanks to Sabah Khan, my fabulous publicist, and also to the amazing Helena Newton, Ellie Pilcher, Bethany Wickington and Catriona Beamish. Many thanks must also go to Kate Nash from The Kate Nash Literary Agency.

405

I would like to give a huge thank you to my parents for their never-ending belief in me and for their constant support throughout everything. It's been incredibly tough, as many others are finding, to be so often distanced from them, but in spite of this as always they have encouraged me to keep going and I am extremely grateful to them for instilling in me such a great love of reading as well as writing in the first place. Their acceptance of these difficult times, as well as their constant loving support throughout the children's illnesses and their incredible ability to just get on with it, fills me with immense admiration.

Loads of love and thanks go to my husband, Keith. He has been really supportive; I have so often shut myself away, scribbling this book and it's not easy having someone talking endlessly about fictional characters and their problems! He has even become pretty handy around the kitchen, for which I am really grateful – this is a role I think he may have to take on full time!

Huge thanks to my wonderful girls; Marianne, Grace, Madeleine and Francesca. Lockdown was tough for all of you, I know, but we got through it and even managed to have some laughs as well as some good times at home (even though I was writing a lot of the time!). Thanks for being so patient about it.

I've borrowed from Marianne's experience as she was apart from me in her residential college for most of lockdown; it was such a long time and so tough not being able to see her, so I felt it was really important to include the plight of those with autism who found the restrictions particularly difficult, as well as anyone who for whatever reason was separated from those they love throughout lockdown.

Aside from her autism – which was only diagnosed in the past couple of years, so often the case with girls – Marianne was born with kidney disease. I know how difficult it has been for her to have endless medical procedures and to feel different from others so I hope I have managed to convey this concept in Jack's character, in his struggle to fit in and eventual realization that he doesn't need to run away from his health condition, he can just be himself.

As for Sophia's epilepsy, I must thank Madeleine for her expertise on this; she has suffered from the condition for the past couple of years. It was a sudden development when she was fourteen, so I felt it was really important to show how challenging it can be to cope with the changes a chronic illness can create when it happens out of the blue. I think there are a lot of preconceptions about epilepsy that once seizures are under control, everything is wonderful, but it really isn't that simple and even when they do work, the meds can have unpleasant side effects. I must add that epilepsy can vary greatly so although Sophia is lucky that her seizures are under control in the story, others may find the condition can make every day a challenge.

I'd like to thank Grace so very much, for being the first person to read my manuscript, for her honest feedback and encouragement and her brilliant beta reader/

editorial skills. Also for putting up with my constant obsession with talking about the book and its ins and outs at all hours of the day and night!

Thanks go to Francesca for agreeing to miss out on bike rides and chances to go out for much of the summer. I hope you enjoy the book and think it was worth it taking up most of my time.

Also no book about lockdown would be complete without a huge thank you to all the key workers who worked tirelessly to keep things going, especially medical staff on the frontline, but also other hospital workers, doctors, bus drivers, shop workers, teachers and to all the other heroes, we owe you so much so thank you.

Finally, thank you to all my lovely readers, for buying this book. I hope it has made you smile, as well as perhaps shedding a few tears and given you a small pocket of sunshine, even if it is only for a while.